# The Levels

Helen Pendry has worked in higher education, research and editing. She has also worked in a zoo, a hostel and a bookshop. Her articles and reviews have appeared in *Planet*, *New Welsh Review* and *Wales Arts Review*, and she has been the recipient of a Literature Wales Bursary Award. She lives in Machynlleth.

# The Levels

Helen Pendry

Parthian, Cardigan SA43 1ED
www.parthianbooks.com
First published in 2019
© Helen Pendry 2019
ISBN 978-1-912109-40-1
Editor: Edward Matthews
Cover design: www.theundercard.co.uk
Cover art: 'Cwmystwyth Mine Memory' by Alison Lochhead
Typeset by Elaine Sharples
Printed by 4edge Limited
Published with the financial support of the Welsh Books Council,
British Library Cataloguing in Publication Data
A cataloguing record for this book is available from the British Library.

Gwych a fyddai cael hanes Celfyddydau Tangnef ymhlith y Cymry, a gwychach fyth a fyddai claddu yn anghof y pwll dyfnaf yn uffern, yr holl hanes y sydd am ryfel a Rhyfelwyr am *Frenhinoedd*.

It would be a wonderful thing to have a history of the Arts of Peace amongst the Welsh, and more wonderful still would be to bury in the oblivion of the deepest pool in Hell all the history which deals with wars and Warriors and *Kings*.

Edward Williams ('Iolo Morganwg'),
translated by Mary-Ann Constantine

Sŵn y dŵr. Bracsaf iddo am ateb.
Dim ond y rhediad oer.

Waldo Williams, 'Cwmwl Haf'

*The air is a cool empty kiss on the skin of his face. He opens his eyes and sees strobing light and sheet lightning. But there's no light down here. His mind is making it up.*

*He's on his back on the rock and he can't move. His right leg twists under him. Pain ebbs and flows through his skull.*

*He'd like to walk home in the light. He knows the way out from level five, even in the dark and without a torch. He knows the incline up to the winch – the winch which was mangled by a rockfall last spring. He knows there's a hole in the roof of the chamber, just above the winch. It was chipped out a century ago by the Bryn Hyfryd rockmen to save themselves the long trudge home at the end of each day through a mile of underground tunnels and then along the valley road. Some of them died before they'd pushed through. Some of them knew they'd die before they pushed through.*

*He can taste metal. He can hear water dripping into a pool.*

# 1

## Holiday Park

Mr Palmer is ahead of me, leading the way up the track between chalets and bare flowerbeds. I drag after him, hands in the pockets of my jeans. There's a glistening on the tarmac like a cold sweat. My boots scuff it. I can hear water splashing over pebbles in the track-side ditch, and below us, in the gorge, another stream gushes between mud banks. Everything is dissolving – sky into earth, trees into sky, my wet wool jumper into my skin.

The static caravans are raised above the track behind jutting decks, their bayed front windows facing out over the valley like ghost ships on the green swell of the hill, their blinds fixed shut against the winter. And then there's a gap in the line of caravans and Mr Palmer stops.

'Here,' he says, and the sound of his voice comes out in a white mist.

There's a ditch of churned-up mud that starts by my feet and ends in the belly of the hill. The only other sign of violence is an uprooted fir tree, flat on the ground. I'm not disappointed – ghoulish curiosity didn't bring me to this hillside in Wales. But I am surprised. On the train I'd tried not to picture the scene of the accident because I didn't want to know what a drone skidding out of the sky on an errant curve could do to a caravan and the woman inside. I tried not to think about twisted steel and shards of glass, of furniture foam spilling out of crushed velveteen cushions. I knew the body would have been removed by now, and I didn't want to see remnants of liquid yellow fat splattered over sheets of fibreglass and MDF. Or blood washed to dark stains by the rain.

'The MoD took everything away. For the investigation.'

Mr Palmer's Puffa jacket makes him look almost as wide as he is tall, and he says 'MoD' and 'investigation' as though words like that explain everything and put an end to questions.

'Did you see it happen?' I ask him.

He sinks further into his warm coat and when he speaks it's towards the muddy space in front of us and not to me. 'It was a godawful noise. And then an explosion, and smoke, and bits floating down, and when I got here ... Put it this way – I won't be getting in a plane for a while.'

What about a caravan? I want to say, but I stop myself. I look out across the valley instead and study a triangle of forestry plantation and a low white farmhouse in the crook of a hill till the red and white tape that marks out the scene of the accident hums in the wind and draws me back to Mr Palmer and the gap in front of us.

He coughs and takes a step towards me. 'Did you know Anwen well?'

I hesitate, and then nod, because it's much easier than telling a lie out loud. I can't tell Mr Palmer I didn't know her at all, that I never met her. I can't tell him I know the man who may have killed her, and that I'm here to find him, not to grieve her. I'm hoping my lack of words will suggest pain and he won't pry any further.

He starts to walk away and I stay a moment, listening to the silence in the space in front of me and to the gale of the world blowing through it. I dig my cold toes downwards, feeling the earth, and in my head I hear Tegid Rhys say *it was my fault*. I turn that phrase over, and again I tell myself it's a stupid idea. It was an accident. That's what they're all saying – the news, the MoD. It was a terrible accident and I have no good reason to question their story.

I try to pull my hands into the sleeves of my jacket but the sleeves are too short so I let the cold embrace me, as though it could freeze the contours of my body and make me feel defined. I know there's a problem with the accident theory: if I don't think Tegid had anything to do with this disaster I wouldn't be standing here by a muddy ditch looking for some kind of evidence that would settle it either way.

When I catch up with Mr Palmer he's half way down the hill. 'Thank god it was out of season,' he says.

'Don't they mind the drones?' I ask him, '– the people who come here for their holidays?'

'I'm sure they will now. But they didn't used to. The drones are quiet. Not like the jets. The jets are really loud if you're not used to them. But even those ... well, people understand, don't they? Our pilots need to train. Our weapons need testing. That's how they protect us from the terrorists, isn't it?'

We've reached the gate across the drive that leads to his dormer bungalow. 'Back to work,' he mutters.

'I need somewhere to stay,' I say. 'Till the funeral.'

He's pushing open the gate and he stops to consider this, and then he turns around and considers me. He's wondering where to place a woman in her thirties who's travelling alone and doesn't have a car. I can see he's not inclined to offer me one of his caravans. 'There's a bunkhouse in town, but I don't think it's open this time of year. There are a few B and B's. You could ask in the newsagents. They keep a list. And there's the Bridge Hotel, but it's not cheap.'

He's ruling out the hotel in my case, which annoys me, so the next thing I'm doing is asking a loaded question. 'Was Anwen living here permanently? In one of your caravans? Isn't that illegal?'

He steps back towards me, sticking out his chin. 'I was doing her a favour,' he says, his voice taut, 'until the council came up with a house. She'd have been out of that caravan well within the time limit.' Then he pushes through the gate and lets it clank shut behind him. When he gets to the house a security light flicks on over the front door and despite the fierce whiteness of its bulb it only adds to the gloom of the afternoon.

I start walking down the drive towards the main road. I know the way back to town – it's a cold two-mile walk along a narrow road without pavements, and the cars don't slow down for the bends, so when he pulls up next to me in a silver four-by-four and offers me a lift I don't decline. But as I climb in the smell of pine air freshener slams the back of my throat and I start to wonder about the wisdom of sharing a confined space with Mr Palmer. I have nothing to say about the dead woman because I didn't know her. It's soon clear though that Mr Palmer isn't going to start a conversation about Anwen. I've told him I'm an old friend of hers, and I don't think he's the kind of middle-aged English man who would cope well with a weeping woman in his car. He'll stay off the subject.

'We had a soldier posted here all last week,' he says, nodding towards the park sign as we pull through the gates, 'which isn't a great advertisement for a holiday park.'

At first I think he means the sign, not the soldier. It isn't a great advertisement. It says 'Sunny Hill Holiday Park in Magical Mid Wales', and under that is a lurid painting of a green hill blobbed with white sheep under a blue sky and a radiant orange sun.

Mr Palmer drives fast on the winding road and I try to focus on the horizon of hills to still the nausea rising in my stomach, but the hills are smudged into the greying sky and I can hardly make out the join. I glance at the dashboard clock and it tells me it's only four o'clock. Even so, a day that's hardly had the energy to show up is being elbowed out by the night. I share its exhaustion and settle back into the seat.

Mr Palmer turns to the pleasantries he's been honing on tourists from England for years. 'Where are you from?' he begins, and I simplify and say I live in London. That starts him off on a long lecture about how Pont Rhith is at least twenty years behind the times. I let him talk. It's easier if he speaks and I listen. It's a role I'm familiar with.

A fine drizzle provokes the windscreen wipers into action and then he's asking what I do in London. When I tell him I work in a hostel for homeless people he says, 'That's the problem with cities: it's where the dregs end up.'

I picture it – the dregs, the sediment, sinking to the bottom of cities, sucked into the black hole at the centre of a swirling galaxy of marine phosphorescence. And then I picture scum floating to the top and to the edges – all the way out to the Celtic Fringe on a tide of property acquisition and greed. I leave my upside-down view of the world unspoken because in his eyes it would be nothing but sour grapes. I have no silver four-by-four. I wear second-hand clothes. I don't own a first home, never mind a holiday home or a hillside caravan park. And right now I'm cold and hungry and I've got nowhere to stay.

I let the swish-swash of the wipers lull me into semi-consciousness and then I hear him saying something about the Welsh hating English incomers like him, and how he wants his children to know there's a bigger world out there, and that most of it speaks English.

'Mandarin,' I say. 'Most of it speaks Mandarin. And after Mandarin it's Spanish.'

He doesn't say anything else after that and we reach the town in silence. When he pulls up outside The Bridge Hotel my stomach lurches, and it's not because he's braked with a decisiveness that betrays his desire to dispatch me onto the pavement. It's because I'm looking at the map on his sat-nav screen – a diagram of fine, red, criss-crossing lines against a black background – and I'm thinking about Tegid. He was a vagrant, a drifter, the sort of man most people avoided and I had to work with because it was my job. If it was wrong to call him crazy, then it was just as deluded to see him as a savant or a wandering sage. He just didn't fit in. He was a man in his sixties who made maps and hated war. I know all that, and I've still come looking for him.

I know something else. He wouldn't have liked the sat-nav's pared-down version of the world. He wouldn't have liked its owner much, either, so I hesitate before I ask Mr Palmer if he knows Tegid Rhys. I'm standing on the pavement, holding the car door open, and he's shaking his head and releasing the hand-break. Then he puts the break back on and leans towards me. 'You mean that bloke who turned up a year or two back and started causing trouble?' He doesn't wait for my answer but barrels on. 'Yes I know him. Always complaining about something, like the names I put on *my* shops and *my* café. He thought they should have Welsh names. He even tried to start a bloody petition, but that didn't work, did it? How d'you know him?'

'He's the father of a friend of mine,' I lie. 'Is he still around?'

'Hope not. It's hard enough making a living in the back of beyond without people like him turning up and sticking their oar in.'

His hand is releasing the break again and I take the hint and lean on the door to shut it. Then I give him a little wave of thanks for the lift. He doesn't wave back.

# 2

## Hotel Bar

The Bridge Hotel has a black and white façade and Georgian windows, and I'm thinking about how much it will cost me to stay there for the night. Then I start walking up the main street, wondering if I'll find somewhere cheaper despite Mr Palmer's advice.

Most of the shops in Pont Rhith are shut and their windows are dark, but there's one illuminating a display of shoes and the Spar glows with ads for sandwiches and fizzy drinks. I smell sesame oil and MSG and garlic before I see the Chinese take-away. My stomach clamps. It's been six hours since the cheese and pickle sandwich I bought on the station. I take an apple out of my bag and then put it back in again. I admire people who eat raw fruit, but I suspect most of them live in California. In Wales, in January, apples should come stewed and covered in a thick layer of crumble and custard.

I keep walking and the shops give way to walls and privet hedges and houses, so I cross the road and walk back down the other side, past a set of steps up to the bolted doors of a chapel and past the frosted-glass windows of a pub. There's no one else on the street and I wonder if the drone accident has driven everyone indoors, or if it's always this quiet on a January evening in Pont Rhith. I wonder what it's like to live in a small town which has suddenly become national news because of a killing. I wonder if people greet each other in whispers, if they glance nervously at the sky, if the hills have taken on a new aura of death.

9

And then I'm outside The Bridge Hotel again, shivering in my damp jacket, and now the entrance porch, strung with white fairy lights, looks like the portal to a magic realm.

There is another option. I have the keys to Tegid's campervan in my bag and a hand-drawn map showing me where to find it. I could have gone looking for it when I got off the train, tramping up forestry tracks into the hills, but it was too late and too dark. It's even later now, and however much I like solitude I realise I prefer it with street lighting. And then there's the smell of chips, and that swings it – I decide to spend one night in the hotel and go looking for the campervan in the morning.

In the lobby the receptionist is busy at the desk with a computer screen, her straight blonde hair hanging down over her face. I ask the top of her head for a room for the night and when she looks up she seems surprised to have a guest. Yes, I confirm. I'm all on my own. No friends. No partner. Not even a dog. When she tells me the price I don't gulp and stammer, I just head straight for the bar.

The bar is a small room with four tables and a large open fire, and it's empty except for the bartender who is drying a glass, polishing the inside and then the outside, flicking the tea-towel around with savage intent. I pick up a leather-bound menu from the stack and order a wild mushroom tarte fine (whatever that is), with shredded leeks (local), cooked in cream (local), and scalloped potatoes (local). The bartender pulls me a pint of (local) bitter with a raised eye-brow, and I wonder if ladies are supposed to sup halves, not pints, in country-town hotels.

At the table closest to the fire I take off my jacket and drape it over a stool in front of the heat. It steams. With my back to the wall and the pint in front of me and the fire warming my frozen feet I start to feel content. The world has turned brown and gold and warm and I slouch back on the bench and stare at the paintings on the opposite wall. There's a picture of a fox hunt with dogs, and there's a picture of bluebells in a wood, and there's a picture of a small farm in the hills, and I wonder why rich people who stay in smart hotels like paintings of hovels in the hills.

A girl with dark hair and red cheeks brings me my meal. She avoids eye contact and scuttles away as soon as she's plonked the food down on the table. The tarte fine, I discover then, is a flat round pastry, and I eat all of it – every last crumb. And I eat all the scalloped potatoes, and the shredded leeks in cream, and then I wish I still smoked and could spend some time fiddling with a roll-up, because I'm on my own in a bar, and I know I don't look like a woman on a business trip.

I notice the bartender watching me so I shuffle about in the contents of my bag and take out the A5 padded envelope. When it arrived at the hostel, addressed in shaky capitals, I'd opened it with a sense of dread, expecting an insane love/hate letter from a resident with stalking inclinations. Instead, a set of keys and a postcard fell out. On the front of the postcard was that bridge – Pont Rhith – in the town of the same name. In Wales. Every postcard Tegid sent me had a picture of that bloody bridge on one side and a plea for me to visit him on the other.

But this postcard was the exception. It was the same bridge, but all it said on the back was *IT WAS MY FAULT*, and under that: *The van is yours. See map for location. I don't need it. Go and find somewhere to settle down with children and animals.*

I roll my eyes. I've read the note ten times and it still niggles me. Sexist crap, I think, from an older man who abandoned a regular life and committed relationships so he could spend his days contemplating more important things – like the speed of light and the structure of the universe and the drawing of maps. He never had any intention of settling down with children and animals. Me though – he thinks I should be wearing a pinny and baking cakes and being the place for some man to come home to when he gets fed up of wandering around trying to solve mathematical conundrums. Not bloody likely.

Not even possible. But he's right in one way. I would like his campervan. The problem is I've got nowhere to put a van: no friends with secluded drives or long gardens, no spare field in the middle of London, no wasteland or backstreet I'd be happy to park it on – it'd be gutted within a week. So his gift is useless unless I leave the city. And I can't leave the city because of my job. My job. That's about it, though. Paid work is the only thing keeping me in London.

And when I get to the end of thinking about my lack of relationships and my wage slavery and being stuck doing night-shifts at a hostel for the rest of my life, those neat capital letters push themselves forward, insisting I read them again: *IT WAS MY FAULT*. And with them comes an image of an unmanned military aircraft smashing into a caravan and crushing a woman's body to death, and I wonder if I'm going to feel OK about taking a gift from a ... murderer?

There's another line on the postcard. It reads: *Goodbye Abby. It's a comfort to know you're in the world.* It's like a punch in the gut. It tells me I'm not going to find him at the campervan in the hills, or anywhere else. It tells me I've left it too late, again.

I take out his map. It's on a sheet of A4 paper folded into three. I spread it out on the table and then I dig around in my backpack for the OS map I bought before getting on the train at Euston. I rattle and squash it till it shows the area around the town of Pont Rhith, and in the process I knock a fork onto the floor. I move my empty plate onto another table and put both maps down in front of me. When the bartender comes over I lean over the maps and pick up the fork from the floor and hand it to him.

Tegid said most maps were made with military and colonial purposes in mind, and Ordnance Survey were the prime example – founded during the Napoleonic Wars when there was a threat of invasion from France. He told me 'ordnance' meant military supplies: munitions, cannon, artillery. He said that the Greek philosopher Anaximander had made the first map of the world in

12

550BC, and from then on, people didn't need to know how a place smelt on a summer's day when the rising heat carried the fragrance of flowers from the meadows, or how it looked when the trees were bare in winter, or how voices carried across swathes of deep snow. They didn't need to know who lived in a place, or how they lived. A few lines on a piece of paper were enough to get a traveller to his chosen destination without getting mired in sensory distractions. A few lines on a piece of paper could tell you all you needed to know about where to get at the gold, or the lead, or the coal, or the slate, or the enemy.

So Tegid drew his own maps. He used exercise books – the kind with small squares used for maths lessons in schools – and when I met him, before he moved into the hostel, he was charting the streets of London, wandering around at night with the exercise books stuffed into two plastic bags. He said he was trying to make maps that would be useless to the military and I told him they were pretty much useless to everyone else too. But he had an answer to that. He said the very structures of our thinking and seeing had been colonised by the machineries of war and domination. In his world, he said, his maps made sense.

They certainly had an effect on me, breaking up the world along unfamiliar lines and at the same time recomposing it, as though he had access to a different colour spectrum and could use those colours to startle or reassure, to reveal the hidden landscape or eclipse the tired and obvious stuff around us. And with the one I have spread out on the table by the fire he has made some concessions to utility. It's for my benefit, I suppose: he wants me to find the van, even if I have to wade through his view of the world to get to it.

I look at the OS map and trace the blue line of the Afon Rhith from its wide estuary on the west coast to a road bridge at the south end of the town. Then the river narrows and there's another bridge which carries the B-road. It looks to me as though the town was built at the point where salt water coming up from the sea gives in to the cold stuff of the mountains flowing down, and I think there must be a word for that point where two waters meet, that point where the river is tidal, but only just. If they taught us that word in geography lessons I don't remember it now. But I know it was an important place when goods were shipped by sea. It's the highest point you can float a boat to up a river on the tide, and then, as the tide goes out, the boat is beached, and you can load it up – with slate, with wool, with logs, with people leaving for a better life on a different continent – before the water comes in again.

Perhaps that's what happened to Tegid, I think. He got beached up here till the tide of his wanderlust came in again and carried him off. I've read the papers and seen the news. No one has even suggested that the drone crash was anything but an accident. There's no murder enquiry. His decision to leave me the campervan and fuck off, just after a fatal crash, doesn't mean he caused that crash. And what did he mean by 'It was my fault'? What was his fault? It could be anything. Maybe he was just trying to let me off the hook for failing to keep in touch with him after he left London. Maybe he was taking responsibility for something patently not his fault. He sent me postcards. I never replied.

I take a sip from my pint and smile to myself. Coming here with the crazy notion that Tegid brought down a drone just proves I'm as unhinged as he is, and if anyone could see me grinning to myself they'd agree. And that's when a man comes in and sits himself on one of the high stools at the bar. He's wearing a tan leather jacket and a beanie hat and he's leaning heavily on his elbows. The bartender coughs and says, 'How are you?' He doesn't get a response. He puts the pint in front of the man and pats the bar beside it as if he's blessing the libation with occult properties.

Without lifting his head the man says, 'I'm here cos nobody bothers me in here. If I want bothering I'll go to the Red fucking Lion.'

I put my pint down and focus on the OS map, moving my attention east of the town, away from the sea and into the hills. I find Mr

14

Palmer's caravan park tucked into a valley. It's only a hill away from the county primary school and a chill creeps through me, despite the heat from the fire: the drone could have come down in a field, scaring a few sheep and ploughing up some dead bracken; instead it crashed into a static caravan and killed a woman; but in another scenario, that chunk of flying metal could have hit a playground full of kids.

I pull Tegid's map towards me. It's in landscape layout and divided into three sections by two vertical lines. I'm looking at the middle piece in the triptych, the one I can make sense of, the one with lines for roads and rivers and little squares for buildings. The other two sections seem to detail tunnels and pools. Maybe underground chambers. I can't tell.

I go back to the OS map and find the old bridge again. The OS map shows that the road across the bridge, leading away from Pont Rhith, joins a twisting A-road which heads north through the mountains, and here the contours condense into patches of dense orange lines, and there are green forests bounded by straight black lines and the random blue lines of streams like veins disconnected from a heart. I find the village called Bethania and match it to the same name on Tegid's map. Beyond the village, on the OS map, is a track that coils around the hill and up through forestry plantations and past a little row of squares called New Cottages. Tegid's map shows the same track as if it's being walked, like a Chinese painting of a single brush-stroke path that leads the viewer from Bethania at the bottom left of the page to the campervan at the top right. To the left and right are watery sketches of trees, and maybe mine equipment – pulleys and wheels – and two-thirds of the way up there's a little house with a blue door and the name 'Raven Davies' written beside it. On the OS map the whole area is littered with the word 'dis': Quarries (dis); Levels (dis); Tips (dis); Shafts (dis). I assume these underground realms are represented on Tegid's map by the outer two pictures in the triptych, with their tunnels and caves and pools.

'Are you going walking?' The bartender is by the table and I find myself slipping Tegid's map under the OS map, as if I want to hide it from his gaze.

'There's a lake here,' he says, putting a finger on the map. 'It's a quarry reservoir. The water is blue. Very blue. You should go to it. Take pictures.'

I register his Polish accent, and the way he's staying by my table to avoid the angry man at the bar. I'd do the same. But I can see the bartender is wary of me too. My hair is shaved short and I have tattoos on the backs of my fingers. I know my fierceness is a bluff I've mocked up in a life that moves between a hostel for the homeless and a single bedsit in a seedy suburb, with some rough pubs and bars in between. And I'm aware my 'fuck off' attitude is probably redundant in this expensive hotel so I try to soften my voice and the hard look in my eyes and I ask him gently if there's a bus to the 'blue pool' from Pont Rhith. It's a delicate operation, this keeping the right distance between me and other people, but he doesn't run away, and he doesn't sit down next to me either, so I think I've finessed it.

'You can take the Number 32 from Pont Rhith,' he says. 'Get off here.' He puts his finger on the map. 'Walk here, here, here.' He traces the B-road to Bethania, and then tracks a path up to the lake. 'No one lives in Bethania,' he says. 'It's a *ghost* village. You must see it also, before the army have it.'

He's wearing small round glasses and he moves like a squirrel – twitching, watching for my responses. 'The army?' I ask.

'They want to train the soldiers.'

There is a smattering of rain on the window and we both glance over. 'I think the weather is better tomorrow,' he says. 'But be careful. There are mines in the ground.'

For a moment I think he means landmines, but then I remember I'm in Wales, not Afghanistan. Not Iraq or Angola, Libya, Vietnam, Kosovo ... I notice the beanie-hat man sliding off his stool

16

and heading for the doorway. The bartender turns towards him and says, 'Take care, take care,' as if he's bidding farewell to a relative off to war.

I wait till he's back behind the bar with his tea-towel, and then I look at Tegid's map again. There's no (dis) on his version of the landscape. Instead there are small shapes like upside-down funnels, and in each of the wider ends of these funnels he's written a list of Welsh surnames in tiny letters: Evans, Jones, Davies, Lloyd ... I can see what he's trying to do. He wants to show me more than industrial ruins on the surface of the world. He wants to show me the way the quarry buildings reach into the ground, down into the past and into the earth. He wants to name the men who spent their lives hacking slate out of those holes and dying from the dust that settled on their lungs. He's speaking to me because he knows my grandfather – my Taid – was a quarryman at a giant open-cast quarry further north. He knows I can picture the landscape slate mining creates, with or without his map to help me. It's a violently scarred landscape, like the lungs of those quarry men.

And there it is – a tiny drawing of the campervan surrounded by disused quarries and straight-edged forests. Tegid's little home in the middle of the wasteland. I find where I think the same spot is on the OS map and curl my finger along the roads and tracks all the way from Pont Rhith to the van. I estimate four or five miles and an hour's fast walking.

Then the bartender is back by my table and taking my empty glass. 'It's very sad,' he says, shaking his head. 'He has to be father and mother now.'

I stare up at him, not sure what he's talking about.

'That man,' he says, relishing the opportunity to impart more local knowledge to a visitor. 'He was with Anwen Pryce, the woman who died in the accident. You know about the accident?'

'Yes,' I say quickly, before he can start giving me the details. 'Terrible.'

'He is the little girl's father. They split up before, but of course he is very sad ...'

'It must be hard for them all,' I say. I didn't know about a child. I'd stopped reading the newspapers and watching the news after the initial reports splashed across London's media. I hadn't thought about all the other people affected by the woman's sudden death. 'How old is the girl?'

He shrugs. 'Eight, nine.'

'Poor kid.'

He nods sadly. And then he rouses himself and holds up my glass. 'Another pint?'

'No,' I tell him. 'Early start and a long walk tomorrow.' And while I'm speaking I'm feeling sick because the dead woman had a daughter. He's turning away when I say, 'An old friend of mine moved here a while back. A man called Tegid Rhys. Do you know him?'

He comes back to my table. 'White hair? Maybe sixty years old? Scar here?' He draws a line down his right cheek, and then he smiles. 'He likes walking, like you. He's always walking. He comes here one time and has a pint. An experiment, he says.' He laughs at that. 'And he speaks a little Polish. But ...' he nods towards the hallway and then leans towards me, 'my boss doesn't like him. This Tegid is ... what is the word ...?'

I can think of numerous words to describe Tegid, but I wait for the bartender's choice.

He beams when he finds it. 'Scruffy.'

At least I know we're talking about the same man. 'But aren't all English people scruffy?' I say.

He colours slightly, not sure whether to agree or disagree. He finds a solution, though, and smiles again. 'I think he is Welsh.'

'Have you seen him recently?'

'I saw him before Christmas.' He thinks about it. 'Perhaps he went home for Christmas.'

# 3

# Hostel

Sometimes I wonder if my obsession with sound comes from being too scared to look and too curious not to know. I'm a child alone in her room who closes her eyes against the frightening things – the monster faces in the patterns on the curtains, the shadows in the corners of the room – and listens to the sounds downstairs: the muffled shouts, the thud of something hitting a wall, a door slammed shut, sobbing in the bathroom.

Now I lie across a king-sized bed and stare at the ceiling. I follow the pelmet to an ornate cornice and then down to curtains of dark-blue velvet whose monochrome sheen makes it hard for me to make scary faces out of the folds. I listen to the soft voices of a couple talking to each other in the next room and to the rush of hot water filling my bath, and I think I'll be fine in this place for one night. I'm going to make the most of my en-suite room and the complimentary bubble bath and the large white towels, because luxury like this usually gives me a wide berth. There's a shared bathroom on the first floor of the building where I live in London, and the bath's enamel is rough and grey. I have a shower in the corner of my bedsit which produces a trickle of warmish water. There's a better shower at the hostel, but the room has no windows and it smells of stale bodies and unwashed clothes however much I scrub it clean.

Hostels, bedsits, stations, airports ... I'd love to add hotels like this one to the list of nowhere places I like to inhabit, but I can't afford to on a long-term basis. Or even a short-term basis. One night is my limit.

I get off the bed and walk barefoot across the soft carpet to the bathroom, climbing into the hot water and sinking under the bubbles. My skin tingles and the heat seeps slowly through to my core and I wonder why someone without status or property or a home or a nation is called a 'nobody'; if there's one thing a nobody has it's a body, and right now my body is happy. My shoulders, hunched against the cold for the last four hours, begin to let go, and I slip further into the water until my lips touch the bubbles, and with the slow release of internal pressure comes space, and into that space rush thoughts. I'm back at the hostel on New Year's Eve a year ago, and I'm going over the details once again, re-running the timeline, wondering if I could have done something to stop Siamak killing himself.

It begins like most other night shifts: I come into the office to hand out pills to the residents on 'scripts, but I've turned up late and Alex, my co-worker for the night, has already dispensed drugs from the cupboard on the wall to help people control their schizophrenia and depression and mania. Siamak, who isn't prescribed anything, is in the office with Alex, and they're leaning over a book on the desk. I watch them from the door. There's blue tinsel around the filing cabinet, and a small fibre-optic Christmas tree on the desk is pulsing electric blue and green light.

'Listen to this, Abby,' says Alex when he sees me. 'Siamak's reading the Persian poet Hafiz, in the original.' His eyes glint with enthusiasm. Alex likes poetry. Mostly he likes Patti Smith, but he'll read anything made up of short lines. I've seen him on a night shift in the office, a book open on the desk in front of him and his lips moving silently as he chews over the words and then pauses to digest them. Now he's holding open a page and saying to Siamak, 'Read this one ...'

But Alex's stunning ability to engage almost anyone in conversation isn't working today. Siamak is preoccupied. He snatches the book out of Alex's hands and turns to me. 'Hafiz writes about love,' he says. 'About God's love for everyone. But you ... when people leave here, that's it. You never think of them again. You cut them off, like this.' He chops the side of his hand down on the desk.

Alex's eyes are wide open, waiting for me to respond. We both know Siamak is talking about Tegid and the postcards he's been sending me. He must have read them – I've been pinning them to the cork board in the office for months, because that's where we put all the postcards addressed to us at the hostel. Because it isn't personal when residents send us mail: it's work. Or that's what I've been telling myself. I've been following procedure.

Alex tries to come to my rescue. 'This is a job,' he says to Siamak. 'Abby doesn't get paid to follow people around the country after they leave.'

Siamak sneers. 'Doesn't get paid.' Then he pushes past me and goes up the stairs, a trail of contempt eddying in his wake.

'Don't worry about him,' says Alex. 'He's having a bad day.'

I shrug. 'Another one.'

I know Siamak's story. Sally, the outreach worker, found him on one of her expeditions along the South Bank. He was on a bridge. He'd decided his life was impossible – that it didn't add up and couldn't be made to. He told her he'd been a bus worker in Tehran, imprisoned and tortured for supporting attempts to unionise. He'd come to England in the back of a lorry and spent two years on the streets, frightened to death and living under a false ID. And then he got tired of hiding and confessed to the police. He didn't know what that would mean. He didn't know it was too late to come clean – there would be no reward for honesty but there would be punishment for having kept quiet. He didn't know he'd never be able to claim asylum because the Border Agency said he'd delayed

21

without good reason, and he'd been lying about who he was, and he should have claimed asylum in Pakistan – the first safe country he reached after leaving Iran. So his claim to stay in the UK was refused. He'd have to go home to Tehran. End of story as far as the Home Office was concerned.

So now he was in purgatory, living in the shadows, hiding at the hostel. He spent a lot of time talking to Tegid, before Tegid left, and he liked Alex, and he tolerated Sally. The rest of us, he thought, could go to hell. We were privileged and useless.

I'm on the sleep-through option that New Year's Eve because I don't have any friends to get drunk with. Alex, I know, wants the double pay to fund his latest community gardening project – to buy a wheelbarrow and maybe a shed. I leave him in the office with his feet up on the desk and the book of Hafiz poetry propped open on his round stomach. Tonight he'll be the one opening the door to any residents who stay out self-prescribing with alcohol until they can't stand up. He'll be ready with his soft Scottish accent and large frame to welcome them in and remove the cans from their pockets. And he's good with the women at the hostel too – even the ones with children who rarely leave their rooms, the destitute ones whose asylum claims have been rejected. Alex, half Scottish and half Pakistani, with a wide halo of black curls, is the one male member of staff they'll talk to. They ask him to fix things: to stop a tap dripping, to help warm up some milk for a crying child, to take the lid off a jar.

The staff bedroom is hot even in winter, so I open the window. I want to hear the river lapping against the bank, but it can't compete with the traffic noise, and even though I'd like to go down to the edge of the water just to hear it slap against the mud, I'm not meant to leave the hostel till my shift is through, just in case there's an emergency. So I lie on the bed and listen to the thin curtain flap in the cold breeze, and I hear Grant outside, singing, and he's probably dancing too, and he'll swig down the last of the can in his blackened hands before he presses the buzzer and comes in, a fringe of super-strength lager foam on his ginger 'tache.

Grant calls me an ear warrior. He adds, 'And not much else.' I don't have Alex's talking skills or fixing skills or all-round being-a-good-human skills. But I can shut up and listen. So Grant tells me stories about his childhood on a farm in Scotland, and how seeing a calf being born beats killing people. He says if he'd known back then what he knows now he wouldn't have joined the paras. Sometimes he comes up behind me and slams his hand on my shoulder and shouts 'Jump!' He's impressed when I don't jump. He says, 'Did your legs wobble, just a bit? I bet they did,' and I don't say, 'I heard you coming because you're drunk.' It's what I don't say that matters.

It's past midnight and I'm nearly asleep when Elsie starts one of her incantations in the room next door. It's a low trickle of sound for most of the time, and then a shout of 'hell', or 'bastard', or 'stop' breaks the flood of her outpourings like a boulder in a stream. I sit up on the bed and wait for her to run out of demons for the night, or the voice to address them with.

I decide listening to music would be better than listening to Elsie but I've left my phone in the office and I think twice about going to get it. Alex is one of the few members of staff suited to the term 'homemaker', which is what we were called for a while. I don't know what we're called now. Service providers? Residential social workers? Whatever the name is, he's good at the job, but I don't trust the way he draws out confidences over cups of tea, lulling people into a feeling of safety so all their defences come down and they blabber on at him about their worries and their hopes. Sometimes he makes bread using a sourdough culture that lives in a wide-mouthed jar in the fridge. When he's on a long shift, the smell of bread baking fills up the hostel's corridors like some house-selling trick. If I go down now he'll want to talk, and he'll want me to talk, and I'll just be rude to him.

But Elsie's disturbing drone continues in the next room, so I put my jumper back on over my T-shirt and wriggle into my jeans. Holding my boots by the laces, I open the door onto the landing and step out and I do a kind of strangled scream because my bare foot touches something warm and soft. I make myself look down and I see a large brown rabbit, and then I remember a note in the logbook: Elsie has a new pet.

Elsie is out on the landing too, her grey hair straggling across her face, her sharp eyes peering at me, and she's coming towards me with a finger jabbing the air. She sees the rabbit and scoops it up and throws it back in her room. But she doesn't follow it in and she's coming at me again, and her finger prods my shoulder and she hisses, 'You let him go. You let him go.' Then those bony fingers grip my wrist and she's yanking at my arm and trying to pull me down the corridor.

I think about throwing her to the floor – it would only take a sharp twist and a bend – but I'm out of practice, and she isn't a threat, so I let her lead me along the landing and I keep the stairs behind me. 'Know your exits' was the main piece of advice given to us on a course called 'Coping with Violence at Work'. It's a precept I've lived by for longer than my career in hostels for the homeless. It's pretty much a way of life.

When we reach the end of the corridor she pushes open the fire door that leads to the stairs to the second floor, still holding my wrist tightly with her other hand. Then she steps aside so that I can see how Siamak's hanging in the stairwell from a mess of silver tinsel tied to the banister and around his neck.

Sally lets me leave an hour early, and for once I cross the Hungerford Bridge with the tide of people retreating from the city after a night of New Year's Eve partying instead of fighting my way against the early-morning commuters. Back at my bedsit I sit and watch the light creep in and then out through the dirty French windows. I don't draw the curtains. I don't turn on the lights. I don't eat or make any words, and somewhere towards evening on the second day of my inertia, when the room is dark and the trees on the street begin to breathe in oxygen like animals, Alex phones and offers me a shift. So I go back to work. And I think I've coped with Siamak's suicide – processed it, moved on. I think I've taken my share of the guilt, but only my share, and now I can forget it.

But here I am a year later in a country-town hotel, my head just above the water in a bath of bubbles, and I know I can't let another one go. I have to find Tegid, whatever he may have done. And it's not because it's my job to care for the world's waifs and strays, or because an old lady with a rabbit thinks I should. It's because I'm out here on the edge too, and I wish someone would bring me in. Strange as it may sound, I think Tegid is the only person who understands that.

I wrap myself in a giant white towel and pad back into the bedroom and open a window. Steam rushes out into the night and the air that comes in is spare and clean and confident. I take a T-shirt out of my backpack and put it on. The couple next door are still murmuring. I wonder if they keep their own fears at bay by staying in fine hotels. I wonder if they feel protected from violence and death by soft furnishings and routine mealtimes.

And then I'm angry. I'm angry that Tegid has left me with a campervan and a postcard and a map. What did he know about me and what I needed or wanted? To settle down? Where the fuck did he think I was going to find a house with a hedge around it? A partner? A family? For god's sake. Didn't he know that the thing we had in common, the thing that drew us together and made us unlikely friends, was our sense of abandonment?

Abandonment. In my experience it comes in two forms: one is abject and forlorn and just about the worst thing a human can feel. The other is ecstatic, free, intoxicating. At some point, we'd both opted for the second form and learnt to love our lack of binding ties. We could both turn intense loneliness into a feeling of freedom, but he was the expert, the master alchemist, the one who didn't seem to have bad days, bad weeks, lost years. I truly thought he'd found a way to turn the sense that we are drifting in an empty universe into a dance through the stars. And I thought he could teach me how to do that too. Instead he just fucked off. It's funny, I suppose, that I hadn't expected that.

I sit on the bed cross-legged and my anger with him abates. My fingers trace the quilting in the lilac bedspread and a thought glimmers inside me. Both forms of abandonment – the ecstatic and the bereft – are the same in the end: cold.

But now I think about it, I realise I have another reason for being here. It's not just about the van, or the guilt for not answering his postcards, or the frantic need to prevent another suicide. It's not even an emotional attachment to someone who became a friend despite my resistance to getting involved in other people's lives. There's curiosity, too. I listen to people, but I don't do much. Even my listening isn't active. I'm not like Alex. I'm just quiet and people tell me stuff to fill up the silence. So I'm fascinated by those who act, who pull themselves out from under the weight of the world and intervene in it.

And maybe that's what Tegid did. Maybe he woke up one morning and thought: that's it, enough's enough; I'm going to put a stop to these weapons. And then he didn't sign an online petition or go on a demo. He didn't start a campaign or complain to the relevant authorities. He went out and shot down an unmanned aerial vehicle … and fucked it up by killing someone.

# 4

## Umbrella

Pont Rhith, says one of the leaflets on the rack in the foyer, is named after the old stone bridge that spans the river at the northern end of town. I take the leaflet to a small table by the wall. The nervous waitress takes my order as if I'm dictating an exam question and I wonder if she'd be happier speaking Welsh. I can't offer her that option. My mother taught me a couple of songs in the language, and a few disconnected words, none of which are 'eggs' and 'mushrooms'.

While I wait for the coffee I read the leaflet's version of the story behind the town's name. Once upon a time, and all that. A beautiful young woman. A handsome young man. He's the son of a peasant. She's a rich farmer's daughter. As children they play together. As adults they're separated by class and a river. They go down to the banks of the river after dark and whisper words of longing across the water.

The beautiful young woman teaches a raven to speak and the bird carries messages of love between the couple. This, the leaflet explains, is a common motif in old Welsh folk songs and tales – talking birds who are messengers of love.

And then one moonlit night a bridge appears – a ghost bridge. The woman puts out a foot. The bridge holds. The man takes a step towards her. The bridge holds. They run into each other's arms and stay there the whole night, parting just before dawn when the bridge disappears into the morning mist. The bridge is there again the next night, and the next, and the lovers meet in a grove of ash trees on the bank. They make plans to run away, to be together forever, and I assume the talking bird is redundant and has moved on because it isn't mentioned again.

On the seventh night it all goes wrong. The couple are betrayed by a jealous steward who works for the girl's father. He persuades his master to follow her through the trees, and when the farmer sees his daughter with her lowborn lover, embracing on the bridge, he is incensed. He takes out his hunting knife, runs onto the bridge, and kills the young man, throwing his body into the river. And at that point the bridge melts back into river mist, and father and daughter plunge into the torrent below and are drowned.

The young waitress sneaks a coffee pot onto the other end of the table. I slide it over, pour the coffee out into a china cup, and keep reading.

The leaflet says the contrite townsfolk and farmers decide to build a real bridge across the river. They use lumps of rock, not shafts of moonlight. I suppose the project also required collective effort, not just dreams and hopes. Even so, the tourist information leaflet seems to suggest it's a mystery the thing stays up, and a couple of years ago a bigger, better bridge was built a little way downstream with European Union money for the regeneration of poorer regions.

A man at another table is telling his companion that he was surprised to find the hotel open. 'Normally,' he tells her, 'it would be closed in January.' Then he lowers his voice and says, 'I suppose it's because of the *accident*. The press and the investigators need somewhere to stay.'

The press and the investigators must have gone home because the only other people having breakfast are an older couple in matching fleeces. When they speak to each other it's in such a quiet way that I can't pick up any of their words and I wonder if the intimate language they're using is just too alien for my ears.

28

I do a lot of listening at the hostel. I make cups of tea and I sit at a table in the dingy subterranean common room and I let people speak. I hear boundless wisdom forged in souls that have endured brutal twisting. I hear lots of human pettiness, and I never drink my tea because I don't like it.

Sometimes, I'm listening not for the sense of the words but the sound of the noise, and I let it resonate in me. Sometimes I can't listen to the sense of the words because I don't understand Eritrean, or Romanian, or Farsi, and that's when I drift back into my other life, the one where I learnt how to take down sounds and play with them. The life where I worked with musicians and singers and composers, turning their output into digital signals, searching for the tones at the heart of their expressions. That was the life I gave up the day I found nothing behind the noise of rampant egos but my own silence, and in that silence I stopped being a sound engineer and started working shifts at the hostel.

When I listen to Tegid downstairs in the common room in the hostel I hear a small Welsh boy whose parents left him at an English boarding school when he was seven years old. I hear a nervous chuckle behind the sophisticated vocabulary. Sometimes I hear a plaintive tone. But mostly I hear deference, even with me. It works like whispering on a wild horse. I'm drawn to him despite myself, and it's the hint of nervousness in his behaviour that allows me to lower my defences. It's harder to admit I may be compelled to protect the lost little boy of seven who was sent away from home. Either way, a connection is made between us.

He's been at the hostel for a week when I sit down with him at a table in the common room and put two mugs between us. He doesn't lift his head. He's scribbling in one of his exercise books. The television hums in the corner, though no one's watching it.

'I was born in Kenya,' he tells me without looking up, without taking his pen off the page, as though he's doing no more than justifying the money they pay me by playing his part in the performance of care we're both engaged in. 'My dad was working there as an engineer. We came back when I was seven and he got a job in London. But he didn't like England, so he took a lecturing post in Canada and left me at boarding school. In the holidays I went to my grandmother's Bed and Breakfast in Criccieth. It was a tall house with large bay windows looking out over the sea. There were plants in white china pots in the bay windows. She told me not to cry. She didn't like noise. I could hear the sea. I loved the sea. Do you like the sea?'

I nod. 'And school?' I ask. 'Did you like boarding school?'

'Most of the boys were headed for the army or the air force, or maybe the navy. So I know,' he says, and his voice is small and bright now, 'how those people think. I grew up with them. You can't reason with them. You can't appeal to their compassion. You can only stop them. Physically.'

He stops scribbling and lifts up a hand as if he's stopping traffic. He smiles at me. His eyes are kind. 'Home has to be the absence of violence, doesn't it? That's the bottom line. Isn't it?'

I stare past him at the pale green wall of the common room. I swallow hard. I realise I've never considered the possibility of a home without violence. Is it any wonder then that I bond to this white-haired man, and search him out when I'm at work? Is it surprising that I invest something powerful in him and begin to listen intently whenever he speaks? That I start to see him as the one who knows where the line should be drawn? That I look at his maps as guides to my own soul? And even when he leaves the hostel – leaves me – I know at some level that his presence in the world – the fact of his existence – gives me a glimmer of hope for a better way of being on this earth.

* * *

I wait to check out of the hotel behind a short man wearing a dark-blue coat. It's made of densely woven wool which doesn't seem practical in the wet Welsh winter, but it looks expensive. I'm busy working out how much money I have left in my account when the man speaks and I recognise his voice. For a moment I can't move and my eyes are fixed on the weave of the coat material stretched across his shoulders. I listen to him using his estuary English like a fishing line, hooking himself into the receptionist's deepest desires, charming the scales of age and experience from her eyes, and then reeling her in. I step back into his blind spot and watch the show. It's the same operation he used on me, adapted for an older woman, and I can't help but admire his skill.

'Mrs Davies, Mrs Davies. I know you're the one who's going to save me. I need a meeting room for this afternoon, and the one I used yesterday was ... well ... come on ... *you* know. It's uninspiring. Right?'

Mrs Davies face is grey and tired and her eyes are watering, but she smiles at this customer as though he's her long-lost son. 'Of course, Mr Rickman. Of course. I know just the one for you. It's on the first floor ...'

The porch shudders in the wind. Daggers of rain strike the windows. The bartender, I conjecture, had faulty information about improved weather.

And now Rickman is admiring the receptionist's felt flower brooch, asking her if she made it herself, and just when he's sure he has her on his line and in the boat, he drops her, flinging her onto the deck with a swift gesture of dismissal. He turns away and heads out, leaving the hotel's door wide open behind him. She stands there, gasping for breath, starry-eyed, not quite sure what's happened, while a cold wind races into the foyer. She hobbles out from behind the desk and goes to push the door closed.

I have to admit he's cheered the woman up, maybe even made

31

her day, and there can't be anything wrong with that. He probably did the same for me, less than a month ago in London.

I think about that day. It's just before Christmas and only a year after Siamak's death. The staff, as always, are expected to enter into the spirit of the season, but this year the sight of tinsel chills my blood and I'm not the only one wondering how bad it has to get before it's not worth carrying on. Still, I'm doing my duty and making paper-chains with a bemused Sudanese asylum seeker – fold, loop, wet the glue, seal, repeat – on the day Rickman visits the hostel. Sally brings him into the common room and says, 'This is Mr ... er ... Ben Rickman ... who works for ... er ... Voluntary Action for Something or Other ... and he wants all your names and personal details.'

The man is wearing a hoody and jeans and he smiles despite the tense silence Sally's introduction has caused. Very few of the long-term homeless are going to volunteer their names and personal details to a white English man they've never met before.

'Sally, Sally,' he reprimands. 'Like I told you on the phone, we're piloting a scheme we hope will help people get back into the swing of things when they're having a hard time. As you know very well, making connections is the most important thing we do in life. And what we're offering here isn't much, but it just may help people keep in touch with friends and family and what's going on in the world.' He turns to the residents: 'And I don't want any personal details – I just need a name. You can write Mickey Mouse if you like.' He waits for the laugh. There isn't one. He stoops down to the bag by his feet and takes out a smartphone. 'And then we'll give you one of these. From Father Christmas.' He beams around the room. No one moves or speaks. 'It's simple. Want a phone? Put a name here. Any name. Then I can sort you out with a network and get you started.'

And that's it. Despite rumours of secret tagging and surveillance, word spreads round the hostel and by the time he's gathered names from everyone in the common room the people who've been hiding upstairs are appearing in the doorway too.

I take the chance to stop looping strips of coloured paper into a chain and watch this man talk his way into the confidence of some of the most reticent people in the city. Then I leave to heat soup and to butter bread for lunch and to do office work, and every time I come back he's still there, talking, moving, joking, taking down names. He's a puppy – a shorthaired golden Labrador that hasn't gone to fat but probably will in the next few years – and even Sally has warmed to him. She's putting another cup of tea by his elbow, looking over his shoulder while he explains for the twentieth time how the phone works.

And then he's sitting himself down beside me on the sofa in the corner of the room. 'Job done,' he says, leaning back forcefully into the cushions. I carry on pretending to read the *Radio Times*. 'What about you? Don't you want a state-of-the-art phone? Or is the boyfriend getting you one for Christmas?'

'I'm staff,' I say. 'I don't need your corporate bribes.'

He acts surprised. 'So you have one of these already?' He flourishes the phone in front of me. 'It'll help you keep in touch with everyone you care about while you're at work, especially when you're on a night-shift and missing out on your social life.'

'I don't have a social life.'

He pretends to be crestfallen. 'Dinner then.'

I look at him.

'Or a pint after work?'

I don't answer.

'I'll get them in if you tell me what you want.'

'I don't want,' I say, and he laughs. I go back to the *Radio Times* and he picks up his bag. I can hear him joking with Grant in the corridor, and then the front door closes behind him. I notice a brief change in the hostel's atmosphere – a lightening, a break in the monotony.

It's a few days later and I'm crossing the Hungerford Bridge after a night shift. There's a cold December wind blowing up the river from the sea and the sky above the buildings is a striated swirl of orange and blue. I feel like the figure in Munch's painting 'The Scream' – I'm the only person going home after work, and everyone else is surging over the river to their offices and computers, and they are silent except for the shuffle of their feet on the concrete.

And then one of the silent people detaches from the crowd and turns to walk back towards the tube station beside me. It's Rickman again. I pick up my pace, and, because I'm taller than he is, he has to jog to keep up with me. This time he's wearing a suit and tie and a smart black coat, but the voice is the same – a flurry of words in estuary English. He says something about Tegid Rhys, and perhaps it's the element of surprise, or my addiction to coffee, but I agree to a doughnut and a cappuccino in a café off the Strand.

He squeezes onto the plastic chair opposite me. He rips open a sachet of sugar and adds it to his espresso, tastes it, and then adds three more sachets.

'Crap,' I say. 'All that phone stuff. It's crap, isn't it?'

'Not if you work for a phone company. It's very useful. It says "We care!" Call it redwash. And all that stuff about us not paying taxes and exploiting the miners in Africa who dig out the rare metals ... well, all that will fade into the background of people's awareness and they'll allow themselves to want what they really want, which is a brand new phone ...'

'So it's PR for a phone company?'

'In a roundabout way. I use what I'm good at to make a living. We can't all be social workers.'

'We can't all be wankers.'

'Ah. Abigail. You are a harsh woman.'

I wince. 'Abby,' I say, just before I wonder how he knows my name.

'There's more to me than my job. Everyone has to earn a living. And not everyone can be as pure as you are.'

'I'm not pure. I'm just disappointed. Benjamin.'

'That's sad,' he says. 'And it's Benedict. Except when I'm hanging out with your sort. Then it's Ben.'

I watch him drink the espresso and start on the doughnut. It's covered in pink icing, and I think his inability to keep still has probably kept the weight off so far. I find it hard to imagine him watching a film or reading a book.

'Seriously though,' he says, 'don't you get attached to the clients?'

'Service users.'

'Service users. Do you get attached to the service users? Is it hard when they leave, move on?'

'People always leave. And if they don't leave they die.'

His expression shifts from cheeky to wistful. 'Yeah,' he says. 'I know about that. My mother died when I was ten.'

I look in his eyes, and then I look away. Shit, I think. Is that true, or is he working me? If he's acting, he's very good at it: sadness and the simultaneous struggle to evade it are hard to fake.

'And I have another motive,' he says, 'for going round the city's hostels with a bag of phones.'

'An ulterior one, I suppose?'

He shakes his head. 'I'm looking for a friend of the family – a neighbour who was really good to us when my mum was dying. You know, he'd help with the practical stuff, like taking me to school and football practice, and getting the shopping in. And his wife was a nurse, and she'd help my dad out with the medicines, and explain things the doctors said. Rhys, they were called. Well my dad told me a few weeks back that they'd split up and the husband – Tegid – had gone off the rails and was living on the streets. I'd like to help him out if he's having a hard time. You know, to say thank you.'

I feel like I've been punched in the chest, but I try not to show it.

I can't believe this PR man, who I wouldn't trust to take care of a pet stone, knows Tegid and is concerned about him. And I feel a twinge of guilt because I haven't answered any of Tegid's postcards and yet this stranger is going to great lengths to find him. A stranger I may have judged too harshly. It's something I've been accused of before. 'There was a man called Tegid Rhys at the hostel,' I say. 'But there's no point looking for him in London. He's in Wales, in a campervan. Last I heard he was parked up in a place called Pont ...'

'Rhith?' And it's only when he says the name of the place out loud that I make the connection with the headlines. Ben Rickman has made it too. He lets out a low whistle. 'That's weird,' he says. 'Wasn't that where the accident was? You know – that place where a drone crashed into a caravan and killed a woman?' He breaks off a small piece of doughnut and looks at it, and then he puts it back on the plate and squashes it with his thumb.

The bright fluorescent lighting in the café makes my eyes sting, and the double-decker bus pulled up outside sounds like an entire building site at work. I need to lie down in a dark, quiet room.

Rickman follows my gaze to the traffic backed up on the road outside. 'I'm going to take you away from all this one day, Abby. Where would you like to go?'

'How about Wales? Seems like a popular choice.'

'Nah. Too wet and cold. Think of somewhere warm and dry.'

'I can't think. I've been on a night shift and I need sleep.'

'I'll text you with my suggestions,' he says. 'Spain? Portugal? Greece?'

'You don't have my number.'

'I know where you work. I'll write you a letter. Dear Abby, How about Italy? Or the Caribbean? But not Cuba. They wouldn't let me in. I'm not pure enough. Love Ben.' He looks at his watch and stands up. 'Got to get to the station.'

'To hand yourself in?'

He grins. 'I'm going to the train station, not the police station, because I'm catching a train to Wales. I'm going to find Mr Rhys, bless him, and make sure he's ok, and then I'll get us a little cottage in the hills because I can see you're intent on moving to Wales, despite the weather. We'll settle down and have kids and grow old together. I'll let you know when I've found the perfect place and you can pack up and join me.'

He stands up, drains his espresso and then takes the other pink doughnut off the plate. He's on his way out the door when he stops abruptly and comes back. He has the doughnut in one hand and his briefcase in the other and then he sticks the doughnut in his mouth and props the briefcase on the table and opens it up. He winks at me and pushes one of his phones across the table.

I don't expect to see him again. We don't live in the same world. But when Tegid's postcard and campervan keys arrive in the post a few days later, I think about Ben Rickman and his dying mother story, and it leaves me with more unease than the usual bullshit pedalled by a male predator. He wasn't after me.

'Is there anywhere in town I can buy a waterproof coat?' I ask Mrs Davies as she processes my bill.

'There's a camping shop.' She leans forward over the desk to mime directions, wincing with the pain the movement causes her. 'I'm not sure they're open in the winter, though.'

'Was that Ben Rickman?' I ask her. 'I haven't seen him for years. We used to work together in London.'

She looks at me and nods but doesn't offer any other information.

'Is he still with the phone company?'

She looks confused. 'He works for the Consortium,' she says. 'Security.'

'Consortium?'

'You know,' she says. 'The army people.'

Another hurl of rain rattles the front windows.

'Take this,' the receptionist is saying, reaching under the desk and pulling out an umbrella. 'I won't be needing it till lunchtime. Just pop it back when you have your coat.'

I take it reluctantly. Handbags, slippers, aprons and umbrellas – they all seem like emblems of a domesticated womanhood I've tried to avoid. But I don't want to reject her kindness. And then I think of something else I could ask her, something that occurred to me in the night about Tegid and his way of being in the world.

'Yes,' she tells me. 'There *is* a second-hand bookshop. It's opposite the camping shop.'

Under the umbrella outside the closed bookshop and sheltered from the wind by the street's single row of buildings, I feel as though I'm standing in a Japanese house with the paper walls pulled aside. I listen to the raindrops tap on my little black roof, and I watch them drip from the umbrella's rim. At the same time I'm breathing the cold, clear air of the mountains. I think about spending the day standing around under this umbrella, watching the silver rain pour past me. The experience is a revelation, and I wonder if slippers and handbags also provide pleasures I've been missing out on in my bloody-minded avoidance of anything comfortable.

The shop's name is embossed in gold across the window: Y Ddalen Ola. I peer through the glass at a display of books on photography and books of photographs – mostly of mountains. In the dimness of the room behind the window I can make out tall bookcases, and I picture Tegid standing there in his frayed clothes, running his fingers over the tattered spines, drawing out what looks to him like a promising tome and leafing slowly through the pages. I'm seeing a ghost, I think, and pull back. I haven't considered he may be dead.

There are a few leaflets stuck to the window of the door. One advertises a parent and toddler morning at the community hall. Another shouts 'Learn to Kill in Wales' in English and in Welsh. It's for a meeting of the 'Campaign Against the MT4S Consortium'.

The shop's opening times are also there in gold on the door and they tell me I need to wait another day, so I go over the road to the camping shop, which is open, and I choose a black waterproof coat from the rack of men's walking gear, and a four-season sleeping bag, and a pair of ski gloves. On the counter by the till are small plastic dragons and Welsh flags on sticks.

*Water drips into a pool. He knows where he is. He shone his lamp into that pool a few weeks ago. He reached in to touch the twisted machinery of an old cart lying just beneath the surface. It wasn't there. It was three metres down. That's because the water here is clear like the air, filtered through the earth and rocks, deprived of light and life.*

*He can move his hand. He lifts it to his head, feeling for the lamp. It isn't there. His head is wet. He tastes the liquid on his fingers. It's blood.*

*He listens to the water dripping. He tries to shout. There's no sound. He wonders if he hears something else. He wonders if he hears someone moving over the rock, if he feels hot breath on his face, if there are fingers tightening around his wrist, lifting his hand, letting it drop.*

*There's no one here. There's water dripping into the pool, and the cool, empty air.*

# 5

## Campervan

At the old bridge there's a gale blowing and I stop to pull up the hood on my new coat. I lean out over the low stone wall to watch brown water pouring through the arch a metre beneath me.

On the other side of the river I trudge a mile on the climbing A-road. With every passing car I'm leaning into the hedge then hauling myself out of it, and in my new waterproof coat I'm like a boil-in-the-bag dinner. Rain drips off the hood and into my eyes and my jeans are plastered to my thighs and my thighs are ice cold. But when I get to the turn-off to Bethania the rain stops and I'm on a single-track lane and there are no cars at all. I walk in the middle of the road and pull down my hood and unzip my coat and let out the heat. I can see the peaks of higher hills towards the north and I feel a sense of nothing much. It's as close to wellbeing as I get, and I'm grateful for it.

Before the road reaches the ghost village, and just before a farm called Allt Wen, I take a track which heads up another valley towards the New Cottages – or towards 'Raven Davies' on Tegid's version of this landscape. It's not signed as a footpath and is probably a forestry track, but it takes a mile off the route by road. I wonder if Raven Davies is a real person, or a figure from slate-mining history, or a phantom of the map-maker's imagination. Or a talking bird who's retired from the messy business of ferrying messages between doomed lovers.

The track takes me alongside dense pine plantation where small holly trees lean out like prisoners trying to escape their cells. The silence seeping out of the forest unnerves me and my city-honed senses switch to hyper alert. It's too quiet. There are no people around. The calm I felt on the valley road, with its high hedges and smooth tarmac, disappears. I clutch my rucksack by the straps at my shoulders, in case of a mugging, and keep telling myself not to be so fucking ridiculous.

Looking back down the valley I can see a cluster of low grey houses snuggled into the bowl of hills, and in the middle of the houses is the hulking shape of a chapel. Bethania. I check the map again, compulsively making sure that the path I'm taking will lead to the New Cottages. It skirts the side of the valley between heaps of slate outfall which look like chunks of the grey sky fell to earth and shattered. Chips of slate clink beneath my feet. Then there's a ruined winding shed, and leading down from that, towards the valley floor, are rails, and on the rails there's a splintered wooden cart fixed on the incline by an iron rope. All of them – rail, cart, rope – are rusted together into one piece.

And then, across the valley and half way up the hillside, there's a square black hole. It has straight sides and a river of slag spilling down the slope in front of it, and whoever cut it out of the hillside made a mess of the view. Even so, I'm compelled to keep staring at it. It's like an invitation to nothing. It is nothing.

When the terrace of houses appears around the curve of the hillside, I can see the New Cottages aren't new at all but as old as the quarries. They're backed into the hillside out of the wind, and probably out of direct sunlight too for most of the year. I approach the gable end of the terrace and see the stonework has been repointed, and there's a blue tarp strapped to the roof. The path takes me round the back of the cottages, above the ground floor windows and above the thick tangle of brambles that fills the narrow ditch between the house and the hillside. I can hear a radio playing inside.

At the other end of the terrace there's a blue estate car parked against the wall and next to it a battered Ford transit. A tarmacked track leads down from the houses to cross a stream on a concrete slab and then curve up the other side of the valley to a road. It all fits in with Tegid's map. It all makes sense now I'm here.

I walk between the cars and push through a rusty gate to the front of the houses. There's a sloping garden with a copse of rhododendron bushes in the middle but nothing to suggest anyone has tended the place in years. The door to the first cottage is painted blue, and the paint is peeling off, and opposite the door is a wood store with stacks of logs on pallets. I knock on the door and wait and I'm cold now that my sweat has cooled inside my clothes. I know from the maps that the cottages are back-sided, facing north, and it's dark and dismal standing in their shadow.

I walk along the slate slabs to the next doorway. It's just an empty frame, and there's no glass in the ground floor window. Inside there's a fireplace without a surround and rusting tins of paint on the mud floor.

The next doorway has been filled in with a stone that matches the rest of the cottages, and the last door in the row is made of solid wood and has a slate nameplate on the lintel. It says 'Murmur'. The radio sound is coming from the roof, and I can hear steady hammering now. When I knock the hammering stops and someone shouts hello.

I back up a little, into the light, and see a man lying on the roof. He sits up.

'Raven Davies?' I ask.

He looks at his watch. 'She's at work,' he shouts down. 'In the forest.'

I don't fancy my chances of finding her 'in the forest' so I decide to come back later, but as I fumble the gate-latch with my gloved fingers the man shouts again. 'Wait. Hang on.' He's standing up now, silhouetted against the grey sky, holding a hammer in his right hand and waving at me with the other. I don't want to hang on; I want to run or grab a weapon of my own. But then he seems to slip, dropping the hammer as he slithers down the tiles. It lands with a sharp crack on the slates next to me. 'Sorry, sorry,' he says as he rights himself and climbs down the ladder. I'm still staring at the hammer when he reaches the ground, and when he lurches forward to pick it up I kick it out of his reach. He pauses, stooped and holding out an empty hand.

He stands up slowly. 'I heard a chainsaw. Up that way.' He nods towards the track rising into the forest. His thick-rimmed glasses have slipped down his nose, and I think I can hear the faint trace of a south Wales accent in his voice. 'That's probably her,' he says, pushing his glasses back up his nose.

I turn back to the gate. I know he's picking up the hammer behind me and I keep walking.

'Are you a friend of hers?' he asks, but I pretend I haven't heard.

The path rises steeply and becomes a shallow stream. I slosh through it until I reach a forestry track which heads upwards through more dense pine plantation. High banks of orange mud dwarf me and, above the mud, pine trees soar into the sky.

I listen. There's no birdsong, only a gentle swishing of the trees and the sound of my boots on the shale, and sometimes the distant whirr of a chainsaw. When I come out of the trees into the light the clouds have begun to break up and there are patches of blue sky. I stop to look back and the forested hills below look like the mossy stepping-stones a giant would use to bound down to the estuary. I pause, and breathe, and something inside me expands and lets go. It's a feeling I remember. It comes with mountains and deserts and night skies. It's the utter relief offered by something – a landscape, a skyscape – that doesn't care about you at all.

I keep walking, up and up, and then to the left of the track is a slope bristling with splintered tree stumps. For a few moments I can't grasp the cause of this devastation. It looks like the site of a UFO crash-landing, and then the words 'clear-fell' come to mind, along with 'desolation' and 'destruction' and 'death'. I've woken up the day after the apocalypse and I'm walking, dazed and in mourning, through a smouldering battlefield, wondering if there's any other life left on earth.

I trudge on. The trees are now deciduous and bare, and the intermittent whirring of the chainsaw is louder and, there's the low rumble of an engine too. I come around a bend to see a tractor parked in the middle of the track. The cab's empty. There's a flicker of movement in the leafless woods. Someone's dragging a log through the undergrowth. When she sees me she drops the log but keeps walking towards me, picking her way over the brambles like a woodland pixie.

'Are you lost?' she calls. She's wearing work clothes – jeans grained with mud and an old jacket worn through to the stuffing at the elbows. Bone-thin and delicate, she has lank black hair down to her shoulders and a baseball cap squashed onto her head. It isn't how I pictured a forester. I imagined someone burly and big, not elfin and slight. She pulls off her gloves and drops them on the ground, then she leans against the bundle of logs which hangs in a cradle of chains at the back of the tractor and takes a pouch of tobacco out of her shirt pocket. She's clearly expecting a long chat with a lost rambler.

I spoil that. 'Raven Davies?'

She goes around to the tractor's cab and turns off the engine. In the silence that follows I hear the distant sound of machinery, the beeping of a reversing truck, and far off, on the side of another brown hill, there are diggers and trucks moving about like toys in a sandpit.

'Chestnut,' she says, pointing at the logs on the back of the tractor before settling against them again. 'It used to be a great clefting wood, but the farmers want their fencing off the shelf now.

45

We've found a use for it, though: pizza oven in The Bridge Hotel. Did you know they cook the pizzas in a gas oven and then finish them off over wood? Gives them the right flavour, apparently.'

She crosses one leg over the other so she can lay the open roll-up on her knee, and then she takes a little plastic bag out of her pocket and removes a lump of resin. She lights up a corner, watches it glow, and crumbles it onto the tobacco, then she rolls up the joint with her fine fingers and looks at me for my answer.

'No,' I say. 'I didn't know that.'

'Is it wood you're after? We've got plenty of Chilean beech.' She waves the joint at the valley. 'It grows fast here and splits when you cut it so it's treated as a softwood, but in Chile it grows slowly and is a hardwood. No idea why.'

'Maybe it's the rain,' I try. I'm used to this. People talk at me whether I respond or not, which is probably why I choose to spend a lot of time on my own.

She shrugs. 'Plenty of rain in Chile. In the mountains.'

She offers me the joint and I shake my head. 'Tegid Rhys,' I say. 'I'm looking for a man called Tegid Rhys.'

She takes a more focussed drag on the joint and squints her eyes at the tiny machines on the far hill. 'There used to be ten gangs working these hills. Now it's all contractors. They come in with their hired machinery, they chop down the trees, and then they go away. But I know every inch of these forests. So does Tegid. That's because he makes maps. They're good, too. Good maps. Have you seen them?'

At least I know we have the same man. 'Have you seen him?' I ask her.

'Hasn't been by for a couple of weeks. You a friend of his?'

'He sent me the keys to his camper van,' I say.

She opens her mouth to laugh, and that makes her cough. I can see gaps between her nicotine-stained teeth and I wonder how old she is. Thirty, I guess, or maybe younger – she has the skin of someone who's worked outside all her life. She drops the stub of the joint into the mud at her feet and stares out over the forest. 'I've got a new boss,' she says. 'An enviro mentalist.' She waits to make sure I've noticed the pause between enviro and mentalist, and then carries on. 'He wants to do things differently, but it seems to me his new ways are just like the old ways, and they didn't work in the end, did they? No one could make any money out of trees. So that's it for forestry, isn't it? If there's no money in it, that's the end of it.'

'I guess so.'

She glances at me. I've stuffed my hat and gloves into my pockets and she's taking in the bristles I call hair and the rows of piercings in my ears and the tattoos on the backs of my fingers. 'Are you from a city?' she asks.

'Uh-huh. London.'

'What's it like?'

'Busy.'

She laughs. 'Not like here then.' She straightens up. 'Back to work,' she says.

She walks towards the trees to fetch the log she left there. I watch her lift one end with both hands and start pulling it over the rough ground towards the tractor. Then, without stopping, she lifts one hand off the log and points along the track. 'I went up to see him a few days ago,' she shouts. 'He wasn't there.'

It's midday and the winter sun is at its zenith. Even so, it's only just over the brow of the hill and it's blinding me. I keep my eyes down on the stony track and go through more clear-fell, where the silence is different from the silence in the dense plantations. I strain to hear it. It's empty and hard, like an accusation, like the anger which comes with grief. On the far hills legions of fir trees are ranked against a depthless sky.

The track enters more forestry and becomes a dark avenue of rutted mud fringed with bright green fronds of moss. There are rusting signs forbidding fires. And then the track and the forest stop abruptly at a five-bar gate. I climb over it and cross sheep-bitten grass to the ruins of a quarry building on the brow of the hill, miles from any house or village. I try to imagine working there, walking all those miles from the nearest home to spend the day digging in a hole. I cross the rounded top of the hill and stop at a sheer drop down to a campervan nestled between three cliffs of slate. It's parked nose to rock, as though the horror will go away if it doesn't look.

I go back down and around the hilltop, taking the van keys out of my bag as I walk, as though I'm on the road from the tube station to my bedsit at midnight and I need to open the door quickly and get in and shut it behind me, or if that fails and I'm not fast enough, to have the keys in my fist as I punch the man following me. But when I get to the van I see I don't need the keys at all – the side door is open. I step over a checked tea towel mashed into a puddle and pull myself into the van. The floor is strewn with papers, and a tin mug juts out of the mess like a half-buried archaeological relic. I climb over the stuff on the floor to a small table at the back and sit down on the bench, taking my backpack off and setting it beside me. There's a shiny red kettle – blackened around the base – in the litter on the floor. I lean forward and pick it up and set it on the table.

I didn't expect him to scrub the van clean for me, but the mess is depressing. There's a brown folder on the table and when I open it up I find it's full of clippings from newspapers. I leaf through reports and photographs of air attacks on towns in Afghanistan. Gaza. Beirut. Drone strikes in Yemen and Pakistan. Stories of women scraping their families off the walls of their front rooms, and soldiers shovelling kids into bin bags in the ruins of a school, and village elders passing out body parts to survivors to give them something to bury.

I put them all back in the folder and close it. Through the back window of the van I can see hills and forests, and beyond those there are mountains capped with snow. I picture a jet on a training flight screaming up the valley, or a drone cruising silently over the forests, and I know he would have considered it – shooting one down.

And then I think of the collateral damage, of Anwen Pryce living in a caravan, trying to make a life for herself and her little girl. I don't know if she had a job, but I can make a guess at the sort of work and wages available to a woman in a place like this: seasonal waitressing, cleaning holiday homes, being on the till in a shop. She would never have been able to afford a house, even if she dreamed of one.

I pick up more pieces of paper from the floor. They look like Tegid's work – notes, equations, maps, drawings and diagrams. There's something on the Geneva Convention of 1983, and a piece about the need to make air-launched bombs and long-distance shells illegal. I laugh at that. Tegid the Dreamer. I could tell him the United States relies on air power to reach distant targets because most of its perceived enemies are very far from its own shores. Just like the British Empire had to rely on ships to police its dominions. And he'd say, with a smile: 'You're right. They aren't going to give them up ... and I'm not going to give up trying to make them.'

I shuffle through more of the papers. An article he's highlighted points out that if infantry soldiers 'accidentally' massacred a family in their home there would be an enquiry. At least. But when a drone misses its target and hits a school or a wedding party, even an official acknowledgement is hard to come by.

I wonder if they'll go beyond official acknowledgements with the accident that killed Anwen Pryce. If it was an accident.

I push the papers away and sit back on the bench. I'm not sure what to do now. I don't know whether to stay in the van or run back down the hill as fast as I can and never come back. Then I see another one of his hand-drawn maps – a beautiful swirl of colour and symbol – and I pull it out of the mess and put it in my coat pocket.

I'm still sat there, contemplating my options, when I hear a car engine. Then the forest gate creaks on its hinges. I climb back over the rubbish and crouch down by the open side door. I think about my exits. I still have the keys in my hand – I could drive out of the quarry – but I have no idea if the van will start. I slide into the driver's seat, and in the wing mirror I see the figure of a man holding a stick. I put the van in reverse and turn the key and the engine sputters to life and the van lurches backwards. I see him dive sideways, roll in the mud and stand up. It seems like an over-reaction, and I want to laugh, but I concentrate on swinging the van around to face through the gate he's left open, and then I lower the window and wait for him. He approaches slowly. I like that – the way he's wary of me. It's a good start. He settles his black-rimmed glasses in front of his eyes and I realise it's the roof man from 'Murmur'. Apart from Raven Davies, he's the only other person I've met since I left Pont Rhith, so I shouldn't be surprised.

'I didn't know it was you,' he says.

'I'll close the gate.'

'You nearly ... '

He has a smudge of mud on his face and he's still holding the stick, and now a small scruffy dog is tugging at the end of it.

And then he seems to work out what he has to do. 'Sorry,' he says. 'I didn't mean to scare you ...'

I watch him and his dog go through the gate. I watch them get into the blue estate. I let the van's engine run until he's disappeared back into the forest, and then I switch it off and listen. The wind gusts around the van and rustles the papers on the floor in the back. I clench my fists on the steering wheel and for a moment I think of going after him. I'm furious he thinks he frightened me, and I want to put that right. But I have no idea what I'll say – or do – to convince him that I'm not some vulnerable female quaking in her boots, and even I know it's close to madness to want to try.

# 6

## Bench

After ten minutes of moving papers and crockery around I sit down on the bench and assess my lack of progress. I'll need bin bags and a more positive attitude towards tidying up. The former is easily remedied if I return to town for supplies. The latter will take coffee or a gun to the head.

The light has begun to leave the hillside, and it isn't the dark and the emptiness that bothers me – it's who else might be up here in it. I look out over the wide valley and see trees and logging tracks, and above the forests there's a smooth-topped hill with a chunk taken out of its side and scree in grey streaks down its green flank. And all the time I'm wondering who's behind me, around the curve of the hill, or coming up through the forest.

I leave the new sleeping bag on the bench and sling my bag on my back. When I slam the sliding door shut three sheep at the top of the cliff lift their heads to peer at me for a moment and then go back to nibbling the grass. I close the forest gate behind me, as though I've already taken responsibility for this patch of hillside, then I run down the track at a slow jog. In the open spaces, between the trees, a fine rain comes down slight and slant from a peached sky.

This time I take a direct route down to the New Cottages and there's no man with a hammer on the roof. I walk as fast as I can, but by the time I get to the A-road it's dark and the rain is pelting down. I'm also wearing a black coat on a country road at night and the cars skim past me without slowing. I take shelter in a bus stop and scan the timetable. It tells me I'm in luck – there's one of three daily buses in ten minutes.

In thirty minutes I'm about to give up and start walking again when the bus swings into the lay-by like a flood-lit spaceship coming in to land.

'Not from round here then?' the driver shouts once I'm sitting down. There are no other passengers on the bus, so I assume he's talking to me.

'London,' I say.

'Yes,' he agrees. 'You look exotic.'

I examine the dripping ghoul that is my reflection in the window. Exotic isn't the word I'd choose. I look beyond my pale face and the cap pulled low over my eyes, and I can just make out the glint of the river as we cross the new bridge.

'Been here before?' he asks.

'No,' I say. 'Not here. But I used to spend holidays up north.'

'Thought I recognised you,' he quips.

He pulls up by the station and stops. 'Thanks,' I mumble.

'No problem,' he says before the doors creak shut. 'I was going this way anyway.'

I check my watch. It may not be too late to catch a train back to London, but when I ask at the ticket office she tells me it *is* too late. So I phone the hostel as I walk along the street and Alex answers. He wants to know if I'll be available for a shift on Thursday because he's doing the timetable. He also wants to know where I am, and if I'm OK, and his kind tone makes me sad. I tell him I'll be away for a week and end it there.

My toes are numb in my boots and I'm hungry. I buy a cheese sandwich in the Spar, and a packet of crisps and a yogurt. It looks like a child's school lunch, so I supplement it with a bottle of beer and walk back down the main street, wondering if the pub has cheaper rooms than the hotel. In the Llew Coch Inn there's a log fire burning at the far end of the room and a huge screen above the bar showing a cage fight. I draw my eyes down from the entangled limbs and ask the bartender if they have a room for the night.

'No,' she says. She's pulling a pint, and her chunky rings point their serrated gems towards me as she heaves on the pump handle. 'Is it just you?'

When I say yes she tilts herself to the right and shouts, 'Mr Ellis!' at an old man at a table in front of the bar. He doesn't respond so she tries again. 'Mr Ellis!'

He turns to face her and grunts. He's wearing a hat with ear-flaps, and his thick grey eyebrows seem to meld with its fur trim. The way he's sitting sideways-on to the table, and still wearing his hat, gives the impression he's ready to leave at any moment. Even so, he's curved a proprietary arm around his pint as if to say, 'This much, it is certain, is mine.'

She finishes pulling the pint and brings it round the bar to Mr Ellis and starts chatting to him in Welsh. He drains the beer he has and passes the empty glass back to her. His thick tweed jacket looks structural – as though it's the scaffolding which holds him upright – and he strains against it when he lifts his arm to put the fresh pint to his lips.

'Are you with the army or the Consortium?' she says, turning back to me.

'Neither,' I say. The two of them confer again, and then, very slowly, as if she's making sure I understand the question, she says, 'Are you a journalist?'

'No,' I say, irritated now. 'Are you?'

She arches her eyebrows. 'You could try Delyth Roberts at the bookshop. She does B and B sometimes. But not if you're with the army or the Consortium. She doesn't like journalists from England, either. Or people who own more than one house.'

The old man chuckles. 'That is true.'

'I'm a residential social worker. I don't own any houses. I'm not with the army, or the Consortium, and I'm definitely not a journalist.'

She shrugs. 'Depends if she likes the look of you then. Just ring on the shop doorbell and she'll come down.'

I can see she expects me to leave, so I ask for a pint of whatever Mr Ellis is drinking and I sit down at his table. He shuffles in his seat, eyeing me sideways.

'So you're a farmer?' I ask him.

He lifts his chin briefly.

'I don't know much about farming,' I say.

His silence is loud with an unspoken, 'No shit.'

'My Taid was a quarryman.'

He stares into the middle distance as if he can't hear me.

'If there's one thing worse than a tourist from England it's one with a Welsh heritage,' I say. He narrows his eyes. 'I don't suppose you know Tegid Rhys?'

'No,' he booms. 'I do not.'

The bartender glances over at us. 'Yes you do,' she says. 'He's the one that wanders around with a daft smile on his face. You know,' she circles a finger by her head. 'He's a bit ... twp.' Mr Ellis ignores her but she doesn't give up. 'Of course you know him. He's living up your way, in a campervan. Or that's what I've heard.'

Mr Ellis still ignores her. He turns to face me directly and says, 'Do I know you?' and then he goes back to protecting his pint, his eyes on the door, his point made.

The bartender raises her eyebrows and shrugs. I finish my pint in silence. I like Mr Ellis, and it isn't mutual.

When Delyth Roberts finally gets to the door – shifting cardboard boxes out of her way – she doesn't seem surprised to see me and she doesn't ask if I'm on my own. She's saying, 'Yes, bach,' before I can ask for a room. 'It's not en-suite but there's no one else here tonight so the guest bathroom is all yours.'

She retreats into the shop and I follow her, turning sideways to pass between the bookcases. We go through to a dark hallway at the back of the shop, and then up creaking stairs. On the landing she lets me into a small room, squeezing between the bed and the wardrobe to switch on a gas fire. When she comes back she hands me a set of keys and I'm suddenly conscious of how I must look to this small, middle-aged woman with her neat black bob and kohl-rimmed eyes. I put my tattooed fingers in my pockets and smile. I feel like a creature that has crawled out from the underbelly of the city and is now blinking in a strange warm light, wondering if it's safe to breathe the air.

I also sense I don't faze her. She's not judging me for travelling alone with a small bag on my back and a man's coat. She says, 'I'll do breakfast at half past eight,' and I see then that the reason she isn't judging me is because she isn't paying me any attention at all. It's as though she's listening to a beautiful piece of music in her head and she has no intention of turning it down for my benefit.

I recognise that expression from the hostel. It's the expression of people who have something precious to protect and who don't trust most of the rest of the world not to barrel through it in a tank. And that's when I decide she knows Tegid, and I'm about to ask her about him when I think of Mr Ellis's response. I'll wait till morning and try to work out a better approach.

Left alone in the room I sit down on the bed, laying out my picnic on a bedspread of tiny lilac, red and purple squares, like the squares in an exercise book coloured in by a neat and pattern-conscious child. Like the books Tegid drew his maps in. And while I eat the limp sandwich I stare at a framed print on the wall of an oil painting – a Victorian version of a Welsh mountain, looming and majestic, Alpine and jagged. But it's not much like a Welsh mountain because Welsh mountains are worn down and cloud-shrouded and this one is triumphant and assertive, thrusting itself up into a blue sky. There is a lake nestled in its craggy embrace, and then I'm wondering what it would be like to be here with a lover, on holiday, but besides a fantasy of fucking on the neat bedspread, which I'm not about to indulge in while eating a cheese sandwich, I can't settle on the idea of love and companionship. I've been on my own for too long. I tell myself, again, that I have adapted over the last two – or is it three? – years to being on my own, and I prefer it that way. And nothing has changed since the man I lived with for a while said: 'Your bags are always packed and by the front door.' Which was true, unlike the other stuff he told me, like 'I'm not sleeping with her or anyone else' and 'I love you'. In the end, it wasn't difficult to let go of something I'd never really had. I'd made up a picture of him, of us, out of the jigsaw pieces I could find, but lots of the pieces were missing, and when he finally presented me with some of the missing pieces the picture turned out to be completely different from the one I'd put together in my head. The one I'd probably wanted but couldn't admit to wanting: the one where we were close, and I was safe.

Tegid was just enough human contact for me after that. Now I think of it, our relationship wasn't the kind either of us could crawl into and curl up in, and it wasn't an illusion either. It was an accidental friendship based on the things we had in common, like the distance we kept between ourselves and other people, like our inability to be anywhere for very long – our refusal to be anywhere at all in case we were called upon to take part in our own oppression, or worse, in someone else's. Staying still always seemed like a tacit agreement with the way of the world, so we didn't stay still. We kept leaving, and we always refused to arrive.

So it's strange that such a fragile connection between two travellers has brought me here. I imagine the tiny current set up between us at the hostel established its own magnetic field, amplified by forces we had no control over. Like Siamak's suicide. Like the drone crash. And now that force field has pulled me to Pont Rhith. The problem is, he should be here too.

* * *

The first time I meet Tegid I'm doing outreach on the Embankment. The shift starts under the cold moon-face of Big Ben, where Sally tells me how she began her own odyssey into the world of rough sleepers. In the winter she'd bring blankets and a thermos of tea for the people hunkering down for the night against cold stone walls. And I can picture her with her grey pony-tail bouncing, thrusting comfort into the shadows, demanding people take what she has to offer them, whether they want it or not. She was a geography teacher, but she quit to work at the hostel full time. Daytime. Nighttime. Summertime. Wintertime. She rarely goes home. Sometimes her girlfriend arrives at the door to drag her away from work, but Sally always seems to have one more thing to do and the girlfriend sits on the desk in the office and swings her legs and waits.

That night it's spring and a warm breeze is blowing through the stone ravines of central London and the white bulbs strung between the cast-iron lampposts flicker behind trembling young leaves.

Outreach, Sally tells me, is her favourite part of the job. I hate it. I hate stopping strangers in the street. I hate trying to start conversations. But I'm being paid to watch and learn, and what I see is the artful construction of cigarettes. She sits on one of the stone steps that lead down from Westminster Bridge and a young lad – an ex-soldier, he says – walks up and down next to her, talking quickly as he climbs and descends, up and down, up and down – a short pause to take the roll-up off her – then up and down again. I lean against the wall and listen while he tells her he saw his best friend's legs blown off and he can't sleep any more. She nods, licks, rolls, hands him another roll-up. And then he stops moving and squats down, out of the light. I can only see the glow of the smoke at his mouth, and when he's finished it he flicks the stub over the wall and walks away.

57

'Same story every time,' she says, and as if to answer the question I haven't asked: 'He doesn't like being indoors.'

I follow her along the wide pavement for a while. In the brief moments when the traffic noise subsides I hear the river sucking at the mud bank. Then she's slowing down and nodding towards a woman struggling to push a shopping trolley full of plastic bags up the kerb and off the road. She's wrapped in layers of fat and rags.

'All yours,' says my boss.

I move sideways across the pavement and mutter hello.

'Fuck off,' she says.

Sally, who hasn't stopped walking, is laughing – I can see her shoulders shake. She set me up. I stare after her and consider going home to sleep. She's a small woman with a fast walk and her accent and confidence were acquired at private school, but, she tells me, she's a class traitor and a member of the Communist Party. I slouch after her.

It must be around midnight when she stops by a bench and sits down next to a white-haired man who's writing in an exercise book. It's late, and I'd like to lie down on the pavement and go to sleep. Instead I sit on the concrete plinth below the bench and hug my knees, staring into the space the river makes in the march of the city's buildings.

The man keeps writing. Sitting on the concrete plinth, I'm closer to his feet than his face, and I can see the frayed hems of his trousers. His shoes are scuffed, split at the seams and sagging. There are two carrier bags at the end of the bench, and both are crammed with exercise books.

'It's only because you're used to it.' I look up and realise he's talking to me. He's leaning forward over his knees and his irises are very blue against the pink of his skin and the white of a scar which cuts down his cheek to his jaw.

'You like being lost because you're used to it. That's what people do – learn to like the things they can't change. But you shouldn't do that. You're still young. You should settle down. With children and animals.'

He's talking to me, but I can tell he doesn't expect me to hear him. And he isn't really looking at me, either: his eyes let everything through. Not in and out, but through, because his eyes are polished and shiny while the rest of him could do with a good scrub.

'Yeah,' I say. 'I will if you will.'

I sense Sally stiffen – I'm doing it all wrong – but he just smiles. 'We need more houses,' he says. 'Don't you think? It would make your job easier. I'm sure they could put houses on the moon, but then all the pipelines and electricity cables running between here and there would get tangled up.'

I stare at him. I assess him. I'm not quite sure if he's teasing me. He's put his head down and he's writing again. I'm pretty sure he's telling us, in his own way, to fuck off, but that's not how Sally sees it. She's nodding at me. She wants me to try again.

'What about solar panels?' I say. 'We could use solar panels.'

I can see her wiggling her fingers against her mouth. The gesture means I shouldn't, in the parlance of our work, collude with insanity, but I'm crap at small talk. I also know that a little more collusion with insanity and I won't have to do outreach work ever again. But it's a fine line between that happy outcome and losing my job altogether. I move up onto the bench beside the man and reach for his exercise book. As I take it he grabs my fingers and stares at the tattoos and says, 'Pythagoras. You have eight fractions scratched onto the back of your hand signifying the Pythagorean scale.' And then he lets go and hands me the exercise book. 'Did it hurt? There are lots of nerve endings in fingers.'

'Not at all,' I say. 'I was drunk.'

He looks out at the river and then points at the exercise book I'm holding. 'I'm using maths to prove that it's possible to travel faster than the speed of light. Einstein was wrong about that.'

All I can see are dense equations in a tight blue script.

'And Pauli's proof that the speed of light can't be exceeded is mathematically incorrect. Look.'

The proof he offers, as far as I can tell, takes place in a world of space and silence. I honour it with my own silence.

'And Stalin decided,' he says, 'after initial reservations, that Einstein was right, so no physicist in the Soviet Union could question Einstein, and anyone who did ended up in a fatal car accident. But it's different now. I'm working on this paper for the Russians. Look.' He jabs a finger at the blue scrawl. 'Einstein has to be wrong, don't you think?'

I look. 'Uh-huh,' I say, handing the book back. 'I think you've got him there.'

He lets it rest in his lap. His fingers are long, elegant and smooth. I guess he didn't have a manual job before he became homeless.

'Anyway,' he says, 'there's another good reason for the speed of light not to be the ultimate barrier to space travel.' He pauses and looks at me.

'What's that then?' I say.

'The aliens would never get here.'

I look at Sally. She's raising her eyes to the fairy lights, but she can't see what I see: his eyes are smiling. We're sharing a joke and a wistful hope for alien company in a world where humans have made themselves lonely. A light wind rustles the new leaves and the edge of the river slaps the bank. We stay there talking for a while, under the street lamp, and then at dawn he comes back to the hostel.

Sally puts my name down for a training course on dealing with clients with mental health problems. In the meantime, I'm officially released from outreach work.

Tegid stays at the hostel for the spring and on into the summer. 'I'm not quite a full shilling,' he tells me, and I tell myself our friendship is about resonance. How else do I explain it? We have nothing to give each other. There's no exchange between us. There's no contract or chemistry or promises, just a shared amazement at the strangeness of being in the world at all. The wonder of it. And the fear.

One day in autumn he upsets everyone by remembering he has a bank account and savings. There's a flurry of discussion about his place at the hostel, but the charity's policy is clear – he'll have to move out. A week later, just as I'm finishing a night shift, he turns up in a campervan and parks it outside. He wants to show me around his new home before he drives it away. He wants to show me the little table he can use to write on and the way the table turns into a bed. He wants to show me the hob where he sits a shiny red kettle and the cupboard with holders for cups and plates so they don't rattle about when he's driving.

Then he comes into the hostel's dining room and says goodbye to everyone while they're slumped over breakfast. A few lift their heads from mugs of tea and plates of bacon, egg and beans, and assess his good luck. Then he bounds up the stairs to knock on Grant's door but there's no answer. 'Tell him I said goodbye,' he says to me.

I'm standing in the office with my coffee and I know I'm no better than the residents at saying goodbye. 'So where you off to?' I manage.

'First I'll go and see Caroline,' he says. 'My ex-wife.' He looks at the floor and frowns, and I wonder if he'd forgotten about her, as well as his savings. Then he brightens up and heads towards the door, still talking. 'And then I'm going west. I'm going to Wales. You should come and visit me. I'll send you a postcard and let you know where I end up.'

But he knows I won't visit him. He knows I won't keep in touch. His cheerfulness falters and he says, 'I'll always have a home in you, Abby, won't I?'

'Yeah,' I say, and I think I know what he means. He means he knows I won't forget him, and that's true enough. I stand on the hostel's steps and give him a brief wave goodbye as he drives off. Then I start walking along the South Bank towards the bridge and the tube station. There's an early-morning mist over the river and a busker is playing by the steps, sitting on an amplifier and plucking at the metal teeth of a kalimba with his thumbs. The instrument's odd overtones hit the air and fade into pure notes that sound like water dripping from an icicle into a tin bucket.

And it must be enough for me to know Tegid is still somewhere in the world because I don't miss him till the following winter when a drone crash in Wales kills a young woman, and I get a postcard with a bridge on the front and that message on the back.

I circle the bed till I locate a bin. The sandwich carton clunks against the sides.

Perhaps Tegid will be outside the van when I go back in the morning, standing there in a trench-coat that's too big for him, shuffling from foot to foot, smiling at me sheepishly because he's changed his mind and decided to keep the van after all. And I'll say – because I'm pissed off about spending money on a night in a hotel and having to listen to Mr Palmer waffle on in his car – 'For a moment I thought you might have shot down a drone and killed a woman.'

His smile will slip and he'll say, with real concern for my twisted soul: 'Violence isn't inevitable. You should know that.'

I take my phone out of the side pocket of my backpack. There are no messages and no missed calls. I curl up on the bedspread and stare at the painted mountain – the curve of its shoulder and the cold blue lake at its heart.

# 7

## Bed and Breakfast

There's a Welsh dresser behind me and a poached egg in front of me. Butter melts into golden puddles on my toast. Through the window I can see the side of the add-on kitchen, and then the land drops steeply away and the view is a long one of the wide valley floor and the winding river and hills steaming with morning mist.

My landlady pushes through the kitchen door with a cafetière of coffee. She sets it on the table next to me and then goes over to the dresser and rearranges a plate. Then she sits down on an old church pew under the window and looks out at the valley. 'Another wet day,' she says.

I slice the toast and the egg. The yolk oozes into the butter. She asks me the standard questions – where I'm from, what I do – but she isn't interested in the answers. She's waiting for something else, as if she already knows I'm not in Pont Rhith for a holiday, and even though I've rehearsed my question many times it still comes out garbled. 'There's someone I know. I think he was here.'

Delyth Roberts waits. She's wearing silver earrings that swoop up in the same direction as the lines around her eyes, making her look amazed. And amused.

I take a deep breath. 'A man called Tegid Rhys,' I say. 'He had a campervan. A yellow campervan.'

She comes over to the table and picks up the cafetière. 'More coffee, bach?' And then she pours herself a cup and goes back to sit on the pew under the window. Behind her the mist is lifting slowly off the hills and a wintry light breaks through the clouds. 'White hair, and a scar ... here?' She runs a finger across her right jawline.

I can tell she isn't surprised by my interest in Tegid. The woman from the pub must have told her I was looking for him. I wonder what I'm going to say next. Will I pretend a professional concern and use words like 'relapse' and 'episode'? They're not my words. My word is 'guilt'. I feel it tugging at me like the strands of a sticky web, drawing me into a complicated mess of human needs and the failure to meet them. The poached egg and butter turn over in my stomach because I stuck all his postcards on the wall of the office, in public, and left them there with the other sad pictures of holidays staff went on: a man in a toga by the Parthenon; a quartet of fishing villages on the Algarve.

Delyth puts her coffee cup down on the pew next to her. 'When I started the campaign, he came to the meetings,' she says.

'Campaign?'

'Against the military training ground.' When I don't respond she says, 'There's an old quarrying village about four miles north of here called Bethania. No one lives there anymore, and a they want to turn it into a mock mountain settlement where they can practise "counter-insurgency" warfare.'

'Who are "they"?'

'MT4S, or the Military Training for Security Consortium. They're doing it for the MoD, but the MoD's privatised all their ...' She stops dead. 'Why are you looking for him?'

I'm not going to voice the insane suspicion that a white-haired man in his sixties, who was fond of writing mathematical equations and drawing strange maps in exercise books, could have had something to do with the drone crash. So I voice the other reason, and it sounds just as improbable. 'He left me the keys to his campervan. Said I could have it. It seems wrong to drive it away without seeing him.'

She relaxes a little and I can see her sum me up. She's thinking I'm like most English visitors – here to take what I want and what I think I'm entitled to – and then leave. Someone whose whole understanding of human relationships comes down to assessing the value of things, and then forcing a favourable exchange. But I'm not quite willing to leave her with that impression. For some reason I want her to like me.

'I'm worried about him.'

She smiles. She massages her left hand with her right hand and gazes out of the window. 'I haven't seen him for ... He was at the last meeting, just before Christmas,' she says, and then she's listening to that melody in her head again.

'He didn't like the military,' I say, trying to bring her back from wherever she's gone.

She looks at me and laughs. 'He hated the jets, and the drones, and when the Consortium turned up with its training-ground plans I think he thought they were trying to annoy him personally.'

I consider this, and, along with the caffeine, a sense of relief surges into my bloodstream. If he felt to blame for the accident, it wasn't because he'd caused it directly. It was because he had a hugely exaggerated sense of his own responsibility for the state of the world. In his mind, he'd failed to stop the war machine, and he'd failed to bring down the military-industrial complex, and therefore every violent death at the sharp end of a missile was his fault. Most paranoid ideas have a grain of truth in them, but only a grain. I can therefore let go of my own suspicion that he had something to do with the crash. I can relax into a fuzzy acknowledgement of our collective guilt for letting stuff happen, and for not stopping the killing and the brutality. We are all to blame. Ah well. Nothing we can do about it. Time for another slice of toast.

'Do you know where the van is?' she asks.

'He drew a map.'

'Perhaps you'll find him there, bach.' She stands up and starts clearing the table.

I tell her I've been to the van already, and he wasn't there, and the place was a mess, and the lock on the door was broken.

She picks up the empty toast rack. She puts it down again. When she says, 'Now then,' I expect something to follow, but it doesn't. She begins to stack the plates. 'Are you coming back tonight, bach?'

'No. Thanks. I'll try the van.'

She raises her eyebrows. 'It's cold.'

'There's a stove,' I say, without much conviction. I don't know how to work a stove.

She gets up and goes over to the dresser, and then she stands there as if she's considering something. 'I haven't seen him since before the accident, and if ... if the van was broken into ...'

'You think something might have happened to him?'

She shrugs. 'It's possible. He was an easy target. He stood out.'

'You mean he didn't belong around here?'

'No. I don't mean that. But he didn't keep his head down. He got involved in things, like the campaign against the Consortium.'

'I can't imagine he was much of a threat to them.'

She doesn't respond. She opens a drawer in the dresser and takes out a leaflet. 'The Consortium are having a drop-in consultation tonight. I'm sure they want to reassure people, after the accident. They want to tell us that having the military here practising for war isn't dangerous. It will be good for us. It will keep us safe and create jobs.' She hands me the leaflet with a gesture of indifference. She doesn't think I'll attend, and she's right. The Consortium's plans have nothing to do with me. But I know she's also right when she says, 'He might turn up,' so I take the leaflet from her and say I'll be there.

Later that afternoon I'm sitting in the campervan passenger seat in my coat and gloves. I've filled a bin bag with rubbish and broken crockery and stacked all the papers and folders and exercise books into piles. I've done this so I can walk from the table at the back of the van to the seats at the front, and not because I'm a great fan of tidiness. My flirtations with purity are more to do with sound than a neat house.

Sound and the human voice. I used to talk to Tegid about that, because he didn't just tell me stuff, he listened too. One time when he was still living at the hostel, we set out at midnight and walked into the morning. I learnt from him that the satellite dishes point south-south-east and that the air has a different smell when it blows in from the sea over the city. By one of London's dark and submerged churches he told me that the altar would be at the east end of the building, so I tried the big wooden door and it was open and he was right – the altar was at the east end. We lingered in the cool darkness for a while, and I tested the acoustics by singing a verse of a hymn I remembered – a song about a still small voice breathing through the earthquake, wind and fire. He liked that. He asked me to sing it again. He said I was someone different when I sang, and I thought I knew what he meant. He meant I was someone better, someone whole. But then he said, 'I wonder how you'd sing if you could find the ground.'

I didn't sing it again. Once was enough.

I try to orientate myself now, sitting in the van, as though knowing which way is north and which is south will give me a grip on this place. A weak light struggles down between the slate cliff and the smeared windowscreen, and there are a few fallen trees at the edge of the forest, and the track from the gate has more puddles on one side than the other. It all suggests the quarry faces southwest – the direction of the prevailing wind. When spring turns up, that's where it comes from, creeping over the earth and warming up the soil. Perhaps Tegid was fully intending to sit here and watch the spring arrive, and then something lured him – or pushed him – away.

Then again, perhaps the isolation and the rain drove him bonkers and he ended up hurling things about in this little box and running screaming into the forest. Perhaps he scribbled a postcard to me when he got to town and then jumped on a train back to the city. Any city. But however much I try to make that story stick, it doesn't work. Noisy madness was never his style.

I take a bottle of water out of my bag and wriggle back between the front seats to the hob. I've managed to find the calor gas bottle and I've opened all its valves. I've congratulated myself on the pre-purchase of matches, and I feel a little surge of pleasure and mastery when the ring lights. I put a mug full of water from my drinking bottle into the red kettle and set it on the flame. I've brought a packet of fresh coffee and I slice it open and savour the first wave of its fragrance. But then my self-satisfaction evaporates: there's no cafetière, or anything else, to filter the coffee with. I search through all the cupboards and then I have an idea. I take a clean sock out of my backpack and spoon the coffee into that. It is, I decide, a mild example of addiction. I've seen more destructive ones.

Sat at the back of the van with my woolly coffee, I look out across the valley and see two yellow diggers moving like feeding insects across a brown patch of clear-fell on the far hill and a tiny logging truck cruising slowly along a track. In front of me, neatly piled up on the table, are Tegid's folders of misery. I open one. It contains a piece about a 2005 attack on a bookshop in the Kurdish town of Semdinli, with background information on how from 1983-1991 the use of Kurdish in public was prohibited in Turkey. It's clearly a subject that interests him, even though it says nothing about drones or missiles. He has written at the top: 'Tyranny demands everyone be understood at all times.'

I close the folder and gaze around the van. This van is how Tegid found a way to be *somewhere* without being anywhere for good, so I can't understand why he's left it. It seems like the perfect compromise between his nature and the social rule that we must all live in a container. But then I look around again and see the same fittings and soft furnishings you'd find in an ordinary bricks-and-mortar house, only here they're in miniature. A little sink. A little sofa. It's as though all the accepted cultural signs of homeliness have been simmered down to something intense and essential. And sinister. There are curtains, for god's sake, on top of the blinds, with brown ovals on an orange background, and the cushion covers on the bench are worn golden velvet with tassels around the edges. It's only the cast-iron stove, with its bodged flue, that says this isn't a desperate imitation of an English suburban semi.

There is always the possibility, I realise, that he came back to find something important that he'd forgotten, and he'd already sent the van keys to me, so he had to break in. And he was in a hurry, and he couldn't find the thing he'd forgotten, so he threw stuff around ...

I pull the curtain aside so I can see the gate at the end of the track through the forest. The rain has stopped and mist steams upwards out of the trees and into the low cloud. I wonder why I don't drive away now. I could go down to the sea and watch the waves pound the shore. Or I could leave the van and go back to London and my bedsit and wait for Tegid to get in touch. But I don't do either. I go to the MT4S public consultation event, because Delyth Roberts is right: it's just the sort of thing he'd turn up to.


A month after he left London, the first postcard arrived from Wales. I stuck it to the cork board in the office. It was a picture of a stone bridge over a mountain river. Others followed, all with the same picture on the front – a bridge of stone arches over a rocky river. On the back he told me to visit, or to get in touch.

I didn't visit. I didn't get in touch. He never owned a phone and he didn't give me an address. In other words: I thought I had good excuses for ignoring his attempts to keep the connection between us alive.

One night in the hostel's office I took a roadmap off the bookshelf above the desk. I leafed through it, amazed to be amazed at the existence of a world outside London. The city had swallowed me whole and obliterated any sense I may have had of the rest of the country. I started at the top of Scotland and moved slowly down the west coast into England and then into Wales. Along the way I paused to stare at the places I knew – the north-west English towns I'd lived in, bits of Manchester, and then the mountains of Snowdonia. There was the village I went to for every school holiday – the place my mother ran to, with me in tow, when she left my dad. It was a place I felt safe in, and cared for, but when Nain and Taid died it fell off the end of the world for me and I never went there again. And all the time I was looking at the map in the hostel office under the bright strip light, I was thinking about the gap between the flatness of its representation of the world and the feelings of nausea and unease – or warmth and love – that came up with the memories attached to the simple names of places. I wanted to tell Tegid about that. I wanted to tell him about the pools of contentment, surrounded by an intense mist of loss, that I sensed in those Welsh mountains, and the grey anxiety – the smell of cigarette smoke and the blank white walls and brown carpets – attached to the names of English towns. It was a personal geography, and it drove me through the world.

Then I looked up Pont Rhith in the index. The road map showed a small town close to the middle of Wales and far to the west. There was a train line running through it, and a river, and all around the town were miles of roadless space: hills, forests, lakes. It looked like a perfect place to disappear into, and then find, with the absence of distractions, that the stuff you thought you'd left behind had come with you.

* * *

It takes five minutes of lurching downhill in the campervan to reach the New Cottages. It's nearly dark and there are lights on in Raven's place. I figure I have enough time to call in on her before I go to the Consortium meeting, so I park up by her transit van and go through the gate.

I have to knock a few times before the curtain at the front window twitches. When she finally opens the door she stares at me for a few moments and then seems to remember who I am. She steps out onto the flags in her socks and peers over the gate at the campervan. 'You found it then?' she says, going back into the house and waving me into the kitchen. She pushes some clothes off a chair so I can sit down, and then she starts filling a kettle at the sink. It takes my eyes a moment to adjust to the room's brightness – it's lit by an unshaded bulb.

'The door was bust open,' I tell her, but she doesn't respond. There's a child's drawing – a stick-figure next to a Christmas tree on a triangular mountain – pinned to the white fridge with a dolphin magnet. I guess it's a picture of Raven because the child has drawn straight black hair and a cap on the top of the stick-figure's head, and she's holding what could be a chainsaw. Or a large comb.

Raven blocks my view of the picture by opening the fridge door and taking out a bottle of milk. She sniffs at it and shrugs. When she moves away I look at the other picture hanging at a slant on the fridge. It's a round face with short stick-up hair on top and two big eyes. The eyes are filled in with a blue crayon and there's a line down the cheek and across the jaw – a scar extending out of the face and into space.

'We used to sit outside the van,' she says, 'so I could smoke. I never went in.'

I catch the past tense but don't challenge it. 'And he told you his theories about the speed of light and the aliens?'

She laughs and fishes the teabags out of two mugs and piles sugar into one of them. 'That and other things. Trees, maps, quarries. Sugar?'

'No thanks. And drones?'

She brings the mugs over to the table and sits down, drawing one foot up onto the other knee. She's a woodland elf, I think, and this is the inside of her magic mushroom house. She takes a tobacco pouch out of her top pocket and starts rolling up on the Formica table, prising the lid off a small tin and fishing out a sprinkle of grass.

There is a delicious, palpable quiet in the brightly lit cottage and I'd like to enjoy it, but I've already worked out that silence isn't something Raven does by choice. The presence of a stranger in her kitchen, though, must have thrown her, because she seems to be struggling for words. She takes a sip of tea. Her folded leg jigs up and down under the table, rattling the teaspoon in her mug. A hyperactive dope head, I think, not an elf. Then she leans forward across the table. 'Last time I saw him,' she starts, 'I'd taken him that letter from the Consortium. I thought he'd laugh. I mean, it was all "Do come and have tea and biscuits with us, what." It had a map on it, too, the letter, with a big circle around these cottages and the quarry where Tegid's van is.'

'And did he laugh?'

She leans back and lights the joint and takes a long slow drag. She's not wearing her baseball cap now and it's left her hair flat against the top of her head. She's tied it back into a ponytail and a strand escapes and falls over her face and she smooths it back behind her ear. 'That's why he's gone, isn't it? He didn't want to live next door to the new neighbours from hell.' It's the most assertive thing I've heard her say about Tegid's whereabouts and her own conviction about the matter seems to settle her and the floodgates of her speech spring open and she's off. 'I grew up in these hills and woods,' she says. 'I could skin rabbits by the time I was ten years old and catch a salmon from the river and cook it on a fire. But the strange thing is, the first time I cut down a tree I heard it scream. I had nightmares that night. It must have been February, when the sap is rising and everything is coming back to life. The next time I cut one down was easier. I don't know if the trees stopped screaming or if I stopped listening, but the thing about people like Tegid is that they never stop listening, and you can't live like that, can you? Not in this world.'

'So you're not part of the campaign?'

She shakes her head. She opens her mouth. She closes it again. 'Not my thing – *campaigning*.'

'But Tegid was involved?'

She shrugs. 'Incomer. Did his own thing.'

I try a polite sip of the tea. The milk's off. It doesn't improve the experience.

'Just take it,' she says then. 'Just take the van. He wanted you to have it. Take it.'

'Uh-huh.' I change the subject: 'Did you know Anwen Price?'

She grins. 'Went out with her in school for about a week. She was mental then. Always in trouble. Drinking, not going to school. She wanted to do – what's it called? – make-up for films, but she ended up working in the hairdresser's. And pregnant. Nice lad Joel, but they weren't right for each other. She was looking for something else. I think she wanted to get out of here, go somewhere better, somewhere more exciting.'

'Don't you?'

She leans towards me over the table. 'I belong here,' she says. 'I can go away when I want to, and I can come back. But Anwen ... she was one of the clever ones at primary school, and beautiful when she didn't cake herself in make-up. She could have done anything, gone anywhere. She had long blonde hair down to here.' She points at her waist, and then she puts her hands flat on the table and sits very still.

I can see she's picturing Anwen as she was – alive, complicated, beautiful. And I feel like I'm picking at one of my own scars, as well as hers, by asking about her. It doesn't help me to know more about the dead woman; it just makes Tegid's possible involvement in her death even harder to contemplate.

I get my phone out to check the time. 'I'm going to that public meeting with the Consortium,' I say, standing up. 'D'you want to come?'

'God. No thanks,' she says, and then she follows me out of the cottage and onto the slate slabs, still talking. 'Zoe. Anwen's little girl's called Zoe. She looks the spit of her mum. Bloody stupid death, wasn't it?' She looks up then as if she's wondering what else might come crashing down out of the heavens, but there are only dark clouds scudding across the night sky.

'Who lives in the end house?' I ask, nodding towards Murmur.

'A boy doing it up for his walking holidays,' she says, 'and I can't burn the bloody thing down because it's attached to mine.'

'Globalisation,' I say. 'We're all connected now.'

'You mean we're all stuck in the same sinking boat.'

When she shuts the door behind me I'm shocked by how dark it is. I walk past the derelict middle house which divides Raven from her neighbour, and then past Murmur. The oak front door looks solid and out of place because everything else up here seems to be crumbling and rotting and falling down. Murmur is different, and in the chink of amber light emerging from between the curtains I glimpse another way of living in the world: rooted and safe. But it's only a glimpse. Houses scare me. When I think of houses I think of the Saturdays my mother spends crying in the bathroom while he slumps in an armchair, satiated like a lion after a kill. I think of hiding in my room and tuning out her gulping sobs and listening to the football he's watching on the TV – the chanting of a whole stadium of men compressed into a thin, mean sound that squeezes out of the telly and permeates the house along with his cigarette smoke. I think of the coiled fury of him as he lurches up the stairs after me. I hear him battering the sides of a mug with a spoon as he stirs sugar into his tea. For me, the sound of tea being stirred is both a prelude to destruction and a summing up of the banality of domestic violence. Menace sticks to little things.

And perhaps Raven is right: when the men with guns said they were coming to play, Tegid just upped and left.

# 8

## Community Hall

The Community Hall is at the top end of the main street. It's an old red-brick school and its tarmacked playground is now a car park. I park the van across two spaces and go in through a door with 'Merched' carved into its lintel.

Inside the hall, deflated balloons dangle from the walls and there's a smell of disinfectant and dust. A scrap of silver tinsel taped to the edge of a windowsill triggers the image of Siamak's face, bloated and dead. I stare at the floor for a few moments. It was an affront to our humanity, as well as his, the way we were blocked by the laws of our land from giving him a safe place.

I blink and look up and focus on the display boards arranged in front of me. They show fashionably matte photographs and crisp black text, and in front of the boards, with their hands behind their backs, are the MT4S Consortium's representatives to the town of Pont Rhith: a pale young man in a grey suit and an orange-faced woman in a skirt and jacket and high heels. They speak to each other and smile. They nod and joke. They laugh lightly.

The public have kept their coats on and are drifting between the boards. A woman in a plastic mac stops to read one. I stand behind her and read it too. Large letters proclaim 'MT4S Consortium and the Environment'. There are pictures of the hills around Pont Rhith, and the village of Bethania, and chunks of text in English and Welsh. The text explains how the area will be protected from damage by the Consortium's development of a military training ground. And not only protected – the land will be improved for the sake of posterity.

I'm finding it very hard to concentrate on this information or absorb it. It's like waiting for the weather forecast after the news, and then realising it's finished and you still don't know if there's a storm on the way, or a week of uninterrupted sunshine, because you started thinking about something else the moment the diagrams appeared on the screen.

I make another effort to focus on the displays and the sounds of shuffling boots and muttered conversations cloud my head. Every time the door opens I turn around to see if it's Tegid, to see if he's come to question the whole event, and protest against it. I force myself to concentrate on the board in front of me and discover that any re-building of the abandoned houses in Bethania will be done using locally sourced materials. The Consortium, it says, will be consulting with sustainable-energy experts to make sure all work meets the highest standards when it comes to carbon emissions. It says soldiers need to train in authentic mountain regions; therefore, the restoration and caretaking work will involve the planting of 2000 indigenous trees.

If the trees are truly indigenous, I wonder if they should be *re*-planted rather than planted, and as I'm ruminating on the meaning of indigenous, I sense another suit next to me and he's leaning down to pull out the right side of the board. It scrapes across the floor and he pushes it back in again, lining it up with the perfect angle he's obviously imagining in his head. When he's satisfied that he has it just right, he stands up. I enjoy noticing how much taller I am than Benedict Rickman. I also enjoy the confusion on his face. 'Benedict, Benedict,' I say. 'Have you moved to Wales without telling me? What about our plans? Did they mean nothing to you?'

He opens his mouth to speak but a large woman wearing a red anorak is requesting his attention by putting her hand firmly on his forearm.

'The hills and mountains of Wales are the sacred lands of the Celtic people,' she announces, and her voice is loud in the hushed hall and her accent is English, Home Counties. 'They are *not* a place to teach people how to kill.'

I notice the MT4S nametag on Rickman's lapel – he's clearly moved on from doing PR for a phone company. I watch him remove his arm from under the woman's hand and step backwards – perhaps because she's taller and wider than he is, and he doesn't want to be overshadowed by her. He glances quickly at his colleagues, assesses their usefulness, and seems to decide not to pass the buck.

'Of course we understand your concerns,' he tells her. 'You care deeply about this country, about Great Britain as a whole, and so do we.' And then he starts to explain that the MT4S Consortium offers world-class training to soldiers carrying out security and humanitarian missions in highly dangerous areas of the world. 'The MT4S Consortium is about helping to make other beautiful areas of the world safe and productive places to live in,' he says. 'Just like this one.' As he speaks, he seems to glow with affection for the woman in front of him, as though he has just recognised her divinity and would bow down in front of her if he weren't in a public place and duty-bound to fulfil his professional duties for the next hour or two.

She shakes her head. 'Bollocks,' she says.

I walk away from them and try to read another board. And another. The big words settle on me: security, economy, local employment, sustainability. They are solid words, and they are all linked with MT4S. Everyone thinks these words refer to good things. Only an idiot would put them up for discussion.

Rickman is watching me, and I wonder if he's working out if I'm still a worthy target for his attention or just one of yesterday's completed tasks. And then I hear a loud voice speaking in Welsh. I edge around the 'MT4S Consortium and the Local Economy' board and see it's Mr Ellis, the old man from the pub, and he's wearing his green tweed jacket and the Russian-style fur-trimmed hat with ear-flaps. He's haranguing the Consortium's pale young lad with a flood of Welsh, and the lad has a look of panic on his face – he doesn't understand – and he keeps taking a step backwards until he's stopped by a display board showing a picture of a stone farmhouse with a wind turbine on its roof.

Rickman comes to the boy's rescue, oozing around the board like engine oil and coagulating at his younger colleague's side in a pool of persuasive energy. 'Noswaith dda, Mr Ellis,' he says, and then he turns to the wider room and announces: 'The MT4S Consortium strongly believes that people should be able to express themselves in their native tongue. Would anyone be willing to translate for this … gentleman.'

'For you,' says Delyth, who has also appeared from behind one of the boards. 'Translate for you.'

Rickman's lips disappear into a tight smile. 'Yes,' he says. 'For me and anyone else who doesn't understand Welsh.'

She turns to the old man and asks him something. He answers quickly, throwing back his head after each sentence as though he's trying to shake off his hat. There's a moment's silence before Delyth takes in a deep breath and starts to speak, staring into the middle distance as if she's reading from an autocue suspended from the ceiling. 'Mr Ellis says the English serpent has had its fangs in the back of the Welsh dragon for centuries.' She pauses. The old man speaks again. Delyth nods at him and continues. 'Mr Ellis says: I'm sure if the government of Her Majesty the Queen of England wants my farm and my land for its war games it will get them. My question is: how much is it worth to you?'

The constriction in Rickman's lips loosens and he squares his shoulders. 'I'm going to be absolutely honest with you, Mr Ellis, and tell you what we want. We want to create authentic mountain conditions for our soldiers. And that means farms and other businesses in the area should continue with their work. That's exactly what *we* want, and that's exactly what *you* want. Any disruption we cause to your productivity will, of course, be paid for. But we don't intend to disrupt anything. We'd like you to see this as just another form of diversification, along with tourism, holiday lets, caravan sites. That has to be a good thing, Mr Ellis, doesn't it? More compensation for farmers. More jobs. More money coming into the area. More money in your pocket.'

And then Mr Palmer from the caravan site is pushing himself forward through the group in front of the board. He's wearing a red tie under a grey bomber jacket and he holds up a hand and opens his mouth to speak and everyone turns toward him. But Mr Ellis hasn't finished yet and Mr Palmer has to wait while the old man continues with his speech. When the farmer stops a few people laugh, and then he looks at Delyth and she begins: 'Mr Ellis says there probably aren't many in this room who know about Saunders Lewis and D. J. Williams and Lewis Valentine and their setting fire to a bombing school on Pen Llŷn in 1936.'

Rickman obviously doesn't know what she's talking about but he understands the implications of setting fire to a bombing school. He moves his attention from Delyth to the old farmer. And then back to Delyth. He's not quite sure which one he's speaking to. He settles on the farmer. 'Mr Ellis,' he drawls. 'The elected Welsh Government fully supports the need for a highly trained British Army, and it's willing to invest in this particular project to the tune of millions of pounds in order to create quality jobs in this area. If you have a problem with that, you will have to take it up with the Welsh Government, and you will need to make sure you vote in the next Assembly elections.'

'Not just the British Army, though, is it?' A man with a ponytail and a denim jacket is standing at the back of the group. Even from where I'm standing I can pick up the smell of rarely washed clothes and wood smoke. 'Who'll be taking your training courses? Any bastard's army, as long as they can pay?'

A young woman by another board shouts, 'Yes, yes.' She has thick blonde dreadlocks and is carrying a backpack, as though she's just stopped off in Wales on a gap-year trip around the world.

But Rickman has prepared for this one too and he looks at Mr PR Junior and nods. The lad clears his throat nervously and states in a monotone that the Consortium is a private initiative working with the Ministry of Defence to provide military training to those who need it. 'We won't be training the members of any army that might pose a threat to this country. We're in the business of promoting human rights around the world. The MT4S site at Bethania will not be supporting or training anyone who abuses human rights.' And then he remembers the key words. 'But we understand your concerns. Thank you.'

The ponytailed man snorts. 'And what's this?' he says, pointing at the wind turbine on the roof of the cottage in the photograph in front of him. 'Total greenwash. Everyone knows a turbine on the roof of a house is bloody useless.'

Mr PR Junior is scanning the room for Rickman and looks relieved when he spots him at the margins of the little crowd, mingling with the public in a way that makes me think of a pickpocket scouting out his next victim. Rickman takes up the baton from where he is. 'Our expert advisers will be up to date on the latest sustainable technology.' And then he's turning to Mr Palmer and speaking as though Mr Palmer has just asked a question, although I can't remember hearing one. 'Yes,' he's saying loudly, even though Palmer's stood right beside him. 'It's a valid concern, Mr Palmer. And the research shows that the development will not have an adverse effect on the tourist trade. On the contrary, the training ground will bring income to local businesses in the low season. It will also contribute to improvements in the local environment – tree planting, conservation work, the clearing up of slate tips and the making safe of disused mines. All of that will actually increase the attractiveness of the area in the high season.'

Mr Palmer folds his hands across his belly. 'As chair of Pont Rhith's Trade Association, and as a town councillor,' he says, 'I'm reassured to hear that the training ground up at Bethania will have a positive impact on local businesses and therefore on the community as a whole. I think we should welcome this development wholeheartedly.'

Rickman looks at his watch. He thinks that's a fitting end to the consultation. 'Please help yourselves to refreshments,' he says, 'and fill in the questionnaire on your way out. We very much want to know what you think about this exciting development. We really need local input and we value your ideas.'

A few people drift towards the table of biscuits and teacups. The ponytail man and the woman with Celtic spiritual inclinations leave, together, and I see Delyth at the door handing them leaflets. But the old farmer, Mr Ellis, is taking a different approach. He's scooping up handfuls of biscuits and putting them in his pockets, and then he's standing by the table and slurping his tea. He doesn't speak to anyone and he's pulled the furry flaps on his hat down over his ears.

I scan the board entitled 'MT4S Consortium and Security'. It details the dangers we all face from international terrorism and rogue regimes. Nowhere is safe, it says. And Wales has its part to play in international security. It talks about the need for training in FIBUA – Fighting in Built-Up Areas – because villages, towns and cities are the locus of war now, not the battlefield.

Rickman's gaze fixes on Delyth, who's handing out her leaflets at the door, and then he's going over to the trestle tables and pouring out a cup of tea and taking it to her. He hands it over with a mock-gallant flourish and she thrusts a leaflet at him in exchange. He takes it and bows. I'm trying to work out the connection between his presence here in Wales and his visit to the hostel in London. When he came to the hostel, and when he bought me coffee and doughnuts, he wasn't trying to pull me, I know that now, and he wasn't looking for an old friend of the family either. He was pumping me for information about Tegid because it was part of his job. I just don't know which part yet.

And then I start to wonder why no one has mentioned the accident, or the drones, and I realise I'm waiting for Tegid, the mad man, to shuffle in with his white hair plastered to his skull with rain water, and his trousers just a little too short and frayed around the ankles. I'm waiting for Tegid to come in and start pinning his own pictures over the matte boards – pictures of massacred wedding parties, of people grieving the loss of their children, of families plastered over the walls of their front rooms, of Anwen Pryce smashed into the boards of her static caravan.

But it isn't Tegid who enters through the double doors and makes everyone look at their shoes – it's a lad wearing a tan leather jacket and a beanie hat. It's the man the bartender in the hotel edged nervously around while I ate tarte fine and chips. It's Zoe's father and Anwen's ex, and as Joel walks up to the boards people move aside to let him pass.

He stops in front of the 'Security' display and stands there assessing the words and the pictures, nodding to himself. And then he turns towards Rickman and says, 'We don't fucking trust you.'

This time it's the PR woman who goes into action, clicking towards him on her high heels. 'It was a terrible, unforeseen accident,' she's saying. 'We are all so very sorry for your loss. The whole country is grieving with you. It's now a matter for the RAF and the MoD. They're doing all they can to find out what happened and make sure it *never* happens again.'

Above the sound of chinking teaspoons and shuffling feet there are ripples of disquiet in the room.

'I'd like to make it clear to everyone,' she says loudly, 'that MT4S has nothing to do with the drones. The training ground we hope to build here will present absolutely no risk to the local community.'

Joel has his hands in his pockets and seems worn out by the

effort it took him to speak out. Delyth goes over and says something to him in Welsh and he smiles weakly. And then she holds up her stack of leaflets and shouts, 'The accident has shown us that those planes are real. They are not happening in another dimension that has nothing to do with us. They have everything to do with us, and we are responsible for saying no to their war machine. Come to a real public meeting tomorrow night. Here. And we can discuss how we're going to stop them building this ... *war school* ... in Bethania.'

There is a moment of silence, and then the young woman with the dreadlocks and the large bag on her back runs up to one of the boards with a plastic bottle in her hands and chucks its contents at the photograph of a little stone cottage with a wind turbine on the roof. Bright red goo dribbles down the board and drips onto the floor.

Rickman is at the door before she can get out, blocking her exit. He holds the door closed with one hand and makes a phone call with the other. The woman looks small and awkward, and I don't wait for the police to turn up. I leave through the kitchen at the back of the hall and take the campervan home to its quarry.

# 9

# Chapel

I greet first light with uncharacteristic enthusiasm. I've been so cold all night that dawn and a slight increase in temperature have been my only hope since the early hours. I'm wearing all the clothes I have with me, including my new coat, and I'm hunkered down inside the four-season sleeping bag with its hood fixed tightly around my head. When I breathe in the cold wet air is heavy on my lungs.

I wriggle a hand out of the bag and open the curtain by my head. There's a strip of white mist above the forest and above the mist the sky is pale blue. To the north the mountains are white with snow. I run my finger over the ridged ice on the inside corner of the window. I need to light the stove. I force myself to shed the sleeping bag and get up, dragging a bag full of old newspapers and kindling from under the bed and setting to work. I managed to get the fire going before, with advice from the man at the garage. I know how to crunch up the newspaper sheets into loose balls and pile the kindling around them in a wigwam. My cold fingers struggle with the match, breaking it in half. I blow on them and try again, and this time the match flares. Once the kindling catches I add briquettes and then close the iron door and watch the flames lick at the glass.

I make porridge with oats I find in one of the cupboards. In the same cupboard is a book on *Slate Quarrying in the Bethania Area*. I take it to the table with the bowl of hot slop and look at the black and white photographs of slate tips and machinery and the men who worked the mines and quarries. These men stare out at me from under their caps and don't smile. In one picture a group of three whiskery, bowler-hatted men pose beside a railcart loaded with blocks of slate – like big-game hunters in Africa bringing home an elephant. In another picture a man sits hunched over a slab with a hammer and chisel, poised to split it in half. And there's a photograph of a mill workshop with lines of men at the benches. A few of the workers peer at the camera through a filter of dust, as though they're staring at the ghosts of the future with curiosity and bemusement, but most have their heads down, ignoring the time that is to come and the attention of their well-fed grandchildren.

There are pictures too of the finished products: not just roofing tiles but a pulpit made of slate, and urinals, and pig troughs, and a billiard table, switchboards and gravestones. And a reusable coffin.

I find a trace of Tegid's presence in the book. There's a pencilled exclamation mark against a passage which says a quarry owner's takings included the profit he made from selling candles, powder and fuse to his own employees. They weren't allowed to buy them anywhere else – anywhere cheaper – and they couldn't do the job without them. And I find one of his maps. It's been folded up and tucked between the pages of the book. I spread it out on the table. 'Map' is not the word most people would apply to this scribbled mess of drawings. It's more like a hypothesis about the landscape. It shows trees with their branches growing out towards the south and the light; it marks ruined quarry buildings as if they were questions; it comments, in tiny handwriting, on the smell of the sweet air in a clearing in the forest where the sun has warmed up the fertile earth. But I know from our wanderings around the city at night that these invitations to experience form a sort of path, and this one leads to the chapel in Bethania.

Perhaps he was offering me a walking holiday, not a home, when he left me the van.

The kettle starts to whistle and I make coffee with the sodden sock, and while I'm drinking it I turn Tegid's map face down and write a list on the back. If I'm going to spend another night in the campervan, I'll need more fuel to burn, and more matches, and a coffee pot or filter papers. As I scribble down my list I notice the paper I'm writing on is headed with the words 'Curved Space Mapping Technologies', and there's a telephone number but no email or website address. That dates it, I figure, to before the 1990s.

It's not surprising that Tegid has a twenty-year-old bit of paper stuffed into one of his books, but it isn't until I'm on the path to Bethania that I decide I need to know more about Curved Space Mapping Technologies. When I go into town for fuel, I think, I'll also find somewhere with wi-fi.

There is a theory that language and music have a common source, and that music came first. For millennia human beings sang to each other, and didn't speak, and I wonder about a world like that. Not a world of badly done musicals – people bellowing out their feelings for each other on city streets or expressing their happiness in sunny corn fields or Alpine meadows – but a world of silence punctuated by soft lullabies and staccato attacks, by resonant longings and collective swoonings of joy and grief. And I think about that as I stand in the ruined chapel of Bethania, in the kind of silence that comes after the singing and shuffling and coughing and praying have stopped. The pews and the slate floor have been ripped out, and there's no pulpit or organ. I look up at the high windows and there's still glass in most of them. Plain, dust-smeared glass, of course, not stained glass. This is chapel. Simple. Pure. Austere.

And I remember how utterly boring it was, in the summer holidays, to be ushered into a chapel like this and hushed for an hour of sermons that made no sense to me in Welsh or in English, and how the singing came as a welcome break. I'd be standing next to my Taid as he nursed his own tenor voice like a baby, and then we'd have to sit still again and listen as the minister preached, slicing and chopping the air with his hands, and contorting his face into monstrous expressions of righteousness and anger. Sometimes I had to stuff my mouth with my fist to stop the giggles getting out.

My Nain didn't go to chapel. She was from the coalfields of the south and somewhere along the line her family had given up on God and gone Bolshevik. I used to wonder why my Taid still believed. He'd lost his older sister to TB, when she was sixteen, and I couldn't understand why anyone would thank God for His wonderful creation when children died from His diseases. But I also knew Taid's religion was a religion of love, not anger or revenge, and he was gentle, and their house was warm. He set a fire before going to bed, and he got up at 5am to light it. There was always the smell of coal and old towels drying on the airer in the kitchen.

I walk into the middle of the dusty chapel over broken slates, and I'm struck by the way the building focuses sound within itself and doesn't send it up a spire to heaven. But it doesn't obliterate sound from the outside world either – it just pushes it to a distance – and I can hear the river outside, and the wind in the trees. And then I hear something else, something out of place in an empty village. It's an oscillating hum, a mechanical whirring, and I realise it's coming from the sky.

I go back out through the vestibule where no hymnbooks line the low bookshelves and no one stands there ready to shake hands with me as I leave, or ruffle my hair with a hand calloused by quarry work or chapped with washing and scrubbing. One side of the arched wooden door hangs open on an upper hinge. I grasp the frame and pull myself back over the 'No Entry' sign which lies flat on the rubble. My eyes take a moment to adjust to the light, and then I see the source of the sound: there's a helicopter hovering over the hill, above the square black mouth of the mine entrance. A line dangles below it, swinging like a pendulum. I'm still looking up into the pale blue sky when a car comes around the bend in the street and heads directly towards me. I move back into the shadows as the vehicle breaks to a stop outside the chapel. I hear someone getting out and walking up the steps, and then he appears in the doorway, a dark shape against the light, craning forward into the shadows. When I step out in front of him he stops abruptly, but with less show than he handbraked the car, and I can see his face now.

'I think this place is perfect for us,' I tell him. 'It just needs a bit of work.'

Ben Rickman flips up his sunglasses and smiles. 'What's the hurry? You gotta give me time to get things organised. Don't you trust me, Abby?'

I laugh. 'Of course I do. With my life. I just know you're very busy with the new job. The big one. The one that will allow you to retire.'

'Exactly,' he says. 'You're getting the hang of this. And when I've completed it we shall be married. You know that, don't you? Fate has ordained it. Why else would we keep bumping into each other like this? And in church!'

He's still in the doorway and that's my only exit, so I say, 'Do come in,' waving him through the broken doorframe like a Lady of the Manor inviting a tradesman into her hallway.

'Ta,' he says. He walks over to one of the inner doors and pushes on it gently as if he thinks someone could be hiding behind it. It creaks open and he peers into the gloom of the chapel and sniffs. I'm watching his back – the long coat, the new military-style haircut.

'So all that stuff about phones for the homeless really was bullshit?' I say.

He runs a finger through the dust on one of the low bookshelves and turns to face me. 'My client was very happy with my work, and

89

I was happy because I found you. Love of my life. Saint Abigail, saviour of the homeless and the broken-hearted.'

'You weren't looking for me. You were looking for Tegid Rhys.'

'You underestimate your attractiveness.'

'And I doubt you have a heart.'

'Ouch,' he says, miming a punch to his chest.

I hear a car door slam shut. I push past Rickman to the doorway and look out. Down on the road there's a huge man in combat trousers and a black jacket leaning against the passenger door of the Range Rover, his arms folded awkwardly across his chest. He's one of those men whose muscles are so big he can't bend his limbs.

Rickman is standing in the doorway next to me, and I like us both knowing I'm taller than him. 'That's Jake,' he says. 'Standard issue heavy. Comes with the job. You should get one.'

'And what exactly is the job?'

'Ah ha. Thought you'd never ask.' He searches through his inside coat pockets and pulls out a card and hands it to me. 'Security,' he says, and then smiles apologetically. 'And I *will* need to ask you a few questions.'

I look closely at the card. 'It says you're Mr Benedict Rickman – a public relations consultant for the MT4S Consortium. It doesn't say anything about security.'

'I'm adaptable. Call it strategic research. There was a serious accident in this area last week. My client needs to know who's coming and going, and why. I'm sure you understand.'

'Strategic research for the MoD?'

'In a manner of speaking.'

'Which manner of speaking?'

He stops smiling then. 'I run a consultancy firm,' he says flatly. 'Just like I told you. We work for the MT4S Consortium, and MT4S is contracted to work for the MoD.'

I stare at him. This man, I think, is the sort of successful person I've avoided most of my adult life. He's probably avoided people like me too, and I'm hoping that puts him at the same disadvantage. But all thoughts of matching him in a fight are blocked out, along with the light, when the hulk arrives in the doorway.

Rickman ignores him. 'You were at our public consultation event last night, but you didn't fill out a form. We'd love to know what you think about our proposed development.'

I laugh. 'You mean you'd love to have my name and address.'

'I know your name, Abby Lockwood. But yes,' he says. 'I'll need to know where you're staying at the moment.' And without changing his chummy tone he says: 'Or I'll have to arrest you.'

I want to say something like, 'Don't be fucking stupid,' but all I manage is a gormless, 'Uh?', and though I'm pleased he doesn't have my surname right – I ditched my dad's name when my dad ditched me – I wonder why he's using it. I'm sure he's done his research.

Jake turns sideways to get in through the door and then he stands with his head tilted slightly to one side and stares at me like I'm an insect he may need to deal with later. I'm picking up the clear impression that any spark of compassion in the man was snuffed out before the age of two. The only defence against him would be a brick to the head.

'I'll have to arrest you under the Anti-Terrorism Act,' says Rickman.

'But the crash was an accident,' I say.

'It's still being investigated, and you knew Tegid Rhys, and I think you know what he was doing up here, and maybe you know where he is now.' He lifts his eyebrows in expectation of on answer.

'Arrest me then.'

He turns around slowly, as if he's thinking about it, and then he lurches forward and grabs my backpack off the floor and throws it to his minder like a rugby ball. Jake catches it and takes it outside and down the steps, and without thinking I'm going after him, taking the steps three at a time, but when I land on the road Rickman grabs me from behind and twists my arm up my back. I watch the hulk upend my bag and tip everything out onto the road, and then he starts going through my stuff: a packet of sanitary towels, a bottle of water, a wallet. He flicks through the wallet and takes out a bank card. 'Abby Hughes,' he grunts.

Rickman looks confused, then he shrugs. 'I bet that pleased your dad. But it doesn't matter now, honey. You'll be Abby Rickman soon enough.'

'I love this getting-to-know-you bit.'

Jake has *Slate Quarrying in the Bethania Area* in his hands and he sticks the rucksack under his arm so he can fan through the pages of the book. The map falls out. He looks at the scribbled schema for a while and then turns it over and looks at my shopping list. The whole inspection is a consummate show of power and he completes it by handing the map to Rickman who lets go of my arm so he can put the map in his pocket.

I turn to face him, but before I can land a kick to his shin he's backed up and started a lecture. 'Go home, Abby. I like you, and this isn't the place for a social worker. Seriously. Take your campervan and go to Snowdonia. Or go back to your job in London. You're good at it, and they need you there, and I really, honestly don't want you to get hurt.'

He starts putting my things back in my bag, carefully, almost tenderly. I'm standing there with my heart thumping and my arm aching and my jaw and fists clenched. 'So the wedding's off?'

He laughs. 'Abby, Abby. If only you'd have me ...' and then he nods to his minder and they both get back in the car.

I watch them reverse up the street till they're gone. The air smells of wet earth and sheep and I'm listening to the river and the helicopter and not the noise in my head. He knows about the campervan. I stand up and start walking down the street, past the row of empty cottages. Their gardens – small squares of brambled earth that drop away to the river – are on the opposite side of the road to their front doors. He knows where I'm staying and he knows where I work. And for some reason he knows my father's surname – a name I haven't used for twenty years. Behind the cottages the hill rises steeply to forest, and at the end of the row there are two large mill buildings. And he was looking for Tegid too, and my worst fear is that he's already found him, because I'm certain Ben Rickman would do a thorough job of removing obstacles to his new employer's plans to build a military training ground in Bethania. I walk past the mill buildings to the end of the village and I look up the valley to the slate tips and hills. I can see a white farmhouse cowering in a curve of a far hill, and in the field beside it there is a scattering of red stones. It takes me a few moments to realise the stones are laid out in the shape of a dragon, and I know in an instant who owns the farm, because I've seen that dragon on one of Tegid's maps. That dragon is Mr Ellis's little act of defiance. I picture him in his tweed jacket, stooped over the stones, carefully pulling away the grass, making sure the red beast is always visible from the road and from the air. It's a two-fingered salute to the colonialists in their jeeps and jets, and it makes me smile.

I stay there a while, watching smoke rise vertically from the farm's chimney, and in the deep stillness of the morning a large bird with a forked tail glides in circles above me and a dog barks in the distance and the helicopter chugs away in the clear blue sky.

*He dreams of rising into the light, of floating along the path over the slate outfall and through the birch scrub to the stream. He dreams of passing the New Cottages and making his way along the forestry track to his campervan in the quarry. He watches himself set the red kettle on the hob and take out a notebook. He's making notes on the Bryn Hyfryd mine. He's making maps of its tunnels and shafts and inclines and adits.*

*He wakes up underground. He knows this giant cave used to be two separate chambers. When the rockmen were told the mine was closing down they started to take away the wall of slate that divided the two caverns. They started to remove the wall that kept the roof from falling in.*

*It was called robbing the pillar. They felt they had a right to do that, even though it made the mine unsafe. They'd worked down there in the dark for years, carving out the tunnels and putting in the rails and chipping out an easier way home. The pillar was easy pickings.*

*He'll make a note about that when he gets back to the campervan. He'll think about all the ways humans rob the pillar.*

*But he's not going back to the campervan unless someone comes to get him. He can't move.*

# 10

## Pavement

As the light begins to fade on the afternoon, I close the curtains at the back of the van and lock the doors from the inside. I don't like the idea that Rickman and his heavy know where I am, but I baulk at moving away. I'm still hoping Tegid will come back, and when he does I want to be the first to see him. Whatever he's done. And I tell myself the strange sense of emptiness – the presence of an absence – is just the way the forest feels to someone from a city teeming with people night and day. It doesn't mean he's gone from the world forever, leaving nothing but a short exhalation and a shimmer of mist and a few unheard protests against war.

I light a lamp and take a book from the stack under the table. It's about something called scientific forestry. I find more of Tegid's pencil traces. He's underlined how after 1919 and the First World War Britain had only five per cent of its forest cover left. But the government, it seems, saw the strategic importance of timber for shipbuilding, and turned to scientific forestry to remedy the situation. This system of forestry had its origins in the colonisation of India, where timber was intensively extracted for railways in the years between 1850 and 1910, and where forests were therefore managed for maximum sustainable yield in fast-growing, monocultural plantations. And then, after World War Two, timber wasn't needed any more for the railways of the colonies, or for warship building. If the state didn't need trees any more, growing them had to be profitable. No more subsidies. Tree production was at the mercy of the markets.

It's dark when I climb into the driver's seat and face the slate wall through the windscreen. I've decided to drive the five miles into Pont Rhith to get enough food and fuel to stay up here for a couple of days. And even though I feel an inner cringe at the thought of my second public gathering in as many days, I've also decided to go to Delyth's campaign meeting. My reluctance to mingle with strangers, or to commit to someone else's fight, has lost out to the fact that I'm still burning mad at Ben Rickman and his heavy for getting in my space and going through my bag.

In Pont Rhith I eat chips and curry sauce from a polystyrene tray balanced on the campervan's steering wheel. A car pulls up on the pavement in front of me and a man and a young boy get out and go in the chippy. It's called The Sunny Sea Fish and Chip Shop and I wonder if it's one of Mr Palmer's concerns.

There's no one else on the town's main street at seven o'clock in the evening, but when I wander down to the Community Hall I see a few people have gathered outside on the pavement. The doors to the building are shut.

'Do you seriously think we're a threat to national security?' It's Delyth's voice, high and strained, and she's talking to a policewoman.

'No meetings. I can't say anything else. You have to go home.' The policewoman has her hands on her hips and she's trying to smile with benign authority, with wobbly results.

Delyth doesn't move. A middle-aged couple are muttering to each other quietly, and then they walk away. There's also the man with a ponytail from last night's public consultation – the one who didn't like wind turbines on roofs. He's tall enough to stand behind the policewoman and look over her head at Delyth. He raises his eyes to the sky and lifts his shoulders to his ears. 'Be in touch,' he says, and then he's also walking away down the street, followed by the woman with long grey hair who invoked the ancient Celts for Rickman and told him he was talking bollocks. 'It's ridiculous,' she's muttering. 'Completely ridiculous.' A young couple with matching woolly hats go after them, and I realise I have now met the sum total of Pont Rhith's opposition to the Consortium's plans – minus Mr Ellis and the woman who threw fake blood at the boards – and most of them have just walked away from their first confrontation with the state.

And then Ben Rickman is pulling up, swerving his Range Rover onto the pavement and climbing out into the road. He swoops towards us in his long coat like a hyperactive little vampire, and he's still wearing sunglasses even though it's dark. 'It's fine,' he announces to the police officer, and her hands fall from her hips and her shoulders relax. 'Counter-terrorism measures,' he says to us, waving a hand in front of him as if he's sweeping away invisible obstacles. 'Time to go home.'

Delyth has moved onto the step in front of the closed doors. 'Counter terrorism?' she says, and the pitch of her voice has shifted even higher.

He doesn't look at her. He just says, 'Given the situation, we're taking all the necessary precautions.' He waits a moment to make sure we understand, and then he's swooping back into his car and driving off. The police officer gazes after him as if she's just been visited by an A-list celebrity, and then she's leaving too, swinging her gadget-laden hips along the street.

'Petrol station,' I say to Delyth, who's the only one left. 'I need to get supplies.' She stays there on the steps in front of the closed doors, clutching her stack of leaflets.

'Mmm,' she says. 'Off you go then.'

I pick up another sack of kindling and a sack of briquettes and food to keep me warm – a tin of leek and potato soup, a tin of lentil soup, and bread and butter and cheddar cheese, and pasta, and more oats, and a packet of chocolate biscuits. There are no cafetières on the shelves, but I find some paper filters that will fit in a mug.

As I get back behind the wheel I notice the hammering man from the New Cottages crossing the brightly lit forecourt. He's wearing paint-splattered overalls and he moves with an ease I hadn't noticed when he was sliding down his roof or diving out of the way of the campervan in the quarry. I surprise myself with that observation. It's as though I'm trying out his physical being for its weight and grace, and I feel a small flicker of appreciation for its fluid assurance. Just for a moment, as I imitate his bearing in my mind, in my body, I sense how it would feel to be substantial, and placed, and still capable of flowing with the currents of the world, and I realise how much I brace myself against the next potential blow. I watch as he climbs into his mud-splattered blue estate, and I wonder if anyone could really feel like that, all the time, or if he's just learnt to move as if he belongs in the world, without question. As his car drives away I see the mournful face of his scruffy little dog peering out of the back window.

Before the bridge there's a tailback and as I pull slowly forwards I can see two soldiers stopping cars in a glare of floodlights. I pull up behind a battered Land Rover. It's Mr Ellis, and he's shouting at the soldiers from behind his wheel. In English. 'Bloody British army,' I hear. 'Going off fighting wars in other people's countries. Why do you boys always want to be soldiers, and not farmers? Heh?'

I can think of a few reasons, but the soldiers are waving him on and I'm up next. I've seen armed soldiers on the streets before. I've been in countries where roadblocks are part of everyday life. When I was a kid we went on holiday to Donegal, with a couple of other families who'd hired a house by the beach, and I remember looking up from the back seat of our car at checkpoint border control towers as we cut across Northern Ireland. But I'm not used to it. I haven't adapted to it like it's a fact of life, and I realise my breathing is tight and fast while the soldiers look at the van's number plate and log it, and then speak to each other as if there's a problem. When they finally wave me on I feel as if I've been let out on probation, and as I drive across the bridge I keep glancing in the rearview mirror, checking to see if they're going to come after me. I can't work out why they've set up the checkpoint now, more than a week after the accident. Or why there was a helicopter hovering over Bethania earlier in the day, or why Delyth's meeting was stopped by the police.

I follow Mr Ellis's old Land Rover all the way up to the New Cottages where he drives a little way up the track to my quarry and then stops. I stop too, because he's blocking my way home. I watch the rear lights go off and the driver's door open. The farmer struggles out and starts hobbling towards me, so I roll down my window ready for an explanation but all he says is, 'So what are you going to do now, eh?' At first I think he's referring to the fact that I can't get my van past his bloody Land Rover, because he's parked it right in front of me, but he just keeps loping down the track, disappearing around the gable end of the cottages.

I'm trying to formulate something more eloquent than, 'Why the fuck have you parked there?' as I get out of the van and go after him. But I also realise he can't reverse back down the track to the quarry, and go home to his farm, until I move the campervan out of his way, so we're both stuck. At the front of the cottages he's opening Raven's front door, without knocking, and he's going in. Then he sticks his head out and shouts at me again. 'Come on, then.'

I pause by the wood store. The still, clear day has turned into a cold, restless night and a breeze is rattling the leaves of the rhododendron by the gate. At the other end of the row a warm light frames the curtains at the window of Murmur. I take a deep breath and follow Mr Ellis into Raven's kitchen.

The old farmer is standing by the table, leaning heavily on it with both his knobbly hands. Raven sits opposite him, cross-legged on a kitchen chair. She's wearing a frayed green jumper three sizes too big for her and she's focussed on rolling up, her head bowed over the table while they fire sentences at each other at great speed. I listen intently but can't understand a word, and I'm painfully aware of the gap in me where the Welsh could have been if my mother had thought it worth passing on. A complicated emotion rises up in me then – an acute sense of loss, mixed with shame. I haven't had to face that feeling in London. In London, I always assume I'm speaking a language that isn't mine. I assume that's how most women feel.

Raven stands up and goes to the fridge and takes out two cans of beer. She swings one at Mr Ellis who shakes his head. I take it instead. Then she sits down at the table again and lights her joint. I wonder if the old farmer minds inhaling Raven's cannabis smoke. He doesn't seem to. He's still leaning towards her over the table, his knuckles white with the effort of keeping himself on his feet.

Raven switches to English. 'Mr Ellis says they found a stash of weapons,' she says. 'This morning. In the Bryn Hyfryd mine. That's why the helicopter was out.'

They both look at me as if I might know something about it, and when I'm silent Mr Ellis grunts and starts putting his Russian hat back on, pulling the flaps down firmly over his ears. Then he glares at me and says very loudly and very slowly, as if I won't understand if he doesn't shout: 'I saw you chatting with that man. That man with the badge. I saw you in Bethania this morning. With *him*.' He wags a finger at me, glaring from under his thick white eyebrows and the fur trim on his hat.

'We weren't *chatting*,' I say. 'He was telling me to leave.'

Mr Ellis grunts again and pushes past me. 'What did your campervan friend do with my gun? Eh?' he says, but he doesn't wait for an answer and I can hear him chuckling to himself by the front door before he bangs it shut behind him. 'Now that's got you!' he shouts into the darkness outside.

I look across the table at Raven. 'What the fuck …?' I start, but she's waving the joint at me. 'No. No thanks. What did he mean about a gun?'

'I don't know,' she almost shrieks. 'Ask *him*, not me.'

I think for just a moment. I think about sharing a beer and a smoke with Raven in her brightly lit kitchen while Mr Ellis waits in his Land Rover for me to move the campervan. It's tempting, but I put my half-emptied can on the table and go after him.

He's standing on the track, looking awkward after his grand exit. I take my chance: 'What gun?'

'That's it,' he says. 'Now you've got it. Come by tomorrow and we'll have a little chat.'

# 11

## Nant y Min

In the night I hear the wind barrelling down the valley before it slams the side of the van. With each new charge it roars through the plantation, violently rattles the gate across the forest track, and shakes the campervan on its wheels. At four in the morning I decide to go back to Delyth's Bed and Breakfast. At five I'm planning to leave Pont Rhith altogether and return to the city where the weather arrives unannounced and already tamed.

But then a grey light seeps over the hills from the east and the gale begins to subside. Little gusts buffet the van as though the beast of the night has retreated into its mountain lair and left its puppies playing in the quarry. I wriggle out of my sleeping bag and go out for a pee. At the edge of the forest a pine tree has been felled by the storm. It sprawls across the fence and onto the tufted grass of the hillside. I squat down between its branches.

Back in the van I pack up the bed and remake the table and open the curtains wide. Then I light the stove and make breakfast: coffee in a mug with a filter paper, a bread roll dotted with small lumps of hard butter. I take them to the table and lift a folder of Tegid's papers off the stack on the floor.

The coffee cools rapidly as I fumble through the clippings with gloved fingers. The subject this morning is drones and death by drones, which 'is swift and efficient' writes one journalist, 'and also murder'. There's a picture of a teenager – a floppy-haired boy with a toothy grin and glasses that cover half his face – who was killed by a drone in Yemen. I stare at him closely – the moment of him, alive – and then move on. There's a piece on US drone strikes in Pakistan, where a legal action charity states 'hundreds if not thousands' of civilians are being killed.

There's a copy of a report by a United States Air Force Chief Scientist and Tegid has helpfully underlined the highlights. It seems the scientist is arguing for greater drone 'autonomy'. In the future, he predicts, the human operator will only decide 'the mission intents and constraints'. He'll leave it up to the drone to find the best 'execution path'. Tegid has underlined 'execution path' twice. The Chief Scientist also extols the virtues of microdrones for 'close-in sensing' in urban areas. I can see how that would have upset my map-making friend. 'The future,' he has written in the margin, 'is war with the people who live in the world's slum cities. It will be fought with drones.'

I finish the coffee and scan a short article on the UK's Reaper drones and their use of Hellfire missiles. Some of these drones, apparently, are in flight every hour of the day and night. And there are notes in Tegid's own handwriting on a sheet of paper torn from a maths exercise book. 'The MoD argues that drone attacks are morally justified because they save the lives of aircrew. The MoD doesn't account for the fact that this makes the decision to attack easier, and therefore makes WAR MORE LIKELY.' But it's the next sentence which has me lifting my eyes from the folder and staring out of the window into the grey sky: REAPER MISHAPS (ie CRASHES) HAPPEN APPROX. EVERY 10,000 HOURS OF FLYING.

And as I look out of the window at the hills and plantations, I remember an afternoon in the common room at the hostel. Tegid is writing at one of the little tables and Billy, a new resident, is watching daytime TV, his empty cask of a body sunk into a high-backed chair, his bony hands gripping the armrests as if he's drifting on choppy water in a little boat. He has a long bald head and folds of skin hang over the dwindled flesh of his neck. I know his wife kicked him out. I know he lost his job as a taxi driver. I know he's sunk into a state as close to death as he can get without inflicting violence on himself – he hasn't got the energy to kill himself. Of course, on that particular day in the common room, I don't know Billy will start on an education programme in September. I don't know he'll meet a young woman teaching on the scheme who will make his eyes shine with little more than the hope that whatever comes around the corner to meet him next may not be all bad. It's all he needs. That little bit of hope will be enough to restart his life.

Sally is in the office doing something administrative with files, so it's my job to 'interact with the residents in a positive way'. I've made cups of tea and I'm watching Tegid write in his exercise book. I listen to the slow traffic on the road outside and to a repeat of an episode of *Midsomer Murders* on the telly. Sometimes I hear the creak of a floorboard above me and I sense the weight of the world carried by the residents upstairs. It's mostly women up there, and children – the ones who try to hide from view because they can't afford to be seen.

Grant comes in and circles the room, muttering. He takes Monopoly off the shelf and brings it over. 'Let's have a fucking game,' he says.

Tegid looks up and smiles. He closes his notebook, sliding it in between the others in the carrier bag under the table.

I feel resistance in every cell of my body. I will clean toilets and mop up vomit. I will make endless cups of tea and never drink them. I will stay up all night listening to people tell me their gruesome, depressing stories. And I will try my best to engage in conversations about the weather. But I don't think I'm paid enough to play a board game. I scan around for an alternative activity. I can't find one. I am doomed.

I choose the counter shaped like an iron and Grant chooses the dog. 'What d'you want to be, Einstein?' he shouts at Tegid, and then he throws the battleship into his lap. Tegid inspects it and shrugs. And it goes on like that for the next three weeks, which is only half an hour in clock time. 'It's your fuckin' turn,' Grant shouts at Tegid, and Billy flinches in his chair in front of *Midsomer Murders*, and I check my watch and wonder if I can make it till the end of the shift without resigning.

Within a few rounds, and despite his lack of motivation, Tegid has bought Mayfair. And then a few rounds later Grant lands on it. I'm staring at the deep blue strip and thinking about fairs in May, and whether they ever took place on the street which is now a synonym for wealth and luxury, when Grant shouts, 'You're supposed to charge me fucking rent.'

Tegid's ice blue eyes dart a look at him. And then he says, very gently and quietly: 'I can't charge you rent. I'm homeless, and you're homeless, and you're my friend.'

I start to laugh, and then I stop. Don't collude, I think. I look at Grant. His 'tache twitches. And then he shakes the dice. For an hour in a basement on the South Bank we move around the streets of London like the birds in the field. Everyone has somewhere to live, and the bank goes bust.

Later that afternoon, when Grant has gone out in search of Special Brew, Tegid tells me about his school, and about the boys who tortured him and the teacher who raped him. 'They can't be reasoned with,' he says. 'You can't beg them for mercy. People like that can only be stopped. Physically stopped.' And although he looks directly at me I can't hold his gaze because the ice over his eyes has melted and I'm looking straight down a bottomless shaft.

Now I focus on the long view through the campervan window. I run my hands over the velveteen upholstery of the bench. I'm putting the scraps of paper back into the folder when I catch Delyth's name in the jumble of words on the back of a receipt. It's followed by a couple of scrawled lines of poetry: 'To Be Charmed ... Seemed enough ambition for anyone with sense. Scant matter with what. Be it only with the serenity of veils at the funeral of a river, or even with the compassion of first snow upon a blackened wood.' Then it says 'Patchen', who I guess is the poet. The receipt is for kippers and milk and a tin of pea and ham soup.

I walk over to Mr Ellis's farm past the New Cottages. The estate is parked against the gable end, and a corner of the blue tarpaulin on the roof of Murmur has come loose in the wind and is rattling against the tiles. I go down the tarmacked track and cross the stream on the slab of concrete that serves as a bridge. The hole in the side of the hill – the Cyclops' eye – watches me. When I reach the road I head north up the narrowing valley, away from the empty village of Bethania, and away from the faint glow of sunlight behind the clouds.

I've been on the road less than five minutes when Mr Ellis judders up behind me on a quad bike, looking like he's been welded onto the seat to stop him falling off. A slack-tongued border collie balances like the lord of all he surveys in a plastic tray at the back, and another lollops along behind, her nose to the ground. The farmer swerves onto the verge and leans forward over the steering wheel and shouts, 'That's right. Up there,' over the chug of the engine and the bluster of the wind. Then he revs the quad and swings it through an open gate, bouncing uphill across the field.

I turn onto the track where there's a wooden sign saying Nant y Min. I pass the red-painted stones laid out in the shape of a dragon in a sloping field next to the farmhouse. The door is open when I get there, so I walk straight into a dark hall. A door on the left opens and there's a barked 'Here'. The dogs are in the yard, so I assume he's talking to me. In the kitchen there's a fire burning in the range, and with the fire and one small window there's just enough light to see the room. There's a small table, and an armchair by the fire, and against one wall is a piano, its lid closed and books and magazines and old newspapers and used envelopes piled on top. There are more books and papers on the stool.

Mr Ellis has sat himself down in the armchair by the fire. He uses his foot to pull out a straight-backed chair from under the table, and he nods at me to sit on it. 'My mother played the piano,' he says, watching me scan the room. 'And my father was a great reader.' Then he cranes his head to look behind me and says, 'My father won that, for his poem.' I turn around to follow his gaze and there's a wooden throne draped in shadows in the corner of the room, its arms and legs carved with creatures and plants and the date of the Eisteddfod etched into its back.

'Nant y Min,' I say. 'What does it mean?'

'Dancing sheep.'

I laugh. 'I know nant means stream. So what does min mean?'

'Piss,' he says.

There's a blackened kettle hanging over the fire on a chain and it's beginning to whistle. Mr Ellis hauls himself out of the chair and swings the kettle off the fire. Then he wets a pot of tea on the range and brings it over to the table and pulls a ribbed cosy over the pot using both his hands. 'I cannot be doing with electricity,' he says. 'A few years ago, on Christmas Day, I was the only one in the valley with a cooked turkey. Everyone else had a power cut.'

'Everyone else?' Apart from Raven and her neighbour, I've not noticed anyone else up here.

He grunts and shakes his head, leaning over the pot to stir the tea. 'They're all gone now. And they want me out too. They say it's for my own good, but the only reason I broke a rib last year was because some fool closed the gate. I was running to one of the cows in the night – she was calving – and some bugger had closed the gate.'

He pushes a mug of tea towards me, one hand leaning heavily on the table. I wonder how old he is. Seventies? Eighties? And I wonder when he last heard anyone play that piano.

Then he starts to tell me how he sees things: they're pulling him away from his life and his land but he's clinging onto them by making a fire up here every day. Every day he makes a fire and he drinks his tea. He checks on the sheep and he gives the dogs a run and he clears the grass from around the dragon. He only goes to that bloody bungalow in town to sleep, because that's what *they* want. They want him to live in Pont Rhith in a bungalow because that makes them feel better. It doesn't make him feel better.

'If you gave me a good-looking nineteen-year-old I'd re-populate Bethania,' he says from back in his armchair by the cackling fire. 'Ten years ago,' he goes on, leaning forward and banging his thigh with the flat of his hand, 'I had a thousand pounds for my wool. This year I had forty-five. Forty-five! I had more in compensation from the MoD.'

'Compensation?' I have no idea what he's talking about.

'For the stress on the animals,' he shouts. 'For the stress their aeroplanes cause the sheep.'

I look at my tea. I'm a little scared not to drink it, so I take a sip. And then I set it back on the table. 'A gun,' I say. 'You mentioned a gun.'

'Went missing,' he says. 'Before Christmas. Before the crash.'

I know what he's suggesting, but I want him to explain it to me. 'So?'

He rolls his eyes and sighs. He struggles out of the armchair and brings his mug of tea over to the table. Once he's settled on the piano stool opposite me he slowly moves the teapot across the table. 'That,' he says, pointing at the teapot, 'is the Pryce girl's caravan at Parc Sunny Hill.' He pushes his mug towards the other end of the table. '*This* is your friend's campervan on Foel y Ffridd.' He picks up a teaspoon and lays it across his mug. 'And *this* is my rifle. Which has gone missing.' And then he lifts up a pen and holds it above and between the pot and the envelope. I watch him shoot at the biro with the teaspoon. I watch the biro dive point-first into the teapot's woolly cover.

'So that's what happened,' I say. 'Tegid used your rifle to shoot down a drone and it crashed into a caravan and killed a woman.'

108

He leans back in his chair. 'Not that I blame him.' He leans forward again, over his tea, and slurps at it. 'Would have done it myself if I could still aim straight.'

I pick up the biro, which was the drone, and I fiddle with it. He lifts his eyes over the rim of his cup and watches me. The silence waits in the room's shadows.

'I don't think you could take out a drone with a rifle,' I say after a while. 'Maybe with a heat-seeking missile, but not a rifle.'

'Expert on weapons, are you?'

'No. Are you?'

'Anyway,' he says. 'The important thing is: what are you going to do about your friend, Tegid Rhys?'

I consider this. I've been considering it pretty much non-stop for the last week, and I still have no clear answers. 'Have you told anyone? About the missing rifle?'

'I'm telling *you*,' he says, lifting up his head and pointing at me like a mad recruiting sergeant for a hopeless army.

I accept the old farmer's offer of a lift into town and cling to the door handle of his Land Rover all the way there. When we pass below the square hole in the hillside he tells me it's an adit – the entrance to a level of the Bryn Hyfryd slate mine – and he tells me not to go near it because I'll fall in and that'll be the end of me. He finally slows down at the road block by the bridge and shouts, 'Who ... protects us ... from you?' at the soldier, and then he swerves across the road and speeds away as if he's playing knock and run. They don't want to play.

I gain stable ground outside Delyth's shop. I want to talk to her about Mr Ellis and his little theory about the rifle and the drone. I want her to tell me that he's prone to paranoia and to winding up women from the city. I want her to tell me that Tegid wasn't capable of acting against the war machine, and that all he could really do was talk and make maps. Stealing a gun and shooting a drone out of the sky? That would have been way beyond his practical capabilities, never mind his inclinations.

But Delyth is dressed in black and locking up and I remember with a shock that it's the day of Anwen's funeral, so I tag along with her, waiting for the right moment to bring up the subject of the farmer's stolen rifle. It doesn't come. Every few steps she stops to talk with someone. First it's an old couple who speak to her in Welsh while I stand there like a moody teenager.

'This is Abby Hughes,' she tells them eventually, and they say hello and what a terrible accident it was. 'She always had time for other people,' says the woman. Her husband agrees: 'Always stopped for a chat.' 'Terrible, terrible,' they say, their heads shaking and their eyes looking at me as if I may have an explanation for the tragedy, or at least the right thing to say. 'Terrible, terrible,' is all I manage.

Then there's a woman with a toddler who tells Delyth all about the time Anwen stepped in to look after her baby when she had to take her mother for chemotherapy. 'She was great with kids,' she tells me. 'She should have been a teacher. Maybe she would have been.' She looks at me as if she's wondering what I do, and then she seems to decide she's not that interested.

The moment I'm alone with Delyth I try to start the conversation. 'Mr Ellis tells me they found weapons in the hills.'

'I know,' she says, but she's stopping again, this time to greet a man in a woolly hat. It's a brief exchange in Welsh and I only pick up Anwen's name. He shouts something over his shoulder as he crosses the road, but I only pick up 'fucking drones'.

I take it as a cue. 'They found weapons. In a mine.'

'That's why they cancelled the meeting,' she says to me then, staring straight ahead towards the big grey chapel where a TV crew are shouldering their equipment and heading up the steps to the open doors. Outside on the pavement two huddles of people dressed in black are smoking and vaping.

Delyth clearly doesn't want to discuss the weapons find with me.

When we get to the chapel steps she goes over to a woman with nicotine-yellow hair, whose face has drooped under her eyes into a series of overlapping crescents. Delyth puts a hand on her upper arm, and while they murmur to each other I look up at the chapel. It's set back from the road behind black railings, between a charity shop and a gift shop, and even though it dwarfs the other buildings it's also strangely invisible, as though it's lurking in the shadows and slowly fading away. I can imagine what's inside: the varnished pews, the large bunch of lilies in a vase by the altar, the IHS embroidered on a cloth. An insipid light will be coming through the frosted windows and an organ will be wheezing out the introductory chords to a hymn. A few old people will know all the words, and maybe even the harmonies, and they will sing weakly against the coming silence. The rest will stare defensively at nothing, waiting for the service to end so they can go home to more diverting, screen-based entertainment in a higher level of comfort.

The people smoking outside begin to stub out their cigarettes and drag themselves up the steps. And then I recognise Anwen's ex, Joel. He's wearing a suit instead of his tan jacket and beanie hat, and I can see the crawl of his tattoos disappearing under his shirt collar. He holds the yellow-haired woman by the elbow, steering her towards the chapel entrance, and as they move a child appears behind them, her huge eyes glazed like a somnambulist's, her hand holding onto her father's jacket. I reel and turn away, as though I have nothing to do with all this grief.

Outside the Spar there's a woman selling the *Big Issue*. She's bundled up in a long skirt and a duffle coat and a headscarf and she's wearing thick woolly socks and sandals. When I give her the money for the magazine she carefully rolls up a copy and passes it to me, and then she squeezes my hand and says, 'Thank you, thank you.' I recoil, pulling my hand away and getting inside the shop before she can say anything else.

The newspapers are on a rack facing me, and the local weekly obviously went to press before the weapons were found – its front page has a picture of the dead woman at a party, smiling blearily at the camera, her blonde hair piled high on her head, her mascara smudged, her lipstick bright red, and in the article beside it Mr Palmer – 'town councillor' – demands the MoD get on with their investigation. There's also a photo of a man with a pushbike who has raised £340 for a local hospice. I scan the nationals. The crash is no longer front page news, but one of them has the weapons story in brief, and as I read it I realise I'm off the hook. I can go home. Tegid wasn't responsible for Anwen Pryce's death. A house in Telford has been raided in connection with a stash of arms found in a disused mine in mid Wales. Two men – both Iranian – have been arrested in a counter-terrorism operation. The police are not ruling out a connection with the drone accident, which is still under investigation.

I buy a copy of the paper along with an egg sandwich and another packet of chocolate biscuits, and then I'm out of the shop and crossing the road again, heading for the library. I pass the closed doors of the chapel and for a few moments I feel relaxed, happy even. I've inherited the campervan from an eccentric mathematician and mapmaker, not a murderer. It wasn't his fault at all. It was the fault of Middle Eastern terrorists. Of course it was.

# 12

## Library

The library is small and T-shaped. One of the open plan wings is full of computers on tables and when I sit down I'm distracted for a moment by the brightness of the place – the primary colours, the strip lighting, the big windows. I feel as though I've wandered into a classroom where all the children have been abducted by aliens and replaced with silent adults staring at screens.

One of the librarians tells me I'll have to wait ten minutes for a turn on a computer, so I stand by the desk with my hands in my pockets. 'Are you visiting the town,' she asks, still looking at the screen in front of her, 'or have you moved here?'

'Just visiting,' I say.

'Because we need proof of address if you want to join the library.'

'I don't want to join …' And then I realise she must know everyone in town, because she knew I wasn't a local. 'I came to visit my uncle,' I say. 'Tegid Rhys. A man with a scar …'

'Yes,' she says. 'He had trouble with proof of address too.'

'Have you seen him recently?' I persist. 'He hasn't been in touch with his family for a while, so I thought I'd check up on him while I'm here.'

She sniffs and shakes her head. But the other woman behind the desk, who is sitting down and only just visible behind the counter, leans around her computer and smiles at me. 'The man with a lake in each eye. That's what my boy calls him.'

'You know him?'

'He's a friend of my ex's,' she says. 'He took us up to the quarry, once, to see the blue pool. And Tomos drew a picture of him afterwards and his eyes were like two blue lakes. So we started calling him "The Man with Lakes for Eyes" ... it sounds better in Welsh.'

'And have you seen him recently? It's weird he's not here. I had a postcard from him, but ...'

She shakes her head. 'Sorry. No. I haven't. Not since I split up with Raven. Sorry.'

'Shsh,' hisses the other librarian to no one in particular. Then she shouts across to a woman leaving. 'Bye Bronwen. See you Thursday evening.' She turns back to me. 'There's a computer free. You have half an hour.'

It's surprisingly easy to find what I'm looking for once I'm online. The Wikipedia entry reads:

> **Curved Space Mapping Technologies** was an early 1980s company which pioneered the design of computer programmes for cartographers. The company's technological expertise allowed it to produce maps of stunning three-dimensional topographical detail. Its partners – Reg Dauber and Tegid Rhys – sold the company and its designs to the US defence contractor SecTec in 1988. SecTec saw the potential for developing the programmes into missile control systems. Later technological developments such as GPS have rendered these programmes largely obsolete from a military perspective.

I click on Tegid Rhys's name. The link says 'Co-developer of early landscaping computer program. See Curved Space Mapping Technologies.' It also says: 'Rhys initially developed the pioneering topographical computer programmes while working for an international aid agency. The programmes were designed to predict

114

the flow of water onto land in areas of the world stricken by devastating floods, but he failed to get funding to put the programmes into use. It was only when he teamed up with Reg Dauber of the Dauber House Publishing Company that the programmes were finalised.'

I search for Dauber House Publishing Company and find it is now an imprint of a multinational media conglomerate. The company's 'History' page tells me it first ran into financial difficulties in the early 1980s but was saved by the foresight of its new owner, Reginald Dauber, grandson of Archibald Dauber, the company's founder. Apparently, Reg was inspired to add 'Mapping' to the company's portfolio after getting lost one day while out hunting in the Cairngorms, and the success of Curved Space Mapping Technologies not only saved Dauber House from oblivion, but also lead to Reg's other ventures, including Total Solutions, a company specialising in groundbreaking designs.

According to the Total Solutions website, the company offers support to designers in their quest for contracts and is particularly interested in designs with potential military application. When I check the contact details for the company, I find it's registered in the Channel Islands. There's also a page about Reg on the site, and photographs of Reg: Reg driving his red sportscar along a coastal road by cliffs of pink granite; Reg standing outside each one of the three houses he designed himself – in Jersey, in Wales, and on the Algarve in Portugal; Reg sailing his yacht; and Reg wearing a suit and top hat and holding his MBE award. There's a long list of his achievements in the design and business worlds, including his development of the mapping programme he sold to SecTec. He is like a full-colour, three-dimensional version of Tegid – bearded, profligate, fat. He is a Tegid who has stepped out of the shadows and announced himself to the world with a megaphone.

I note down the contact details for Reg's company, and then I sit there for a while, watching my half hour of internet access ticking away. A man who has the squat build of a rugby player stands at the desk with a stack of crime books. His voice booms in his wide chest as he jokes with the librarian. 'I'm sure I've read these before, but I never remember who did it.'

I check my emails. They tell me I could buy some printer cartridges or sign an online petition that will change the world. I don't do either. I stare at the screen. Just an hour ago I was convinced someone else was responsible for the drone crash, and Tegid had nothing to do with it. Now that sense of relief has leaked out through my boots into the library's worn carpet. He didn't just hate the military-industrial complex, he'd helped to furnish it with a key technological advance. He'd helped to make killing from a distance easy, and the worst thing was, he'd never intended to. I feel the blood drain from my face and a chill creep over my skin. Tegid wasn't in Pont Rhith by mistake. He'd followed his own maps here.

I key in 'Benedict Rickman', refining it with 'public relations'. On his company's website there's a photograph of a faceless man marching resolutely along a grey city street in a long coat, and even though it's a grainy shot I recognise him from the frenetic style of movement, frozen mid stride. The 'About Us' blurb plays with the initials PR without ever saying overtly: we're fixers. 'You want the Public to understand the Reasons for your actions. You want to Persuade and Rule opinion. You want carefully Planned Research into where any opposition to your company's projects may come from. And you want that opposition Pre-Rendered harmless before it affects your interests. We'll help you achieve these aims. Professionally and Responsibly.'

I wonder then if Tegid was a Person with Reasons to obstruct Rickman's plans. I already know he was looking for Tegid, and if Tegid the homeless madman really had managed to bring down a drone and cause the death of a local resident, that would not be good PR for Rickman's paymasters. A military consortium would be keen to project an image of power, control and safety; it wouldn't want to look vulnerable to the activities of a lone bloke. If Tegid came out of hiding to tell people the 'accident' was his fault, that sort of information would have to be handled carefully. And maybe it would be better if he didn't turn up at all.

It's late afternoon and Delyth is sat behind the bookshop's counter, her fingers working a crochet hook around a deep blue yarn. She's changed out of her funeral clothes and is wearing a pink fleece.

'Was it windy last night, bach?' She squints at her crochet, and then she reaches across the counter and flicks on a lamp.

'There was a breeze.' I'm obviously not being offered tea today, or a seat, so I stand in front of her, holding the newspaper with its terrorists-in-Telford headline behind my back. 'How was the funeral?' I ask.

'Great fun,' she says, and then she considers me. 'Palmer gave a lovely speech. In English. All about the potential in this town, especially among the young people, and how we must all work to realise that potential by creating secure work and homes for all.' She rolls her eyes. 'And I suppose that's exactly what he's trying to do by buying up all the shops and cafes and starting his building firm. I just wish he'd put Welsh names on his shops. It makes a difference, you know, to the high street, and to how people see the town. But he won't listen to me.'

It must be Pont Rhith's evening rush hour because I can hear traffic on the road outside. Delyth is pulling at her crochet, and then leaning back and holding the woolly knots up to the lamplight to inspect them closely.

'Anwen's sister said a few words,' she carries on. 'And she cried. And one of Joel's buddies shouted a bit. And the minister, of course, she told us about love and hope and about talking to Anwen through Jesus now ...' She trails off and lays the crochet in her lap. She looks shattered, and then she says, 'It's all in pieces, this place.

What can you say when things are in pieces? Everyone looks at each other with mistrust and fear, as if we all want different things.' She glares at me – 'That's the biggest lie of all' – and she deflates back into her chair.

I bring out the newspaper and put it down in front of her, noticing for the first time a pot of pink hyacinths on the counter. Their thick smell feels like a frantic assertion of life against death. She tips her head forward slightly, glances at the article, and then settles back into her chair and continues with her crochet.

'So it wasn't him,' I say, pointing at the headline. 'Terrorists did it.'

'Handy,' she says, and when I shake my head she snaps: 'Think about it. They plant the idea that foreign terrorists – preferably from the Middle East – are responsible for the crash, and suddenly a military training ground sounds like a great idea. Because we're in danger! The tentacles of terror reach everywhere – even into the hills of Wales! We need a well-trained army to protect us!'

I laugh. 'Sounds a bit conspiracy.'

She considers me, and then she gives me one of her faraway smiles, like a children's storyteller about to embark on an educational yarn. 'There have been rumours for years about weapons stashed in the hills. People think they've been there since the 1960s – IRA stuff, Free Wales Army, MAC. The Consortium could have found them or planted them. They've been surveying every tree and mine shaft in the area.'

'What's MAC?' I ask.

She sighs. 'In English? ... "Movement for the Defence of Wales".'

She picks up the crochet hook again and stabs it through a loop and throttles it with a yank of wool.

'We've lost this one,' she says then. 'You watch the bulldozers move in now. When ... *if* the truth comes out about the weapons, about the accident, it will be too late. They'll have their training ground up and running before we have a chance to stop it. Because people are frightened, and fear is a powerful thing.'

'So what about these men they've arrested … these terrorists from Telford?'

She stares at me with her kohl-rimmed eyes. She's trying to be patient, but it's been a long day. I change direction. I take the receipt out of my pocket, the one with her name on it in Tegid's handwriting and the lines from the Patchen poem, and I lay that in front of her on top of the newspaper.

She stares at the creased receipt for a few moments and then reads out loud: 'To be charmed seemed enough ambition for anyone with sense …' She stops and turns the scrap of paper over as though she's more interested in the kippers and milk than the poem. I watch her face but there's no change in her expression. She puts her crochet down on the counter and stands up and goes over to one of the bookshelves and pulls down a tattered paperback. She flicks through it and presses it open and passes it to me. It's the Patchen poem. 'He used this place as a library,' she says, 'taking out books and then bringing them back when he'd read them. He hardly ever bought one. But then I never expected to make a living out of secondhand books. This shop was somewhere to let the dust settle after my divorce. I was a teacher. I have a decent pension. With that and the occasional B and B guest like you, I get by.'

'Are you from Pont Rhith?' I ask. I don't want her to stop telling me the personal stuff, so I say it quietly, picking up the book of poems and leafing through it.

'No,' she says. 'I grew up in Bethania.' She says it as if they were completely different places, and not four miles apart. 'And then I moved to Cardiff to train and to work and I came home when I retired because I wanted to live in a place where I could use my own language every day.'

'And can you?'

'Just about. But the town has changed. There wasn't a word of English in the primary school playground when I was a child. English is all you hear now.'

She's watching me, wondering if I understand. I think about some of the people I work with – the refugees and asylum seekers. They're people who've been forced to leave their homes and their cultures. They're people who've been torn from familiar sounds, foods, clothes, and ways of being with each other. But how would it feel to sense your world seeping out of your surroundings without you going anywhere? To have it trickle away over the years until you're living somewhere you don't recognise any more, among people who speak another language when they greet each other?

I keep my eyes fixed on the poem in front of us, in case I put her off. 'So how did you meet Tegid?'

She glances at me, and then she picks up her crochet work again. For a moment I think she's going to go back to listening to that music in her head and leave me with nothing but her silence and an enigmatic smile. I slump a little – she's not the only one who's tired. 'He came in the first time asking if I had a book on the slate quarries around Bethania,' she says. 'And that was probably the only book he ever bought from me. I slipped in a postcard of an M. E. Thompson sketch of a man splitting slate in a quarry workshop. A few days later the postcard arrived in the post with a thank you on the back. And an invitation to his campervan for tea.'

I notice that the black jacket she wore to the funeral is draped over the back of her chair. 'Did you go?'

'It wasn't just books he failed to buy. His clothes were worn out. He lived on scraps of food – some of it dragged out of the skip at the back of the Spar. He walked everywhere, and, on top of all that, he seemed happy, which was an insult to everyone else. He refused to play along with the whole buying stuff thing and we thought he should be miserable as a result. But he wasn't.'

'So you didn't go? For tea?'

She stares at me. 'Sometimes I wonder if a man so insensitive to the coercive messages of consumer capitalism is also plain insensitive. I've met a lot of political types. I even married one, and underneath all that talk about wanting a better world there's usually a raging ego. But I never quite made up my mind about Tegid. I still haven't.'

From the way she looks at me I can tell she hasn't made up her mind about me either.

She leans down under the counter and brings out a postcard. It's a pencil drawing of a man splitting a block of slate with a hammer and chisel. Splitting slate was something my Taid did before the dust started to affect his breathing and he went to work on the railways instead. But long after he left the workshops he still had the skill. He made a 'book' of thin slate pages bound together with orange twine for me. It's one of the few things I carry with me from place to place, and I want to tell her about it. I don't.

'Look,' she says. 'No mask. That man would have been coughing up his lungs a few years later. But there are no pencil drawings of that. When there's no work, any work seems noble. Even work which kills you. Or kills other people. That's what we're up against, isn't it?'

The door rattles and we both look towards it. It's the wind. I put my hands in my pockets and she continues with her crochet. The postcard lies on the counter between us and I wonder if I'm supposed to pick it up and read it. I slide it towards me and turn it over. Tegid has drawn a map of how to find the campervan in the quarry, and he doesn't want Delyth to linger on the way there or become distracted by a sensory experience of the landscape – it's clear and direct in a way that makes me laugh. Military precision, I think, when it comes to inviting an attractive woman over for tea.

I feel I have to reciprocate now and tell her something. 'He didn't do it,' I say, 'but he felt responsible for it. He felt responsible for every airborne missile attack of the last thirty years.' And I tell her about Curved Space Mapping Technologies, and the computer programme he designed to track floods.

She listens. She crochets. And then she shakes her head. 'It doesn't rule him out, though, does it? A man crippled with that kind of guilt. A man determined to put things right.'

'But if that was his plan,' I say with a hint of desperation in my voice, 'there'd be no point keeping quiet about it, would there? He'd have gone public.'

'What if it went wrong, bach, and someone died? Or what if they couldn't allow him to go public because it would make the Consortium look like a liability?'

'Is that what you think? That they've bumped him off?'

She shrugs. Then she stands up and starts heading towards the door. 'I think I'll close early,' she says, flipping the sign. 'I don't know why I bother opening at all in January.'

Before I start the long walk back to the quarry I go to the Spar for supplies. It's dark and cold and the *Big Issue* woman is still there, swaying from side to side, and then stamping her feet. A loose gaggle of kids have gathered on the wide pavement in the light from the shop window. In the middle of the group there's a boy on a bike, and when an army truck trundles past he shouts, 'Watch out! You're going to crash!' One of the girls sniggers.

I buy a jar of pesto, a packet of grated cheese, and a bag of salad and a bottle of red wine. And I'm thinking about Sally and her outreach work – her flasks of hot tea, and her tobacco and papers – and I guess she must have had an influence on me after all because on the way out I stop at the hot drinks machine. The milky tea gurgles and splutters into the cardboard cup, and then the machine goes back to rest with a satisfied clunk. I take up a handful of sugar sachets and a wooden stirrer and stuff them in my pocket.

But I don't have time to hand the tea to the *Big Issue* woman because a car pulls up outside the shop and the driver starts shouting stuff out of the window. 'Fuck off. Get back to where you came from. Murdering bastard.'

For a moment I think he's shouting at me, but then I see the swaddled woman rocking from foot to foot and peering up the dark street to the side of the shop as if it might offer an escape route. I go and stand in front of her. I'm taking the sugar sachets out of my pocket and listening to the car door open behind me. I can see the man's reflection in the shop's window. He's tall, and wide, and he's still shouting as he blunders across the pavement towards us. I crouch down to put the tea on the floor-tiles under the window, out of the way, and then I turn around, still crouched, and let the fury in me turn into something cold and fluid. He shoulders in with his head stuck forward and all I have to do is stand up under him, lift him off his feet and watch him drop to the floor. There is a moment of stillness and then he's heaving himself back up and taking a swing at me. I step aside and let him follow the thrust of his punch into a rack of flowers in plastic pots. He's floundering among the vegetation and water, pushing himself up and stumbling about and getting ready to lunge at me again, but now there's another man between us and he's holding out his arms to contain – or shield – the lad, and he's saying something to him. The man is round and bald and short, and he's wearing the shop's logo on his fleece. The big lad listens to him. He shakes himself down, and then swaggers back to the car.

'It's not worth it,' the shop man shouts after him. And then he turns to the *Big Issue* woman and says, 'Off you go then. Hop it.'

The lad gets into the car and I can see Joel in the passenger seat, still in his funeral suit. He grips the dashboard as they accelerate away.

The *Big Issue* woman keeps her head down as she sticks her magazines into her bag and lifts the strap onto her shoulder. I pick up the cup of tea and hold it out to her. She looks at it for a moment, and then takes it off me and starts walking away.

'And don't come back,' the shop man shouts after her. 'Understand? Don't ... come ... back.'

I go after her. She walks slowly, and she doesn't acknowledge me when I fall into step beside her. We're nearly at the station when she breaks the silence. 'He is not a terrorist,' she says, and I think she's talking about Tegid, but then she goes on to tell me her brother has been arrested because of the weapons they found in the hills. She says he used to sell the paper in Pont Rhith, and now she has to do it instead, and she doesn't want to. She hates it. Her back hurts, and it's very cold, and nobody speaks to her. She doesn't want trouble. She hasn't done anything wrong. He hasn't done anything wrong. But no one's going to believe them. No one ever does.

When we reach the station she stops speaking and walks away from me to sit on a bench under the awning. I watch her sink into her big coat, the shawl wrapped tightly around her black hair so only her face shows. She puts her bag on the bench beside her, to make a barrier, and she takes the lid off the tea and sips at it.

I stand on the platform and look at the orange numbers on the screen in the eaves of the roof. There are sixteen minutes till the next train east and I could go home too. I could go back to my bedsit and my job at the hostel. It would make more sense than trying to track down a missing man in a place I don't belong, getting into fights with local lads over stuff that has nothing to do with me.

I watch a woman drag a wheeled suitcase up the steps of the footbridge one at a time. She crosses the bridge over the track, her golden hair, backlit by the station's lights, billowing in the wind. I wonder if she's Anwen's sister, going home after the funeral. She lowers the case slowly down the steps on the other side and wheels it along the platform, and then she disappears through the door of a waiting room.

I walk down to the end of the platform where there are no lights and no roof and a cold wind, funnelled up the estuary from the sea, smacks me in the face with a smattering of rain. And with the cold slap comes an inner flush of heat. I'm suddenly ashamed of fighting with that boy. Fighting is something I did in my teens, to stay sane. It taught me I was flesh and bone, and not someone else's idea of a girl. It taught me I wasn't very strong, or fast, or skilled, but I had a right to take up space in the world, and to defend that space. It taught me that the intention to defend myself was often enough to stop someone hurting me.

The ground at the end of the platform dips down to the track and a 'No Trespassing' sign. I stare into the darkness along the steel bars, and then I turn around and walk back to the benches. I look at the screen. There are now twelve minutes until the next train and I'm still not sure whether I'll be on it. I work with the homeless, and I have no home, because the alternative, I know damn well, scares me more.

I squat down beside the *Big Issue* girl. I can see how young she is now: sixteen, or eighteen at a push. 'Do you know a man called Tegid Rhys? White hair, blue eyes, a scar across here.'

She looks straight ahead across tracks splattered with lumps of toilet roll. 'He talks to my brother,' she says. Then she smiles. 'He speaks some Farsi.'

# 13

# Murmur

It takes over an hour to walk back to the quarry. The cloud has cleared, and there's a half-moon rising over the hills, and I don't need my new torch until I reach the avenue of trees at the end of the track.

In the van I take the red kettle from the hob and set off in search of the stream. I've heard its urgent whisper in the gorge below the forest and I'm beginning to understand the terrain around Foel y Ffridd, so I cut off the track well before it descends towards the New Cottages and take a path over the slate outfall. The shingle clinks under my feet and the white bark of the birch trees glows in the moon-light. Where the trees' lower branches have been discarded there are black circles which look like random eyes in the night.

When the path enters plantation again I follow a barbed wire fence along the edge of the gorge until the slope looks safe enough to descend, then I climb over the wire and start to slither down through the slushy black remains of last summer's bracken, gripping the kettle in one hand and steadying myself with the other. Tough strands of bramble grasp at my shins and ankles. When I reach the bank of the stream I stand there for a few moments, watching the full load of black water driving around the curves of the gulley, coursing between and over the rocks, and then I step out onto a slab and dip the kettle into the force. The water pours messily into the spout, gushing over my fingers till they ache with cold. And as

I sit there on my heels on a rock in the stream I think about Tegid, and I feel a fierce and unexpected yearning to see him settled down with Delyth, living out his life in Pont Rhith with the bookshop owner. It's a disconcerting thought. It tells me I'm not altogether immune to the idea of a love that brings lonely souls in from the cold and pins them to life.

I put the water to boil on the gas ring and light the lamp on the table. I set a fire in the stove. Then I cook pasta on the hob, dressing it in pesto and finely chopped cheese – finely chopped because there's no grater in the campervan's cutlery drawer. I open the wine and I'm thankful it's a screw top because there's no corkscrew either, and when I've eaten all the pasta and cheese out of the pan I realise I don't have enough water to wash up in so I put 'big water container' on the list of things to get next time I'm in town.

Sitting at the table I doodle on a scrap of paper, drawing trees and the paths between them, and I sing to myself in a quiet hum and sip at the wine from a plastic beaker, and I begin to think I could live like this a while longer, up here in my house on wheels in the clouds. At the same time, I realise I haven't closed the curtains and I'm no longer listening intently to the sounds of the forest as if every swish and rustle, every crack and creak, were the sign of a predator on my trail. I'm comfortable with the non-rhythms of the wind and the trees and the creatures out there snuffling about in the undergrowth.

Which is why I don't notice the car until its headlights hit the campervan's back window. I keep still and watch. I'm expecting to see the man from Murmur climb out of the driver's seat, but the figure that lurches into the beam of the car's lights doesn't move like him. It's the lad from the shop – the one I floored just a few hours ago – and now he's standing in front of his car, leaning back on the bonnet with his arms folded. I slide down off the bench, out of sight.

Nothing happens for a moment, and then the passenger seat window shatters and a rock lands in the footwell. I'm up and wrenching open the side door, ready to flatten him again, but I stop at the top of the steps. He's laughing at me. He's satisfied he has my attention. I watch his breath condense in the headlights. He's taking little glances behind me, into the van – he wants to make sure there's no one else in there before he tries anything. I do the same, checking his car for mates. It looks like he's on this trip alone.

'*He* got the message,' he says. 'Now you can fuck off too.'

'If you tell me where he fucked off to I'll go find him.'

He unfolds his arms, stepping forward. 'How should I fucking know?' and the words are slurred. He's been drinking. Then again, so have I.

'She was a friend of yours,' I say. 'Anwen?'

'Fuck off,' he repeats, and then he's picking up another rock. I have sympathy for him – he's Joel's friend, and he was probably Anwen's too – but I don't want the van destroyed. I take the steps down from the door in one jump and run at him. This time he's ready for me, rooted to the ground with his big feet, and I'm as insubstantial as the vapour we're exhaling into the night air as he throws me off with one arm. I land in the mud on my knees, closer to the open door of his car than he is, and I reach in and snatch the keys from the ignition. Then I'm running towards the gate and the forestry track, stumbling over rocks and ruts, and it's bloody dark in the forest and suddenly I'm totally sober and exhilarated.

There's another 'Fuck!' when he realises what I've done, and then I hear him lumbering after me. I can hear him grunting and cursing in the dark avenue of the plantation, and then I come out of the forest into bright moonlight and I can see him a good twenty metres behind me. I find the narrow path down to the New Cottages, jarring a knee in a dip, but he isn't fast – he's too big for speed – and I have to wait till he comes out of the trees to let him see me, and then I carry on, limping down the slate outfall and through the birch saplings. He's close now and shouting, and I hear, 'Bitch' and 'Stop you fucking bitch' and I want to stop and laugh, but I keep going. When I reach the lower track I turn up towards the New Cottages and batter on Raven's door. There are no lights on and no answer, and I suddenly see the flaw in my plan. But there's a line of orange between the curtains of Murmur. I run along the row and thrust the car keys through the letter box in the oak door just as the rock-wielding drunk staggers around the gable end. He's got me by the neck when the door opens and I just manage to say, 'He wants his keys back, please.'

The man at Murmur is standing with his back to the stove and I'm sitting at his oak table, leaning forward over my arms, waiting for my heart to stop pounding.

'You don't look like the type to make enemies,' he says quietly.

I raise my head from the table. 'Is that a challenge?'

He shrugs. 'Just a theory. Wrong one.'

He's wearing a grey T-shirt and black combats, and he's chewing his lip. He wants an explanation, and I probably owe him one. 'Thank you,' I try. 'For saving me.' My gratitude doesn't sound convincing. I guess I don't like being rescued.

The kettle begins to whistle and he makes two mugs of tea, mashing the bags against the side of each cup with a teaspoon before lobbing them into the sink. Then he adds two heaped spoons of white sugar to each one. 'Good for shock,' he says as he places the brew in front of me, but it's his hand that's shaking, not mine, and it's his tea that slops onto the table as he sets it down.

I look around the room while he gets a cloth. The table is nestled between beech-topped kitchen units and a stove which glows in the recess made by the stairs. At the other end of the room is a sofa where the scruffy dog is curled up with its chin on a cushion. It's not asleep, though. Its eyes are wide open and staring at me. There's a basket of chopped wood by a pine cupboard, and in a corner of the room is a small bookcase – OS maps and guidebooks and books on building and DIY as far as I can tell. There's also a whole shelf of bird books. I look at him again as he mops up the spilt tea. He's a twitcher, I think, and I wonder if I've made a mistake coming here: an evening scrapping with a thug would be better than sugary tea with a birdwatcher.

He sits down opposite me at the table and hunches over his mug, grasping it tightly as if he's trying to still the tremor in his hand. A resident at the hostel once told me that only criminals, guitarists and probation officers take two sugars in their tea. I look at the loaf of freshly baked bread on a cooling rack between us, and I take another quick look around the room for a telly or for something plastic made in China, but there's nothing to break the illusion of countrified middle-class taste.

'Owen,' he says. 'Name's Owen.'

'And you're from the Valleys.' I'm hoping to puncture his *Country Life* pretensions with an observation drawn from listening intently to the submerged undercurrents of his accent. He just shrugs and smiles. He doesn't mind being rumbled.

'And I couldn't wait to get out,' he says. Then he looks towards the closed front door as if he's studying it for clues. He fiddles with his glasses. 'So what's with your friend?' he says.

'Friend?' I realise he thinks it's a lovers' spat and I laugh. 'Do you have friends like that?'

He turns his gaze on me. 'I just ...'

'He's upset,' I say. 'He thinks some Iranian refugees killed a friend of his.' It isn't much of an explanation, and we both know it, so I relent a little and tell him about the *Big Issue* lass, and the little disagreement I had with the boy outside the Spar. I also want him to know I can usually take care of myself.

'And you're staying in that campervan?' he asks. 'In the quarry? On your own?'

'Only a couple of men have bothered me so far.'

He sits on his hands and curves his back forwards slightly, as if he's trying to get away from a bad feeling in his gut. 'I was walking the dog. Noticed the gate was open.' He gives me a hopeful smile. 'Being neighbourly ... Checking ... It's how people are up here. They look out for each other.'

'So you know Tegid Rhys? The man who was living in the van?'

He shakes his head. 'Seen him around ... not to talk to.'

'Not that neighbourly then.'

The dog shuffles about on the sofa, exhales loudly, and closes its eyes. Then it opens them again and stares into the middle distance. Owen adjusts his glasses, as if their thick black frames are weighing on him, and then he puts both hands flat on the table. They've stopped shaking and I notice they are large hands, and the knuckles are scuffed. Building work. Or something like it. He hasn't spent much time in an office.

'Do you live here?' I ask. 'All year?'

'Peace and silence,' he says.

I laugh. 'Till the drones and the jets come back and they build an army training ground on your doorstep.'

He stands up then and walks over to the stove, squatting down to open it and push in a chunk of wood. 'I don't mind the jets,' he says, without turning round. 'I was in the army. I'm ... I was a squaddy. We were in a town. It was being shelled from the hills. All the time. Day and night. They didn't care what they hit. Schools, hospitals, houses, the marketplace. But they stopped when they heard a jet coming. The shelling stopped ... So I like that sound. It's a good sound.'

'The cavalry's coming.'

He stands up slowly. 'It's no different from you stepping in for that woman today. Protecting her because she couldn't fight back herself.'

'Cos that's what they're for, is it, the army and the airforce – protecting the weak?'

He sits down at the table again and squints at me. 'That's what

I was there for.' He brushes a patch of flour around the table, making spirals with his fingertips.

I start to feel bad about my attitude. He opened his door to me. He persuaded an angry man to go home and leave me alone. And then he made a cup of sugary tea for me. 'It's a beautiful valley,' I say, 'and a lovely cottage.'

He looks up. 'I got two cottages for the price of one. No one wants to buy a house in a war zone – even a pretend war zone.'

'Except you,' I say, and then bite my lip.

'Where you from?' he asks then. 'You talk like a college girl.'

'Nowhere.'

'Not possible,' he says. 'London?'

'I've moved around a lot.' He won't go in any of the boxes I've set up for him, and now he's trying to find one for me. I wonder whether he has a family, away from this hideout in the hills – a wife and kids stashed away in the city. There are no photographs of people on the bookcase or the walls.

He sees me assessing the room and looks around it himself. I'm jarred by the wistfulness in his gaze. It's as though he loves the place and longs to live in it but knows he can't.

'You're not staying here, are you?' I ask, amazed by my own certainty.

'What? Yes! I'm going to do the place up and then look for work. Maybe in an outdoor education centre. Something like that.'

I'm not sure if he's trying to convince himself, or me, but I know I want to get out of the place. It's like being on a studio set for a country cooking programme, and it's giving me the creeps. I stand up. 'Thanks ... for the tea,' I say, looking at the full mug.

'You can stay. If you want.' He motions vaguely towards the sofa.

I think of the broken window at the van, and the cold clear night, and the likelihood of another rock coming in through the windscreen before dawn. But I decide I couldn't push the sad little dog off the sofa even if I could stand being in the fake cottage for a night. 'I just need a piece of plywood,' I say. 'Or cardboard and some tape.' It's a demand disguised as a list. Like most lists.

He disappears up the stairs and returns with a piece of wood and a small box of tools, and then he's putting his coat on and the dog is by his heels, and they both look at me expectantly, standing by the door, the dog wagging its tail, the man raising his eyebrows and smiling. It makes me laugh, so I let them walk back with me, and we go up through the forest without speaking much, drawing the cold damp air that rises in a thin mist between the trees into our warm lungs.

The lost recognise each other. I've seen it before. And if they're really stupid they try to set up home in each other, as if being the same is a guarantee of success, rather than a double curse. It makes no sense. It's like building a house in a cloud, without a plan or any practical knowledge or experience. It will fall down.

And I've heard it said that a daughter isn't, as Freud suggested, attracted to men who remind her of her father. She's drawn to those who echo the one her mother loved most. In my case, that wouldn't be either of her violent husbands. My mother loved her father the most: the man with sea-grey eyes and slate-scarred hands; the man who scared away the demons and the monsters, and never summoned them up; the man who spoke gently to children and shouldered his own pain without ever passing it on.

But my Taid wasn't a soldier, I tell myself. Not even a damaged one.

# 14

## Spa

At first light there's something moving around outside the van. I mull over the possibilities. A sheep? A man with a brick? A line from a dream echoes around my head: I think we've had it.

It could be Owen and his dog, come to check I've survived the night with a broken window and a thug on the loose. I'm not sure what to think about that last option. It isn't entirely intolerable. I put my coat on over the clothes I've slept in and shuffle to the door.

Raven is out there on a log she's dragged over to the van, smoking a roll-up. I go and sit next to her, huddling into my coat, my hands in my pockets. There's a tightness in my head and I know why – I finished off the wine. Owen helped me pick the glass out of the footwell and off the front seats and wrap it in newspaper, and then he held the plywood to the window frame as I taped it up. And then he went home with his dog and I drank the wine.

And I remember now that I folded another sheet of newspaper around the broken glass, and as I folded it I scanned a piece about the arrest of the suspected terrorists in Telford – and perhaps that's why I dreamt about Siamak, the Iranian who hanged himself. In my dream we were outside a classroom in a college building, sat on a sofa. I know, in the dream, that he should be inside the classroom, in his English class, and I'm worried he'll be in trouble, that he'll be in danger of reprisals if his absence from the class is discovered, and I'll be in trouble for not forcing him to attend. When the other students start to come out I look at him and say, 'I think we've had it.'

I look out over the hills and forests towards the mountains. The sky is pale blue and empty, and Raven, for once, is quiet, sitting on the log next to me with her elbows on her knees, drawing on the roll-up, her cap pulled low over her face. And in this great expanse of trees and grass and sheep I understand why people might gravitate towards the nearest human being. I understand why Raven is sitting outside my campervan on a cold winter morning, waiting for me to come out for a chat. I decide to tell her a joke – the joke Alex, who was half Scottish and half Pakistani, told me one night at the hostel. 'Tonto and the Lone Ranger are riding across the prairies when they see Cheyenne warriors on swift horses pounding towards them from the north. They wheel around and gallop south but coming from that direction are the Comanche. They turn again and head east, but the Cherokee are charging towards them from the east, so they try west, and from the west come the Apache. The Lone Ranger and Tonto pull their horses to a halt. They are completely surrounded, and the Lone Ranger looks at Tonto and says: "I think we've had it, Tonto." And Tonto says, "What d'you mean 'we', Pale Face?"'

Raven laughs. 'I get that,' she says. 'Feeling like you're living your life undercover just cos it doesn't suit other people to see who you really are.' And then she waves the roll-up at me. 'He wouldn't let me smoke in the van. Anyway, it's better out here than in that box.' She looks out at the hills as if she's only just noticed them.

'Have you always lived here?' I ask her.

'I belong here,' she says, as if I've just accused her of something. 'I like the city, but I don't want to live there. I tried it once. Worked in a factory for a bit.' Her eyes widen as if she can hardly believe it herself. 'In Bristol. I stayed with my mum for a few months and got a job in a factory.'

'What did you make?'

'No idea.'

She goes quiet again. My head pounds. 'I met your ex in the library,' I try.

'She's alright,' she says. 'It wasn't her fault. It's her family.'

'She said her lad – Tomos, is it? – liked Tegid.'

She grins. 'Followed him around all the time, asking for stories, asking him to draw maps. Kids know, don't they? They know more than they're supposed to know. He's a great kid, Tomos.'

I decide I need coffee, so I go back into the van and put the kettle on, and as I wait for it to boil I watch Raven through the window. She throws the end of her roll-up into a puddle by her feet and then fidgets about on the log. She could be waiting for a bus.

The coffee spills onto my cold fingers as I step down out of the van. I hand her one of the mugs and she looks at it, then she puts it down on the ground beside her. 'Fish,' she says. 'Tegid had fish for breakfast.' She says it as though she's confirming to herself that strange people who live in campervans and talk about aliens also consume strange things for breakfast. 'Said it was good for the brain.' She laughs. 'I don't think he needed any more brains.'

The coffee is bitter and warm and I hold the mug with both my sleeved hands and listen to Raven talk about trees, and forestry, and about her mother. She was an English hippy, she tells me, searching for something in the Welsh wilderness. She looks at me as if I might be doing the same thing. 'Don't know what she expected to find,' she says.

I shrug. 'Maybe she wasn't looking for anything. Maybe she was running away?'

She laughs. 'Yeah. That's right. And the only thing she found was my dad – a grumpy drunk bastard. I think she thought he was Celtic and mysterious, just cos he never said anything. So in the end she had to run away again. She went to Bristol with a hippy who talked all the time. I don't blame her. It wasn't much of a life here, looking after me all day, cooking his dinners while he was out in the forest or down the pub.'

I want to say it can't have been much of a life for a child either, being left with an alcoholic father, but she's already swept that story

136

aside and moved on. Now she's talking about Tegid. 'He tracked the height of them. Every time one of those jets went over he'd jump up and do some kind of measurement and calculation with this gadget thingy he had. Then he'd shout, "Seventy feet! That one was just seventy feet above the ground." And I remember the first time he did it I said to him, "Is that allowed?", and he said, "No! They're not supposed to come down lower than a hundred feet, even here." And I said, "No – I don't mean that. I mean, are you allowed to track them?"'

She chuckles to herself and I picture them together. Tegid, with his boarding-school education, was never inclined to equate the law with morality. In Tegid's experience of life, the establishment turned a blind eye to abuse and bullying, or carried it out, so obeying their rules was something you did out of fear, and not because you thought the rules were just. But that expensive education – what he called 'training for trench warfare and subduing the natives' – also taught him things they couldn't take back later: how to ignore his own fear when he needed to, and how to value his own opinion. And Raven? She was someone with nothing much beneath her feet or behind her back except fresh air. She'd need to be mindful of the rules – their rules. She'd know the cost of breaking them.

'I didn't find any calculations and readings in there,' I say, taking a hand out of my coat sleeve and waving it towards the van. 'Just maps and notes.'

'He put them on his computer,' she says.

There's a blood-curdling cry at the edge of the forest and I jump up. 'What the hell …?'

'Buzzard,' says Raven, not moving.

I sit back down on the log and fold myself into a huddle. 'There wasn't a computer in there either,' I say.

'Must have taken it with him.'

I glare at her. 'D'you know where he is?'

She leans back into the space behind her. 'He said it was his fault. Said he was going to make sure the girl was alright.'

'What girl?' Maybe it's the hangover and the cold, but for one moment I get an alarming picture of Tegid besotted with a younger woman. So that's what he meant by 'his fault' – he got some girl pregnant and then ran away.

I must be staring at her in horror because she gives me the same look she gave the coffee. And then slowly and loudly, as if I don't fully understand the language she's using, she says, 'The girl whose mother got killed. Anwen's little girl. Zoe.'

I look out over the legions of dark green fir trees towards the mountains and I feel a stupid sense of relief. He didn't get a woman pregnant. He got her killed. And then he tried to make up for it by paying off her daughter. 'So you think Tegid shot down a drone with a farmer's rifle and killed Anwen?'

She looks down at her feet and moves them around in the mud. 'I don't know about a rifle. But he mapped the forest, and then he started on the old quarries. If there was anything down there, he'd have found it.'

'You mean the weapons?'

She shrugs as if to say, 'Work it out for yourself,' and for the first time I feel annoyed by the way none of Tegid's friends seem to trust me enough to tell me the truth, but I still get pushed around by Rickman and by Joel's mate. 'What d'you know about Joel, Zoe's dad?' I ask her.

'He used to work with me before he got laid off. Now he does bits of contract work. Spends most of his time in the pub. Why?'

'A friend of his put a brick through the van window last night.'

She turns to inspect the campervan. 'Guto Martins? He's a dickhead,' she says. 'I'll sort him out for you.'

I shake my head. 'It's fine. It's sorted.'

She shrugs. 'Well. You know where I am.' And then she's standing up, leaving the coffee on the ground. 'Got to shift some wood,' she says, and instead of turning towards the forest gate, which everyone else seems to come up through and go out through, she heads in the opposite direction, climbing the steep slope beside the quarry and disappearing over the brow of the hill.

I drive the van away from its mooring, scratching a note on a piece of slate, just in case. 'Back soon' it announces to the hills and sky.

At the New Cottages I get out and leave the engine running. I want to put the roll of duct tape and the handsaw on his step and run, but Owen hears me and opens the door. I pass the tools to him with a quick, 'Ta for the help.'

He follows me to the van and holds the door open while I climb in. 'Sleep well?' he asks as I yank the door out of his hand and shut it.

I wind down the window a little. 'Fine,' I tell him, conscious that I need a wash and a change of clothes.

'I could cook something,' he says. 'If you come round tonight.' And when I don't respond he mumbles, 'Just pasta. Nothing special. Just food.'

'I can cook pasta myself,' I say. 'On a gas ring in the van.'

He smiles then. 'Then it won't be pasta. I'll use the oven.' He passes a scrap of paper through the window. It has the address of a caravan sales site on it, and directions. 'I think they do repairs.'

I chuck the paper on the dashboard. 'And I'm vegetarian.'

I hear him say, 'Figures,' as I wind up the window, and I wonder if I should have said no. I don't want to lead him on. Or me. But I can't think about it because the puddles in the track are fringed with ice and I have to concentrate till I reach the main road. When I get into fifth gear for a few minutes, the plates in the cupboard rattle and my sleeping bag slides off the back bench. The world seems to have woken up after days of slumber and it's now open-eyed and expectant under the cloudless sky.

Sally once said I wouldn't know a potential relationship if it came up and punched me in the face. I think she was referring to

Alex, who'd been lingering in the office at the end of his shift and trying to talk to me about music, poetry, and the vegetables he was growing on his allotment. But she was wrong. I could tell Alex was interested. He saw me as a challenge, a project, and he desperately wanted to nurture something cold and self-contained. I told him to get a cat.

I find the caravan sales site just out of town, downriver, and they tell me it will take a day or two to get the glass. I leave my number with them and drive away. On the road back to town I pass a billboard showing a photo of a woman's blissful face framed by a head towel, and the words 'spa' and 'heated indoor pool' hurl themselves at me. I turn the van around and go back, chugging through the iron gates and up a long snaking drive to a holiday resort nestled in the hills.

At reception I buy a swimming costume from the minimal choice and the man slumped in a swivelling chair behind the desk hands me a large towel and a locker key. In the changing rooms I shower first, relishing the smell of the gel from the dispenser on the wall. A steamy heat fills the cubicle and I stay there, under the blast of hot water, for a long time. The costume, when I put it on, is high-legged. I try tugging it down as far as it will go but it's not designed for women who don't wax their bikini-line every week. I walk quickly to the poolside and plunge in. The water is warm and there's no one else in the pool, but there are two women in the Jacuzzi, keeping their hair and make-up out of the bubbles as they talk. I front crawl the first five laps and then settle into a steady breast stroke, and then I catch a glimpse of Ben Rickman through the glass windows that divide the pool from the gym. He's on the running machine, leathering it to some track on his phone. I don't wave. I put my head down and keep swimming.

As I rack up the laps in the small pool I think about Tegid. I try to picture him wielding a weapon, aiming it, firing it, and I can't.

140

He was a watcher, a listener, someone who waited for the small spaces in the middle of other people's noise to allow him to speak. He never muscled in, even on a conversation. And yet, and yet. He told me once that it took him nine years of boarding school to figure out that even bullies need to sleep. He didn't tell me what he did with that knowledge, only that he was expelled for acting on it.

One of his postcards just said: 'Are you still there?'

I hold the side of the pool in the deep end. I push my feet against the wall, gripping the rim with the tips of my fingers, bowing my body into an arc and letting my head dip down so that my face is close to the surface of the water and my breath blows across it like a miniature tropical wind ruffling the surface of a tiny ocean. For a moment I'm thinking about sinking to the bottom of the pool and staying there. But the water keeps me half afloat and I decide I have to find him, whatever it takes and whatever he's done, because we recognised each other and were not appalled.

I start with a pot of coffee and free wi-fi in the resort's bar, where the sound of harps playing Welsh folk tunes dribbles out of the speakers and there's a list of spa treatments in a frame on the table (hot stone massage, Indian head massage, full body massage). Once the waiter has retreated to the kitchen the place is empty. My intention is to contact Reg Dauber – Tegid's old business partner in Curved Space Mapping Technologies – but I've been distracted by a copy of the local newspaper in a rack on the bar. It's caught up with the weapons story and the front page screams 'No Welcome in the Hillside for Terrorists'. Not till the end of the article, on the third page of the paper, is there an acknowledgement that no clear link has been made between the jet crash, the discovery of the weapons stash, and the raid on a house in the Midlands occupied by asylum seekers from Iran.

I turn to the letters page. A Mr Briand points out that nowhere is out of reach of the tentacles of terror. And then there's the letter

Delyth predicted: 'Isn't it time the good people of Pont Rhith played their part in making the world a safer place? We should give all our support to the MT4S Consortium in its attempts to build a training ground for our brave soldiers. It's the least we can do.' It's signed by Mr Palmer of Sunny Hill Holiday Park.

I pull up the internet on my phone and look for contact details for Reg Dauber through his company's website, and then I write him an email. I tell him I'm a social worker, and that I'm worried about one of my clients. Given his state of mind, I say, I'm concerned for his safety. I've been looking for anyone who could possibly help me find him.

And then I delete it. Tegid never mentioned Reg Dauber. I'm guessing they weren't close. And when I look again at the pictures of the man on his company's website – in front of his houses in the Channel Islands and in Portugal, on his yacht in the Mediterranean, driving his flash cars – I decide appealing to his compassionate side probably won't work either.

I say I'm a freelance journalist. I tell him I'm writing a series of features on great designers. I would very much like to interview him. I tell him I'm currently on a research trip to Wales and would be more than happy to visit him at his Abersoch home, which I believe he designed himself. And then I add: 'I'm also trying to track down your one-time business partner and co-developer of the computer programme which brought you such great success – Tegid Rhys. I would be delighted if you could shed some light on his current whereabouts.' But my instincts tell me to delete that bit too and to stick with the 'great designers' line.

I hit send and stretch my arms above my head. I catch a faint smell of shower gel and there's a pleasant ache in my shoulders.

# 15

## Kitchen

It's when I leave the A-road and start up the valley towards Bethania that I notice the small red car behind me. It's still there on the track up to the New Cottages, and when I stop outside 'Murmur' it draws up beside me. I watch the driver check her lipstick in the rearview mirror before she gets out. She comes over to the van as though she intends to inspect it for contraband or refugees: she notes the number plate, moving her lips while she reads it; she stoops abruptly to peer underneath at the bodywork. I climb out and wait for her to finish her survey. The twilit sky is beginning to cloud over, and there's a sudden smattering of icy rain. A planet has appeared just above the eastern hills.

'Is this Tegid Rhys's campervan?' she asks, her hand on the patched wheel-arch. I'm wondering if I want to answer when she stands up and holds out a hand and says, 'Gemma Scanlon. Journalist with *Gwalia News*.' The hint of self-satisfaction suggests this is her first job on a real paper – she's young, maybe mid-twenties. I try to look impressed, and probably fail, and her hand falls limply away.

'Yes it's Tegid Rhys's van,' I say, following her around to the sliding door. 'Does that count as news?'

She doesn't reply. She walks back to her car, picking her way carefully between the puddles on her high heels and retrieving a brown handbag from the passenger seat. I don't know much about handbags but from the way she wields it in front of her I think it must be an expensive one. And then her face unfolds into a wide smile and she's walking towards Owen who's opened his door and is standing there silhouetted against the soft light from the kitchen.

He doesn't move to let her in and she has to stop in front of him. I start to feel a little sorry for her – she's not getting a warm welcome at the New Cottages. 'I wasn't expecting to meet Miss ...' she waves a hand towards me, but I don't fill in the gap, 'here. I was coming to see how you were getting on.'

She twists a strand of her hair around her forefinger while she speaks, and even though she's as tall as he is in her heels, she's somehow contorted herself to look up at him. I've stopped feeling sorry for her – I'm shivering with cold. 'Owen won't mind if we come in,' I say, and he steps aside to let us through.

'What a beautiful place.' She walks over to the sofa and lightly brushes it with her hand before sitting down. I pull out one of the chairs at the table and turn it to face her. Owen stays standing, leaning against the stove with his arms crossed. 'Have you done it up yourself?' she asks him, and her wide smile makes my own jaw ache.

'Tegid Rhys,' I growl before Owen can start a rundown on his DIY prowess. 'You wanted to know about Tegid.'

She turns to me then and the smile fades. She'd prefer to be talking to Owen and not to some shorthaired woman in a man's mountaineering jacket and muddy boots. 'I heard you were in a *fight*,' she says. 'Outside the Spar. I've heard the man you attacked doesn't want to press charges, but the manager thinks he should. Do you have any comments?'

I consider her. I wonder how she knows it was me in the fight, and I wonder if the Spar had a CCTV camera or if the whole town knows who I am, because I'm a stranger. 'I think the woman he was harassing should press charges,' I say.

She snorts. 'Well then. Maybe you know something about Tegid Rhys's relationship with the Iranians who were selling the *Big Issue* in town.' She turns back to Owen. 'You know they've been arrested under the Prevention of Terrorism Act?'

I laugh then. 'I'm sure Tegid bought the *Big Issue* in Pont Rhith. Lots of people buy the *Big Issue*. That doesn't make them supporters of terrorism.'

She crosses her long legs and leans forward. She has a notebook out but doesn't seem to be writing in it. 'It's just something people are saying. They're wondering where this Mr Rhys is now, and who you are. They want to know why you're living in his van. That's all.'

I meet her gaze. And then I decide we could be allies, whether or not she'd like the idea, and I'm pretty sure she wouldn't. I reel out my piece about being a residential social worker, about Tegid living at the hostel, about his disappearance. 'I'd like to know where he is too,' I say. 'And you're the right person to find him, being a journalist. You could run a "missing person" piece in your paper.'

I've provided the professional acknowledgement she needs and she leans back into the cushions, pulls her bag onto her lap and takes out her card to give to me. 'Email me with the details. And I'll need a photograph.' Then she turns back to Owen: 'Maybe I *can* help your friend find this man she's lost.'

I wince at the implication of fault on my part, and I glance at Owen who appears to be enjoying her performance. He's let go of his folded arms and they've swung to his sides, and there's a hint of amusement in his eyes.

She stands up and rearranges her scarf, and then she's moving around the table towards him. He pulls himself away from the stove and goes towards the door. I flounder for a moment under the clear impression that these two have played this little power game before. 'The trouble with people who escape to the hills,' she purrs, 'is they think they can get away from it all. But it always goes wrong. No one can escape themselves, can they?'

Owen opens the door for her and the cold air floods in. 'Sorry,'

145

he says. 'I didn't cook enough for three. You should have told me you were coming.'

She pauses on the threshold, reluctant to leave the warmth of the cottage, and then she's pulling her handbag against her thighs and opening it again.

'Ask Tim Jones about your friend,' she says to me. 'You know him, don't you? Calls himself a green anarchist. Lives in a commune in Cwm Bychan?'

I shake my head.

'Ah,' she says, 'here it is.' She comes over to the table and slaps a piece of paper down in front of me while Owen pushes the door closed and then leans his back on it, watching us. The paper is a printout of an article about a group of women who were arrested for 'disabling' a fighter jet in a British Aerospace factory in the 1990s. She lets me scan it and then she puts it back in her bag. 'One of those women,' she explains with an air of triumph, 'was going out with Tim Jones at the time. He was part of the group that planned the whole thing, before he moved here and started growing vegetables.' She looks at Owen. 'You see the connection? Violent acts of sabotage.' Then she turns back to me. 'He'll know where your friend is hiding.'

Owen smiles and opens the door for her again. She looks out into the darkness and puts a hand on his arm. Her nails are long and painted a silvery blue. 'I know it's ridiculous,' she's saying, looking up at him with her eyes wide, 'but I do find those road blocks scary. Are they really necessary?'

I'm focussed on her voice now, trying to work out how she's producing the effect – it's as though she's breathing in rather than out while she speaks, keeping her chest inflated.

'No idea,' he says.

146

I keep my coat on despite the heat from the stove. A glass of red wine is placed by my elbow. The dog slides off the sofa, stretches, and then clatters across the stone floor. It rests its chin on my leg, looking up at me with shiny brown eyes.

'What's he called?' I ask.

'She,' he says. 'He's a she. And you can call her whatever you like. She's deaf.'

I scratch behind her ears and her eyes implore me for something, quietly and without any hope, before it's too late. And perhaps it's the wine, and the warmth, and the dog's soft jowls against my thigh, but I start to relax. I take off my coat and fold it over the back of my chair. I lean back and watch Owen at the stove. He's searing mushrooms in butter and garlic, and I can see his shoulder blades move beneath his white T-shirt. An ex-squaddie who cooks and goes bird watching and gets tremors when he's faced with a fight. I keep watching.

When he turns around I look away and focus on the little window behind the sink. All that's visible through the glass is a tangle of brambles illuminated by the house lights. It reminds me of a tropical display case in a zoo – a tank where the snakes try to hide from the stares of children scoffing ice creams. It seems odd to put a window into a ditch, but I suppose it would let in a little extra light if the brambles were cleared.

He's pulling a tray of steaming roasted vegetables out of the oven and placing thick discs of white goat's cheese on top. Then he puts the tray back in the oven and takes the kettle off the stove and pours hot water over a bowl of couscous.

I take a sip of wine. It isn't the bargain basement stuff I buy. It's more like the wine my father would have at the table – smooth and deep. It suggests a communion rather than a student party. It also suggests indebtedness, something I may have to be grateful for later. I set the glass down.

'So there's another suspect ... according to our local journalist,' I say. I'm hoping he'll tell me more about this anarchist, Tim Jones. Or more about Gemma Scanlon. He chooses the first option.

'Lives at the Shed,' he says, taking the mushrooms off the heat and squatting down to pull the roasted veg out of the oven. 'It stands for something. Sustainable Housing Environmental ... something. Design maybe.'

He takes two plates out of the warming oven and starts dishing out, scraping oily melted cheese out of the corners of the tray, adding the mushrooms and the couscous. He sets one plate down in front of me. 'Ten miles by road. Two or three over the hills on foot.'

There is silence as I contemplate the hot food. It didn't come out of a tin, or a jar, and that means I have something else to be grateful for. My appetite struggles with my desire to keep out of his debt and my hunger wins hands down. This isn't going well.

'Do you want to go? Tomorrow?' he says.

For a moment I think he's asking me if I want to leave, to go back to London. For a moment I think he's already noticed I have, like my ex used to say, my bags permanently packed and by the front door. And for a moment I have the horrible feeling he'll try to persuade me to stay. I take a gulp of the wine while I scrabble around for an answer.

'To this SHED place,' he says. 'To ask Tim Jones about your missing friend Tegid.'

And then I don't like the suggestion that he's inviting me along. I can find my own way there. I put down my fork and sit back in a manner I hope will be off-putting, but he's concentrating on his food and misses my little act of withdrawal from the conversation.

'Why do you need to find this Tegid man?' he asks after a while, still not looking at me.

'I collect father figures and dismantle them,' I say. 'When I've finally got enough bits I'll put together a decent one, but he'll probably turn out like Frankenstein's monster and I'll have to kill him.'

He laughs. 'Fair enough. None of my business.' He curls over his food again and I watch him push his glasses up his nose.

I fork a gobbet of beetroot into my mouth. 'I liked him,' I mumble. 'And I let him down.'

He stops eating and stares at me. 'You can't save other people from themselves, you know.' He's waiting for me to look at him directly, as though it's vital I understand this bit of useless advice.

'He left me his van. And as far as I know, he doesn't have anywhere else to live. I'd just like to know he's OK, and that it's OK for me to take it. I'm not in the business of *making* people homeless. I leave that to the landlords and the state.'

It seems to work, as an explanation. He clears the plates to the side and goes to the oven. 'We could walk over to SHED in the morning,' he says with his back to me. 'Give the dog a run.'

'And do some bird-watching on the way?'

He chuckles. 'You've found me out.' And when he comes back to the table I realise how hard it is not to trust a man who makes home-made apple crumble with custard. I try anyway, leaving when I've emptied the bowl and walking back to the van alone.

*A good rockman could read the slate with his fingers. Where he found a weakness, he drove in a long chisel to cleave the slab away. If he couldn't find a weakness he had to insert explosives and that ran the risk of blowing the slab into small, useless bits. Cleaving left a smooth surface; where gelignite had been used, the surface of the rock was wrinkled.*

*In this way the rock spoke to those who could hear its language.*
*Now it is silent.*

*Long before the quarries and mines, the rock was eloquent with runes and rituals.*

*Now the stone circles are dumb too.*

*A rhoddaf i chwi galon newydd, ysbryd newydd hefyd a roddaf o'ch mewn chwi.*

*I will give you a new heart and put a new spirit in you.*

*A thynnaf y galon garreg o'ch cnawd chwi, ac mi a roddaf i chwi galon gig.*

*I will remove from you your heart of stone and give you a heart of flesh.*

*Is that the Bible? Eseciel. He thinks it's Ezekiel.*

*He stares sightlessly upwards, sprawled across broken slate with his leg bent backwards and his arms spread out, a black star in the dark underground.*

*And his heart turns from flesh to stone.*

# 16

## SHED

The clear sky has meant a hard freeze and in the morning the puddles on the track by the New Cottages are solid. I scuff around on the ice, waiting for Owen. There are icicles on the low eaves and I snap one off. It lies in my palm like a glass dagger then slides off and shatters on the flagstones.

At the other end of the terrace Raven is out too, zipping up her padded jacket, banging her gloved hands together. She looks at my backpack and the map sticking out of my pocket. 'Going for a walk?' she calls. Then she's taking out her cigarette papers and walking towards me. 'I'd go with you, but I've got to make sure some of those enviro-mentalists can get into the top wood next week without getting themselves killed by brambles,' she says. 'The boss wants to show them what he's been doing up there.' She kicks my splintered icicle with her foot. 'I suppose it could work, this new way of doing things, but ...'

She stops. Owen is locking his front door, the dog at his heels, binoculars round his neck. When I turn back to Raven the gate is clanging shut behind her and she's already on the path to the forest.

Owen shrugs. 'Busy woman.'

'I don't think she likes you. You should try cooking for her.'

'Yeah. Works on some people.'

I want to say I didn't think I was being worked on, but I keep quiet.

We set off along the farm track that crosses the stream and the

151

road, and then it's a slow climb up the other side of the valley. My blood stays close to my vital organs, leaving my extremities to fight for themselves. My face aches with the cold and I hold my fleece around my chin with a gloved hand and wish I had more fat on my bones.

We're silent as we cross the icy slabs of the slate outfall, moving upwards at a slant towards the black hole in the side of the hill. I know the path passes to the side of the adit, and I keep glancing up at the square black hole, drawn to its blank, one-eyed gaze. I tell myself it's just a sign of the harm humans have done to the hillside; I tell myself it's a scar, not a threat; I tell myself it's not going to suck me in with a ravenous avenging fury.

The dog has her nose to the ground and occasionally stops and looks back at us, waiting for reassurance. She finds a dead jackdaw between some rocks, its wings spread out as if it's been crucified to the frozen ground. A rime of white frost edges its black feathers. She snuffles it for a moment and then scuttles on.

The path skirts the mine's mouth and continues upwards, rising steeply to a dam that plugs the opening of a small valley. I start scrabbling up the scree, sending little avalanches of shale backwards down the slope. Owen keeps a safe distance behind me. When I get to the top I climb onto the dam and walk out along it, stopping halfway across to look out over the valley. I can see the New Cottages on the opposite hill, and Mr Ellis's farm at the top end of the valley. I can see the dragon picture he's made with his red-painted stones in the field beside the farmhouse. And in the other direction, downriver, I can see the village of Bethania. It's nestled tightly into the hills, with only the valley road as a way in and out for vehicles. A few sheep fields surround the cluster of buildings, and beyond those there are forests and rocks. I'm sure it's the perfect place to practise mountain warfare.

I turn round to look at the small reservoir behind the dam. The water is a deep blue colour that reaches down inside me like a bass sound, resonating in all the empty spaces of my being, filling them up with its own cool calm. Owen is taking photos of the water, crouching down on the dam, quiet and focussed. I turn back to the valley and sense the tug of the air, the pull to jump, to fly, to fall.

When he's finished snapping we push our way through leafless trees to the top end of the small reservoir. And then we're following a stream out of the valley and onto still-rising ground that is frost-hard. Our boots make no impression on the mud and my bones jar with every step. Then, when we crest the hill, there is a wide area of flat moorland between sharp-cornered forests, and the earth is boggy. We pick our way over tufts of reedy grass, crunching through the thin seal of ice into the mud beneath. The winter light disperses through a veil of mist.

The lake, when we reach it, is half-covered with a sheet of opaque ice that ends in a sweeping curve against black water. Owen goes to the edge of the lake and squats down. He's taken off his gloves and he's picking up a stone and skidding it across the ice. I watch his fingers return to the pebbles beside him on the shore, searching through them, feeling for the one with the right shape and texture. And then the low sun breaks through the clouds and lands a smudge of bright light on the lake's still surface and a large black bird flaps slowly towards the far shore and then turns around and comes back again, as though it's looking for something it's lost.

'Cormorant,' he says. I brace myself for a bird lecture and he tells me that millennia ago the sea came all the way into these hills and the cormorants haven't forgotten that: they still make the long flight from their hunting grounds at sea to roost on cliffs that are now miles from any ocean.

'Old habits die hard,' I say, picking up my own skimming stone and sending it across the ice.

I take the map out of my pocket and he points to the location of SHED. It's near the head of the next valley, maybe two miles away. As I fold the map up and put it back in my pocket I realise I would never look at a map out in the open in London, where lost people are targets to be picked off by vultures. I always pretend to know where I'm going, even when I don't.

We continue along the path that skirts the lake. The mountains to the north are gathering thick grey clouds and as we descend the hill it starts to hail. It's like walking into flying gravel. I lower my head and wonder why anyone would want to go walking for fun, and even with my eyes down and my hood pulled tightly closed over my hat I can still see the sheep, weathering it all, their quiet resignation like a woolly judgement on our endless running around.

I remember Tegid in the common room one Sunday morning – the smell of frying bacon drifting through from the kitchen and a church service droning on the TV and a congregation warbling through 'The Lord is my Shepherd'. He leans toward me over his mug of strong brown tea and says shepherds do indeed love their charges and keep them fat and happy and safe from harm ... until they take them to market to be slaughtered.

The hail and wind dissipate once we're in the valley. I lift my head again and take down my hood. We're trudging along a track with a dry-stone wall on one side and a wooded hill on the other. A grand house comes into view through the trees: three storeys of Georgian windows and a steep slate roof. It doesn't look like a farmhouse, and I guess it must have been built for a quarry manager or owner. The more recent occupants have added solar panels, and there's a patch of dark earth dotted with the stumps of brassicas to the side of the house.

The track feeds through a gate onto a lane where we pass a yurt and a converted minibus. Owen tries to look into the minibus but there are blankets pinned up against the windows. A chicken does a high-legged strut in front of us, and then wiggles into the hedge. Owen grabs at his dog and puts her on a lead.

As we reach the yard outside the house we have to stand aside to let a car pass. Gemma Scanlon winds down the window and, keeping her smile and attention firmly pinned on Owen, says, 'I suppose you're used to this sort of terrain.'

'Couldn't be more at home,' he says, pulling on the dog's lead to keep her away from the car.

'Seen one mountain, seen them all,' she laughs, and the window goes back up. She gives him a little goodbye wave and I watch her hatchback lurch down the lane, past the yurt and the minibus and out through the gate.

'More visitors?' shouts a man standing in the doorway of the house, leaning against the frame with his arms folded across his chest. 'Takes a bloody RAF disaster to put SHED on the map these days.' He shakes his head slowly and strands of lank grey hair swing across his lined face.

I take a tentative step toward him over the muddy yard, a little worried he might pick up a rifle and demand we get off his land. But he just lowers his head to inspect us and says, 'And that, of course, begs the question ... "whose map"?'

I recognise him now from the Consortium's public consultation event. He was complaining about the roof-mounted wind turbine, and then he was on the pavement outside Delyth's cancelled meeting. And I know Gemma Scanlon is right about one thing – this green anarchist would have known Tegid.

'Who are you two with?' he says as we get to the door. 'Army, Consortium, newspaper?'

'No one,' I say, glancing at Owen for confirmation. He's standing next to me in his walking gear – thick socks, blue waterproof coat and trousers, binoculars, and bobbles of white hail stuck to his woolly hat – and he looks nothing like a soldier.

Tim lets out a long sigh. 'Come in, come in,' he says. 'And the dog too. I don't really care who you are. We don't get many visitors these days. We used to get loads of 'em. They were all coming up here to ask us how to grow turnips on a slate tip and how to rig up solar panels out of radiators and how to shit in the woods. Does everyone know how to do that stuff now?'

He doesn't wait for an answer but leads us down the hallway and into a back room. The pot plants on the windowsill block out most of the daylight, and there are magazines and books piled on the floor and chairs. On the sofa a woman sits amid a jumble of throws and threadbare cushions, her legs tucked up beside her, looking as if she's just come out of a deep trance. I recognise her too: she was channelling ancient Celts at the Consortium meeting, and she told Rickman he was talking bollocks.

Tim introduces us to her: 'Here are some more people here to arrest us for shooting down drones with home-grown cabbages.'

She chuckles, and her voice is raucous when she says: 'Perhaps we did it with one of our highly-trained combat ducks. They use ducks to test jet engines, you know. They chuck them into the works to see what happens when a bird gets sucked in. I'm serious. They do.'

'Ours don't fly, remember?' He turns to us: 'We clipped their wings and then found out Indian Runners don't bloody fly anyway. Clues in the name, I s'pose.'

I feel they could go on like this indefinitely, sharing jokes about ducks and vegetables, so I break in: 'I work in a hostel for the homeless in London and one of our ex-residents has gone missing. Tegid Rhys. His name is Tegid Rhys.'

'Tegid? Bloke who lives in the campervan on Foel y Ffridd?' he says.

I nod.

'Just cos you live in the hills doesn't mean you've gone missing,' he says.

'No one seems to have seen him since before Christmas.'

'Oh,' he says. 'OK. Have a seat. Brew? Sorry, I'm a bit distracted. Seems I'm a suspect in this drone crash thingy, which is fucking ridiculous. Not that I haven't thought of downing one, but it's the jets that really get me. Here I am putting solar panels on my roof, growing my own fucking vegetables to reduce my carbon footprint, and then a couple of those noisy bastards buzz my roof. It's like they're taking the piss. Can you imagine the emissions they're putting out? More than a year's worth of bus trips to Pont Rhith and back, I can tell you. And what about the embodied energy in a thing like that ...'

He's on his way out through the door while he's speaking, and when it closes behind him there is silence. The woman on the sofa pats the cushion beside her. I sit down and sink further into the sofa than I was expecting to and have to struggle to sit back up. Owen finds a low three-legged stool in the corner of the room and the dog nestles in beside him, tight against his boot. There is a tall and shiny metal cylinder beside the two of them which glows orange through a small glass window and looks like a machine from an advanced civilisation. I'm staring at it when Tim returns with a tray of mugs.

'It's a stove,' he says. 'State of the art biomass. We got it cheap because we're testing it. Doesn't work very often, so you've come on the right day.' He hands out the mugs. 'I'm Tim,' he says, raising his eyebrows at me. 'Tim Jones.'

'Sharon Moonstar,' says the woolly woman.

'Abby Hughes,' I say and look at Owen. He's much too big for the little stool he's sitting on and has to realign himself on it before he can speak. 'Owen,' he says, and leaves it at that.

Tim squats down by the stove and puts his mug on the stone floor. 'Shooting the bloody things out of the sky won't help, though, will it?' He peers in through the window of the stove and seems to be satisfied it's still working. 'Food – that's what we need to sort out. We need to make sure there'll be food when the oil runs out. Because let's face it, we're only a few missed meals away from total social meltdown.' He stands up and comes to sit between me and Sharon on the sofa. I try to make room for him, but I'm

157

trapped in a dip in the cushions and we end up with our thighs squished together. He doesn't seem to mind.

Owen shakes his head. 'Not in this country. There are organised structures in this country.'

Tim Jones looks delighted: he has an adversary. 'You mean the government and the army? You're right in one way. Food *will* be shipped out to England once the establishment starts running out of supplies. And it will be shipped out under armed guard.'

'Why bother then?' says Owen. 'Why bother growing your vegetables if they're just going to take them off you the minute there's a crisis?'

'Ah. Good question.' Tim takes a deep breath. 'Because it's revolution disguised as organic gardening. It's putting people back in control of their lives, and the individual back at the centre of the universe. It's about the individual making decisions, making plans, and working with the earth.'

I sink back into the sofa and nurse two feelings at once. One is of general despair, and the other a tiny glowing ember of hope that I may be getting somewhere in my search for Tegid. He must have been here; he must have known these people; he must have argued with them. And if he had any plans to take drastic action, it's just about possible he told Tim Jones.

I notice a fixed smile on Owen's face. He's decided not to go any further. Then he looks at me as if he's asking for permission. He turns back to Tim. 'Tegid Rhys,' he says. 'D'you know him?'

Tim takes the diversion genially. 'Tegid. Yep – we met him in a few of those meetings against that military training ground they want to build down in Bethania. Intense bloke,' he says. 'Had a thing about the jets and the drones. He'd always bring them up, whatever we were talking about. And it was always at the end of the meeting when everyone else was ready to go home. "What are we going to do about the drones?" he'd say. And then he'd tell you something you really didn't want to know about kids getting blown to bits by missiles.'

'But you haven't seen him in the last couple of weeks?'

Tim shakes his head. 'He wasn't at that bloody stupid public consultation thingy, was he? Strange that, now I come to think about it. Would have been just his cup of tea.'

I watch flakes of snow spiralling onto the window pane. They're falling fast, and they've already formed little heaps of white on the crossbars. I'm thinking about how fruitless the walk over the hills has been, and how cold the tramp back will be.

'Will you let me know if he gets in touch with you? Or if you hear anything, think of anything?' I fish a pen out of my coat pocket and look around for some paper. Tim tears a corner off an envelope and hands it to me.

I'm writing down my number when Sharon says, 'Spain.' I've been trying to work out what the motif on the front of her jumper is. I think it's a mouse, but I'm not sure. It could be a squirrel. 'He's gone to Spain ... Went on the train.'

Then she begins to explain, in great detail, how you can travel by train from Pont Rhith to Barçelona in twenty-four hours. She's going on about the times and the connections and the possible routes through France until I start to wonder if she runs an eco-travel business on the side.

My words, when they come out, have to impose themselves forcibly on her talking timetable. 'Spain? For a ... holiday?'

She shrugs. 'Said he had something to sort out. Good time to choose, if you ask me. If you stay here in the winter the moss and the mould start to grow on you.'

The snow crunches under our boots as we set off down the lane. I'm striding now, back along the walled track and up towards the lake. But I don't slow down. I want to know why the hell I'm in Wales in mid winter looking for a man who's on holiday in Spain.

And while I'm asking myself that question, I decide to come out with the other one I've been mulling over all day. I pick the highest point on the route, in a blizzard, to pull down the hood that's been fixed tightly around my face and shout: 'The journalist. The one with the shark smile. How d'you know her?'

He keeps his head down in the fierce wind and I catch something about a friend of his in England who put him in touch with her. Knew her from college. Reckoned she'd be informative. She grew up in the area. Speaks Welsh. So he rang her up. They went for a drink. Wouldn't call her a friend. More like an acquaintance.

I put my hood back up over my woolly hat and stomp on ahead of him. I'm thinking the snow and the roaring wind don't make much difference to the way I hear him: he gives me snippets of information that never seem to add up to anything, and the truth falls through the gaps between his words.

'I prefer cold and distant women who are hard to keep up with.'

I hear that. 'I'm going at my own pace. Sorry if that's too fast for you.'

I sense him stop behind me. 'Are you?'

# 17

## Cae Neidr

When we reach the New Cottages the wind has ebbed. Owen and his dog leave the path and go in through the gate by Raven's place. I keep walking. At the start of the forest I stop and look back and the cottages are far away, distanced by the snow and the layer of stillness it's drawn over the world. It's about three centimetres deep here in the valley, and it's falling lightly now, on my face and on my coat. The snow is the world's lullaby, or a lament for another universe where life thrives through its connections and isn't poisoned by one greedy species. I hum along, weaving strands of my own soft tunes into the quiet.

I told Tegid about that – my inclination to complete the soundscape by adding a rhythm, a drone, or a line of melody. He said he did the same with scenes. If he was struck by the lines in a landscape – the way a road and a bridge and the river and the edges of buildings met each other – he'd place himself in the right place to complete the scene. Or sometimes he'd add himself to a tableau – a family having a picnic in the park, or a flock of pigeons by a statue – in a way that made the picture complete, or funny, or interesting for that moment in time and from his point of view. He called it guerrilla art. He said it was self-entertainment.

We were on our way to Primrose Hill, I remember, on my day off, when he told me about that. It was summer, and I'd suggested going to Kew on a river boat because I liked the clammy warmth and the fusty smells of the Palm House, and the hiss of spray from the watering system, and the Latin names of the plants, and the overtones of abundant life and heat.

He laughed and looked at the floor and said he'd rather not. He said all that lovely warm comforting stuff just smothered the colonial undertones creeping like a parasitic ivy through the foliage. Or words to that effect. And when I said that probably ruled out most of London he said there was another reason he didn't want to go. He had a personal problem with glass houses and he pointed to the scar down his right cheek. So I took him to Primrose Hill instead, to see the city spread out along the skyline. On the way there, walking past the mansions and black steel gates of St John's Wood, he told me the story.

'I went through a glass door,' he said, and he rolled up his sleeve and showed me the ridged white lines on his right forearm.

'You fell through a glass door?'

'Well. Not exactly fell. I drove through it.'

'In a car?'

'On a lawnmower. I'd been allowed to use an empty greenhouse at school to grow some seedlings, and some of the older boys didn't like that. They thought I was strange. They locked me in and they took my clothes. It was nighttime and I was afraid of the dark back then. I didn't like the sounds of the night, or the shadows. And I didn't want anyone to find me there in the morning, with no clothes on, in a glasshouse.

'There was nothing in there with me except my seedlings, a bag of compost and a sit-on lawnmower with the keys in the ignition. So I drove the lawnmower out through the doors and the glass fell down on me. I should have thought of that – how the glass would fall down on me. It was like a shower of razor blades. I didn't think it through properly. I just wanted to get out.'

He told me he was probably nine or ten years old, and that he ended up in hospital where they stitched up the biggest cuts and sent him back to school. 'And the boys who put you there?' I asked him. 'What happened to them?'

'They liked me even less. But I made plans.'

'Even bullies need to sleep?'

'Exactly.'

When we got to Primrose Hill he turned his back on the view of the city and squatted down and scrabbled about on the floor instead. He was enthusing about the brass plaque on the ground commemorating some eighteenth-century Welsh poet called Iolo Morganwg. And he didn't try to complete the scene, either. He just got in the way of all the tourists taking pictures as he tried to keep their feet off the plaque while he read it.

I didn't ask him what he'd done to stop those boys at school, and to get expelled, and he didn't tell me. It didn't seem important at the time.

There's a bark from the field below. A man is standing completely still and at a slant, like a megalith marking the movement of the sun over the white field. He's leaning heavily on his stick and two dogs are running towards him, and then away again, and then back towards him. From the Russian fur hat and the parka coat I recognise Mr Ellis. I climb the barbed wire fence and head towards him, worried he's having a heart attack, but as I approach he starts moving, heading upland towards his farm.

When I catch up he turns his craggy face towards me and says, 'It's not fit for a dog to be out,' and keeps walking, stooped over his stick, his furry earflaps jigging up and down. 'That's what my mother used to say. "It's not fit for a dog to be out. Send your father."'

'So why are you out?' I ask.

'The silly buggers try to find shelter,' he says, stopping to wave his stick at the sheep. 'They huddle into hollows and against the walls, and then the drifts get them. It's as though they want to be buried alive. I've spent all morning trying to drive them into the open.' He rummages around in a pocket and brings out a handkerchief and wipes the drip from his nose. 'But it isn't going to snow anymore. I have wasted my time.'

'Have you heard a forecast?'

He chuckles. 'No bach. I can hear the stream. And the mountain looks far away. That means it isn't going to snow anymore.'

'Oh.' I listen and I look. I can hear the stream chattering at the edge of the field, and then, while I'm trying to work out if the mountain looks further away than usual, a fast-moving fleck in the sky catches my attention and rapidly expands into an arrow. The jet crests the gap in the hills above the farm and then the sound catches up. It's a roar that hurts my ears and shakes my insides, and I flinch because the plane comes so close I think it will take my head off. Mr Ellis keeps walking as if he hasn't noticed the sky being torn apart, but the dogs' bellies are a little closer to the ground, their backs flattened, and their chins are pushed forward as if they're gritting their teeth.

As the sound dies away Mr Ellis is telling me that Raven came over in the morning and offered to help with the sheep, so he sent her out with feed. And then his voice is drowned out by another jet ripping through the sky above us. He carries on talking anyway and I watch his mouth move without hearing a word, and then as the roar fades away I pick up the end of what he's saying, '... she'll eat her own fleece.' He stops and looks at me for a response, then shakes his head and starts walking again. 'If she gets buried in snow, she'll scratch at the ground, and then she'll start eating her own fleece.'

'Does that happen a lot?' I ask him.

'Only when they're buried in the snow.'

'I mean the jets.'

He shrugs. 'It's one of their favourite routes.'

'It's bloody terrifying,' I say.

'It's the sound of peace,' he says. 'That's what the man from the army told me when I complained.' He chuckles to himself. 'Bloody fool.'

164

I think about Tegid then with the farmer's rifle, and those jets skimming the roof of his campervan. He would have been tempted, I'm sure of that, but I can also see the planes are so low and fast a pilot wouldn't have time to eject before hitting the hillside. Tegid would have thought about that too. He'd have gone for an unmanned aerial vehicle instead, with no pilot to worry about. 'Mr Ellis,' I say. 'Did Tegid really shoot down that drone?'

'And nation shall not lift up sword against nation, neither shall they learn war anymore,' he says.

He's stopped to kick at a patch of snow in the field next to the farmhouse. One of the dogs jumps at the crystals flying from the man's boot, catching bits of ice in its mouth. I'm not sure what Mr Ellis is doing till I see a red-painted stone appear under his foot. I crouch down and use a gloved hand to dust the snow off the other rocks in the dragon. The red paint looks faded and grubby against the white snow.

Mr Ellis has stopped kicking at the stones and is watching me, leaning on his stick. 'We've always called this field Cae Neidr,' he says. 'It means field of snakes. Which is why I put a dragon in it. I've never seen a snake.'

My knees are getting wet but I'm intent now on uncovering all the stones, and maybe it's my willingness to work which prompts him to say more as he looks out over the valley. 'They say you should live as if you're going to die tomorrow, and farm as if you're going to live forever. The problem is, this place has more ghosts in it than living people, and I can hear them all. I can hear the men at shearing time, swearing and joking. I can hear the women calling them in for tea and cake and a cold ham salad. I can hear the families by the piano singing hymns to God and ballads to love and the land. I can hear the poets reciting poems that make you weep and poems that make you laugh, and the lads telling blue jokes, and the girls telling them off. And you know, I'd be happy enough to join them now. I'm already half gone. The problem is, the sound of those bloody jets drowns out even the ghosts, so there's nowhere for me to go, is there? Even the dead aren't safe. Your friend with the campervan understood that.'

'Did he do it?'

He chuckles again. 'No bach. That was not the plan.'

'So what was the plan?'

He taps the side of his nose. 'It doesn't matter now,' he says. 'He's gone.' I follow his gaze across the valley towards the yawning hole of the mine adit in the side of the hill. Then he turns away and heads for the house.

I stand up. I think I've uncovered all the red stones, and that the dragon is now revealed to the sky, but it's hard for me to tell from where I'm standing, on the ground.

# 18

## Moonlight

At the van I sweep the snow off the step with my gloved hands and slide the door open. Now that my reason to stay here has gone on holiday I look around and see a cramped, cold space and wonder what the hell I'm doing in a fibreglass box in a disused slate quarry in January. And then I realise with a wave of dizziness that I have no real reason to be anywhere else either, and I understand why people have pets: a dog who needs feeding and walking, a budgie's cage to clean out, a cat to call us back and quilt us into the world with its kneading paws.

But maybe Tegid was different. Maybe he really didn't need to belong anywhere. The opposite, in fact: he chose to break all ties of kinship and friendship, and, like a Celtic saint, throw himself on the sea winds, drifting without hope or expectation towards his place of resurrection. And right now, I think, with another surge of irritation, he may have washed up outside a café in Catalonia where he's sipping freshly made lemonade and watching the sun go down over the Mediterranean. He's not thinking of Wales, or drones, or missile-guidance systems. He has a few postcards on the table in front of him. He knows the first one should be to Delyth, but he's not sure what to say to her. 'Hello,' he tries. 'How's the campaign?' But there's no point struggling for the words to address her with. He isn't going back. Not yet. Maybe never.

The afternoon passes slowly. I light the stove with the last of my wood and huddle in my sleeping bag on the bench, watching the day fade over the snowy hills. I drift in and out of sleep. I think of the ways Tegid could have taken revenge on those sleeping bullies at school, and I wonder if he came to Wales thinking he could catch the military-industrial complex snoozing in the mountains like a gorged dragon. I wonder if he thought he could creep up on the beast and deliver it a devastating blow. And then I remind myself he's no longer implicated in the drone disaster and I can let that idea go. He didn't do it. Middle Eastern magazine-sellers from Telford are to blame, and he was probably on holiday when it happened.

It's nearly dark when the stove goes out. I have no more wood. My breath condenses in the cold air of the campervan, so I get up and find a couple of plastic bags and go out foraging like a character in a Brecht play, tramping through the snow after a war, wrapped in layers of coats and scarves, looking for something to burn to keep warm. But the wars are far away now, not here, and the dangers I face are mostly psychological. If I really wanted somewhere warm to go, I could turn up at Owen's cottage, or Delyth's Bed and Breakfast, and beg for shelter.

I kick at a fallen branch buried under the snow and try to lift it up; it frays into soft black splinters. I'm not going to find the kind of wood you can burn in a stove in this dank forest; I'll have to keep warm with hot coffee instead. I go back for my new water bag – a bag I can fold up when it's empty and put in my pocket – and I take it down to the stream in the gorge.

There are thin shelves of ice over the edge of the water and the stream is rippling along an inch or two beneath the glassy sheets, racing as if it's trying to escape its own imminent immobilisation. I lean out beyond the ice and let the water run into the bag. And then, over the noise of the stream, I hear a car revving to escape a snow-filled dip, and I know enough about the landscape now to wonder why a car would be driving up or down that track on the other side of the gorge – there are no farms or cottages up there. Its headlights sweep the pine trees as it pulls out of the dip, and then it's rolling slowly downhill towards Bethania. I start to cross the stream on the ice-polished rocks and I make a clumsy jump to the opposite bank and drop the water bag and my left foot slips into the water. I watch the bag float away on the stream, then I stagger up the slope, my foot squelching in its sodden sock. Brambles snag at my calves and I have my arms out in front of me to push away the branches of the pine trees. I get the feeling that something in the forest is waiting, marking time, and I'm as alert as I've ever been on a city street at night. But I can read nothing from the forest sounds and they're the opposite of music now. A thin branch whips against my face, just under my left eye, and when I draw my hand away from my cheek there is blood on my glove.

At the track I listen again, but all I hear is the laboured sound of my own breathing. I bend over, my hands on my thighs. The air in the forest is so wet and cold that my lungs ache with each in-breath and the toes of my wet foot are already numb. Then I pick up the distant hum of another engine. I think it's a tractor.

I give up chasing the car and think instead about asking Raven for some wood, so I can re-light the stove and avoid frostbite. From the sound of the tractor she can't be far away. I walk in one of the snowy ruts left by the car until I get to a point where the track widens out and forks and it looks like the car turned around. There's also a shed, and a workshop with open sides. There's an axe in there stuck in a chopping block on a bench. I very much want to be back at the van, making coffee, getting warm. The tractor sound is coming from higher ground, so I carry on up through the trees, struggling to lift my tired legs through the deep snow, and only then wondering why the forester is out at night, working in the dark.

I come out of the dense plantation into an area of clear-fell. The white discs of the stumps glow in the moonlight, and the bleached and leafless branches between them are piled up like heaps of bones. Running through the ghostly devastation is a dry-stone wall – a relic from another way of life, before the forests, before the mines.

I'm not sure where I am, and for some reason the sense of being lost compels me to walk faster, as though getting away from here, which is nowhere, will lead me to somewhere.

I find the tractor, at last, close to the top of the hill near a clearing in deciduous woodland. I scan the trees on either side of the track for Raven. I see the chainsaw first, sticking out of the snow, then the slumped shape in the undergrowth. When I get to her I kneel down in the snow and take off my gloves and pull on her arm. Her eyes are wide and unblinking and her head is thrown back and there's a gash in her neck. I press it. I know it's too late. I smooth a strand of her hair back and the black hair and the black blood trickle into the snow together. I touch her cold cheek and I can hear a 'no no no' coming from my own mouth.

I let go of her arm and it flops into the snow. I take out my phone. There's no signal, so I start running down the hill, following my own tracks, going for help to the nearest place I know.

I don't see them lift Raven's body off the hill, but Owen tells me a helicopter comes. I picture it like a giant nocturnal bug spooling her into its bulging stomach and flying away.

I'm sat by the stove with a towel wrapped round my waist. My jeans and socks are drying on the oven's rail. Owen is levering off his boots by the door and then banging them against the frame to release the snow. I watch him shut the door and set the boots on the floor by the wall, then he comes over to the table, pulling his phone out of the pocket of his coat and laying it on the oak table.

He notices me looking and says, 'I gave them co-ordinates. Makes it easier.'

'You had a signal? I didn't have a signal.' I don't like the fact that he's taken things out of my hands.

'Satellite phone,' he says.

I watch the dog sniff at his boots, collecting incriminating evidence about the walk he's just been on without her.

'How did you find her?' I ask.

He smiles then. 'Followed your tracks.'

I think about that for a moment, and then I stand up quickly and the towel slithers from my waist. I kick it away and start pulling on my damp jeans and socks. 'There was a car up there,' I say. 'It stopped by the sheds, but I didn't see any footprints. I wasn't looking for footprints. I wasn't thinking about footprints.'

Owen is shaking his head and putting out a hand as if to stop me leaving. 'She shouldn't have been working after dark. She shouldn't have been out there on her own. It's dangerous. It was an accident,' he says.

I stop lacing up my wet boots for a moment. 'I know,' I say. 'Another one.' And then I'm opening the door. It's stopped snowing but the cold is shocking and I stop for a moment on the threshold.

'There won't be any tracks left,' he's saying. 'It's been snowing for hours.'

I know he's right, but I step out into the dark and slam the door shut behind me. The rescue vehicle has churned the earth to slurry and the moonlight makes everything look strange. I switch on my torch and wave it at the track.

'The helicopter,' he says when he catches up with me. 'The helicopter will have blown the snow everywhere.' He's panting. 'And the mountain rescue team – they'll have messed it up. Come back to the house. There's nothing you can do. It's pointless.'

I keep walking. I have no words for what I'm doing, only a furious energy. I let it take me. When we finally get to the clearing the first thing I see is Ben Rickman's Range Rover, with its headlights illuminating the clearing. Rickman and his friend – the hulk he calls Jake – are lurking under the trees. But I don't see the Alsatian till it lunges at me. Jake yanks it back just before it takes hold of my arm with its spittle-flecked teeth, and then Owen is between me and the dog. It whines, writhing on its short lead, and its handler has to lean back hard to stop it going for me again.

171

I take my eyes off the hound for a moment and look at Owen. He's a pool of seething menace and it wouldn't surprise me if he pulled out a gun and shot Rickman between the eyes. But all he says is, 'Get that fucking dog away,' in a low voice.

A smirk lifts the corners of Rickman's lips as he looks from Owen to me. The mud and snow haven't smudged his long coat, although I can see the hems of his trousers are dark with meltwater. He puts his hands in his pockets and assesses us. 'We're done,' he says.

Jake drags the dog around to the back of the Range Rover and pushes it in. Rickman stays where he is. 'I told you to go home, Abby,' he says then, shaking his head. 'We could give you a lift to town, but you'd have to sit in the back with the dog.' Then he turns to Owen. 'Looks like you know what you're doing.'

'Tosser,' says Owen.

Once the Range Rover is out of sight I turn my torch on Owen. The tension has fallen away from him and he's just a twitcher again, out on a nighttime expedition to find owls and tick them off his list. And then he shrugs, as though he's mystified by their decision to leave and was about to invite them back for tea. 'Come on,' he says. 'Let's go.'

'What did he mean? What's he leaving to you?' I shine the torch in his face.

'Fuck knows,' he says, shielding his eyes. 'But I think he fancies you.'

'Jesus.' I turn the torch away slowly and sweep the beam of light over the clearing. I don't want to be distracted by Rickman's games. I start circling the site like a starving animal looking for something it buried in a season of plenty, before the snow came. I find a footprint that isn't mine and I call Owen over and make him place his boot in it like some goretexed Cinderella. I lift up his waterproof trouser leg to see the match, and that's when I start to laugh, because he's right and it's pointless and Raven is dead. He puts his arm around my shoulder for a moment and I lean my forehead against his jacket.

Perhaps it's the closeness of death that softens me, but I let him clean and patch the weal beneath my eye. His roughened hands are gentle, and they tremble as he works. I search his face for the rage I saw on the hill, but it isn't there. All he wants to do now is clean my wound and patch it up, like a nurse. He catches me looking at him. 'Beautiful,' he says, and, 'All done.'

I want to lean into him then and stay there. But the pain that comes with the return of feeling to frozen limbs pushes me out of his house and back up the hill to the campervan.

# 19

## Skin

There is knocking on the van door in the morning. I let him knock and I let him leave.

The rain splatters on my fibreglass box and I pull the sleeping bag up under my chin and think of Hundertwasser's 'skins'. The first skin, the Austrian architect says, is our epidermis, and the second our clothes, and the third is the houses we live in. And then, around those three skins, there is the social environment – our communities and countries – and beyond that there's the planet – the biosphere, the air we breathe, the earth's crust. And I think my skins are all full of holes and I'm trying to patch them up like a crazy woman trying to sew up the sky.

I pull aside the curtain by my head and look out at a world sliding disconsolately downwards. Most of the snow has gone and there are just pockets of the stuff in hollows. One patch is splattered yellow with the pee of Owen's nameless dog. It's as though the dusting of snow has made a bit of the doggy world visible to human eyes. It's always there, of course, that world of pungent smells, that map of the animal world, but the snow lets humans see it too.

I snuggle back into the bag and feel my will to keep going melt into the mud of the hillside. It's as though the snow is still heaped up outside my front door and I'll need a shovel to clear my way through it, so I lie there a long time, not moving, and when I finally heave my way out of the bag I can't make coffee because I have no water and I can't light the stove because I have no wood. I climb into the driver's seat and start the engine.

At the road block I hand a young soldier with pock-marked skin and shaved hair the papers I find in the glove box. 'Name and address?' he says.

'Why?'

'Precautions,' he says.

'Against what? More accidents?' But before I can give him my details he's stepping back from the van and waving me on as if something more important has come up.

In town the snow is grey slush in the gutters. I park up by the police station, which looks like an abandoned bungalow in a piece of wasteland. The copper who moved us on from Delyth's cancelled meeting takes my statement, writing slowly with large looping letters. I slouch in the plastic chair opposite her, because slouching is the only posture the chair allows. Occasionally she coughs, sits forward, and puts the pen down. Then she rubs her hands together as though she's massaging muscles that have worked too hard. I can see my unsmiling reflection in her large glasses. Her plucked eyebrows rise high above the frames like the sketched wings of seagulls.

I tell her about the car on the track and she writes something down, but she doesn't say anything.

When I ask about Raven she tells me she didn't know her. 'I'm not from round here,' she says. And then, 'We're not treating her death as suspicious. It was an accident.'

Delyth's shop is closed when I get there, but I knock on the door and wait. There are yellow smears on the front window, like large dollops of bird shit splattered across the shop's name and mingling with the rain. She eventually appears behind the piles of books and packages stacked in front of the door and motions for me to go

175

round to the side of the building. I find my way through an archway that connects the shop to a row of houses and I go down some stone steps to a high wooden gate. I can hear the sound of terracotta pots being dragged across paving, and then the drawing of bolts. When the gate judders open a breathless Delyth says, 'Come in, bach. I had a delivery and it's all piled up by the door. I've not sorted it out yet.'

In her kitchen she puts the kettle on. 'How's the van?' she's asks. 'Warm enough?'

There's a bustle about her I can't quite read. She's as edgy as I am, and I assume she's heard about Raven. She has a Welsh-language radio station playing, and she doesn't bother to turn it off.

'They're saying she'd been drinking and smoking dope ...' I start.

She's pouring boiling water into the pot, and then she picks up a teaspoon with a red dragon moulded into the handle. She stirs the pot and then waits for a moment, as if she's reading an orchestral score; when it gets to the part that says 'tap teapot', she raps the lip twice.

'She drank too much,' she says. 'And she smoked too much weed. She was worried about her job. She was depressed about splitting up with Jane, and about not seeing Jane's little boy anymore. And forestry is dangerous. She made a mistake. That's what happened. Those chainsaw things ... they kick back. It only takes a small nick, you know. She shouldn't have been out there on her own at night. That was stupid.' She pauses and lowers her head, as if she's run out of the school teacher explanations and with them the energy to hold herself up.

'There was a car up there,' I say. 'Before I found her.'

She pours tea into the two mugs on the table, but she doesn't sit down. She stands with her back to the window, leaning against the sink. I think she must be listening to the radio. There are two voices on it now – a man's and a woman's – and they're laughing. I'd like to understand what they're saying, so I can share the joke and the funny side of life, but I don't dare ask Delyth to translate. I watch the steam rise from the pale brown stuff in front of me.

'They'll have their training ground,' she says. 'People are scared, and we've been told over and over again that if we prepare constantly for war we'll be safe.'

She reaches for her mug and takes a sip. Then she turns away from me to look out of the window at the wide valley. It's drizzling.

'He's in Spain,' I tell her.

'Who?'

'I spoke to a woman at a housing co-op called SHED. She says Tegid went to Spain. For the winter.'

Her mouth is open now and then she starts to laugh. 'Well, there you go then ... And not even a postcard.'

I suppose it is funny.

'And is he ... is he coming back?' she asks, sitting down beside me at the table.

I shrug and her amusement drains away. I can see she's hurt. She stands up and gestures for me to follow her. We go out into the hall and through to the shop. It takes a few moments for my eyes to adjust to the dim light. She puts a hand on my arm and points towards the window. 'Eggs,' she says. Then she goes behind the counter and turns on the shop light. She lifts a hand to shush me while she starts up the computer. 'Look,' she says.

It's a picture on a Welsh news site of the bridge at Pont Rhith. 'Consortium reassures nervous locals' reads the headline. I scan the article. It quotes an MT4S representative saying, 'Pont Rhith needs jobs and our troops need proper training in order to protect us from the scourge of international terrorism.' A Pont Rhith councillor offers 'wholehearted' support for MT4S: 'Most local people are in favour of the Consortium's plans because we're happy to do our bit to make the world a safer place. And if it brings in much-needed jobs too, all the better.'

I see Mr Palmer's name. 'There have been concerns,' says the local councillor, 'particularly about safety. And about protecting our beautiful environment. But overall the planned development is a good thing. It means more jobs, and more people spending money in our shops, and the area the Consortium wants is unsafe for walking or farming because of the quarries and mines. This new development will put it to good use and bring Pont Rhith into the 21st Century.'

Delyth points a finger at his name. 'He means his new building company will benefit from the contracts.'

I keep reading. A small minority of people in the town are opposed to the Consortium's plans, it says, and Delyth Roberts, proprietor of the bookshop The Last Page, says the development is an insult to Welsh culture with its history of principled pacifism.

She picks up the mugs. 'They obviously didn't have room for all the other things I told them.'

'And you think someone didn't like what you said and threw eggs at your window?'

'People are angry. They want jobs. They're not thinking about the bigger picture.'

'Seems a bit extreme, though, throwing eggs at a bookshop.'

'You stick your head above the parapet and you get fired at.'

I turn the screen away and listen to her pouring my tea down the sink. The voices on the radio continue to laugh and joke with each other. She has her back to me again when she says, 'What will you do now, bach? Wait for Tegid to come back from his holiday? Or go home to London? Or is there someone else you're chasing now?'

I stare at her back. I get a flash of small town vertigo. But her knowledge of the company I'm keeping shouldn't be a surprise. I'm more surprised by her tone of disapproval. She sounds like a chapel-goer with a hat pinned tightly to her perm and a twist in her critical lips.

'I'm not *after* anyone.'

'I just hope you know what you're getting into,' she says, wiping her hands on a towel.

I want to say, 'I'm thirty-six for god's sake,' but my mouth is clamped shut, and then she seems to gather herself together. She comes over and sits down and puts a hand on mine. 'Sorry, bach,' she says. 'But why would anyone buy a holiday cottage up there? Now?'

'It was cheap,' I say, removing my hand from under hers. It's not as if I don't share her mistrust of the birdwatching ex-soldier. I'm annoyed with her because I do.

She leans her elbows on the table and her head in her hands. 'Raven,' she says quietly. 'She had a good heart and she was brave. And she knew where she belonged.'

'I liked her too,' I say, knowing I can claim none of those qualities.

A silence settles on us. Now there's a traffic report on the radio. I wonder how I know it's a traffic report, given I don't understand a word. It must be the tone – or the monotone – and the speed, and the naming of places and roads. It must be the whirring of helicopter blades. 'Did Raven say anything about ... about her neighbour?'

She doesn't lift her head, and I can't tell if she's heard me or if she's listening to the radio, or trying to remember something Raven may have said about Owen, or wondering if she should tell me anything at all now I'm dallying with the enemy. 'Go home, bach,' she says in the end. 'This isn't a good place to be right now. Come back in the summer and have a nice holiday.'

While I'm waiting for the van window to be fixed I go to the café on the main street and linger over a fried egg and mushroom sandwich and a cup of instant coffee made with steamed milk. My coat drips rainwater onto the floor. The windows are steamed up and there's a constant clatter of cutlery and voices, and the coffee

179

machine hisses, and I can think of no other environment that would reproduce more closely the sounds a baby must hear in the womb.

I let the place lull me, and I think about my options. But then I think about Owen, and I remember the feel of him as he stood beside me tending the cut on my face, and I reach for the cup of coffee and its little handle slips in my cold fingers and the hot frothy suds spill over the table and onto my lap. I stand up quickly and the waitress is there with a cloth, and although she doesn't smile she says, 'No problem' and goes to fetch a mop. I dab at the wet patch on my jeans with a handful of paper napkins. My thigh skin stings.

I sit down on a dry chair and try to remember what Rickman said to Owen in the clearing. Something about knowing what he was doing. And that smirk. And then I'm considering where I'll park the van if I go back to London. I can't see a solution to that problem because it won't be secure in the city even with the window fixed and proper locks on the side door. The waitress puts another coffee on the table. 'Diolch,' I say.

I take out my phone and there's a message. I don't recognise the number and my first thought is it's Owen. I breathe in deeply and brace myself for whatever is coming. But it's not him. 'Hello Abby,' it says. 'This is Sharon Moonstar from SHED. Made mistake. T went to the Algarve. Portugal. My friend Jan went to Spain. She had a great time. The trains were all on time ☺'

It doesn't make any difference. I can't imagine Tegid lying beside a pool with a plastic bag full of exercise books beside him in Spain *or* Portugal. And then I remember Reg Dauber and his houses. One of them, I'm sure, was on the Algarve.

When I get to a computer in the library there's an automatic out-of-office response from Dauber from the day I sent my request for an interview. It says he's away on business and that urgent queries will be forwarded to him by his PA. That makes me laugh. I'm sure Mr Dauber has the technology to access his emails wherever he happens to be on business. The reference to his PA is just another way to tell me how important he is.

But the chance to show off one of his houses is clearly an urgent issue because the next message, sent a day later, is from the PA: 'Mr Dauber is returning to Abersoch for the weekend from his villa in Portugal and would be able to arrange a short interview on Saturday morning at 11am. Directions attached.'

# 20

# Marina

I don't wait till Saturday. I set off as night falls, driving through steep-sided valleys and pine plantations, the mass of the mountains a dark presence above and beyond the forests and fields. Most of yesterday's snow has melted, but the north-facing sides of the trees gleam with a coat of white. For a while I'm tailgated by a car with its lights on full beam, the glare aimed straight into my side-mirror. When the road eventually straightens up the car surges past and I watch its red-lit rump disappear into the darkness.

I have run away. I know that. I have two days to get to Reg Dauber's house, but I didn't want to spend them parked up in the quarry thinking about Raven. Or about Owen. I need to get away, just to be able to sleep, and I'm very tired now and my eyes are sore from watching the winding road. After less than an hour driving I pull into a parking bay and switch off the engine and the lights. The darkness is total. In the passenger seat I eat a cheese and salad sandwich and text Owen. I tell him I had to see someone and when I get back I'll make him dinner: powdered soup and beer. His answer is prompt: 'I'll bring a packet of crisps. Where are you?'

I don't reply. I make up the bed and close the curtains. For a while passing traffic rocks the van, and at one point a car pulls into the lay-by behind me. It stays there, engine running, for a few minutes, and then drives slowly past and back out onto the road. Then the only sound till morning is the wind in the trees.

It's still dark when I wake up. I drink coffee in my sleeping bag while dawn percolates through the clouds and over the hills. Through the trees to my left the hulk of two concrete bunkers comes into view across a black lake. The road map tells me the buildings are Trawsfynydd, a disused nuclear power station. I've slept in another bit of this land that has been ravaged for its uses and abandoned to its scars.

When it's properly light I get out of the sleeping bag and pack away the bed. I find a bread roll and eat it in the driver's seat, staring out at the hills. My Taid told me about a poet from here who took the name Hedd Wyn – White Peace – and who died in the trenches at the end of the First World War. A few weeks after he was killed in battle the poem he'd submitted to the National Eisteddfod won the Chair. They draped it with a black cloth. And I begin to understand then why I've stayed away from Wales with its tales of tragic heroes who run fast and die young and who write like angels and are killed in battles they would rather not fight. I didn't know what to do with those sad stories, and I can't redeem the dead.

On the map I see a fair-sized town at the mouth of the estuary. I need to go shopping. I need to find the kind of clothes a features journalist might wear when she interviews a successful businessman and designer in his Abersoch mansion. It's a challenge I am woefully unprepared for.

I'm standing in front of the mirror in a charity shop changing room. The light is harsh, and the image reflected back at me is odd. My jeans and jumper are in a pile on the floor and I'm wearing a tailored grey jacket over a pale blue shirt and a short grey skirt. My shaved hair is the main problem, but I've thought of a solution to that: I tie a silk scarf around my head and inspect the result in the mirror. I look like a pantomime version of a peasant grandmother coming into town to sell a cow, so I take off the scarf and wonder how else I can soften up my hard edges.

Through the beige curtain I can hear the women at the till chatting in Welsh and I feel a sudden need for a mother – someone kind who will take me under her wing and tell me what to wear. It wouldn't be my own mother. She didn't approve of dressing up. Clothes were there to cover up nakedness, to keep you warm, and to be 'smart and presentable' for work, just like food was 'to keep you going'. You weren't supposed to enjoy it. And just for a moment I feel a twinge of sympathy for my father, with his rampant appetites and his lust for pleasure.

I pull myself together. I have a job to do. Earrings, I think, and makeup. They will divert attention from the bristly hair and the tattoos on my fingers. There's nothing I can do about the tattoos, I think, except wear gloves all the time, and that would look weird.

Then I realise I'll need a handbag, and I'm very pleased with myself for remembering that part of the standard girl costume. I change back into my old clothes and fight my way out through the curtain. It seems to be stuck on its runner and by the time I've pulled it free the two women at the till have gone quiet and are staring at me. I keep my head down and start going through the wire baskets by the door, pulling out shiny black bags with gold clasps and things with tassels on. They don't seem quite right for a journalist, but it's stretching my shopping patience – which never lasts more than ten minutes – to find the right one. I have no idea what I'm looking for and in the end I decide to rely on the assumption that Reg D. won't either. I get something just big enough to hold my camera and a notepad and a pen or two.

'That's a lovely colour, isn't it?' says the woman at the till as she folds up the suit. I'm not sure she's actually noticed the colour, but I agree with her anyway.

Exhausted by the whole experience I go in search of a café that makes good strong coffee even in the low season, and I choose a place with big windows onto the street and I linger there with a cappuccino, relishing my anonymity and the whole day I have to waste till I meet Mr Dauber. I watch strangers walk by in their waterproof coats and thick scarves, hats pulled down over their ears. And then I realise I'm still looking for Tegid. I'm still expecting him to walk around a corner, bouncing lightly on his toes like a little boy, a question in his gaze, a smile on his lips. I'm still waiting for him to appear in a crowd or come up behind me and tap me gently on the shoulder. Even here, I'm looking out for the man with a lake in each eye.

His clothes were from charity shops. He used to give money to charities even when he lived on pennies. 'I don't know what they mean about "compassion fatigue",' he said to me once. 'I see starving children and I think they should be fed.'

I'm getting in the van when I notice my mud-encrusted boots and I have to go back to the shops and find some high heel strappy things. All the self-satisfaction I felt on remembering the handbag is replaced with weary resignation. The reality is, I'll look fucking ridiculous.

In the afternoon, with the cheap girl clothes and makeup stashed in a cupboard, I drive the van west towards the faint glow of a setting sun and a seaside town on the Llŷn. I've booked a hire car from a garage on an industrial estate just outside the town. I park up within sight of the garage's closed gates, ready to pick up a hatchback in the morning.

The small industrial estate is next to a marina and I turn the van so the back window faces out over the yachts and the motorboats moored to the boardwalks. A heron lands on a flat metal bridge and stands there with its back to the water, staring inland, as though the hills give it the meditative comfort human beings get from looking out to sea. 'Look at all that nothingness,' it's thinking. 'Makes me feel calm just staring at dry land.' Red-brown seaweed surges against the mortared rocks of the marina wall, and beyond the marina there is the town, packed tightly around a yellow chapel.

The scream of a child being murdered wakes me in the night. I lie there with my heart thumping and my breath racing, scrabbling around in my sleep-fuddled brain for an explanation. I slowly put together the clanking and the wailing sounds with the boats in the marina: the wind has picked up and it's whistling through the rigging of the yachts, vibrating the wires that hang from the masts and slapping them against fibreglass and wood.

Zinanna. It's the Arabic word the Palestinians use for the sound of Israeli drones. It means 'whining child'. Tegid had underlined it in one of the articles he'd cut out and filed. It stuck in my mind because it was the name for a sound, and I'd tried to imagine it – the high descending pitch, the way it would play on your nerves, demanding attention, provoking anxiety.

When I fall asleep again it's not surprising I dream I'm on a boat. It slips out to sea beyond the breakwater and then the cold waves are over me and the surf is sucking me down. I have to decide to let go, to let the water flow through me, to stop struggling and sink.

And then I'm awake again. There are footsteps outside and a shuffling by the van door. I hear the grunt of a large dog being choked on its lead. I lie still. I'm waiting for the knock on the door and the instruction to move on. It doesn't come. I circle around inside the van, shifting the curtains on each side, but there's no one out there. I hear a car start up, but I can't see it. I go back to bed and curl up in my sleeping bag as if its soft folds could offer protection from a man with a dog. But I don't go back to sleep. I stay awake, listening to the boats creak and rattle and whine in the marina, and at first light I get up and get dressed, scraping the new tights onto the cold skin of my legs, buttoning up the shirt, smoothing down the short skirt. I sit in the passenger seat and put makeup on in front of the tiny mirror behind the sunshield. I'm doing well till I poke myself in the eye with the mascara stick, which draws tears, which smudges the eyeliner I've already carefully sketched across my lids. I have to wipe it all off with a damp tissue – rubbing my skin red to remove the stuff – and start again.

When I finally look as close to a confident professional as I can manage, I dig my camera out of my backpack and cradle it in my hands. It was a present from my ex. Of course he gave me a camera – he was a photographer. But now I think about it, I was a sound engineer when we met, and I never gave him a digital recorder as a present.

I switch the camera on and look at the screen. I've never used it before, but he tried to teach me how, in a café on my birthday, toggling between menus while I looked over his shoulder with glazed eyes saying 'Uh-huh'. It wasn't what I wanted him to teach me. I wanted him to teach me how not to care. I took the drugs he offered and drank the beer and the whisky. Whole weekends never made it into my memory. I slept at one party rolled up in a beer-soaked carpet, and at another in the bath. I vomited in other people's wastepaper baskets. He was a good teacher and I was a keen student, but I still preferred the mornings after the parties when the light came in softly between half-drawn curtains, saturated with the sounds of the street outside. I preferred those quiet mornings, when I knew where he was – next to me, and not in some other woman's bed.

I hear the clank of metal and see a man opening the gates to the garage. I swing my handbag onto my shoulder and follow him into the yard and to the car hire office. I feel uncomfortable in my clothes and shoes and I think: maybe one day Tegid will thank me for this charade. And in that instant, I know my self-imposed education in not caring didn't work. I do care, in my warped way. I care about Tegid, and I know that the thin, honest connection with my lost friend is the only thing stopping me from walking into the sea.

# 21

## Mansion

I find the entrance to Reg Dauber's place on a small private cul-de-sac above the town. The iron gates are open and under the house name is a No Turning sign and a No Trespassing sign. In my hired hatchback I drive down the gently sloping drive between scots pines and evergreen bushes. The mansion, when it appears, is a modern house, a house of glass and chrome and black and silver. It's the sort of house that demands to be kept clean and shiny, and I'm sure Reg has an army of servants to respond to that demand on his behalf.

I park in a recess between neatly-trimmed shrubs and walk over to what I think is the main entrance. The wind is fierce and cold and without my big coat on I'm shivering as I press the bell. I wait. I wonder if I have the wrong house, or the wrong door, and then a woman opens it slowly and tells me to come in. She's wearing an apron and a fixed smile, and her accent and appearance suggest she's from the Mediterranean, in her fifties, and tired. She leads me through a hallway lined with gilt-framed oil portraits of men and women with pale faces and thin lips, and then into a room big enough to turn the van around in, without having to reverse. When the woman walks silently away on the thick carpet I stand there facing a wall of glass and a panoramic view of the grey sea.

'Five letters: blank, E, blank blank A,' commands a voice from the other side of a low bookshelf. I can see the top of a head, and two tanned and sandaled feet sticking out into the expanse of cream carpet. 'She cooked up music for who?'

I skirt the bookshelf and step carefully down two wide steps. I'm still not used to my heels and I wobble. He's sitting at the end of one of the room's two long sofas, glasses on his nose, pencil poised over the *Daily Telegraph* cryptic crossword.

'Delia,' I say.

He harrumphs. 'I don't see ...' He puts the paper down next to him on the sofa.

I put out my hand. He doesn't attempt to hoist himself forward out of the cushions when he shakes it, and I nearly tip over onto him as I lean forward to make contact. I pull back quickly and he waves me towards the other sofa. I perch on the edge of it, keeping my feet as firmly on the ground as the stupid shoes will allow.

'Delia Derbyshire,' I say. 'Pioneer of electronic music. She arranged the Dr Who theme tune.'

'Well I wouldn't know about that,' he says. 'How would I know about that? Can't stand electronic music. I could have been a concert pianist, you know. Put that in your article.'

I take out my notebook and a pen and resist the urge to mime 'concert pianist' with my lips as I scribble it down.

'No recorder? Good good. Can't stand those things. May I offer you coffee?' Before I can answer he's pressing a button and saying, 'Coffee in the lounge.'

I notice he isn't looking at me at all and I begin to relax about my tattooed fingers and cropped hair. I inspect him instead. He's the same age as Tegid – early sixties – but less haggard. His brightly patterned shirt is stretched over a large stomach and he's wearing shorts. I assume that's because he likes to keep the house hot, despite the winter wind and the big windows and the warehouse size of the room. His face is round and his eyes are small behind his glasses, and he has a moustache. A moustache and no beard.

'Let's get on with it,' he says. 'What d'you want to know about me?'

I've prepared my approach. 'Our readers,' I say, 'would love to know how you turned a single brilliant idea into ...' I wave my arm around the room, 'all of this.'

He takes a deep breath, settles himself into the cushions, and from then on, as long as I keep nodding and smiling and gasping with amazement, he keeps telling me about himself. The sycophantic questions stagger out of me, peering around like beings raised from a hundred-year sleep, as reverent and eager to please as small children. The tired looking woman brings in coffee and I stem the queasiness caused by my own dishonest behaviour by taking sips of it black. At some point, while Dauber's voice drones on, my concentration slips and I begin to drift into the wide sea outside the window. I pull myself back.

'And Tegid Rhys? What was his part in your highly successful design business?'

He goes quiet, his eyes fixed on the Persian rug between us. He looks as though he's searching for a lost page in the script he was working from. He can't find it.

'Your business partner?' I try. 'Or was he an employee?' I smile as widely as my lips will allow and tilt my head to one side, giving thanks again to Scanlon for her expert demonstration on how to wield hyper-femininity in the pursuit of information. The only tool I lack is long enough hair to curl around my fingers. I use my voice instead, teasing him out with a soft, breathy tone. 'I may be wrong, but my research mentions he played a key part in Curved Space Mapping Technologies, and I'm just wondering ...'

'He was a topographer, and he was good with computers.' He coughs. 'But he had no business sense. He couldn't see the commercial value in anything.'

'So he didn't build on the mapping programme's success in the way you have?'

'I've had no contact with Tegid Rhys since he left Curved Space more than twenty years ago. I've no idea what the man is doing.' His voice is raised and he's fidgeting now.

190

I don't push it. I let him settle. He picks up the crossword and goes about erasing something very carefully with the rubber on the tip of his pencil. I look at a small bronze statue of a naked dancing woman on the shelf behind him. From this angle it looks as if she's dancing on his head. 'From my research he was last seen at a hostel for the homeless in London.'

'Was he? Well I'm not surprised about that. You can't help a man like Rhys. God knows I tried. I told him to pull himself together or face the consequences.'

'You tried to help him, but he didn't listen to you?'

He glances at me and I look down at my notebook to avoid his gaze. 'We were at school together,' he says. 'They say opposites attract and we were complete opposites. I don't think he was capable of enjoying anything. Money would have been wasted on him.'

I know the interview is in danger of being abruptly ended for the simple reason I'm not asking questions about Mr Dauber and his genius, but I risk it anyway. 'So he left the business? He just walked away from all that money?'

He shrugs and shuffles about on the sofa, and finally he sits up and leans forward. 'People have tried to tell me,' he says slowly, '– people like my first wife – that he had some sort of moral objection to selling the programme to SecTec. But I owned 51% of the business. I had the controlling share. And it's a ridiculous idea anyway. You don't stop wars by refusing to design anything the military may possibly use at some point in the future. For God's sake, it's practically the only way you can get funding these days.'

I watch him set the coffee cup back on its saucer, and then place it on the tray on the table beside him, and then he rearranges the jug and the sugar bowl and the cafetière to accommodate the coffee cup in an arrangement that seems to calm him down.

'And that's what you do now?' I say. 'You specialise in finding finance for the development of military designs and inventions.'

'Believe me – if I didn't someone else would.'

'Like old ladies,' I laugh. 'If I didn't mug them, someone else would.' He stares at me. He stares at the cropped hair and then at my tattooed fingers. 'Which is why they need protecting,' I say quickly. 'And why you're giving your support and expertise to the MT4S Consortium.' It's a guess but it seems a good one.

He stares into the middle distance. He clears his throat. He claps his hands together with a dull thud and rocks himself forward. 'Excuse me for a moment,' he says, and he pushes himself out of the sofa, stands up and puffs his way around the bookcase and out of the door. I listen to him walk down the corridor. A door is opened and shut. I get up and put my coffee cup on the tray and then I wander over to the huge window. There's a species of palm to the side of the lawn and it's waving around in the wind like a child's toy windmill. A seagull is stamping about on the grass. I've heard about that. They patter on the ground with their feet and fool the worms into thinking it's raining, and the worms come up to the surface and get eaten.

Beyond the lawn is the slate-grey sea and I fall into it, replaying my dream. I let the sea's steely currents lift my frozen limbs and wash my glassy eyes.

'You came to see the house. Allow me to give you the tour.' He's back, and now he's turning away, expecting me to follow him.

'So many achievements,' I mumble as we pass cabinets of awards and shelves of artefacts from his years in business. 'You certainly have the right to relax and enjoy yourself now.'

'Oh I don't have time for that,' he snaps.

Even so, he seems to have time to display his wealth to me: the swimming pool, the library, the orangery ... I take the requisite photographs and I let him advise me on the best angles from which to capture his property at its best. Every time we stop he tells me a story which involves an argument with an architect or a designer or an engineer, and every story ends with Reg D. being the one who

192

was right. When we come close to the front door for the second time I spot my grey jacket on a stand and go towards it. 'Tegid Rhys,' I try for the last time. 'Has he ever tried to contact you?'

'I heard he split up with his wife. Lovely woman. A nurse.' He pauses. 'Which is a great job for a woman.'

I take my jacket off the stand and notice the fur-trimmed coat beside it. If the second Mrs Dauber was also a nurse I can't imagine she is now. 'It just seems strange that he wouldn't want a share in the profits?'

'He refused to sign anything,' he barks, and then he squints a little, as if his brain is having trouble moving from my interest in his achievements to any other possible motives for my visit. 'Goodbye, Miss ...'

He leans past me to open the door, but before his hand reaches the handle I say, 'Do you know why he was expelled from school?' I can't leave without any information at all.

'I do indeed,' he says, and for the first time he looks at me directly. He feels on safe ground now, and I brace myself for the worst. 'He threw a smoke bomb into a prefect's room and locked the door from the outside. The terrified boy woke up thinking his room was on fire and jumped out of the window and broke his leg. There was no proof Tegid Rhys was responsible.'

'But they expelled him anyway?'

'A week later he went into another prefect's room with a gun and pressed it into the boy's temple till he woke up, and then he "explained" things to him, apparently. It wasn't a real gun, of course. It was a starter gun. But that's why he was expelled. You see ... he was never stable. He was very clever, but he was never quite right mentally.' He reaches round me to open the door again.

I say, 'Well, thank you, Mr Dauber, for taking the trouble to see me,' and I'm stepping onto the tiles when I stop, because Ben Rickman is there.

This time he doesn't look at all surprised to see me. He holds out his hands, palms up, and says, 'Abigail, Abigail. Up till now I've been more than willing to forgive your interest in other men. But really. What has this old geezer got that I haven't? A moustache? Is that it?'

'An inability to lie?' I say.

He falters for a moment, and I can see he's trying to work out what Dauber may have told me. 'I'm sure Mr Dauber has been most obliging. Lovely man. Generous to a fault with time and personal information.' He's looking at Dauber while he speaks and he's shaking his head, telling him off for blabbing at this pseudo journalist all morning.

I push past him. 'I can see you two have lots to sort out.'

'You'll always be my "got-to-go" girl,' he says as I pass. 'But you should scrub up more often. It suits you. I'd just advise you to close the curtains in that campervan of yours when you get undressed. You never know who might be watching.'

He turns to look at me from inside the hall, and then he shuts the door in my face.

I put my hand against its solid wood. I breathe deeply. Then I give the door a kick with my high heel shoe and wish I had boots on. The sea wind blasts around the side of the house and pierces my thin clothes. I feel tiny, and I know I'm meant to.

# 22

## Ditch

I take the hire car back to the garage at the marina, and as I walk across the tarmac to the campervan I'm looking for a security guard with a dog, or a man in a black Range Rover with a pair of high-spec binoculars. But the car park is empty except for a woman strapping her toddler into the back seat of a Volvo estate. Even so, once I'm in the van I lock the door behind me and close the curtains.

I'm doing up the belt on my jeans when there's a rap on the door. I flick the curtain aside. It's Rickman and he's wearing shades and he's pulled up the collar on his coat as if he thinks he's a spy in a film. He's obviously cold, too, with the wind blowing in off the sea. I open the side door and I'm looking down on him even more than usual because he's on the ground and I'm in the van. I don't invite him in.

'You never mentioned you were a journalist. My Abby is a very talented woman.'

'I'm not your Abby and I'm not a journalist. I'm a residential social worker.'

'Ah yes. And you're looking for one of your missing clients.'

'Service user,' I say. 'And he was a friend of your parents, too. Remember? He helped out when your mother was dying, or that's the story you told me over doughnuts and coffee in London.'

'It wasn't a complete lie,' he says. 'Except the friend bit. Oh, and the dying mother bit. She was alive and well last time I checked.'

The yachts are still clanking against their moorings, and their rigging whines in the wind, but in the daytime the sounds are as seasidey as ice cream vans and children playing in the sand. I lean out of the door and look around. I can't see Jake, or the car, or the dog.

Rickman removes his shades and sighs. 'I need to let you know, Abby: Mr Dauber is not happy about the interview. He says it was harassment. He says he may take it further.'

I shrug. 'It made me happy. He was very useful.' It's a lie. I'm acutely aware that my little performance for Mr Dauber has yielded nothing, and that forcing myself to wear a skirt and high-heeled shoes has been worth fuck all. I'm no nearer to finding Tegid than I was before I paid his old business partner a visit.

'So what did he tell you?' he asks me then, and I realise I have him on the back foot for the first time in the short history of our relationship.

'That Tegid Rhys was trying to get in the way of the Consortium's plans. That he was asking Reg for money – the money Reg should have given him when he sold the business.' It's a guess.

Rickman stares up at me and shakes his head. 'Nah,' he says, starting to turn away. 'He didn't tell you that.'

'And he said you were hired to sort out any problems. To dispose of any problems, in fact.'

He comes back to the door of the campervan. A seagull squawks from the top of a mast in the marina. Rickman gives it a hard stare. 'You think,' he says then, still watching the seagull, 'that just because you live in the shadows and own nothing and do nothing, no one with power can see you.'

I don't want to admit it, but he's right. It's crazy to think a shuffling mathematician with no fixed abode could fancy himself a match for the likes of Dauber and Rickman. Right now, Tegid's probably dead in a ditch in Portugal, or down at the bottom of a

196

mineshaft in Bethania. And if I'm not careful I'll be joining him there.

But then I realise I'm not completely unconnected. I get out my phone. 'I haven't seen my dad in ages. Must give him a call.'

He laughs. 'Mm. Good idea. I've been meaning to have a chat with Mike Lockwood myself. I need to let him know my intentions … with regards to you, of course.' He laughs again.

'And what are those intentions?'

He feigns surprise. 'Well marriage, of course. And children. Or a dog if you prefer.'

'I'd prefer to marry a dog.'

'Oh Abby, my Abby. You resist me now, but one day you'll know I'm the one.'

'The one I need to shoot in the head at point blank range?'

'Mmm,' he says. 'Well. Let's keep in touch,' and he's burying his hands in his pockets and walking away.

I close and lock the door again and then climb into the driver's seat. I watch the yachts shift around on their ropes. I haven't discovered anything new about Tegid from Dauber or Rickman. The only thing I really know is that Tegid didn't tell me the truth about his reason for driving the campervan to Wales. 'I'm going home,' he'd said. 'It's time for the wanderer to return.' But he must have known about MT4S and its plans to turn a Welsh mountain village into an army training zone before he moved himself to Pont Rhith. In fact, the military training consortium was probably the very reason he went there and holed up on land they were planning to use, waiting for a chance to sit on a digger or chain himself to a gatepost. And not just because he wanted to dismantle the military-industrial complex all by himself – he also wanted to stop his old business partner profiting from the whole thing. He wanted to be a spanner in the works of the smooth running of Reg Dauber's wealth-and-glory machine. And the drones? The drones would have kept his wounds open, telling him with each fly-past that the bodies piling up on the other side of the world were his fault because he hadn't stopped Reg selling his computer programme to SecTec.

A politics fuelled by personal hatred. It's a heady combination, and one I understand down to my bones. I know exactly what it's like to despise everything that someone close to you has come to stand for.

My phone's still in my hand. I call the hostel. Sally is cool and business-like and asks no questions about where I am or how I am. I'm thankful for that. She books me in for an overnight shift on Sunday, and that's the easy bit done. Then with clammy fingers I dial my one connection to the heart of the beast and arrange to meet my father for Sunday lunch in Hampstead.

It's a forty-minute detour to the slate quarrying village where my mother grew up. It's where I was sent as a child when things got too hard for her. I didn't complain.

I'm not sure why I decide to pay it a visit now. Maybe I'm searching for a deeper connection with the country, and stronger resistance to Rickman's attempts to unsettle me and send me back to London. Or maybe I just want to match the sense of loss inside me with a picture of that loss in the outside world. The drive takes me north, further away from Pont Rhith, and I'm not expecting to find anything or anyone I know in the village. My mother was an only child, like me, and as soon as she could she left for London and the promise of a better life, escaping, or so she thought, the drudgery her own mother had endured – washing clothes and scraping vegetables and dusting oak dressers day in and day out.

And now the old people are dead, and I have no real connection to anyone in the village. I'm sure it would be better, in my state of isolation and anger, to avoid it altogether and head straight back to Pont Rhith. But I keep driving into the snowy mountains, and they come in closer like the ghosts of those long dead relatives, and behind them the sky is duck-egg blue and in the gutter there's brown slush.

Tryfan is the first mountain I can put a name to. It's like a stone lion at the gateway to the realm of my childhood because from then on the landscape is deeply familiar. There's the lake and the falls, and the car that's been behind me for an hour pulls into a lay-by and stops. They weren't following me. They were walkers or climbers headed up to the slabs and ridges. I keep going down the pass, picking out the perfect mountain from the range on my left – the one shaped like a kid's drawing of a mountain, like the one on Raven's fridge.

The brutal slate-tip just outside the village has been softened by the snow and by patches of new vegetation. I pull off the main road onto a track down to a bridge and park by the entrance to a caravan site. I watch a woman come over the bridge on foot with a bag of shopping. I avoid her glare and when she's gone I get out. The river is loud – a noisy, fast-moving mountain river that races over the rocks and is nothing like the slow, field-skirting river at Pont Rhith. I run my hand over the top of the low slate wall of the bridge, searching for my name among the hundreds etched into its surface. I came here late one afternoon with my Taid, when the weather had been wet for days and he'd been told to take me out for a walk. When we reached the bridge, I leaned over the wall, my belly on the cold stone, my arms dangling in the space above the river. I didn't know why he was carving my name into the rock, but I understand now. It was so I'd come back one day to find it. It was so something of ours would remain here after all the people had died or moved away for work.

I scan the professions of undying love and the dates which span the twentieth century. But even as I search through them a part of me has already decided my own name won't be there. He'd carved it too lightly. He'd used the plastic casing of a biro. I don't want my absence confirmed so I give up looking and trudge back to the van.

'You can't park there.' The woman with the shopping bag has returned – without the shopping bag but with a husband.

I don't bother responding. I get in the van and drive away, and that's when the sense that I'm trespassing starts, and as I get closer to the village it becomes stronger. I pass the football ground where Taid played as a boy and as a young man, and the bakery where he bought bread – preferably with a burnt crust. It's boarded up now. I realise then that my Nain hardly ever left the house, even to shop, and that she spent most of her life indoors, dusting surfaces that were already clean and watching soap operas on TV.

I pass the pubs that used to be closed on Sundays, and the chapels that used to be open on Sundays, and the betting shop which is open all the time. I know my feeling of dispossession isn't unique. Every bit of the world – earth and air and sea – seems owned now, private, and the rent most of us struggle to pay for our right to stay put will never be enough. I know my condition of dispossession is mild compared to Siamak's, and the millions of refugees like him who are forced to move across the planet with nothing but the clothes they are wearing to places where the language they think in is no longer of any use to them, and the memories they hold on to can't be shared with anyone who understands them.

I drive down a side street to the house at the end of a terrace where my Nain and Taid lived. The yard wall has collapsed, so when I pull up I can see into the little garden. The grass has been replaced with concrete, the lobelia border with rubble and rubbish. In that shed Taid kept letters, in Welsh of course, from his seventeen-year-old sister. She was dying in a TB sanatorium on Anglesey. 'May I buy gloves for the winter?' she asks her parents. 'I had a whole egg. I don't have to share one with my brother.'

When my mother moved us to the States to be with her new husband, Taid dreamt he stowed away on the plane. The female steward found him hiding in the toilet. I can imagine him, in that dream, quietly explaining to her that his love for us was more important than an unpaid-for air ticket. He would have expected her to understand that. It made sense to him.

I don't get out of the van. I open the window and listen to the river.

# 23

## Bedsit

It's dark when I pull up by the New Cottages. Owen looks surprised to see me, and then I think he's going to hug me, so I turn away quickly, walking towards his car and saying, 'I'm going to London for a few days. I need a lift to the station.'

He stands there a moment, considering, and then he shrugs and pulls on his coat. I'm already in the passenger seat when he gets in. There's a layer of ice across the screen so he climbs out again and goes back into the house, returning with a jug of water which he sluices over the glass. The window turns from white to black.

Once we're driving he starts fidgeting in his seat like a man on the verge of making a marriage proposal. It's an endearing sort of nervousness.

'London,' he says, pondering the notion of the place as if he's never thought about it before. 'Theatre? Museum? Changing of the Guard? I know – you're going to see the Queen.'

I laugh. 'I'm running out of money. I need to do a shift at work.'

'But you can't go yet. You owe me dinner.'

'I know,' I say. 'Soup. You can choose the flavour.'

'I'll bring a spoon.'

'You won't need one. It'll be in a mug.'

I look at him, the side of his face, the way he's squinting through his glasses at the road and biting his lower lip. And then he says, 'They think Delyth Roberts was involved in arson attacks on

English estate agents in the 1980s – the ones selling second homes in Wales. She was being watched.'

I stare at him. I know he's giving me something – stepping towards me out of the shadows – and it's vital I keep him there, in the light, where I can see him. 'And how do you know that?'

He grins. 'I have my sources.'

'Ah,' I say. 'Gemma Scanlon.'

'I guess they were also interested in her friends. People like Raven Davies. So you were right,' he says. 'Someone could have been following Raven that night.'

'And did they kill her?'

'Unlikely,' he says. 'What would be the point? But who knows. Things can go wrong.'

I owe him something now, if only to keep the gates open to the information he's holding. 'I'm going to visit my dad,' I say.

He nods and considers. 'And your mum?'

'She lives in the States. With her second husband. My dad's in London being a politician of some kind. Any kind that happens to suit him this year.' I wonder if I'll tell him anything else. 'They divorced when I was twelve, and not because he hit her and had affairs, which he did. He dumped her because she didn't fit in with his new image.'

'What about you? Did you fit in with his new image?'

'I stayed with her. When she met a Yank who was willing to step into the bullying husband role she moved to Colorado to be with him. She took me with her.'

'Brothers? Sisters?' he says.

Now his agitation seems more like a spy who's desperate not to blow his cover by asking too many questions – and that sort of nervousness isn't endearing at all. I look at the river as we cross the new bridge. Its black surface is coated with smears of orange light from the street lamps. I can see a shale beach on the far bank. It's a good sign – the train won't be cancelled because of flooding. 'No. And you?'

'Both parents dead,' he says. 'Dad from a heart attack, Mam from lung cancer. It's not a healthy place where I come from. I probably had a longer life-expectancy in the army than staying there.'

'If you were a general. Were you a general?'

He chuckles, and then he's slowing down as we approach the road-block. 'And I've got a younger brother. Does something with computers in London.' The soldier waves us through without looking at us and I wonder if Owen ever gets stopped. 'Why did you come back from the States?' he asks me.

'I was sixteen.'

'So you came to live with your dad?'

'God no. I came back to drift about and torment him from a distance with my spectacular inability to be a shining success despite everything he's done for me.'

We pull up outside the Victorian façade of the station and as I reach for the door handle he says quietly, 'You'll drift back here, won't you?'

'Home is where the van's parked,' I say. For a moment I'm held in his gaze, and it isn't a bad place to be. But I can't stay there. 'Were you the one keeping an eye on Delyth and Raven?' I say, to break the spell.

His eyes widen behind his glasses. 'No,' he says. 'No. Wow. That's really paranoid.'

I flinch. I've heard that before. My ex was fond of putting my suspicions about his promiscuity down to paranoia. But there's always a grain of truth in paranoia. Working out which grain is the difficult bit. I struggle out of the car with my bag and he's winding down the window as I walk away. But I don't listen to what he's saying, and I don't look back.


I open my eyes on the morning in a dingy bedsit, conscious of the wide empty space between me and the opposite wall. It takes a moment to realise I'm back in London and that the empty space is only a couple of metres wide – it feels huge because I've been living in a campervan. I stare at the rubber plant on the kitchen counter. It's lost all its leaves and the ringed stalk that sticks up out of the pot looks like a skinny phallus. It was a house-warming present from my ex, who must have felt guilty for lying so much and telling me his affairs were all in my head. I deprived it of light and water and kind words. The result is hardly surprising.

It's difficult to get myself out of bed and over to the hulking wardrobe, and I blame my lethargy on getting in after midnight and not being able to sleep. But I also know that a basement bedsit on a grey Sunday morning in London is a powerful incubator for depression, and I consider giving up altogether and going the way of the rubber plant.

I open the listing cupboard door and shuffle through the clothes I've dumped on the floor inside. I try to keep my mind fixed on my mission, which is to get useful information out of my father. That means I have to keep him even-tempered. That means I have to avoid annoying him. That means I'll have to wear a dress. I go rummaging around for one in the shadows and find I have far more of them than I have ever worn or will ever wear. I choose an electric blue thing that doesn't need ironing. It has long sleeves, but I'm still cold when I put it on, so I cover up with a baggy black cardigan which ruins the whole effect. I figure it will keep me warm on the way to the restaurant and I can take it off when I get there.

I make coffee, of course, and I drink it black because there's nothing that looks like milk in the fridge, and while I sit on the stool at the counter next to the dead rubber plant I wonder what kind of plant I would cherish and not starve to death. I imagine an olive tree with grey-green leaves. Or a singing ringing tree with silver pears for a princess who refuses to smile.

205

# 24

## Restaurant

I'm late and he's waiting outside the restaurant when I arrive. He lifts his eyes to the sky and then turns and pushes through the glass doors without greeting me. I follow him in, already aware of the bulletproof vest I've wrapped around my vital organs.

'I didn't bother to book – you're too unreliable.'

We're greeted by a man who tells us there are no tables available. My father leans over him and asks to see the manager, and then we wait. It's not exactly neutral territory, this place: it's one of his skins, not one of mine, with its tables swamped in thick white tablecloths and weighed down with huge white plates.

'No problem, no problem, Mr Lockwood,' the manager is saying. 'Come this way.'

The waiter is relegated to taking our coats and the manager himself leads us between closely-packed tables to the back of the restaurant. I wonder if my week in the hills has lowered my immunity to loud noise because the effect of thirty-odd screeched conversations bouncing off the mirrored walls and marble floors, combined with the clinking of glasses and cutlery, is painful. And then I realise I'm hyper-alert, waiting for the tiniest sign of danger from the man in front of me. I take a deep breath. I can protect myself. I'm not a child. And this is a public place.

The manager drags out a heavy, high-backed chair for me. 'Normally we ignore Mr Lockwood,' he says as I sit down, and my father smiles because it's patently not true, 'But because he has ... a lady's company ...' – he raises his eyebrows – 'we've found you a quiet corner.'

'I'd like to ignore him too,' I say, 'but he's my dad.' The man's smile doesn't slip. He just nods approval of that relationship too and wishes us a pleasant meal.

Once we're both planted behind our huge menus I begin to wonder what the man meant by 'quiet corner'. I have to lean forward to hear my father say, 'It's nice to see people don't feel compelled to dress up for dinner these days.'

'At one time you didn't either,' I say. 'But that was when you were a Labour MP pretending you were down with the masses.'

'Ha. Ha. Ha. And that's precisely why I defected to the Conservative Party. They're inclined to arrange far more events with dress codes.'

'And how is life with the Tories?' I ask, without a hint of interest in my voice.

'Excellent,' he says. 'Excellent. I had no idea what I was missing.'

The waiter has inched up to the table with his notepad and pen and I listen to my father demanding large amounts of rare meat in two courses using a strange diction which I think is his attempt to gentrify his Yorkshire accent while at the same time maintaining its fashionable and endearing qualities. I pick salads, and refuse wine, and I feel a strong desire to become a hermit on a Western shore under a leaden sky.

'Still with that unemployed photographer of yours?' he asks.

'Are you divorced? Again?'

'Yes. Fancy free and ready for fun. So let your friends know ... I'm available.'

'I don't have any friends.'

'Ah yes. There is that.'

I pick up the fork. It's like a giant's fork, huge and silver and heavy in my hand, and it makes me feel like a child at the table, waiting for the slaughter to begin, waiting to see who will be cut down first. Then again, the fork could be a magic weapon for killing the giant. I pass it from hand to hand, testing its weight and shape, wondering where I should stick it in for the most painful and fatal effect.

'I'm looking for someone,' I say.

'I could let you go through my address book.'

'He won't be in your address book. He was a resident at the hostel.'

'Homeless?' He shakes his head. 'It won't do you any good, you know, hanging around with losers. At some point you have to face the fact – life is for living.'

'Is that why you dumped your family?'

He shakes his head and smiles. 'If you want to get on in life, Abigail, you have to learn not to care too much.'

This is the closest I get to paternal affection – advice that hardly seems to apply to me at all – so I'm silent for a moment, testing it, wondering if it's enough to live off for the rest of my life. And then the food arrives and I see he's lost none of his appetite for slabs of bloody flesh.

I take a deep breath and sit back from my salad. He forks steak and potatoes into his mouth and washes it down with a swig of Châteauneuf-du-Pape. I start to float and scatter, as if I'm becoming shards of light glinting from the chandelier above our heads. I pull myself back. I focus on the feel of the chair under my thighs, my feet in my boots.

'The MT4S Consortium,' I say. 'What do you know about it?'

He stops chewing and says through the food in his mouth, 'What the bloody hell are you involved in now?'

'MT4S. A consortium of defence contractors. They're building a military training zone near a town called Pont Rhith in mid Wales.'

He closes his mouth. He reaches for the red wine and takes a sip. 'Whatever you think you're doing, Abigail, I'm telling you to stop. Now. You're way out of line.'

'And you battered your wife.'

The wine comes spluttering out of his mouth and he grabs at a serviette to mop the mess off his chin. He scans the tables around us. 'This missing man of yours?' he says when he's recovered his breath. 'He wouldn't be a topographer called Tegid Rhys?'

The name seems to find a momentarily free bandwidth between the various hums and clatters of the restaurant's background din, and it echoes around the room for a second. But no one looks across at us. No one puts up a hand and says, 'I know him!'

He sighs. He puts his glass down firmly on the table and smooths out the smeared napkin with one of his surprisingly small hands. I realise I'm going to get a lecture, and for once I'm intending to listen. But all he says is, 'You're not the only one looking for him.'

'Meaning?'

'Anti-terrorist cops. I wondered why they were asking *me* about him. I thought it was because I'm on a defence subcommittee. I should have known it had something to do with *you*.' He's shaking his head again. The bags beneath his eyes wobble.

'And have they found him?'

'No idea.' He's raising a hand to attract the attention of the waiter. I pray he won't snap his fingers.

'But you could find out, couldn't you? A man in your position?'

He gives up trying to attract the waiter and turns his gaze on me. 'I'm flattered you think I have such influence,' he says, 'but my powers don't extend in that direction.'

'Really?' I say, scrabbling for some leverage, and failing to find it.

And then he changes the subject and asks if I've heard from my mother.

'She phones from time to time.'

'And what does she have to say?'

I shrug. 'No idea. I don't listen. I just say "yes" every five minutes.'

He laughs drily. 'Nothing's changed there then.'

'But she's moved on from saving the world's suffering children to rescuing dogs.'

'Always the most morally superior person in the room,' he says, and he sits back with an air of self-satisfaction which I would like to deny him.

'I guess people don't change,' I say. 'Her new husband has turned out to be a bully.'

I watch him crunch his teeth, and then I glance quickly at his hands. They are both on the table, where I can see them, and they are thrumming the tablecloth. They may be small hands for such a big man, but I have felt the power in them. I know what happens when they close into fists and find someone smaller and weaker to pummel.

A violent pain stabs me under my ribs in the pit of my stomach, and I know that the only way to ease it is to lie down flat on my back. I get up and find my way to the toilets. Beyond the white door to the ladies there's an anteroom with a black leather sofa and a vase of white lilies in front of a mirror. I take a couple of fluffy white handtowels off the pile by the sinks and fold them under my head and lie down on the marble tiles.

I stare up at the recessed lights in the ceiling. A mist of air-freshener squirts out of the wall. In a few moments the cramped muscles in my stomach have relaxed and the pain is gone, but I stay there until I hear a toilet flushing in the next room and then I get up and busy myself at the mirror. A woman in a tight black dress passes behind me and frowns. I look at myself. I see my father's hooded eyes and his height, and the same dark hair, and I'm hit by the powerful sense that I can't, or shouldn't, exist at all. It's such a strong sense of my own impossibility it nearly slams me back onto the tiles for good, but then another woman comes through the door from the restaurant and she smiles and says hello, as if I'm not monstrous, as if I'm ok.

When I get back to the table the waiter is there. I decline dessert but my father orders berry tart with cream, and I watch him scoop out the red filling and then slowly break up the pastry, eating one small piece at a time. I know it's his comfort food. Until he was seven he'd thought his real mother was his sister. When he was nine she married a man with a chain of furniture shops. She was going to send for her little boy when she was settled. She never did send for him. So he was brought up by his grandmother, who fed him and loved him.

It was easy to see the currents of allegiance and ambition fighting it out inside him – the desire to stay wrapped up in the warm, nurturing world of his grandmother's terrace house, and the fierce need to prove himself to the mother who left him for a wealthy man. Or that's the story my own mother told me when she wanted me to pity him the way she pitied him.

He sees me watching him eat the pie. He knows what I'm thinking. 'Did you love your grandmother?' I ask him.

'She's dead,' he says. 'And so is her world.' Then he glances at me. He must have seen the chink that pity has opened up in my armour because he's pulling a small stack of notes out of his wallet and handing them over the table to me.

'I've been hearing rumours,' he says, 'about a possible peerage.'

I don't move. I know exactly what I'm being asked to do, for money, and suddenly I know I have some influence over him after all. I hold up my hand to block the bribe: if I'm going to be silent about his wife-beating, I want something in return.

'Tegid Rhys,' I say, and I watch him very carefully. It's as though a bomb is going off deep inside his chest and a shockwave of anger is racing through to the surface, urging him to batter me to a pulp, or knock my block off, or skin me alive, or tell me my life won't be worth living when he catches me – all the threats I've stored in my tense muscles for the last thirty years.

'You really don't get it, do you, you gormless numbskull?'

I match his glare, but the connection between my brain and my mouth is severed, and all I can do is swallow.

'You're a bloody irritating waste of space. Do you really believe your stinking homeless man is more important than the fact that this country could be on the verge of war with a *rogue regime*?'

I shake my head, and as if from some great distance I hear myself say, 'I think my homeless man is more important than your fucking peerage.'

He looks down at the money in his hand, and then he stands up, scraping his chair over the floor with the force of his rage. He puts the notes on the table in front of me and presses them down with his hand. I hear the air escape from his mouth. And then he's turning away. I know it's the only way he can stop himself from hitting me, and this time he has to stop himself – because we're in public, because he knows I'll fight back, and because he really, *really* wants to be Sir Lockwood.

'I'll text you if I hear anything,' he says.

# 25

## Café

I'm in the hostel's office and I can hear the faint sound of voices on the TV in the common room downstairs. The fluorescent light above me buzzes in the key of E, and I'm too hot. I take off my baggy cardigan and lay my head on my hands and close my eyes. I have dispensed the night's drugs to the residents and my sole function now is to respond to an emergency. I hope there isn't one.

'Did the mountains help?' Alex stands in the doorway holding out two mugs – like offerings, or defensive weapons. For some reason I think of Kung Fu Panda – a large cuddly creature with unfeasible fighting skills and an innocent wisdom. 'Was it good to be on your own for a while?'

I lift my head slowly. He is one of the few people in the world who has heard me say that I don't like tea and registered it. He's made me a coffee and set it down on the desk in front of me.

I swivel my chair to face him. He's standing by the wall now, his hands on the radiator behind him, leaning forward slightly.

'Err ... Help what?'

'Well, they say a suicide affects as many as seventeen people. It affects them deeply. And anniversaries are particularly difficult.'

'You too then.'

He gives me a smile of solidarity and nods. 'It wasn't your fault.'

I doodle in the margin of the log book in front of me and feel very tired. And then I stand up and take down the dictionary from the shelf above the desk and settle it on my lap. 'Suicide, it says here, is "the act or an instance of killing oneself intentionally."' I flick through to 'M'. 'Murder, on the other hand, is "the unlawful, premeditated killing of one human being by another." All very simple, really.'

He frowns. 'I don't …'

'If someone is driven to suicide by circumstances beyond their control, then the people who control those circumstances must be murderers.'

He's shaking his head. 'That would make all of us murderers. To a degree.'

'Drones have killed two thousand people in Pakistan since 9/11. Some of them were children. Is that murder?'

He smiles bleakly. 'I know what they call that,' he says. 'They call it "collateral damage".'

I don't smile back, but I know I'm being unfair. None of this is Alex's fault. My foul mood has much more to do with the indigestible dinner I had with my dad than Siamak's suicide. But I can't seem to let it go now I've started. 'A drone on a training flight in Wales crashed into a caravan and killed a young woman. Was that an accident?'

'Err … I suppose so. Wasn't it?'

'What if someone shot down that drone because they objected to the "collateral damage" going on in Pakistan and Yemen, and they had no intention of killing a young mother on a caravan site who was living there illegally because there aren't enough affordable homes in rural Wales for the people who live and work there to buy?'

'I suppose that's collateral damage too, then,' he says. He doesn't ask what on earth I'm talking about. He just waits. But he's stopped smiling. I can see he has no intention of letting me hurt him, but he still thinks he can save me. And I want to save him the trouble of trying.

'Perhaps it would be better if I told you about my childhood and my crap relationship with my parents?' I say.

'I'm not your therapist,' he murmurs. 'But I would like to be your friend.'

I lower my head over the log book. For a brief moment I think I'm going to cry. And then I realise Alex's compassionate nature may be useful to me after all. In all the months Tegid spent at the hostel, he must have talked to Alex, and told him stuff. If he talked to me, he would have talked to a warm and friendly person like Alex. 'It's Tegid Rhys,' I say. 'I've been trying to track him down and he seems to have disappeared off the face of the earth.'

'Why d'you want to find him? I thought he'd sorted himself out.'

I don't answer that. 'What did you know about him? What did you know about his reasons for being on the street, and then for leaving the hostel?'

He thinks about it, and his expression becomes serious. He's rehearsing his professional opinion. 'I thought he was a classic case of emotionally useless male falling apart after his wife kicked him out. And then, with a little time in a safe place, and with some kindness from us, and from you in particular, he got himself back together and returned to the world. Although I was a bit worried when he said he was going to visit the ex on his way to Wales. I thought that might cause a relapse ...'

I hear a shout on the street outside and a wheelie bin being trundled along the pavement. 'Do you know where his wife was living?' It seems obvious to follow Tegid's trail to her, if that's where he went first after the hostel.

A smile breaks out on Alex's wide face and I feel the wave of its warmth as it hits the rocky shore of my personality. 'Manchester. Her husband is a gynaecologist at a hospital in Manchester. He's from Pakistan. Like my Dad. Which is why Tegid told me his surname. He was interested in names, and languages, wasn't he? I think he could speak about ten different languages.'

I push a piece of paper towards him across the desk and he leaves the radiator and comes over and writes the name down neatly, in

215

capitals, in the middle of the page. 'Thank you,' I manage, and he beams at me again. I turn away and start up the desktop computer. I listen to him going up the stairs, his boots clicking on the metal runners till he reaches the carpet on the first floor. Then I go online and start searching through the names of gynaecologists at Manchester hospitals.

I sleep on the morning train to Manchester and when it arrives at Piccadilly I walk down the platform as though I haven't quite arrived. I stop to watch a pigeon flutter onto a rafter and then I go in through the glass doors onto the concourse, where the sounds of a thousand feet on hard surfaces replaces the rumble of the trains and confuses my senses, and I find myself wondering if I need to buy a silk shirt or an expensive salad, while all I really need is a pee. I search through my pockets and wallet for the right coins to get me in the toilets.

More awake after the brightly lit toilets, I find the café Tegid's ex-wife suggested and buy a cappuccino and take it to a brown sofa. I resist the urge to curl up and go back to sleep. Instead I stare at the wall and at the large sepia photograph of Italian women sat around a table with their smart handbags, laughing stylishly. And I let my eyes flit across the faces of the other customers. A man is instructed by his wife to wait with branded carrier bags at a table; a thin woman in sharp-edged glasses sits up very straight at a small table, reading a book over her latte; two men in suits lounge on another sofa, their legs spread wide, hands on their bellies, their coffee cups already empty. A spiky-haired waitress removes their cups. They watch her arse as she walks away.

Then there's a woman coming directly towards me. 'It wasn't difficult to recognise you,' she says, unwrapping a long scarf from around her neck and taking off her coat. 'You are ... distinctive.'

'Thank you,' I say, without getting up, 'for agreeing to see me.'

She lays the coat over the back of the chair and holds out a hand. 'Caroline,' she says.

'Abby,' I say, touching her hand without getting up. She notes the tattoos on the backs of my fingers.

'Let me get you another coffee,' she says. 'Cappuccino?'

'Espresso. Double.'

I watch her then at the counter: a small woman in her fifties with blonde hair falling to her shoulders in soft curls. She's wearing a dress patterned with little flowers and a cardigan that accentuates her curves. When she speaks to the grim-faced barista taking her order her hands flutter in front of her.

At our table she settles herself behind a tall glass of hot chocolate topped with whipped cream, and like the cream she seems to froth out into the space around her, moving towards me as gently as foam. I look at my espresso – dense and dark within the thick walls of its little white cup.

I try to picture her with Tegid and decide she's an ageing version of a public schoolboy's fantasy female – the sort every friend's sister must have looked like in bromide-suppressed dreams. I'm not immune to her softness myself, and when she speaks her voice is low and quiet. 'So,' she says, 'my ex-husband is missing and you think I may be able to help you find him?'

'And can you?'

She puts a hand to the blue stone pendant suspended just above her cleavage. 'I need to let you know from the start that I stopped running to his rescue a long time ago. I had to. For my own sake as much as his.'

'So why did you agree to see me?'

She smiles and folds her hands in her lap as though she's trying to close down some of her natural openness. 'I like the sound of your voice, Abby. And I thought I could help you. In a broader sense.'

I laugh. 'I just want to find Tegid. That's all the help I need.'

'Well,' she says, 'if he's in Wales, as you say, he'll be in Criccieth. That's where his grandmother lived.'

I shake my head. 'He was in Pont Rhith.'

'Oh,' she says, and her hands begin to flutter again, as if she's trying to draw something in the air. 'Isn't that the place ...'

'Uh-huh.'

She stills her hands by taking hold of the glass of hot chocolate. 'You think he did it, don't you? You think he brought down that drone?'

'Do you?'

She stirs her chocolate with a long teaspoon and then looks directly at me. 'It's possible.'

I wasn't expecting her to say that. I was expecting a swift denial. 'But he was a pacifist,' I counter. 'He wouldn't have risked it. He wouldn't have risked hurting anyone.'

She smiles. 'I don't mean to pry, but are you in a relationship with him?'

I lean back into the sofa. 'No,' I say, 'if you mean a sexual relationship. I work in a hostel for the long-term homeless and he was a resident. We were friends.'

She nods. 'I'm sorry to hear he was on the street again.'

'Again?'

'He was homeless for a while after he came out of prison.'

I'm aware the espresso cup on its way to my mouth has stopped halfway there.

'He didn't tell you?' she says. 'He went to visit Reg and ended up waving a frying pan around in his kitchen. He said he didn't hurt him, and never intended to, but there was a court case and Reg had good lawyers. Tegid insisted on defending himself, of course. He went down for a few months, for Actual Bodily Harm.'

'What was he trying to do? Kill him or cook him breakfast?'

'Do you know about Reg?'

'I know he sold Tegid's landscaping programmes to SecTec. But I didn't know Tegid had attacked him!'

She shrugs. 'He wasn't trying to get money out of him, although

Reg owed him a fortune. Tegid thought the money was tainted. So I don't know why he went to see him, or what he hoped to get out of it.'

'Revenge?'

She shakes her head. 'I've always wished Tegid well. He's a good man, and in some ways I'm sorry he didn't get the bastard.'

It's hard not to smile when she swears.

She lifts the glass of hot chocolate with both hands and takes a small sip, and then she puts it back on the saucer and sighs. 'We're carers,' she says, 'you and I. Nurses and social workers. We find it hard to believe that there are people in this world who really don't give a shit about anyone else.'

'But ...'

'I don't mean Tegid,' she says quickly. 'But he was perfectly capable of recognising a psychopath when he saw one. And for that you have to have a shard of ice in your own soul, don't you think? We, on the other hand, are always taken by surprise when people are evil.'

I've had too little sleep and too much coffee and there's a metallic taste in my mouth. I try to relax and focus. I close my eyes, and I see the space in a line of caravans where a young woman died when a drone careered out of the sky and smashed into her soft body. And I see the little girl outside the chapel, her eyes wide with the horror of sudden, total separation from the one who adored her. I open my eyes to erase the image. 'He must have been difficult to live with,' I say.

She laughs wryly and her blue crystal earrings dance around. 'We met when we were students,' she says, 'demonstrating against the bomb. It must have been the early 80s, I suppose, and he was a postgrad running the CND group. He was so ... so committed and ... fearless. He'd stand up to anyone. The first time I saw him, he was arguing with a policeman, on a march, and I decided he was the kind of man I'd marry. One who could stand up to authority. But in the end I realised – or my counsellor helped me realise –

that I didn't have the energy to look after him, and work, and have children ... and I wanted children. A lot of the time he needed looking after, you know. He could never hold down a job for long. He was too pure to compromise with the world, and by the time I reached thirty I was ready to fall in love with someone else. Someone willing and able to be a husband and a father.'

I can't imagine Tegid in a job. Any job. 'So what kind of work did he do, after Curved Space?'

'He did part-time lecturing at the university. He taught 3D cartography – that sort of thing. I thought it suited him. I thought it would lead to something more permanent. But then he started changing the syllabus and excluding anything with possible military applications. And then he started telling the students they'd been picked for the course in the first place because they could calculate missile trajectories and not consider the consequences. He stopped grading their work. Then he found out where most of the funding for his department was coming from and he started a campaign to break the university's links with arms companies. But he was on a short-term contract, and the university didn't ask him back. After that he did some freelance computer work – coding and things. But he said the whole atmosphere around computers was saturated with power and he didn't like that either.'

I can certainly hear him saying those things. 'And you didn't agree with him, I suppose?'

'I was worried about our future, about how we'd survive. I was always worried, because someone had to worry about those things and it wasn't going to be him.'

I lean back into the sofa, away from her gentle common sense. She seems to have done a lot of thinking. She seems to have worked things out. 'And you don't know where he is now? He hasn't contacted you?'

'No,' she says. 'You're the only one who's been in touch with me. And that woman from the newspaper.'

'Gemma Scanlon? And what did she want to know?'

'She wanted a photograph. For a missing person piece.'

'So you knew he was missing?'

She doesn't look at me, and then she's reaching for her coat. 'I didn't want to come here and spend the whole time talking about *him* or any other man. I came here to help *you*, because when you phoned I was concerned and I thought I could help you. And I also wanted to help myself. I've had years of therapy, Abby, and now I'm training to be a counsellor myself, and the more I understand the choices I've made in my life, the better. I wanted to tell you that it can take a lot of courage to acknowledge your own need for love and safety. There has to be something in return, Abby, in every relationship. That's what I wanted to tell you.'

'You have no idea what I need,' I say, 'but I can tell you it isn't a big house in Cheshire.'

She doesn't take the bait. She holds out her hand instead and grips mine. Her hand is cold. 'It was nice to meet you,' she says. 'I hope you find what you're looking for. I just wish it wasn't my ex-husband.'

# 26

## Home

I wake up when the train stops. All the other passengers are putting on their coats and pulling their bags off the racks and the guard is moving through the carriage repeating the same message over and over again: the track is flooded further down the valley, before Pont Rhith. There will be buses, she says. We need to wait on the side road. I close my mouth and release my squashed face from the window. Then I get my coat and bag and stagger out onto the dimly lit platform. Moments later the train pulls away, leaving us with nothing but faith in the guard's promises and wild rumours about where the rescue buses may or may not stop to collect us.

A cold hour later one small coach arrives on the side street beside the station, but there isn't room for everyone and only the determined manage to shove their way on. I watch their faces at the windows as the bus pulls away – headphones on, gazes fixed to the back of the seat in front of them. Among those left on the pavement are a woman with two young children and an old man with a small suitcase.

I walk down to the main road where there's a garage with a shop, and I linger there in the warmth over the chocolate bars and crisps. I text Owen and tell him the invitation to powdered soup is off. He says he'll cook instead. And he'll pick me up. I don't turn him down.

* * *

I'm too tired and cold to talk so I sit in his car in silence, watching the road ahead as it twists through the hills. In half an hour we're passing Mr Palmer's caravan site where the red and white tape has migrated down the hill and is now strung across the entrance. The town, when we drive through it, is dead. Even the Spar's lights are out and the pubs and the hotel have closed their doors for the night.

Owen says he's checked and the flood waters have receded with the outgoing tide and we'll be able to cross the old bridge. Even so, he has to mount the pavement to avoid the deepest part of the spilled-over river.

I wonder if it will be like coming home – over the hill and into the valley, up to the cottage where the stove is lit and a dog sleeps on the sofa. When he parks up against the gable end the first thing I'm conscious of is Raven's absence at the other end of the terrace – the darkness in her kitchen, the unseen drawings on the fridge door, the unused wood in the store outside. And when I walk into Owen's cottage I'm struck, once again, by the sense that this is a mock-up of a country retreat and he has no intention of living in it permanently. His real life is somewhere else.

I sit on the sofa and he passes me a glass of red wine. It's the travelling, I think, that makes me feel like a smashed battery with my wires hanging out, acid corroding my vital connections. I have reached the end of my not belonging and there's nowhere else to go.

He's setting a pan on the stove and somehow it's easier to confront him when his back is turned. I begin to tell him about the atmosphere of places, about the resonances found in a high street bank, compared with those in a chemist's, or a café, or a chapel. 'And each time we move into a new place,' I say, 'we need to mark the transitions with rituals that confirm we haven't slipped through the gaps in this world. We don't want to know the earth is our last skin, and beyond that there's nothing. We hold on to each other with "hellos" and "goodbyes". And we drink. We take in fluid to confirm our fluidity, to tell ourselves we are still in our element, even though the places we go to are all different and demand different things from us. We drink tea when we visit other people's houses and we drink tea when we get to work and when we get home, and we drink beer and wine to mark our arrivals in bars and restaurants.'

He's turned slightly towards me but I've no idea if he's listening. He stirs the pot and I keep talking, my tongue jangled loose by the hours on trains and the lack of sleep and the caffeine overdose.

'But not anymore,' I'm saying. 'Now everywhere we go is the same place. It's called Tesco's. The bank, the butcher's, the chemist's, the bookshop, the newsagent's, the grocer's, the café. And if somewhere isn't a supermarket – the library, the chapel, the home – it's going to be closed down or assimilated into a supermarket very soon. To save us the trouble of transitions. To save us the awkward sense that there are different worlds possible – in-between worlds, nowhere worlds, somewhere-else worlds. Or nothing.'

He picks up the wine bottle from the table and comes over to me. 'So now we can drink whenever we like,' he says cheerfully, refilling my glass. And when I don't smile he says, 'Just a thought.'

I hold the red liquid up to the amber light. I notice he isn't drinking. 'It's not real, is it? All this ... hominess came off the shelf in a supermarket. Why? Why go to the trouble?'

He sits down beside me on the sofa and sets the wine bottle on the floor. The dog leaves her basket and pads across the floor. She leans against his leg and he ruffles her ears as she sinks slowly onto his foot. 'I was in the army. I left. I'm starting a new life. It isn't easy. It doesn't come naturally. But I'm trying.'

'Huh,' I say. 'And you haven't even bothered to name your dog.'

'Her name is Kova,' he says quietly. 'I found her tied to a drainpipe at the back of an empty house. Inside the house were the bodies of a woman and two children. At the side of the house was the body of a boy. I think he was going to the dog when they shot him. Or maybe he'd tried to hide her, and he was running back to his mother and sisters.'

I can hear Kova's breathing, and the lid on the pan on the stove begins to rattle. He stands up and goes over to it.

'I don't know if she went deaf before or after they shelled the village,' he says. He brings the pan over to the table and I watch him dish up a thick stew of vegetables and lentils. 'And I don't pretend to know how to stop moving,' he says. 'Or how to live a normal life. But I need to try. Don't you?'

I can't quite manage an answer, but I sit down at the table. I pick up the knife and start slicing the bread – for something to do while I think. And then I decide to tell him everything I know about Tegid. About how he mapped the mountains and the quarries, and how he worked out the angles and trajectories of missiles aimed at drones. And I tell him about Reg Dauber, and Curved Space, and the topography-mapping computer programme that was used to bomb people on the other side of the world. And I tell him about my meeting with Tegid's ex-wife, and about Ellis-the-farmer's missing rifle.

He's been dipping a thick slice of bread into the winey juices of the stew, and now he holds it still and lets it drip into the bowl. 'A farmer's shotgun wouldn't work,' he says. 'A 50-calibre sniper rifle, maybe, but not a farmer's shotgun.' And then it seems to dawn on him. 'The stash they found in the old mine?'

'Why not? He was mapping the mines. He'd have known what was down there.'

'Unless the people who found the weapons put them there in the first place.'

I laugh. 'And why on earth would they do that?' I speak steadily and look directly into his eyes, trying to assess if he knows something I don't.

He shakes his head, and for a moment I think he's going to tell me to give up and go home. To stay out of it. I think he's going to lay down the law, for my own sake. But all he says is, 'You should tell them. If you think Tegid Rhys shot down that drone, you should tell them.'

'Them?'

'The police.'

He's suggesting that it's safer to be found than to be lost, but I've never been so sure about that. 'Why should I tell the police? How would that be better for Tegid?'

'If you have your suspicions about Tegid, then they do too. Bring it out in the open. Tegid's in far more danger where no one can see him.'

I look at the mess of veg in my bowl. I can't eat it. I'm swimming in my own confusions, struggling with the sense that I'm about to betray a friend in an attempt to keep him safe. 'And you?' I say. 'Would it be better for you if I tell them?'

He frowns. 'I can't see it makes any difference to me.'

It's still dark when I wake up in the morning. I listen to the rain insisting against the glass – insisting without saying anything – and behind the rain the wind moans, and I'm close against him, and I've slept that way. But then I'm wriggling out from under his arm and he doesn't stir as I find my clothes and take them downstairs. While I'm dressing by the stove Kova comes across the floor towards me, her claws tapping on the stone, her tail wagging, her head low and her eyes beseeching. I scratch her behind the ears and then she goes back to her basket and nuzzles her flank for a while.

I put on my coat and sit down on one of the wooden chairs facing the heavy oak door that leads out and away from here, and the fingers of my right hand, with their scratched-in tattoos, play silent tunes on the table top ... like his fingers played over my skin in the dark. And in my morning reverie I feel the afterglow of being wanted, of those few moments of feeling required on this earth, in this one place and no other.

It's an illusion, I think. It's like this cottage in the middle of an army training ground, with its stove and its beams and its basket of freshly chopped wood. But now I'm wondering if an illusion could keep me warm, if I let it. A little bit of me thinks an illusion could be a start, not an end. I'm letting myself think we could maybe bring a home into existence, without a blueprint, because neither of us have one of those. Step by step. Brick by brick. With work. Like the bridge they built in Pont Rhith when the fantasy one disappeared. In this place. With these people.

I get up and fill the kettle and set it on the stove. I hear a text message arrive. I find my phone in my coat pocket and take it over to the table and sit down. It's from my father. 'Ur homeless man blackmailing gov scientist. No longer issue. Leave alone.'

I shudder. I'm not going to leave it alone, and I'm not going to the police. Instead I dig Rickman's card out of my wallet and I call him.

# 27

## Meeting Room

When Owen drops me off outside the hotel I tell him I'll find my own way back. I want to talk to Rickman on my own and I don't need Owen holding my hand. A flicker of concern crosses his face, but he accepts the dismissal.

I go to the bar and ask for a coffee. 'How was the walk?' asks the bartender as he sets the cafetière down in front of me. When I look at him blankly he says, 'You were going walking. To Bethania and the blue pool.'

'Oh,' I say. 'It was great. And I didn't fall down a mine.'

He presses the plunger down on the coffee. 'I hope not,' he says. 'Enjoy.'

I take out my phone and re-read the message from my father. 'Leave alone.' I understand that's an imperative, not an abbreviation. But 'No longer issue' is the bit that makes me squirm. I can only imagine how they might have solved the problem of Tegid Rhys.

Rickman comes in while I'm stuffing the phone back in my bag. 'I knew you'd come begging for me one day ... and I've found us the perfect room in this lovely hotel.'

I stay sitting at the table and pour myself a cup of the coffee while he waits at the door. I hear him sigh. I stir in some cream and then I pick the cup up off its saucer and follow him.

He stays ahead of me as we walk up the stairs and down a narrow corridor and into a dark room at the back of the hotel. A square oak table dominates the small space and there are three chairs set against each side. 'Not very comfortable, I know, but necessity is the mother of invention, and I'm very inventive. Shall we start on the table?'

'I'll finish my coffee first,' I say, setting it down in front of me.

He goes to sit beneath the whiteboard on the far wall, and I search for the light switch and find it behind the door. I flick it on and a fluorescent strip hums into action and keeps on humming.

'It does that,' he says.

I turn it off. There's enough light from the window.

He tells me to sit down and I stay standing. He tilts his chair backwards against the wall and spreads out one of his fine-fingered hands on the table in front of him to steady himself. I realise I'm working out where his centre of gravity is, just in case I need to tip him. And I've already worked out my exits – I stay between him and the door.

'I think Tegid Rhys may have shot down that drone,' I say, and I watch his face for a reaction.

He's still smiling. In fact he's beaming a fake appreciation of my manifold qualities and an intense interest in every word I say. 'Abigail ... It's extremely unlikely that a man working alone could bring down a large unmanned aerial vehicle. He wouldn't have the right equipment.'

'He mapped the mines.'

'Ah.' He nods his head. 'I can see where you're going with that. You think he may have used weapons stashed there by another terrorist organisation. Well, I appreciate your concern, but I think your vivid imagination may be running away with you.' He looks at his watch and stands up. 'Thank you, Abby Lockwood, for letting us know, but it's best if you leave this to the professionals.'

'Lockwood isn't my name,' I say. 'I'm surprised my father didn't tell you.'

His eyes narrow. 'Abby *Hughes*, then. Why all this fuss about a homeless man? I'm sure he doesn't want your misplaced concern. There's absolutely nothing to say the crash wasn't an accident.'

'Then why the finger pointing? Iranian terrorists, eco-activists, Welsh nationalists? Why are you trying to suggest it *wasn't* an accident?'

'We don't control the press. They're free to make their own conjectures.'

'You don't control them, no. You just feed them irresistible tit-bits, and then you stand back and watch them stoke the fear.'

'You flatter me,' he says, and for the first time I notice the piercing in his left earlobe. He was a skateboarder. Or a surfer. Or he liked to dress like a skate-boarder when that was the image to conform to. I bet he has an iPod somewhere with a large collection of indie music on it. And now he has a collection of meditation tracks on his phone to improve his concentration. Of course, he's left behind the skating, the surfing, and he's the slick fixer for the boys with the big money. 'It's part of my job to manage the press, Abby.'

'And Tegid Rhys?' I say. 'Have you managed him? Have you removed him from the picture, because it's much better to suggest foreign terrorists are responsible than a middle-class white man who designed computer programmes and had principles. That way you can use the fear you stoke to get what you want: more money and support for your war machine. And then when things calm down you can tell everyone it was an accident, as long as Tegid Rhys doesn't appear with another story.'

He gets up and walks around the table towards me. He stops when he realises coming any closer will emphasise our height difference. 'This is serious stuff, Abby. We know terrorists have been active locally. They've used the outdoor education centre here for team-building exercises. It's not propaganda. It's fact.'

'Is that what gave you the idea for the MT4S training ground? A place to train our own terrorists? I mean soldiers.'

230

He ignores the jibe. 'This part of the country has excellent terrain. I want it used to support and train *our* people in the dangerous security and humanitarian work they're doing in similar mountainous regions across the world. Don't you, when you're not busy feeling morally superior to everyone else?'

'And you work for Reg Dauber as well as the MT4S Consortium?'

He's silent. And then he's reaching into his jacket pocket for his phone and pawing at the screen. I assume this means he has more important things to attend to than a conversation with a residential social worker. I'm well aware that the only reason he *has* been talking to me, and not offering to give me a lift out of town – anywhere out of town – is because I happen to be the daughter of a politician. 'I have a portfolio of concerns,' he says, without looking up.

I lean against the door jamb and watch him. He looks tired. Perhaps things are getting on top of him. 'Do you enjoy this work?'

He shrugs. 'I must be doing something right – they pay me a fortune. In a few years' time I'll be able to retire to a surf shack on the beach in Thailand and have a beautiful young wife to attend to all my needs. Or I could buy a cottage in the Welsh hills and find a girl with a sturdy pair of walking boots to move in and do the cooking.'

'I'd poison you.'

He shakes his head. 'We're not that different, Abby. We're both trying to survive. I'm just doing it with more humour and success than you are. And more style, obviously.'

'Style? You look like a Labrador in a posh coat.'

He laughs. 'That's funny, and I'll tell you why. We had a Labrador crossed with a Whippet when I was a kid. We called him Sandy. He had a white triangle on his chest and when you stroked it he'd grin and his eyes would roll back in his head. I loved him to bits. But he just couldn't stay home. He was always racing off. He came up to the primary school once and stole the football from the middle of a game. I thought it was hilarious.'

I watch him. I can see him as a little boy with a dog.

'And then one day, when I came home from school, Sandy wasn't there anymore and my mum said my dad had taken him to the vets. He was too much trouble. They'd put him down.'

'Fuckin' hell. That's a bit extreme.' I'm not sure I believe a word he says.

'I know,' he says. 'I hated my dad for years.'

I'm looking at him closely then. Perhaps he's right and we have more in common than I thought.

'And I cried buckets.'

'Maybe you do have a soul.'

'Mm. Maybe. But I also learnt a lesson.'

'Go on.'

'Running wild isn't the same as being free. You've got to be clever if you want to be free. And you've got to have power. And that means you've got to have money. Lots of it.'

I pick up my coffee and flick the lights on and I'm walking out when he says, 'You're not clever enough, Abby. You're running wild and you think you're free, but you have no money and you have the wrong friends. Let me list them: Tegid Rhys – a man convicted of harassment and threatening behaviour towards a contracted MoD scientist; Tim Jones – involved in planning the sabotage of Hawk jets in the 1990s; Delyth Roberts – frequently imprisoned during the 1970s for Welsh-language activism, and under surveillance since the 1980s for involvement in suspected arson attacks on English estate agents.'

I laugh. 'Is that all you've got on me? My mates?'

He's still pawing at his phone as if it holds the key to everything. 'And then there's Siamak Hamidi – suspected Iranian spy, and Sally Campbell, member of the communist Fifth International. Those two are much more worrying. They're the reason we're going to have to look more closely at that hostel of yours. I'll be speaking with Counter Terrorism, and Immigration. I think we could get the place closed down pretty quickly. For reasons of national security, of course.'

'You've forgotten Mike Lockwood,' I say. 'One-time union leader, then a Labour MEP, and now a Tory MP in search of a title and a seat in the Lords.'

He smiles. 'You have friends in low places and enemies in high places. That doesn't make for a comfortable life.'

'Comfort isn't one of my ambitions,' I say, but inside I'm reeling. He's worked out my dad won't come to my rescue. And if he closes down the hostel, any number of fragile lives will crack. Suddenly my own rootlessness seems less like a curse and more like a privilege.

The cafetière is still on the table in the bar. I refill my cup. I sip at the cold coffee, but I don't sit down. I want the caffeine to hold up a defence against the greyness that is crashing down through my head and sinking through my body in a wave of thick sludge.

The local paper is folded up neatly by an abandoned teapot on the next table and I pull it towards me. On the front cover is a grainy picture of Tegid. He's young and he's smiling, and he's wearing a trench coat that's too big for him. Dark curls appear from under his woolly hat, and he's holding up a CND banner. It must be his ex-wife's photo, and I can see now why she took him under her wing. All he needs is a guitar on his back and he'd be the epitome of the doomed young poet: androgynous, angelic, 'touched', and ready to be sacrificed by the patriarchy for failing to be converted into the standard model of masculinity.

'MAD SCIENTIST HAD SIGHTS ON DRONES' reads the headline, so my attempt to bring the theory into the light has been pointless too. It's already there, for everyone to see.

Was he mad? I look at the picture again. I can certainly see awkwardness: the ever so slight hunching of the shoulders and the

233

child-like turning sideways to deflect what might be coming at him. There is glitter in his eyes, and a frown line between his brows. It's a frown of bewilderment – he has no idea why anyone would want to inflict pain on him or anyone else. There's a problem he can't solve, even if he spends his whole life trying to work it out, and the problem is: should he fight back, and risk becoming just like them? Or should he curl up in a ball and let them carry on with their abuse and brutality?

'Have you seen this man?' it says underneath the picture. I read Scanlon's article. Tegid Rhys, it says, was living in a campervan parked illegally on Foel y Ffridd. He'd been seen stealing food from skips outside a local supermarket. But the real scoop comes later in the article. He had contact with 'Welsh extremists and suspected arsonists', as well as the Iranians whose flat in Telford was raided. There's a number to call if anyone has any information on him.

For his own good, I reckon, as well as theirs, and maybe that's true and Owen is right. I'm pretty sure he'd be safer in prison than providing a target for fixers and vigilantes.

I put the front page of the newspaper in my pocket and leave the hotel. I want to speak with Delyth, but when I get to the bookshop it's closed and banging on the door doesn't bring her out. I go to the petrol station and buy powdered soup and beer, and then I start the long trudge back to the campervan. I don't phone Owen. I want to walk and think. Slowly. Between hedges. I cross the old bridge and this is what I think: I can leave Gemma Scanlon to do the rest of the work – to find Tegid and flush out the truth. I can slink away and watch from a safe distance and see what falls out at the end.

I'm only a few minutes along the A-road when Mr Ellis's Landrover rattles up beside me. He's wearing the hat with the furry earflaps and he hugs the steering wheel and stares at the road ahead while he waits for me to climb in.

'And what are you going to do now?' he says when we're moving.
'About what?'

'About these soldiers coming here and using my land,' he shouts. 'About your friend with the campervan who's gone missing. About the accident which wasn't an accident.'

I hold on to the door handle and try to fix my gaze on the old farmer as we bounce over potholes and swerve between verges. There's nothing I can do about any of it, and I know that now. And I don't understand why Mr Ellis thinks I can. Or why he feeds me stories about Tegid borrowing his gun and shooting down drones. 'It was all rubbish, wasn't it?' I say to him.

'What?' he shouts over the noise of the engine and the wind whistling in through gaps in the floor and bodywork.

'All that stuff you told me,' I shout back. 'All that stuff you did with the teapot and the biro in your kitchen, showing me how Tegid shot a drone out of the sky with a farmer's rifle. It was bollocks, wasn't it?'

He screws up his face, closing one eye. 'A little white lie,' he says.

'And the big dark truth?'

'It was Raven Davies. She had my rifle.'

'Why would she have your rifle?'

'She wanted to shoot a rabbit. She said it was eating her lettuce.' He chuckles to himself and then stops. I wait. 'But your friend ... Tegid Rhys ... came by with the gun, just after the accident. He said Raven had done something stupid. He said Raven was drinking and going on about losing her job. She thought her boss was going to sell the forest and that she'd get laid off.'

'And Tegid?'

'He said it was his fault. He said he'd given Raven the idea. Said he'd even shown her how to shoot one of those death machines out of the sky.'

'Have you told the police?'

'Huh,' he says. 'Last year the alternator on my generator was stolen and the police turned up two days later. "Next time I'll get

235

on my knees and pray," I told them. "It's quicker than waiting for you lot."'

I laugh, and I wonder if he navigates the valley road by memory alone – he certainly doesn't look at it.

'I've told *them*,' he says, using his thumb to gesture back down the valley towards Pont Rhith. 'I've told that Rickman.' He spits out every consonant in Rickman's name. 'They can dredge the quarry reservoir if they like. That's where it is. That's where my rifle is now.' Then he stops looking at the road and turns to me. There's a glint in his rheumy eyes. 'It's like Caledfwlch ... or Excalibur to you. It's down there waiting for King Arthur to come back for it.'

'Diolch,' I say, 'for telling me,' but I still don't believe a word of it. It's easy to blame Raven now she's dead. And Tegid, who isn't here.

'S'dim ots,' he says. 'No one's interested in what an old Welsh farmer has to say.'

# 28

## Puddle

There's no light on at Murmur and the door is locked, so I get in the campervan and rest my head on the steering wheel. My options are limited. I could take the van to London and see how long it lasts, or I could leave it in the quarry. Either way, I know I need to give up my search for Tegid and go back to work before I run out of money, or worse, find myself in a hopeless battle to save the hostel from Rickman's attempts to close it down.

Maybe Mr Ellis was right, and if anyone shot down that drone it was a stoned and drunk forester facing redundancy. And one day, maybe, Owen will phone me and say, 'Hey. You know what? That old man you were looking for has turned up, out of the blue, and he says he's sorry for all the trouble he's caused by disappearing just after a military drone crashed into a caravan and killed a woman. He says he thought you'd just take the van and be happy. He didn't expect you, of all people, to go chasing after him.'

Or perhaps I'll be doing outreach one night on the Embankment, and he'll be sat on a bench under a string of white bulbs, and when I sit down next to him he'll say, 'If X is any set, then there exists at least one set, the power set of X, which is cardinally larger than X.' And I'll wait patiently for the explanation of what on earth he's on about. 'Infinity,' he'll say, his eyes glinting. 'Cantor's set theory shows that infinity means anything is possible. Even justice. It means there could be a world where children don't die of starvation or diseases and where they

237

aren't blown to bits by bombs. It's not impossible. Nothing is impossible.'

And I'll say, 'But can we get there from here?'

And he'll laugh and shake his head. 'Probably not. But that doesn't matter. Even a new starting point is possible.'

Or maybe Tegid will be dredged from the Thames one day when I'm not looking, and I'll get a message from his ex-wife: 'I'm afraid he threw himself off a bridge. Sorry. I know you were fond of him. If you'd like to talk about it, I'm here to listen. Just pick up the phone.'

I lift my head off the steering wheel and sit up. I'm staring straight over the valley at the square black hole of the mine adit halfway up the opposite hill. I lift my right hand and cover the hole with it. I'm not sad to see it go. It's like a reminder of depression, a shadow lingering just out of sight in the background of a sunny day, something I just have to live with but can never afford to engage with, unless I want to go under.

A compulsion to drive back up to the quarry, like some giant yellow homing pigeon, has me turning the key in the ignition. It's an act of blind faith in Tegid's return to leave the van in the quarry when I go back to London, but that's what I've decided to do. Taking it with me would be like admitting he was never coming back, and I'm not quite ready for that. The van lurches and creaks over the ruts and rocks. A mug slides off the table at the back.

When I enter the forest I have to turn on the headlights – the sun is obscured by the dense trees and the clouds. The ground is sludgy after all the rain and the front wheels slide about. I shift gears and concentrate, so I don't get stuck. When I get to the gate it's wide open and there are fresh tyre marks in the mud, but whoever was in my lair has gone now – there is no other vehicle on the hill.

I park the van face-in to the cliff and then walk over to the forest gate and close it. It's a feeble attempt to feel safer. I look up at the grey sky and consider Mr Ellis's conviction that it was Raven who shot the drone down with the old farmer's rifle. If Owen is right about guns – and he should know about guns – then that wouldn't be possible, and Mr Ellis is using a woman who can't object to fulfil his own fantasies of fighting the coloniser's army. On the other hand, Tegid may have shown her the weapons in the mine. He may have told her exactly where to find what she needed.

I walk back to the van slowly. The wind is cold and the air smells of sheep and earth. I realise leaving the campervan in the quarry when I go back to London will serve another function: it will give me a reason to come back, to breathe in the air, which smells of sheep and water and rock and peaty earth, and to expand into the space which stretches out over the hills and forests towards the mountains and the sky. It will also give me a reason to come back and see Owen, without having to stay with him. It seems like a good compromise between my desire to connect and my desire to run away.

In the van, I set a fire in the stove using some of Tegid's squared maths paper. The lines and vectors curl, blacken and fall, and then there's a shout from the forest and Owen is out there, climbing over the gate with Kova tucked under his arm. They walk towards me across the mud and shale – two conglomerations of earth minerals and water that have risen up to walk around for a while on the surface of this planet.

He's brought freshly baked bread and cheese and a bag of cherry tomatoes and a pint of milk and some coffee, and he follows me into the van and sets them down on the table. But Kova refuses to come in, staying at the foot of the steps with her head down, straining backwards against the lead. Owen stops pulling at her and squats down in the doorway, trying to coax her in, his fingers mussing under her nose. I wonder if it's the smell of calor gas and woodsmoke she objects to. Or if it's me and my ambivalent attitude to the man she loves. In the end she lies down outside, her head on her paws, the surface of her brown eyes shiny in the wintry light.

239

I make coffee with my gloves on while Owen slices and butters the bread. And then we sit at the table and look out towards the mountains. Sometimes he lifts his binoculars and tells me the name of a bird. A strange feeling seeps into me with the grey afternoon and I wonder if it's a sense of wellbeing. I wonder at its low intensity, its quietness, its lack of drama. I imagine how we would appear to anyone looking in at us from the outside. They would see a couple having coffee in a campervan. It's a picture I shouldn't be afraid of. I let it be.

But I'm not about to take up bird-watching. Something tugs at the corner of the safety blanket I've wrapped myself in, asking for my attention like a hungry child whimpering from the cold shadows of the world. I stand up and take the plates to the sink. I pick up a brown folder of Tegid's clippings which I've left on the draining board. I've already looked through it. I know what's in there.

There are pieces about the training of Saddam Hussein's elite troops in the 1980s at the US Army's John F. Kennedy Special Warfare Center and School at Fort Bragg. At that time, the US was worried Iraq might lose its war with Iran so it wanted to make sure the Iraqis were trained in 'unconventional warfare.' If the country were invaded and occupied by the Iranians, the Iraqis would need to know how to fight back. 'Unconventional warfare,' according to the school itself, 'is the development of a resistance movement following an invasion.' It's all about training people to overthrow a government or occupying power. Tactics include dramatic small-scale attacks and guerrilla warfare. The training includes the difficult and dangerous art of learning how to make improvised explosives and weapons. All the sorts of skills the Iraqi insurgents turned on the Americans a few years later.

And Fort Bragg also trained Nicaragua's Contras. It trained Pakistani officers who were then expected to pass on their acquired knowledge to Afghanistan's anti-Soviet mujahideen. Same story: chickens coming home to roost with bombs under their wings.

It's clear from Tegid's scribbles that he believes the Consortium's planned training ground at Bethania will serve a similar function to Fort Bragg – the training of potential terrorists in the name of Western 'security' and continuing arms sales, because a government or dictatorship under threat from trained insurgents also needs weapons, and the whole circle of profit and death will go on perpetuating itself.

There's more in there. Notes on fundraising activities, during the 1970s and 1980s, by Irish Americans in support of the IRA – an activity supported by the US government and senior US politicians, even after the bombing of pubs full of civilians in Birmingham and Guildford. Even after the near assassination of Margaret Thatcher, who was, after all, the elected Prime Minister of one of the US's closest allies.

I don't open the folder in front of Owen. I stick it in the cupboard above the sink with the mugs and plates. I know what's at the back of that file. It's a list of the weapons found in the Bryn Hyfryd mine shaft. It's an inventory of the stuff Tegid thinks was channelled there via the IRA to an armed group of Welsh nationalists. The list includes a 50-calibre sniper rifle.

Owen is worried Kova will freeze to death huddled up by the van door so he takes her home as the light fades. I've told him I'll pack my things and come to his place for the night, before I get the train back to London, but when they're gone I sit in the passenger seat and stare at the rock face. I have been living in a factory in the middle of the mountains – a factory that used to make slate and still pumps out wood, and the flesh of sheep. And if the Consortium has its way, its next product will be fighters and bomb makers.

I decide to make more coffee, but there's no water left. I spend a few minutes looking for the water bag and then remember I dropped it in the stream and it floated away. I take the kettle instead. It's nearly dark, and even out in the open, where the trees have been felled, I strain to see the ground I'm walking on in the half-light, and some of the ditches are deep and full of brambles. A thorn snags on my jeans, tearing a red line through my skin from the back of my knee to the top of my boot.

I try what I think is a direct route to the stream and stumble down a steep slope with the kettle gripped in my hand. At the bottom of the slope I come to a fence. An empty fertiliser bag is caught on the barbed wire and flaps in the wind. On the other side is a sheer drop to the stream, its white water squeezed between the rock sides of a gorge, then dropped down a twenty-foot fall to a deep pool. I start walking along the top of the cliff, next to the fence, till I find an old tree, its thick trunk sliced a third of the way through by the barbed wire. A few crisp brown leaves cling to its branches. Deep rifts in its grey bark look like the shapes of running animals, or ancient messages written in a pictorial language I don't understand.

I use the tree to help me clamber over the fence and onto sodden heather. By the time I reach the stream my legs are soaked and all I'm thinking about is getting water and making coffee back at the van. I struggle along the narrow bank to the pool at the bottom of the fall where the force of the water creates a hiss that submerges all other sounds. It's a relief, this drowning-out of the rustling that goes on in a wood at night, and my grasping thoughts dissolve in the pulsing flow.

When the kettle is full I climb slowly back up the hill through the plantation, sweating now in four layers of clothing, taking the longer route back to the forest track and the green avenue. Clutching the kettle in one hand I take my torch out of my coat pocket with the other. In its beam silver droplets glisten on the bearded moss at the side of the track.

I'm almost at the gate at the end of the forest when a hollow thud resonates through the ground and up through my body. An orange glow appears in the sky above the hill. I drop the kettle and start to run, climbing over the gate and racing across the mud, and as I round the hill into the quarry I can see the van is a fire box, dark smoke pouring through its shattered windows, flames snaking into the black sky. The heat is intense, and I stop and remember the calor gas bottle under the sink. I'm turning away when it rockets through the roof and sends smouldering debris down from the sky and onto my shoulder, burning through my coat and singeing my skin. I pull the coat off and hurl it into a puddle and then I sink onto my knees, my hands shielding my face from the heat, the animal heart in me hurting from the loss of my shelter. Then I'm up and running again, down the track through the wet forest with the crazy idea that there is still time to save it, if I can get help.

I cower on the doorstep of Owen's place hugging my knees. The door is locked. I pull my wet coat around me and lean my head against the oak frame and close my eyes. A warmth creeps over me, and I'm by the coal fire in the kitchen of my Nain and Taid's house, and I can smell old towels drying on the airer, and boiled cabbage and Knight's Castile soap. My Taid is sat in his chair by the fire and he's speaking to me in his first language, which is neither English nor Welsh, but a very simple language of love. I don't understand what he's saying, and I know I'll never speak that language fluently, however much I try. I know I'll have to learn it the hard way. I'll always stumble over the words, because it's not my native tongue, and I'll make mistakes, and give up, and try again, hoping for patient teachers and kind fellow learners.

Then I'm being hoisted away from the coal fire by hands under my shoulders and I struggle to stay put, on the threshold of the house, where I've moulded myself into the cold stone step and the doorframe, and where I'm dreaming of warmth. But someone's making me move, and then I'm being hauled inside and rolled onto the sofa. I make myself sit up straight and I stare at him. There's a blanket wrapped around me and I'm bloody angry and he's asking me something but his voice is drifting away, and I'm not sure if he's talking to me or into his phone.

Do you need a doctor?

No.

I'll drive you to the hospital.

No.

There is whispering and one of the voices may be mine. It's a dance of shared sounds. Sh sh sh. Stay stay stay.

# 29

## Fire

When Cocteau was asked what he'd save from a burning house, he said the fire.

I drift in and out of sleep, half aware I'm not in a sleeping bag and can stretch out my legs under the luxury of a wide duvet. I can hear Owen downstairs setting the stove and filling the kettle at the sink. I turn over and the burn on my shoulder scrapes against the sheet, and that's when I remember the van is gone. Fear jolts through me. I've lost my den. And then, almost immediately, I feel elation. I'm free of it.

When Owen comes into the room he's holding out a cup of coffee. I sit up and take it, wrapping the duvet around me and leaning back on the wall, and then not leaning on the wall because of the burn on my shoulder. He sits on the edge of the bed with his back to me. I try to read his back. I think about reaching out and placing my hand on it. I wonder if I need to start believing what he says now. I wait for him to say something. He might say something.

He says, 'D'you think I set fire to your van?'

I don't remember accusing him of that, but maybe I did. 'I don't know where you were last night.' I say. 'You weren't here.'

'I was in town,' he says.

He's turned around to face me and I'm trying to read his expression, but it's dark in the room and he's in deep shadow. There's a lamp by the bed, but it isn't on, and the small recessed window only offers the murky light of a winter morning. I can see why you wouldn't need curtains in a north-facing house in a deserted valley, but their absence chills me, and I pull the duvet up closer to my chin. I start to wonder if he destroyed the campervan to get me to leave, and, if that's the case, he'll also need to make sure I don't move in with him now. 'I need to find somewhere to stay, till I've sorted things out.'

'You can stay here,' he says.

I feel a moment of relief, but then I start to wonder if I was meant to go up in the fire with the van. There's a constriction in my throat so I take a sip at the coffee. It's too hot. I set the mug down on the sanded floorboards next to the bed. 'I need to go back to work,' I say, scanning the room for my clothes. 'I should go back to London.'

He's still for a moment, and then he says, 'They're drying. I'll get them.'

I listen to him talking to Kova in the kitchen. Whatever else is a lie about him, it's true he loves his dog. When he comes back into the room he puts the clothes and my coat on the bed and then he stands by the window, looking out over the valley while I pull on my jeans. I can see past him to the hillside with its scrubby trees and its river of slate spoil and the grey sky above it. It all looks cold and empty. And beautiful.

'They've scared you, haven't they?' he says when I'm dressed.

I laugh. I want to say, 'What d'you mean "they"? Shouldn't it be "we". And who are you anyway? Tell me that.'

He seems to pick up the gist of my silent response because he's shaking his head and frowning. 'You're not scared of *me*, are you?'

I stare at him. I try to imagine speaking out the answer to that question. I can't. My fear has become a way of life, ingrained in my sinews, and not admitting to it is one of the ways I look after myself. He doesn't move from the window, but I see his jaw clench and his lips go thin. He doesn't like my silence.

I pick my coat up off the bed. It seems to have survived being dunked in a puddle and dried above the stove, although there's a large brown-rimmed hole at the shoulder where the white padding shows through.

'What happened to you?' he says then. 'I mean, I know what happened to me. Fucking war happened to me. But what happened to you? Really. Why are you so ...'

'Nothing,' I say. 'Nothing happened to me.' And I think: not one thing. Lots of things. That's what it takes. Years of attrition. I start pulling on my coat, edging it over the burn at my shoulder. Then I go through the pockets. My wallet is wet but intact, but my phone ... my phone was in the van. I unzip an inner pocket and feel for the folded paper of Tegid's map. It isn't there. I'm sure it was there – a map of the mine, a guide to the underworld – and now it's gone. I think about asking him where it is. I open my mouth, and then I shut it again.

'You'll ring me,' he says, following me down the stairs, 'when you get to London?'

I don't have a phone and I don't have his number. I say, 'Yes mum,' anyway.


I walk to town, counting my steps when I get agitated and trying to breathe with them – three paces in, five paces out. It doesn't work. Most of all I want a cigarette, as if I haven't inhaled enough smoke in the last twenty-four hours; as if a little more self-destruction would make me feel any better. When I get to the Spar I buy sandwiches for the train and I pick up a tabloid newspaper. On the fifth page there's a spread about Pont Rhith and the sinister Mr Tegid Rhys. It repeats most of Scanlon's article, but it also contains a line straight from the mouth of Ben Rickman. Tegid Rhys, it seems, was in close contact with people under surveillance for possible involvement in arson attacks by Welsh nationalist extremists in the 1980s.

I decide to catch a later train to London and go and see Delyth first, and when I get to the bookshop she's at the door flipping the sign to Ar Gau.

'I'm going back to London,' I say.

'Cardiff,' she says, looking at her watch. 'Just for the weekend. My train's in ten minutes.'

I tag along with her towards the station. We're pushed into single file on the narrow pavement between the slate wall of the churchyard and the cars on the road, but once we've crossed over I can walk beside her. I have the newspaper open at page five and I start to read it out loud.

'Uh-huh,' she says.

'What do you mean – uh-huh?'

'Can't you see, bach? They're going through every organisation or group that could possibly oppose the Consortium's plans. And I'm bloody insulted that it's taken them this long to get round to the Welsh nationalists. But I'm not surprised. We're not much of a threat these days. Most people think the battle's won – we have a government, of sorts, and they think we've saved the language. What more could we want?'

She's slowing down and stopping to talk with an old couple. There's lots of shared concern and arm patting. The man turns to me and asks in English if I'm enjoying my holiday, despite the weather. The stooped old lady in a grey mac and headscarf smiles up at all three of us, waiting for my answer.

'I was enjoying it,' I say, 'until someone set fire to my campervan.'

Their smiles run like paint in the rain. 'Oh,' he says. 'That's terrible. Terrible.'

Once we're walking again Delyth is quiet for a while and then she says: 'Perhaps it would be surprising or interesting if Tegid had come into contact with people active in the defence of Welsh culture and the Welsh language if he'd been living in ... Peru. But this is *Wales*.'

She's not in a great mood and I can see I'm not helping. But then she glances at me. She assesses my crumpled, singed coat, and seems to take pity. 'There was a time I used to go to prison for a rest, you know. It's bloody hard work trying to save a language and a culture from extinction. I'm not surprised I'm on their lists.'

I decide to take advantage of this expansiveness. 'But ... were you really an arsonist?'

'Are you asking me if I set fire to estate agents in England who were selling second homes in Wales?'

'Well did you?'

She laughs and shakes her head. 'They've still got no idea who was responsible for those fires. And that must really annoy them.'

We stop outside the ticket office and she starts looking through her handbag. 'But if they suspect you,' I manage, speaking to her back as she walks towards the doors, 'I don't understand why they'd also suspect Raven Davies.'

She turns around to face me. 'She loved her work in the forest, and she'd have done anything to hold onto it. She also drank too much and smoked too much dope. But ...' She looks at me then.

'But?'

She's walking back towards me across the pavement. 'You know more about her neighbour than I do ...' It's a query, and it cuts right through to the stuff I don't want to know about Owen. I stare at the wet pavement. She's waiting for a response and I want to say, 'You're wrong about him,' but it won't come out.

'Raven knew she was going to be a suspect because she was born a suspect. She was working class and Welsh and gay.' She puts up a hand as if to silence me. 'Now I'm going to Cardiff, and then I'll come back and go to her funeral. You should go home.'

I'm standing there on the pavement outside the station, fighting the urge to refuse to do what everyone is telling me to do. Because they're right. I should go back to my bedsit and my job. I have no business being here.

249

And then I see Joel, Anwen Pryce's ex, walking down the street with his friend, the brick-wielding thug Guto Martins. I don't bother to say goodbye to Delyth because I'm going after the boys. I'm sure, in that moment, that the ruddy-faced bastard set fire to my van. I follow them into the Llew Coch and then stop, repelled by the silence and the cold. A weak grey light comes through the frosted windows and there is no fire in the grate.

The two men are settling themselves behind their pints at a table in the corner and all my focus is on the fat one. 'You destroyed my van,' I say quietly. 'Why the fuck did you do that?'

He hears me but he doesn't look up. 'I didn't,' he says, turning to Joel. And then he says, 'But I should have.'

I lean in a little closer, over their pints. 'You should have?'

'Because he killed her,' he says, looking past me with his little piggy eyes. 'And you know it. It was him killed her.'

I watch his fingers tighten around his pint glass the way I'm sure he'd like to tighten them around my neck. I shake my head. 'The van was mine, not his. He gave it to me.'

He leans back and stares at me directly. 'And who the fuck are you? You come here asking questions about *him*, but you don't want to know about Anwen? Or her little girl. Your type never fucking does.'

Joel is looking at me now, but I don't meet his gaze. Even so, I can sense the quality of his silence: it's the silence of someone who's been forced to be quiet for so long it's become a state of being; it's the silence of someone who has given up waiting for anyone to hear him, and now he's just waiting. I've seen it before – that listless patience – in the refugees at the hostel. And now that I've sensed it I lose the urge to get even with his friend. I sit down opposite them. 'I'm just a residential social worker,' I say. 'I work in a hostel for the homeless in London. That man was one of the residents and he disappeared. I came looking for him. That's all.'

Guto splutters beer back into his glass and looks at his friend and laughs. Joel grimaces and shakes his head, and then he raises his pint to his lips and I can see the black Celtic knotwork tattoo weaving around his wrist and up his forearm.

I get up slowly, unsettled by their laughter.

'He had *you* fooled then,' says Joel.

His big friend puts a hand on his arm and says, 'Don't talk to the bitch,' but Joel shakes it off.

I sit down again and Joel carries on speaking, staring down at the table and fiddling with a beer mat. 'I got a cheque from him. In the post. A few days after the accident. There was a note saying it was for my little girl and he'd try to get more.'

'Did you go to the police?'

'They didn't want to know. Said he was just a mad man, and if he wanted to give me money they wouldn't interfere. So I cashed it.'

Guto leans in towards me and hisses: 'I guess ... your friend ... felt guilty.'

I ignore him. 'How much?' I ask quietly. 'How much did he give you?'

He stares at his pint. 'More than a fucking tramp should have.'

# 30

## Winding Shed

I don't get the train back to London. I keep walking – out of town, across the new bridge and north along the A-road. I start to run, and the tarmac slides away beneath my feet. When I turn onto the track to the New Cottages I finally slow down and walk. Below me I can see Bethania's hollow chapel and its cluster of empty houses and the low roofs of the old slate workshops. I can see the slag tips and pine plantations on the slopes, and the square black hole in the side of the hill.

Owen's car isn't at the cottages, and when I knock on the front door there's silence inside. I go back to the track that runs along the back of the houses and throw a chunk of slate through the kitchen window. The sound of breaking glass echoes across the valley, and then all I can hear is the shushing of the wind in the forest and a bird cawing.

Because the terrace is built into the hillside, the track at the back is higher than ground level and there's a deep bramble-filled ditch between my feet and the bottom edge of the window. I need something – like a plank of wood – to bridge the gap, so I go round to the front of the cottages again and into the derelict middle house. There are no floorboards left on the ground floor and the middle floor is absent altogether.

Back outside I squint in the light. I'm listening hard for the sound of a car coming up the track. I can't hear one. I look out over the garden, over the grass and rhododendron bushes, over the fence to the stream. The garden hasn't been tended for years. Nothing has been cultivated here since the New Cottages were new. There's no vegetable patch. There's no lettuce for rabbits to nibble on, and therefore no need for Raven to shoot them. More white lies from Mr Ellis.

I go to Raven's woodstore and heave out a long, split log – flat on one side and rounded on the other. I drag it to the back of the cottages and push it over the ditch and in through the broken window. I take off my tattered coat and lay it along the wood and start crawling along it. The log wobbles. I wriggle back onto the path and stand up. For a moment I hesitate, but I know I've already gone too far, so I get back on the log. I use a gloved hand to sweep shattered glass off the frame and I climb in through the window and into the sink.

Once I'm standing on the stone floor it's too late to consider I may be making a mistake. I don't really know what I'm looking for, except conclusive evidence that Owen is not on my side. I can't think what that evidence would be. Detailed notes on the comings and goings of Raven Davies and Delyth Roberts? A large box of matches and instructions on how to set fire to a campervan? Tegid's map of the mine – the one I had in my coat pocket, before the fire?

Kova is there, looking at me from her basket. She gets up and comes over, shaking her haunches, head down. She didn't hear me break in, of course, and she didn't bark when she saw me. I rub her head softly till she's had enough and goes back to bed.

I tell myself there's evidence everywhere in this cottage that Owen isn't who he says he is. This is a show home. But it's not enough evidence. I'm sure lots of city people fill their rural retreats with symbols of a rustic life they have no intention of living – the oak table, the china water jug, the stone floor and Belfast sink. All supported, of course, by central heating and mains electricity.

And then there's his name. Owen. It sounds like an undercover cop's bright idea for a regular Welsh bloke's name. And I realise then that I don't know his surname.

But it isn't enough. There needs to be something else to justify my betrayal. I go over to the low bookcase and squat down. I pull out a stack of OS maps and open them up one by one. They're all pristine – unsullied by rain and muddy fingers. They smell of print, and when I fold them back up they snap into place along the manufactured creases. The only map that's been used is the one we took with us to SHED.

I put them back on the shelf and sit back on my heels, listening again for the sound of a car on the road across the valley. The house creaks and Kova wheezes in her sleep.

I go upstairs. There's a hatch into the roofspace in the bedroom and a stepladder propped against the wall at the top of the stairs. I fetch a head torch from the hooks by the front door and climb the ladder into the attic. The blue tarp over a hole in the roof rattles against the tiles, and I can't hear anything except its flapping. That makes me nervous, so I quickly sweep the torch across the boarded floor. There's a box of tools and a pair of gloves and a box of nails and a radio. That's all.

I retreat down the ladder and put everything back where I found it, except the torch, which I put in my pocket. There's not much I can do about the smashed window. And then I look at Kova curled up in her basket, and I wonder if she's a prop too. I wonder if he'll leave her, or give her back, or pass her on, when he bores of this attempt to settle down, or when this little mission comes to an end and they send him somewhere else to keep an eye on another poor activist they've decided is an enemy of the state or of some corporation's profits.

He's moved her basket in front of the stove, and I kneel down beside her and tickle her ears. I know now that I'm not staying, and that I've just blown all my chances of coming back. Still, and for once, I slow down and say a proper goodbye. She can't hear me, and she looks at me with resignation, and in the sheen of her eyes I can see all the ghosts of all the people I have lost. They raise their

254

contorted limbs towards me before I bury them quickly in another layer of mud and ice. I scratch her under the chin. And then I'm reaching over her head and opening the heavy iron door of the warming stove. There's a piece of paper drying on the rack and it's Tegid's map, a little singed around the edges, but still readable.

I spread the map out on the floorboards and trace my finger over its markings. It's a map of the Bryn Hyfryd mine, from its huge square adit in the side of the hill, through its network of tunnels and shafts and chambers and levels. But I'm still not sure if its presence in Owen's stove should lead me to condemn him. Perhaps he was drying it for me. I fold it up and put it in my pocket, and then I'm climbing back onto the sink and out of the window.

I start to run along the path through the slate workings and shale tips towards the Bethania road down in the valley, but I stop abruptly when I hear a car. It purrs to halt, and although I can't see it I'm guessing it's stopped in the lay-by where the two valleys meet and the path to the cottages splits from the lane. I climb over a collapsed slate wall into the shelter of a roofless winding shed, navigating over the rubble, ducking under a thick and rusted iron rope attached to a drum. At the far end of the shed I climb onto the tumbled rocks of the wall, but I still can't see the road.

And then I hear another car. I listen as it pulls to a stop in the same lay-by, and then I risk it. I leave the shed and climb across the slag-heap till I can see down into the valley towards the village. The men are the size of toy people, but I can tell it's Rickman and Owen. They stand together by the black Range Rover for a few moments, then Rickman gets back in his car. Owen stays there, and when he looks up I shrink back and then turn away from him and start to traverse the slag heap. I want to get back on the path, and away from Owen and Rickman, but the shale slides beneath my feet and I fall against it, cutting my hand. I push myself back to upright and stagger. I'm fighting to stay on the higher ground, to get back to the path to the New Cottages, and then I give up and go with gravity and the moving shale, still trying to get away from the parked cars, but sinking further below the cottages with every step. When I reach the bottom of the scree slope I'm close to the stream, and to the shelter of the trees that line it, and I make my way quickly to the slab bridge.

The burn on my shoulder stings as I run and there's a deep gash across the inside of my fingers from the slate. I slow down to walking so I can put on my gloves to soak up the blood, and then the road enters woodland and I hear another engine. I cut into the trees and listen and wait. This time it's the farmer's tractor, so I push through the wood to the fence and wave at him. He doesn't see me. I follow the fence upland till it leaves the trees and reaches a gate. I try waving at him again and the tractor stops and he climbs down slowly from his cab and crosses the field towards me.

'She didn't have any bloody lettuces,' I shout when he gets close enough to hear me.

'No,' he shrugs. 'And the girl couldn't have shot a cow at five yards.'

'Another white lie?'

'Wishful thinking,' he says. 'But if you want a job doing, you should do it yourself.'

'Did you?'

He looks towards the mountains, and to the gap where the jets appeared on the day it snowed. There's a globule of liquid on the end of his large nose. He uses a crumpled handkerchief to wipe it away, then he dabs at his eyes with it.

I take the singed piece of paper out of my pocket and hold it out to him. It rattles in the wind but he doesn't look at it. 'I think it shows the mine,' I say, nodding towards the square hole in the side of the hill above us. 'I think there's something in there.'

He fixes his rheumy eyes on me. 'Then you'd better go and find it,' he says.

# 31

## Mine (dis)

I leave the road and start up the path which rises through scrub and over slag towards the Bryn Hyfryd adit – a black mouth above a triangle of vomited rock. The branches of the birch trees vein the slate outfall with lines of dark red, but the leafless saplings offer no shelter from the wind. I put my head down and my hands in my pockets and I walk fast. I don't need a map to get to the black hole – it's been taunting me since I arrived in the valley with its silent scream, and I know exactly which direction to take, even when the adit disappears from view.

I gain height quickly. Bethania and the silver strip of the river are soon below me. I have to negotiate a wide patch of slate slabs and that slows me down. And then I stop dead. I'm listening to a sound above the gusting wind that chills me to the bone. I try to understand it: two notes, one after the other, sliding across a semi-tone, over and over, like an unoiled seesaw in a disused playground. Its unearthliness empties me out and refills me with cold terror, and I know in an instant that this is the kind of fear that drives people to pacts with the devil. Right now, I would do anything to feel safe and warm and protected by the men with the biggest guns, whatever the cost. For a few moments, in that state of fear, I long for the roar of a manmade jet to drown out the wailing and to tell me that I'm not the only human being left on earth.

And then the sound stops, and I hunch up and scurry on like a small animal hoping to be passed over by predators. I calm myself with the steady crunch of my boots on the path and the rhythm of my laboured breathing. I step over the wing of a large bird – there's no sign of the rest of its body – and when I reach the barbed wire fence at the edge of the forest I follow that. Then the wailing sound starts again, louder this time. I crouch down and scan the hillside and the valley and the scudding grey clouds in the wide sky and the edge of the plantation ahead of me, looking for the source of the tuneless keening. All I can see are a few trees that have been uprooted by the wind, their grey roots stretching out from the mud like random arms searching for something to hold on to.

And then I see it: a dead pine tree at the edge of the forest. Its trunk is dry and brown and most of its branches have gone. It's leaning against the tree beside it and when the wind gusts the two trees – one dead, one alive – scrape against each other like a monstrous violin played by a phantom bow. I walk past the dead tree quickly, and where the fence corners I turn away from the plantation and start to clamber uphill over slate spew.

It's slow going – stepping from one chunk of stone to another – and the slabs wobble and slide beneath me. A shower of sleety rain mottles the slate, and then another jolt of fear goes through me. I see a hunched figure – a person in a grey mac with a backpack on, huddled against the wind on the side of the hill, waiting for me. I picture Raven's head on the rock, trails of black blood from her neck wound mingling with her hair. But it isn't a person. It's just a rock that's been wedged upright amongst the spillage. I keep climbing.

When I stop to look back I catch a flicker of movement on the valley road. I think it's Rickman's car. It stops by the start of the path, a hundred metres further down the valley, but I know it's him. He gets out of the car and stands where I can see him, and from his posture I think he's watching me through binoculars. Then he waves. I don't wave back, but I get the message. He knows where I am, and where I'm going. I watch him get back in the car, do a six-point turn, and drive back down the valley.

258

I push myself to move faster, and the last twenty metres to the adit are hard going. The path is steep and follows a narrow railtrack of rusted iron. When I reach the vaulted entrance to the mine and stagger onto flat ground I'm panting. I'm also out of the wind and my heavy breathing echoes around the inside of a cavern the size of church. I turn around and look back, out at the valley framed by rock. I take out Tegid's singed map and study it closely. The way into the mine from the adit is down a ladder in a shaft which plunges through five levels to the base of the hill. And on the lowest level there seems to be another exit, another way out.

The shaft is at the back of the cave and I get down on all fours to crawl to its edge. I take Owen's head torch out of my pocket and put it on, but I can't see anything except the sides of the shaft and the ladder. I pull back, scared of the drop into nothing. I pick up a stone and chuck it into the hole and after a few seconds there's a chink. I have no idea if the ladder is intact, but I push my gloves into my pockets and grasp the top rung and slowly descend into the void.

My hands are cold on the metal and they keep slipping in the blood oozing from the cuts on the insides of my fingers. The air in the shaft is surprisingly warm. I pick up a sweet smell on the updraft. I know that smell. At the hostel, before the rabbit arrived, Elsie kept a python she fed on mice. We had to order them for her by post, and we kept them in the freezer with the sausages and burgers and defrosted them when the snake needed feeding. Sometimes the snake wasn't hungry, and the mouse would rot in Elsie's warm room and the smell would seep out into the corridor and drift around the hostel. It's that same smell of rotting flesh wafting up the shaft now.

At one point the metal ladder ends and is replaced with a wooden one lashed to it with rope. For about eight rungs I'm climbing down on something that sways about and creaks under my weight, and I hold myself tightly against it and I move very slowly, and then it lists to one side and I stop breathing. For one moment everything is still, then the ladder peels away from the wall and I'm falling backwards, only to be met almost straight away by the ground which hits my right foot and then my bum. I lie back on the wet rock, holding bits of the wooden ladder above me, and I start breathing again. Then I push the thing off me and slowly stand up. I didn't die in the fall, and I'm too shocked to feel the bruises, but I have another problem. There is a four-metre gap between me and the first rungs of the metal ladder, and what's left of the wooden ladder won't bridge the gap. I'll have to find the other way out.

I sweep the space at the bottom of the shaft with the head torch and find the source of the putrid stench. It's a suppurating sheep in a puddle of water. I scan the chamber and see there are three tunnels leading off it. I get out Tegid's map and try to match it with what I'm seeing. Two of the tunnels appear to be blocked, or he hasn't bothered to explore them. The other leads far into the hill and to the chamber on level five where there may be another way out. I choose that one, stooping between the rocky floor and the jagged ceiling and moving as fast as I can over the uneven ground.

I hit my forehead against a low beam and reel and stop. When the shock and pain subside I listen. There's dripping water. I have to steady myself against the tunnel wall and I feel a strong desire to lie down. The roof of the tunnel has dipped lower since I left the shaft and the walls have converged so that now I can easily touch both sides with my hands. I turn the head torch off. I'll use it in short bursts, when I need to, to save the batteries. But I also turn it off so I can listen, and pick up all the sensory signals Tegid put on his map.

Tegid was here, I think. And while I find that thought comforting in some ways, I also know I'm relying on a madman's view of the world to find my way out.

I keep my hand on the right wall as the tunnel forks and twists.

I trace the scars made by axes and chisels and I move very slowly now, feeling with my feet for the ground. I taste the air: it is stale and wet. Everything down here is wet, and the sound of dripping water is constant. I slosh through deep puddles and my feet and legs are wet and the walls are cold and wet, and I have no idea how far I've walked from the shaft, or if I could ever find my way back.

My foot clinks on metal. I switch the torch back on and pick up a small horseshoe-shaped piece of iron. It's the heel of a man's – or a child's? or a woman's? – boot, a remnant of a life spent digging down here. I check the map again and match my senses against its dense details: the way the sound of dripping echoes around a small chamber where the tunnel briefly opens out and there are candle stubs in a rock alcove; the place where an abandoned cart has lurched onto its side; an acrid smell at the point where I need to choose the left fork. He marked it all. I'm doing OK. At some point soon I will see daylight, and there will be an exit, because he drew a gap in the hillside with rock on one side and trees on the other, and I hope to god it wasn't just something he imagined, something he thought would be a good idea in a better world.

And then the map fails me. I walk into a boulder. There is a wall of stones behind the boulder and they completely block the tunnel. I look at the map again, trying to work out if he drew this rock fall, but it isn't clear. There are the words 'altar' and 'east-side', and a line moving towards trees and a sun. That's all I have to go on.

I consider going back to the bottom of the shaft and shouting for help, but I'm not sure I know the way back, so instead I shout at Tegid, and the sound echoes back up the tunnel and dies away. I turn around and sit down. Is this it? Is this where I finally learn to scream, to bellow out my lungs, when I know damn well no one can hear me? I cup my hands around my mouth: 'Where the fuck are you?' I shout. And then I'm quiet. I know I'm not going to hear him shambling along the tunnel towards me. And I'm no longer waiting for him to appear in the beam of his own lamp, an expression of diffidence on his face, saying: 'I have something to tell you about the wonders of this world, so please don't hurt me.' I know he's not there to hold out a hand in the dark and touch me gently on the arm and tell me I'm not alone. Because I *am* alone. It's just me. In this fucking pit. Forever.

All I can hear is the echo of my own voice. Even the sound of dripping water has stopped. And it dawns on me that this is an appropriate way for me to die. I could curl up and sleep in the protection the mountain offers me from everything out there. I could sink down and never get up again. I could stay in the rock's cold womb and never return to the struggle. It has a certain appeal. It makes a kind of sense.

I curl up on the wet shale against the wall of the tunnel. I think of St Melangell, the woman who hid a hare under her skirts to protect it from the hunting dogs of the Prince of Powys. My Taid told me the story, many times, because I asked him to. Melangell slept on a stone bed in a cleft of the rock near the land the Prince gave her – he was so impressed with her courage and compassion – to build a sanctuary for all those fleeing persecution. When you are very tired, a rock bed is enough, and I'm very tired, and I pull my coat against me and the cold from the ground seeps through it and into my bones.

When I open my eyes, there's nothing. I strain to hear something, but the silence is like no silence I've ever heard before. It's an emptiness that could wait forever to be filled, without expectation, without hope. I'm not ready to join it yet, and lying on cold wet stone no longer feels saintly, it feels disgusting. I roll slowly onto my front and push myself up.

I turn on the head torch and take a look at my situation, and then I start back the way I came. This time I'm going to try a different turning at each fork, in case I've made a mistake and misread Tegid's scribbles. The first tunnel I go into forces me to stoop even lower than before and then to crawl along the wet shale. The cut across my fingers re-opens, and I'm deciding I can't picture Tegid squeezing through this small space, and that I should try to back up before I get stuck, when I sense the walls and roof recede from me. I stand up carefully, shielding my head with my hands. The torch light doesn't illuminate much of the space in front of me, but I can tell it's big from the way the sound of my voice is thrown when I shout. I'm in a cavern the size of a cathedral, and a cathedral, of course, would have an altar on the east side.

I sing with my still small voice, and I listen to it resonate around me. I turn slowly, revolving and singing and listening, and my sound – pure, rough and full of longing – pulses into the belly of the hill. And that's when I know which way to go, like a bat, checking and correcting, listening again, moving again, edging along the cavern's wall until I can see dim light filtering through a curtain of brambles in the roof of the cavern, and I can feel the colder air of the outside world against my face. I start to climb up over the rocks towards the light and the air, and then I look down.

I'm on a platform at the top of a steep incline that cuts to a deeper level of the mine, and there are the rails of a small track disappearing down into the dark, and a rusted rope attached to a winch which has been half crushed by fallen rocks. And there's that sweet smell again. I start clambering down the track, following the rusted rails a good twenty metres further into the earth, and at the bottom of the incline there's a pool. He's sprawled beside it, his eyes wide open and the skin of his face stretched back over his cheekbones.

I still want to save him, and I can't quite believe he's beyond my help, but this lump of decaying flesh bears only a strange resemblance to Tegid. This thing isn't the man I knew. It's just the casing. I creep closer. I find a head torch jammed between two rocks a few feet below him. And then I try his coat pockets. There's a pen and a folded exercise book. There's nothing written in the book. No note, no map to show me where he's gone, or tell me why.

I put them both back in his pocket. I tell him I'm sorry I didn't write or visit. I'm sorry he was on his own in the world. I tell him I'm on my own now, and if I believed he'd gone somewhere else I would go with him, to keep him company.

I haul myself away from the body, back up the incline to the winch, and then up further over the rocks to the opening and out into a narrow hanging valley where the grey light of the winter afternoon is blindingly bright after the dark of the mine. I run down the hill through the woodland, sliding on the mud between the trees, contouring the hillside till I see Bethania. Then I head upland, away from the road, under cover of the forest, towards Mr Ellis's farm. I hear a car on the road and it sounds like Rickman's Range Rover. I'm damn sure he knew I'd find Tegid down there. I'm almost certain he put him there – or drove him there. If there's something, anything, in that chamber which links him to Tegid's death, he'll want to make sure no one finds it.

I keep to the pine plantation, searching out avenues wide enough to run through, heading upland towards the farm. Once I'm above the house I wait at the treeline and scan the fields and the tracks and the vehicles parked in the yard. I can't see anything other than Ellis's Land Rover and his quad and trailer, so I run for it, over the open field, and the dogs start barking from a cage by the barn.

Mr Ellis opens the back door. He doesn't say a word but nods towards the small whitewashed barn. I'm halfway across the yard when I hear Rickman's car on the farm track. Mr Ellis pushes me into the gloom of the barn through a half-open door and then grabs me by the arm and pulls me over to the far wall. My eyes strain to adjust to the dim light but Mr Ellis goes straight over to a tarp and lifts up a corner. I scurry under it and curl up. I listen to him walk slowly across the yard to the house, and I listen to Rickman's car lurching up the track.

'Good afternoon, Mr Ellis.'

I hear Mr Ellis grunt and then mutter something in Welsh.

264

Rickman tries again. 'We may have a security incident on our hands. Mind if I take a look around your property?'

'I do mind,' says Mr Ellis. And then he gives a sharp whistle and I hear the scrabble of paws on wood and a few moments later a low growl.

Rickman doesn't say anything, but I can imagine the look on his face as he stands there confronting the dog and the old farmer. He won't like being blocked, but he'll smile. 'Another time, then,' he says, and the confidence in his voice appals me. He's not worried. He's not left anything to chance. I hear him get back in his car and turn it around. Once the sound of the engine has faded Mr Ellis is back in the barn, lifting up the tarp so I can crawl out.

'I found Tegid,' I say.

He shakes his head as if he's not surprised at all, as if he knew all along, but he doesn't say anything. He starts lifting up the tarp again and throwing it further aside. There's a metal box under it, and he cranks open the lid and beckons me over.

'Look,' he says proudly.

I think I know what I'm looking at.

'A long time ago,' he says, 'before I inherited the farm, I worked in the quarries. I still have some dynamite. And before I go to join my parents in heaven, I will use it.'

I stare at him.

'Your friend ... my friend ... we were going to blow up the dam at the quarry reservoir. We worked it all out. We knew when to do it. In September. In September the sheep are still on the ffridd, out of harm's way. Tegid knew all about water. He knew which way it would go when it poured out of the lake. He knew it would drown Bethania. He knew it would destroy their playground.'

He bangs down the lid of the box and starts pulling the tarp back over it. 'But now he's gone and I'll have to do it myself. Unless you fancy giving me a hand?'

He doesn't wait for an answer – he's limping out into the yard. I follow him, and he points at the Land Rover and grunts, 'Get in, then,' and he disappears into the house. He comes back out a few minutes later with his fur-lined hat on and keys in his hand. 'I phoned the police,' he says. 'To let them know where he is. I'm sure they'll be here in a day or two.' Then he throws a damp towel at me and points at my head and I try to clean the blood and dirt from my face and hands and hair as he drives straight across the field towards a gate. I get out and open it, and then we head along a lane, into the foothills of the mountains, travelling away from Bethania and away from Pont Rhith.

It's a couple of hours of driving over moorland tracks and 'B' roads, and Mr Ellis doesn't say much, so I'm left to the misery of my own thoughts about how Tegid died down there. And I wonder if Rickman is busy making sure nothing about the death points to him or his clients.

It's dark when we come down from the hills into a town across the border. Mr Ellis pulls up outside the police station. He takes some money out of his wallet and hands it to me. 'For your train ticket.' And then he's giving me a re-used envelope. I stare at it. It's more tape than envelope. 'Now bugger off and don't come back till September.' He reaches over and shakes my hand, like a craggy chapel elder saying goodbye to a member of his flock.

# 32

# Garden

My laptop's open on the yellow duvet in the staff bedroom. I've looked at the contents of the memory stick many times since I peeled it out of Mr Ellis's old envelope. It's undoubtedly Tegid's work. It holds files of figures and calculations and graphs and diagrams. But they have nothing to do with jets or drones. They calculate the volume of water in the quarry lake and they trace the probable route a flood would take if the dam failed. He maps this route in all the possible permutations of the flood's flow, given the realities of gravity and the topography of the valley. He knew how to do that. He knew how to map the way flood-water moves over land. He concludes that a dam break at the reservoir would drown Bethania – and the MT4S military training ground – in water and shale.

He leaves little to chance. There are notes on when the tide pulses up the Rhith valley, and when it sucks the water back down the estuary to the sea. When the tide is fully out he calculates that the riverbed next to the town would be capable of dispersing all the extra water flooding down from the quarry reservoir. The town would be safe. And he's picked the dates in the year when this low tide happens in the night. He doesn't want to drown a farmer out on the hills at dawn, or ramblers enjoying an early start to their day's walk on a bright autumn morning. He notes when the sheep are on the ffridd – the higher summer pastures – and therefore not in the valley. His only reservations relate to the host of little creatures that live between the rocks and slate and on the scrubland in the valley. And he's well aware of the history of drowned villages in Wales. This one, though, is already empty. This one, he thinks, is better drowned than used for war.

The date he chooses for the deluge is a Sunday in September.

In another file there's stuff about dynamite and how to use it. There are poems he's copied down, including the one by Patchen that he wrote out for Delyth. Poems of love and delight, mostly.

And photographs of trees.

And there is a video of the sea. Just the sea. A blue sea. It could be the Mediterranean. It could be the Algarve. I watch that film of the sea again, because I'm convinced it's telling me something. But all I get are waves – endless rippling waves.

It takes my father a day to phone the hostel. I assume he's spoken to Rickman. Maybe I shouldn't have come back to work, but I had nowhere else to go. Disappearing, I've realised, takes resources, and I don't have any.

He wants to see me, he says. He'll meet me after work on the South Bank. When I get there he's leaning on the river wall, looking over at Westminster as though he's surveying the next conquest in his long campaign for success and recognition. I know I'm an obstacle in the way of those ambitions. A small obstacle. A minor irritant. But one he'll need to remove.

I lean on the wall as well, but not too close to him. I look at the sky above the Houses of Parliament. It's matte grey, with streaks of charcoal and patches of bright shiny white. It's a sky which reflects the sea and the watery world of sailing ships. I pull my jacket closed under my chin. After the stuffy heat of the hostel I'm shivering.

'I can't help you anymore,' he says. 'I always said you were on your own once you turned eighteen. I thought you understood that.'

'So why did you want to see me, Mike?'

He turns to look at me and pretends to sum me up. 'The trouble with you middle-class kids,' he concludes, 'is that you think you're special. You want to be musicians, photographers, activists. But you're not special, Abby. You need to accept that and get a boring job and get married and have kids.'

'OK,' I say. 'Will do.' I can hear the gale of the world again, as though I'm on that hillside caravan park in Pont Rhith in January, when I stood next to the site of another catastrophe. It's a silent gale which roars up the Thames without rippling the water. It makes no sound at all as it rages around the Houses of Parliament and blasts its way through the city. It is nothing, and its nothingness is so loud it can't be heard.

I start to walk away. 'Wait,' he says, and I stop like a well-trained dog. 'You won't be testifying at the inquest into Tegid Rhys's death.'

'That's not up to you.'

'The thing is,' he says, 'no one's going to miss a homeless man. Except you. And there are more important things to consider.'

'Your peerage, I suppose?'

'National security,' he says.

I laugh. 'I don't understand how ...'

'You're not meant to.'

'... how killing Tegid Rhys would protect national security. But I can see how Tegid Rhys might reduce Reg Dauber's wealth by demanding the money he was owed. And I can see how Tegid Rhys might give the MT4S Consortium a headache by messing with their plans and telling the truth about the drone accident.'

My father shakes his head. 'It was suicide, Abigail. The coroner will confirm that.'

'I have reasons to doubt it.'

'None of your reasons will stand up in court,' he says, not looking at me. 'Particularly if your performance at Reg Dauber's place is mentioned. And your work record. We've seen the reports: you have a tendency to collude with clients who have mental health problems. And your relationship with Tegid Rhys was ... well ... too personal. We've spoken to his ex-wife.'

'You don't scare me.' I look at him – the bulk of him as he leans

269

on the wall. He's always been willing to use violence, or the threat of violence, and he scares me to death.

And then comes the 'for your own good' bit. 'I know you think I can pull strings,' he says. 'But there are some people I have no control over. People like Benedict Rickman.'

'So that piece of river slime is working for you now?'

'He's been very helpful. And he's concerned about you.'

I'm looking at Mike Lockwood MP, and it's as though he's far, far away, and I'm in the sky, high up above the buildings. This man who towered over me all my life now looks tiny and desperate. Desperate to be recognised as the man he wants to be, desperate to prove himself better than the man his mother abandoned him for, desperate to stop the gale of nothingness sweeping him into space with all the other debris of human ambition. I can't help it. I start to laugh. 'D'you know why Einstein was wrong about not being able to go faster than the speed of light?'

'No idea,' he says.

'Because the aliens would never get here.' Then I land the hardest punch of my life – harder, I'm hoping, than all the ones I've pulled – into his stomach. And I walk away.

One hot night in July, Sally sticks a newspaper under my nose. 'Isn't this where you went,' she says, 'for your little holiday?' She's pointing at the 'News in Brief' section. 'Pont Rhith. Is it nice?'

I'm at the desk in the office, making a frame to go around a picture one of the residents has drawn of a cottage in the hills.

I look sideways at the report. It says the MoD investigation into a drone crash that killed a woman near the town of Pont Rhith, mid Wales, has reported mechanical malfunction as the cause of the accident.

'Yes,' I say. 'It's picturesque.'

* * *

I think about Owen. I wonder if I made a mistake. I wonder if I punished him for a crime he didn't commit, the way Prince Llewellyn killed Gelert because he thought the dog had killed his child. But the blood on Gelert's jowls wasn't the baby's. The blood came from the wolf Gelert had valiantly slain to protect the child. I banish those thoughts because they don't do me any good, and it's just as likely Owen was the army's loyal dog, not mine, and the blood was Raven's. Or Tegid's.

Besides, it's not as if he's tried to find me.

It's August when I visit Alex at his new job. I stand by the gate to his community garden, and I watch him crouched over the dark earth between rows of vegetation. He looks up and sees me and smiles. He's grown a big black beard, as well as cabbages, and he looks more like a bear than ever. He's also triumphant. He's holding up a handful of small, soil-flecked spuds as if they're a new baby he's just delivered. 'It's not locked,' he shouts, pointing at the gate.

He fetches a stripy deckchair from a shed and gets me to sit on it while he washes the potatoes at a tap against the wall. Then he puts them in a blackened saucepan with some water and sets about making a fire in a tin bucket. I watch him pile up a wigwam of cardboard strips and kindling, sitting cross-legged on the mud. When the fire is lit he sets the pan on top to boil, and I sink into the chair and listen to him tell me about the garden, and the groups who come to work in it. And about his girlfriend, who is pregnant.

'You seem so ... at home,' I say, 'wherever you are.' I watch him, wondering if it's true or just something I imagine about other people.

'What ... even though I'm not from round here?' He's laughing at me.

'You know what I mean.'

271

He leans back on his hands and looks up at me. 'No one really belongs,' he says. 'We're all just passing through. There's no point waiting to feel welcome. No one's going to say, "Come in. Make yourself at home."'

I stare down at the bowl of tiny steaming potatoes he's passed to me. He settles himself in another deckchair and skewers one of the little spuds with his fork and puts it in his mouth. I watch him savour it, closing his eyes with only slightly exaggerated relish.

'How about this then,' he says, when he's stopped chewing ecstatically. 'The system we live in – or capitalism – deprives people of their place in the world. So we have to make a place. We have to create a centre and give it a bit of gravity, so people have somewhere to fall towards. We have to make promises and keep them. And to everyone we meet, we have to say, "I'm glad you came".'

'Thank you,' I say, not entirely convinced.

'You're welcome,' he beams back.


The sense of sight dominates our world. Everything is spectacle. In my own life I've been clinging to sound against the grain, trying to listen before I look. But I'm obviously losing the battle because it takes me another month to go back to that video of the sea and turn up the volume. The recording is poor quality. I work on the hiss and two voices emerge. Perhaps it's an argument. It could be Tegid. It could be Reg Dauber. But I'm not sure. Perhaps Tegid is asking for his share in the profits from the sale of his programmes, so he can give the money away to the victims of his abused invention. Or perhaps Reg Dauber is saying fuck off, and if you don't I have friends who will make you. No one will miss a crazy homeless man. They'll make sure it looks like an accident, or suicide.

But I don't know. Not for certain. And all the equipment I can access fails to clarify it. All I can hear are the cadences of their exchange and the result of their performance is rough and inconclusive and full of mutual hate.

272

## 33

## Tidal Reach

It's a Saturday in early September, and Sally's lent me her car for two weeks while she's on her honeymoon in Italy. She's persuaded her wife that they should go on the train, because Sally's opposed to flying on the grounds of its high carbon footprint, so I'm surprised to find the car is an old petrol-guzzling Mercedes.

Mr Palmer isn't impressed with my desire to lay a bunch of wild flowers at the site of the drone crash – he's installed a new static caravan in the gap left by the accident, and he doesn't want the owners to have their holiday disturbed by reminders of violent death. But he says I can place the flowers discreetly under a patch of shrubbery on the other side of the lane.

Although it's after the school holidays, the park seems more than half occupied and the little gardens that surround each plot are bright with begonias and primulas. I don't linger. I ignore Mr Palmer's request for discretion and lay my bunch of wayside flowers next to the stump of a tree beside the new caravan. I listen to the wind in the trees and the stream in the valley, and I think of Anwen who was here less than a year ago, washing up the breakfast dishes after taking her daughter to school, and then getting out her college books and laying them on the table by the window, ready to work.

I arrive in Pont Rhith in the early afternoon and the town is busy with people going from one antique shop to another or lingering over lattes at the pavement cafés which have sprouted up all along the high street in the sunshine. I find Delyth outside the Spar and she's holding out her hands in mock despair and rolling her kohl-rimmed eyes towards the shop's automatic doors. 'The tourists have eaten all the veg!' she says, and then she moves towards me across the wide pavement with her arms wide open. I rest in her hug for a few moments, against the warmth of her.

We go to the bookshop and while she's unlocking the door I look at the new posters stuck to the glass – a Noson Lawen, a string-quartet concert, a visiting theatre company. Inside, the bright sunshine of the street fades to sepia and melds warmly with the sanded floorboards and the pine bookshelves. I sit with her, behind the counter, and the shop bell rings more in an hour than it did in a week in mid-winter.

Between serving customers buying books on wildlife and slate-mining, thrillers and romances, nature writing and transport, Delyth tells me the Consortium offered funds to modernise the primary school. 'Bribery and fear,' she says. 'Works every time.'

I ask about the little girl, Anwen's daughter. She tells me she's living with her father now and he's bought Raven's cottage, and the one next door, and he's doing them up. 'So your soldier is their neighbour,' she says, and before I can protest that he isn't and never was 'my' soldier, she's saying, 'and maybe I was wrong about him. He's helping Joel with the renovations. And he has a job teaching at the outdoor education centre down the road.'

A man with a 'tache hands her a book on steam railways and she slides it into a paper bag and folds down the end neatly and they talk about the old Bethania to Pont Rhith line. He thinks it should be re-opened as a tourist attraction.

She shakes her head. 'Not with a military training ground at one end.'

The man obviously doesn't know about the military training ground so Delyth tells him. It's clear she hates the place. It's also clear the man would love to take a look at it and log the specifications of any shiny new weapons on view at the site. I stand up and go over to her notice board. All the leaflets are for cultural events – music, art, theatre – and most are Welsh language. But in the middle of the board is a small index card with a large number on it. Underneath the number it says, 'Civilian deaths from drone attacks'.

'And Mr Ellis?' I ask when the man has gone. 'How's Mr Ellis?'

'Not too good, bach. He had a stroke and he's in a nursing home. I don't think he'll last long. And the farm's up for auction – none of his younger relatives wants it. I think the Consortium are bidding for it.'

I go back to my seat behind the counter and take my laptop out of my bag and fire it up. When the shop is empty I say, 'Mr Ellis gave me a memory stick. It's Tegid's.'

She looks at me, and then she goes to the door and locks it and turns over the sign. She leads me through to the kitchen and puts the kettle on. When the mugs are on the table I show her the poems on the memory stick. 'He was a romantic,' she says.

'Maybe,' I say. 'But he wasn't a suicidal romantic.'

She takes a sip at her tea. Her face is fixed. 'No,' she says. 'But the inquest thought so.'

I go back to the laptop and pull up the film of the sea. I turn up the sound and she listens carefully to the hiss. She says she's certain one of the voices is Tegid's, and that he's asking for something. Demanding something. She has no idea who the other man is, but she thinks he's angry. 'Did you give this to the inquest?'

'It isn't clear enough,' I say, although that isn't the only reason I've held onto the memory stick. 'You can't identify the voices. You can't hear the words properly. But I think it's Dauber. I think Tegid's demanding his share of the Curved Space money.'

She shakes her head. 'Dauber's safe if that's all you have to connect him with Tegid's death.'

'He's safe from *them*,' I say, 'but not from me.' I don't tell her I've thought about borrowing a gun from Mr Ellis and paying Dauber a visit. Or that I've planned to kidnap him and seal him into the chamber where Tegid died. They're only fantasies, but I hate to think of Reg D. raking in the cash from the MT4S Consortium while his old friend and partner crumbles into dust.

She looks at me steadily for a few moments, trying to assess whether I'm serious or not. 'Maybe it's my age,' she says, 'but I've decided to focus on strengthening the things I love rather than fighting the things I hate.'

I stare at the mug in front of me. 'I don't like tea,' I tell her.

'Oh. Sorry. Coffee?'

'I didn't show anyone this,' I tell her while she tips away my tea and makes a coffee. I open up the files of topographical diagrams of the quarry reservoir and the Bethania valley. When she comes back to the table I show her the route the flood water would take if the dam failed. And I show her the calculations for just how much dynamite it would take to blow up the dam.

She's quiet for a while and then she shakes her head and says, 'Stunts like that need to be tied to something, Abby. They need a wider political movement behind them with the courage to carry out real social change. Otherwise they're just more mindless acts of violence. And there's more than enough mindless violence in this world.'

I disconnect the memory stick and place it on the table. 'You can keep it,' I say. 'Just in case you manage to get that political movement off the ground.'

She laughs wryly. 'In my dreams.' And then she picks it up and hands it back to me. 'But you could help me try.'

I pass it back to her. 'I'm not an organiser.'

'I'll teach you.'

I stare at her. I realise I'm not responding and that she's offering me something important. 'I think my place is with the homeless and the lost,' I say. 'But if I change my mind, I'll let you know.'

Delyth has told me the old bridge is closed. It isn't safe and there's no money to repair it, so I drive up to Bethania along the main road and over the bridge which the Consortium has reinforced to make safe for construction vehicles and heavy artillery. The water is low and there are wide pebbly beaches on the southern bank.

I park in a lay-by just before Bethania and walk. On the sides of the hills the rowan trees are heavy with clusters of crimson berries and I can hear the whir of crickets and the muted sound of birds whistling in the forest. At one point a red kite flies vigorously across my line of vision.

And then a jet hurtles into the valley with a grinding roar that is utterly outside me and forcing its way in – as harsh and persistent as a drill. When it's gone the after-hum echoes around the bowl of the hills like a distant thunderclap. And then its partner roars over, and for a while afterwards the world looks shocked and drained of colour. The creatures have stopped singing and whirring and clacking and buzzing and there is a flat silence.

I keep going up the valley road. The square black hole of the Bryn Hyfryd adit looks smaller than before, and its edges are softened by a fringe of summer vegetation. When I get to the gate across the track which leads to Mr Ellis's farm I see the sign has been replaced. It no longer says 'Nant y Min'; it says 'Farm No. 1'. I go back down the road and take the track which crosses the stream on the concrete slab and rises to the New Cottages, wondering what I'm going to say to Owen, if he's there.

There's no blue estate parked against the gable wall of the New Cottages. Instead there's a yellow skip brimming with junk. I peer in through the window of Murmur and it's dark inside. I can't see any bread on the table or fire in the stove. There's no dog basket. The props have been returned to base, their function fulfilled.

The middle cottage has been cleared out, ready for renovation, but nothing much has been done to Raven's place, and the peeling blue door is locked. There's a patch of tatty rose-bay willow herb by the woodstore, its 'silk' hanging out and its leaves shrivelled and orange-brown. I pick one of the closed pods and slit it open and scrape out the silver threads with my nail.

Then I go down through the rhododendrons to the stream at the bottom of the garden, where I can hear the distant buzzing of machinery – the diggers and generators at work on a Saturday morning recreating a Welsh mountain village around a derelict chapel in a steep-sided valley.

Under one of the rhododendron bushes is a small wooden cross and a mound of fresh earth. The spiky lettering says, 'Kova, who was happy here.' I kneel down and pat the soil. 'Me too,' I say, and then I get up quickly and climb over the fence at the bottom of the garden, as though I'm worried I'll end up buried next to the dog if I stay any longer.

I'm heading down across the field to the concrete bridge when I see his car. I stop and watch him park by the gable end and get out. He goes round to the boot and starts pulling out a sack. I walk back up the field and climb over the fence, catching my T-shirt on the barbed wire and struggling for a moment to release it. When he sees me he edges the sack back into the car and wipes his hands on the front of his jeans.

'It was you, wasn't it?' I say, before he can speak. 'You were the one watching Raven and every other potential trouble maker in the area. That's why you knew about SHED and Tim Jones. That's why you were friends with that journalist, and with fucking Ben Rickman.'

He looks at me and shakes his head.

'Did you kill her too? Did you get rid of Raven. Was it a little job you were doing in your retirement? Were they giving you a payoff for whatever you did in the army? Something easy, this time, for a man with post-traumatic stress. Was the cottage thrown in? And the dog?'

He shakes his head again, and then stoops back into the boot and starts edging the sack out.

I feel wrong-footed by his reaction. He should be angry, defensive. He should be spouting a ready-made story. But I'm fixed on my version of the truth – the one I've been working on for months – and I'm not ready to let go of it yet. 'I saw you with Rickman,' I say. 'Were you working for him?'

'No,' he says into the back of the car. 'He's a twat.'

I nearly laugh.

He straightens up and assesses me. 'He told me you two were involved, back in London. Seemed to think that made us mates.'

I stare back at him. The sack is still leaning against his thighs. 'You didn't try to find me.'

He sighs. 'Look,' he says. 'If someone tells me to fuck off, I'm not going to stalk them. I can take no for an answer.'

I wonder when I told him to fuck off, or if he's just referring to my general demeanour. Or the fact I put a rock through his kitchen window.

'I'm not your enemy, Abby,' he says. 'And if you're going to go through life never trusting anyone, you might as well ...' he waves vaguely towards the far hill, 'jump in that lake up there and drown yourself.'

I start to walk away. I can hear him heave the sack onto the slab outside his front door. I hear the door open. I'm climbing the fence again when he shouts, 'Where are you going now?'

'To jump in the lake.'

# 34

## Reservoir

Close up, the water of the reservoir isn't cobalt blue; it's clear. I take off my boots and socks and sit on a slate slab at the edge of the water. I let my toes ripple the surface. I've spent three hours setting the dynamite Mr Ellis left for me in a box in the woods. I've used all the knowledge I gleaned from Tegid's notes, and from the internet, to drill holes at the base of the dam and shove the explosives in. Now all I have to do is wait till four in the morning, when there is a moon but still no sun. Then I'll light the fuse, and a half-constructed training ground for counter-insurgency warfare will disappear under gallons of water and shale.

I sit on the slate and swirl my feet around in the cold water. A bird rustles the leaves of an old oak tree on the far bank. A sharp longing to be held pulses through me and has my fingers gripping my thighs. I try to crush the feeling. I think about living in a north-facing cottage with an ex-squaddie, and maybe a dog, and I know I could want that. I pull the box of matches out of my pocket and lay it beside me on the slate slab.

And then I think about the soldiers playing their war games in Bethania, and the jets screeching down the valley, and the drones cruising over the sheep fields and plantation forests. I think about watching the little girl next door grow up, without a mother, and I think about Delyth's patient, persistent campaigning for change. I wonder if it's possible to hold onto all these things at once and be happy, at times, in the middle of it all. And I'm not sure I have the courage for that kind of everyday happiness.

I take off my jeans and shirt and lay them next to the box of matches on the rock. Then I wade out into the reservoir on slime-covered slate. The bones in my feet and ankles ache with the cold. The sides of the reservoir slope steeply and I'm up to my thighs in water within a few steps. I plunge forward and swim out and in a few moments the cold is almost bearable and I turn on my back and float, cupped by the reservoir and the hills, open to the sky, displacing my body volume of water against the dam – the dam that, if it failed now, would send me and a flash flood surging down the valley and smashing into the machines and buildings at Bethania.

I think of Tegid telling me to live simply, with children and animals. He was offering me a map to my own heart because he couldn't find the one to his own. He said purity and abstraction were fine, but they started with flesh and blood and earth, and that's where I should start. Even our notion of time – a beautiful abstraction – was rooted in our physical experience of the world. At the dawn of human history, when we lived in the forests, we knew the past was under the ground. When our lives depended on the earth in ways we couldn't deny or ignore, we knew the ground was the source of everything, because everything grows out of the ground, just as everything rises out of the past and is formed by it.

The future, on the other hand, was around the bend in the forest trail, or over the next mountain – it was all the places we couldn't see and could only travel towards. It was where we were going, and if we were wise animals we would plan for the journey and prepare for the future; we would use all the information we had at our disposal to avoid hunger, pain and disaster.

I paddle my hands at my sides and stare up into the pale blue sky, and then I turn on my front and swim out further, into the middle of the reservoir, and the cold stiffens my muscles and constricts my breathing. A little bird trills from the reeds by the bank and dives under the water. And what about the present? What did Tegid say about the present? I think he said it was the air around us. It was our breathing in and out. It was the wind in the trees and the singing of birds. It was a note of music blown over a reed, and it was the whisper of voices around a fire at night.

And as I swim I realise Tegid missed out water. As I move through it, I decide water is our deep understanding of another dimension, like a visceral memory of life before birth. Water is our sensory knowledge of another way of being, beyond our ordinary lives on land where we breathe in the air of the present and follow a track into the future from our past in the earth.

And if water isn't the past or the future, or the present, then it has to be the place and time of dreams and possibilities, and out of the water will come a beautiful new world. Or monsters.

I hear a low rumble and a moment later a jet comes banking through the gap in the hills and up the valley towards Mr Ellis's farm. It rips away a layer of the earth's aura as it skims the fields. I take a deep breath and sink under the water and when the second machine hurtles through the sky above me all I hear is a muffled purr. I think of staying there, under the water, and I think of Owen and I think of drowning, because I trust no one and let no one in. The cold water streams over my skin and I know what I have to do.

I walk home in the night.

# Acknowledgements

I'd like to thank Literature Wales for a 2016 Writers' Bursary (supported by The National Lottery through the Arts Council of Wales). I'd also like to thank: Diane Bailey and Geoff Young at Pen'rallt Gallery Bookshop for a special place to work, buy books and meet readers, writers, thinkers, artists, activists, loafers and browsers; Rhiain Bebb and Ruth Roberts Owen for being bridges between languages and cultures (a fo ben bid bont); Julia Forster for her generosity with time and advice; Mark 'Moley' Waite at Corris Mine Explorers for a guided tour of the slate mines; Gwyn and John Pendry, Megan and Robert Jones, Lottie and Arthur Kingdom for a history and a conscience; all at Parthian; Alison Lochhead for art work which acknowledges the human cost of war, abandonment and exploitation; Cerys Hafana Hickman and Huw Arthur Hickman for music and laughter; and Marcus Hickman for a place to be.

Books which have been useful include: David Abrams, *The Spell of the Sensuous: Perception and Language in a More-Than-Human World*, London, Vintage Books, 1997, for thoughts about the physical roots of our abstract notions of 'time' – past, present and future; Tristan Dooley, *The Natural Navigator*, London, Virgin Books, 2010, for tips on navigation; Vijay Mehta, *The Economics of Killing: How the West Fuels War and Poverty in the Developing World*, London, Pluto Press, 2012, for his information on 'unconventional warfare' training at Fort Bragg.

The epigraphs are from: Mary-Ann Constantine, *The Truth Against the World: Iolo Morganwg and Romantic Forgery*, Cardiff, University of Wales Press, 2007, and Waldo Williams, trans. Tony Conran, *The Peacemakers: Selected Poems*, Llandysul, Gomer, 1997.

Alison Lochhead lives in west Wales. She works primarily as a sculptor and has exhibited widely in the UK and internationally since 1977. Her artwork reflects upon her experiences living in several countries and advocating for women's rights – fighting social injustice and inequality throughout the world. Alison is a member of the Royal British Society of Sculptors, Sculpture Cymru, Sculpture Network, and 56 Group Wales. The title of the collograph used for this cover is: 'Cwmystwyth Mine Memory'. The print looks at the scars on the landscape and from deep within the mines.

Website: www.alisonlochhead.co.uk

## Women Who Blow on Knots
Ece Temelkuran
ISBN 978-1-910901-69-4
£9.99 ● Paperback

Winner of Edinburgh Book Festival
First Book Award

PEN England Translates Award

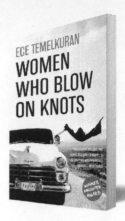

## The Golden Orphans
Gary Raymond
ISBN 978-1-91-210913-5
£8.99 ● Paperback

'Intense, unnerving and brilliant.'
– *The Spectator*

## Bad Ideas \ Chemicals
Lloyd Markham
ISBN 978-1-912109-68-5
£7.99 ● Paperback

A Betty Trask Award Winner

PARTHIAN